SHATTERED SHELL

BRENDAN DUBOIS

SEVERN RIVER

PUBLISHING

Severn River Publishing
www.SevernRiverBooks.com

ISBN: 978-1-64875-407-4 (Paperback)

ALSO BY BRENDAN DUBOIS

The Lewis Cole Series

Dead Sand

Black Tide

Shattered Shell

Killer Waves

Buried Dreams

Primary Storm

Deadly Cove

Fatal Harbor

Blood Foam

Storm Cell

Hard Aground

Terminal Surf

To find out more about Brendan DuBois and his books, visit
severnriverbooks.com/authors/brendan-dubois

This is for my brothers:
Michael
Brian
Neil
Dennis
Stephen
A finer group of men I have never known.

FOREWORD

There's an old joke that if you want to make God laugh, announce that you're making plans. If so, writers must be at the top of the line in giving the Almighty amusement, for we're always making plans.

The same happened to me after writing and publishing my first two Lewis Cole mystery novels—DEAD SAND and BLACK TIDE—to a great publishing line, Otto Penzler Books, which was part of Macmillan Books. I was working with top talent, getting great reviews and feedback, and I had a grand plan where I could write a Lewis Cole novel every year, building up my fan base and making a bit more money with each book.

Cue God going: "Hah, hah, hah!"

Publishing has always been an uncertain industry, and there was a shake-up in publishing in the late 1990s that struck home for me. Not to get into any gory details, but after the dust had settled and the wounded had been taken away, my publishing line no longer existed.

Bummer.

That meant I was an orphan, and my agent at the time worked hard to find another home for Lewis Cole, which took a fair amount of time. But I used that time to a greater advantage, for if I couldn't find a publisher for book number three in my series, I sure as heck wasn't going to write the fourth. So while I waited to hear on this publishing hunt, I decided to take a leap and write a stand-alone thriller, my alternative history novel, RESURRECTION DAY, which has turned out to be one of my most successful books ever.

There's a lesson in there, about lemons and lemonades, but I think we can skip that lesson for now.

While RESURRECTION DAY was being revised and getting ready to be eventually published in 1999, my agent contacted me and said that the incredible and talented Ruth Cavin of St. Martin's Press—who began her editing career at the age of 70!—had agreed to take on Lewis Cole.

That was a head-spinning time... to sell my first stand-alone thriller, and to find a home for my main man, Lewis Cole.

I hope you enjoy this third book in my series. It took longer than it should have to get published, but I still like to think it was worth the wait. And I hope you understand that I've not changed the time and place of the novel: there are no cellphones, home computers are expensive, and only the very first stirrings of the Internet were coming alive.

And one more note... in some ways, this was the most difficult of my Lewis Cole novels to write, although I'm proud of every single word. I'll explain more later.

1

Though I didn't have a watch on, I'm sure it was just after ten p.m. when on a cold Friday night in January the Rocks Road Motel in Tyler Beach, New Hampshire, gave up its soul and died. Its death was well-attended, with about forty or so people there—some working, some watching—and I was standing about seventy feet away when the roof collapsed with a crackling boom. Then there was the roaring sound of the rushing flames, reaching up to the freezing night sky, feeding on the oxygen. The sparks were bright orange and quick, and they moved up into the night like fireflies looking for a home. The crackling sound of the fire, the creaking of the timbers, the rumbling of the fire truck engines, and the echoing noise of the police and fire radios all drowned out the sound of the Atlantic's waves, about a hundred feet away.

It hadn't been long since the fire had been called in, and I stood outside the ring of firefighters from Tyler and Falconer—our sister town to the south—as they struggled through the snow with their heavy turnout gear, air packs, helmets, and boots. A ladder truck had its spindly aerial ladder over the collapsed roof and a deluge of water flowed into the fiery mess. Three other pumpers, two from Tyler and one from Falconer, were parked on the narrow street, their rigid hoses twisted through the snow.

I shrugged against the cold, wearing a green parka I had bought the previous summer at the Eastern Mountain Sports store in North Conway, when a companion and I had stopped on our way up to the White Mountains for a day climb. As I stood in about a half-foot of snow, I pretended the fibers still contained a faint breath of that hot summer day when I had made my purchase. My gloved hands were in my pockets, along with a reporter's notebook, and I had a Navy wool watch cap pulled over my ears.

The hotel was near some cottages and another motel, the Dune Wave, and no lights were showing from any of the buildings. The tourist season was gone, and the bulk of the businesses and motels were closed up until April or May. There had been mild winters in the past when some places remained open during the short days and long nights, but this season wasn't one of them. Winter had struck early and hard, with a blizzard two days before Thanksgiving and a storm nearly every week after that, and though Christmas was only a few days past, most people were already heartily sick of winter.

Before me a couple of firefighters crunched by in the snow, icicles hanging from their helmets, their faces puffy and red from the cold and exhaustion, carrying another length of hose. It had not been a good winter so far for Tyler Beach and its firefighters. Since those first snows, four motels had burned to the ground—including tonight's victim—and none of them had been accidental. All had been arson.

The cause hadn't been determined yet for this fire, but I had that feeling, and I could tell from the nervous and edgy look of the firefighters that they had the same feeling, that the Rocks Road Motel would soon join the list. It just made sense. And though no one was saying the words tonight, it was plain to see what was going on.

An arsonist was at work in Tyler, and so far the winter promised to be a long one. I shifted in the snow again, saw the little clouds from my breath, and waited. A woman stepped away from a couple of firefighters and came over to me. She had on a blue down jacket, jeans, and knee-high leather boots. A metal clipboard was in gloved hands, and she wore no hat. Though the light was bad, it was still easy to make out the brown hair of Diane Woods, sole detective for the Tyler Police Department. Her face was scrunched up from the cold and what looked like frustration. Diane has a wonderful smile and light brown skin, marred only by a short white scar on her chin that came from a fight when she was a uniformed cop, but this evening she didn't look particularly happy. I didn't have any envy for anyone who got on her bad side tonight.

She stood next to me and stamped her feet in the snow and said, "I, for one, Lewis Cole, am getting mightily sick of this crap."

"I can imagine," I said. "I'm not having much fun, either."

"Where's your notebook?" she said, a slightly demanding tone in her voice.

"In my coat."

"Not taking any notes?"

"Don't need to right now," I said, keeping my hands in the parka. "Just observing the scene, and I don't need a notebook for that."

"Hah. Seems to me you're getting lazy. Maybe I should call your editor."

I smiled, thinking of the retired admiral who was editor of *Shoreline* magazine and pretended to be my boss. "Go ahead. Knowing Seamus, he'd tell you to go to hell."

"Maybe." She angled the open metal clipboard and used a tiny black flashlight to illuminate her notes. There was another crackling and groaning sound as a few more building beams collapsed, and it seemed like the deluge gun from the ladder truck was at last having an effect. The flames were dying down some and the steady heat on my face was beginning to diminish. From near the fire scene I made out the quick shots of light that came from a camera strobe, and I knew that the *Tyler Chronicle* was on the scene.

"What do you have, Diane?" I asked, keeping my eye on two people, a man and a woman, the man carrying a camera bag.

"What I have is what you and everybody else here has already guessed," she said. "Empty motel goes up in flames. Possible arson and will become a definite arson once Mike Ahern and the guys from the state fire marshal's office get in there to poke around."

I shivered as a breeze came by, salty-smelling from the ocean.

"This guy's good. He gets the fire working so the building is fully involved by the time the first engine's on the scene."

"Unh-hunh," and she motioned with the flashlight to a man standing in the snow, holding a woman in his arms. The woman's face was buried against his shoulder, and he was shaking his head and kicking the snow with one foot, over and over again.

"That there's Sam Keller with his wife Amy," she said. "Owner of the Rocks Road, and he doesn't know it, but his life is going to get even worse tomorrow."

I nodded in understanding. "When the investigation gets into high gear."

"Yep. And when Mike Ahern starts talking to him tomorrow, he's going to think that God's got a week's worth of punishments ahead of him and that God's only begun on day two. Look. There's Ahern now."

A squat man in fire gear came over to the couple, but unlike the other firefighters, he wasn't wearing an air pack. He talked some to Sam Keller, but I wasn't sure if Keller even comprehended what he was saying. The man then turned around, and a light caught the reflective letters on the rear of his turnout coat: TYLER in big letters, and underneath that, in smaller letters, AHERN. Mike Ahern, fire inspector for the town of Tyler, and one busy man these past few weeks. I felt even sorrier for Sam Keller at the sight of having Mike Ahern talk to him. Ahern had a short fuse, and every businessperson whose motel had been destroyed had come under sharp scrutiny and even sharper questioning by Ahern as the investigation started. But for all of his efforts, and those of Diane Woods and the state fire marshal's office, there had been no evidence that any of the businesspeople who owned the motels had a part in the arson.

Usually it's easy to tell there's a lead when arson destroys a business. A day or two's worth of fact-checking, and if a guy's up to his ears in debts, if all of his mortgage notices are printed in pink, and if not-so-polite men in suits come a-visiting from banks, then that guy's vulnerable to the siren call of fire. One quick blaze and one fat insurance check later, you're back on your feet, breathing hard but breathing more free. Except these business-people, blind to the mountain of debts and the ringing phones from bill collectors, ignore the quiet, squat guys like Mike Ahern and the very tough women like Diane Woods, and then end up several months later appearing before a Wentworth County Superior Court on charges of conspiracy to commit arson.

But that wasn't happening here. None of the owners had business problems. One or two were even considering expanding for next year. Which meant something worse, that the arsonist was a nut, that he wasn't following any particular agenda and was just burning down buildings for the hell of it.

That thought made for a lot of cold nights these past weeks. I looked over to Diane and said, "How's things between you and Mike?"

Diane ducked her head, like she didn't want me to see her expression, and she said, "A bit of an improvement. I don't worry now about checking my Volkswagen for bombs every morning, and he's gotten to at least returning my calls after the third try."

"Oh," I said, not wanting to add anything more, and Diane nudged me with her shoulder and said, "I should get back to work, and make the most of a ruined evening."

"Previous plans?" I asked.

She winked. "A date, and one that was going to be—if you excuse the pun—an extremely hot one."

"There's always the weekend."

"Thank God for that." She looked around, perhaps to see if anyone was within earshot, and then she asked, "How goes the column you're writing on these arsons?"

I shrugged. "About as well as your investigation. We've both been down those same roads, and I don't think either of us is missing anything. But I'm still, um...I'm still doing the research."

She touched me with a gloved hand, her voice still low. "Glad to hear that. See you later."

Diane walked away, stumbled a bit in the snow, and went over to Sam Keller and his wife and started talking to them. Diane looked good, she looked skilled, and she had been my companion that day when I had bought my EMS parka up north. Yet spending the day on a mountain peak had not changed anything between us, for her heart belonged to another, and that was all right. I walked a bit nearer to the motel. The wind shifted and the smoke was thick for a moment, making my eyes water, and I coughed.

When I was out of the smoke I came up to a man and woman talking to each other at one end of the unplowed parking lot that belonged to the motel. Paula

Quinn, reporter for the *Tyler Chronicle*, gave me a little half-wave, holding her notebook in one hand and a pencil in the other. A reporter who carries a pencil in the winter is a good reporter, for the new ones forget that ink can easily congeal in cold weather. Paula was experienced and Paula was good, but in her talks with me, she still expressed the same old frustration of having a big talent in a small town. She had on a black wool coat and red beret that looked nice on her long blond hair but probably didn't do much for giving her warmth. Paula has a bit of a pug nose and her ears have a tendency to stick out of her hair just when she wants to look serious, and tonight the poor things were red with cold.

"Glad to see *Shoreline* is being represented here tonight," Paula said, giving me that smile of hers that managed to tickle something deep inside of me. "If the *Chronicle* has to be out here freezing, at least your magazine should be here, too."

"Thanks for the invite," I said. "When did you get here?"

She gestured to the bearded man at her side. "Jerry and I drove in a couple of minutes after they sounded the alarm. Message came over the scanner that this place was going to three alarms."

A little imp of the perverse came to me, that voice that tells you to jump when you're standing at the edge of the Grand Canyon. This time the voice was telling me to ask Paula just what she and Jerry had been doing before the fire alarm came in, but I managed to resist. I just smiled and said to Jerry, "Getting your fill of pictures?"

The man next to her was wearing a green, heavy down jacket with a bulky camera bag slung over one beefy shoulder. He had on jeans and, like me, Canadian-made Sorrels on his feet. His face and nose were bright red, and his brown hair was almost as thick as his beard. Jerry Croteau, sole photographer for the *Tyler Chronicle*, and a man I was beginning to dislike for no good reason except that he was spending time with Paula Quinn— both on and off the job. It disturbed me, and it shouldn't have, for I had no formal hold on Paula. Just some pleasant memories and odd hopes. It shouldn't bother me, but it did. Sorry for the contradiction.

His smile was almost as wide as his beard. "Got a bunch of great ones when we first drove up. It was a hell of a scramble, with the hoses being dragged across the snow, and even though it only took a couple of minutes for the first truck to roll in, the roof was fully involved. Got some great shots of a couple of guys trying to ventilate the roof with axes, with the fire backlighting them. Gonna try to sell them to AP tonight."

"Sounds pretty good."

He nodded enthusiastically. "It does. Paula tells me you might be doing a piece on the arsons for your magazine. Let me know if you need anything. I also shot some color."

There was a smart-aleck remark in there about taking advantage of someone else's misfortune, which I left alone. Instead, I looked at Paula and felt that funny little tug and wished that I felt comfortable enough to rub those cold ears.

Instead, I played professional and said, "Hear anything about arson tonight?"

She moved her feet, shivered, and said, "Not officially, but you can tell from the way the guys are working. They're tired and I think they're also scared. Firefighters are macho, but they get scared when an arsonist is working. Look at their faces. There's the story there."

There was another crackling and rumbling as another portion of roof caved in. More water was being poured onto the motel and the building was being transformed with each minute. When I had arrived, hard on the heels of the police cruisers and the fire engines, the building with its empty swimming pool in front and the two rows of balconies almost looked majestic, the flames and smoke pouring from the roof, so many men and women working desperately to save it, the lights from the vehicles making the white paint and black shingles look almost new.

But with the center and the roof gone, with the exposed beams and flying shingles and broken glass and hanging wire and pipes, the Rocks Road Motel looked sad and pathetic, like an old woman who had been hit by a car and who was lying dead in the road, pocketbook in her hands, before the EMTs could cover her with a blanket.

Jerry took another picture and shook his head. "Who could blame them for being scared?" he said. "Read once about arsons in New York City. Sometimes the arsonists, they'll cut holes in the floors and cover 'em with linoleum, so the firefighters fall through when they go in. Bad enough to go in a burning building, must be ten times worse when you know someone's busy setting the fires and setting you up."

"True enough," I said. "Good luck in getting the story. It's time for this magazine writer to get going."

Paula nodded and said, "Lunch soon?" and instead of looking at her, I quickly caught a glance of Jerry Croteau, seeing something pass over his face. Maybe it was concern, maybe it was jealousy, and maybe it was just a passing wisp of smoke.

"Sure," I said. "I'll call you."

I left the two of them there, and they bent heads together to talk, and I wondered if my name was coming up in the conversation.

IT TOOK a few more minutes of walking through the snow and looking at the backs of firefighters' turnout gear before I found the man I wanted. Mike Ahern was sitting on the hood of his car, smoking a cigarette. His fire helmet was off and the top of his sweaty head steamed in the cold air. He was writing with some difficulty on a notepad, wearing fingerless gloves, and he looked up at me and went back to work as I came over.

"Wish you'd change your mind about an interview, Mike," I said, standing in front of him. His pullover pants and fire boots were wet and black with soot and debris.

"And why's that?" he said, not looking up again from the pad. "What advantage would I have in talking with you?"

"Maybe not an advantage to you, but an advantage to others. Readers of my magazine. People in town. This is becoming a story, whether you like it or not."

"Hah." He put down the notepad and stretched. Mike was about as tall as I was, but was easily a foot wider, with thick forearms and hands. His black hair was trimmed short and was streaked with gray, and on the side of his face, above his left ear, his skin bore the shiny and wrinkly marks of burned skin that had not healed well.

"Let me tell you this: I don't have to tell you anything," Mike said, removing his cigarette and pointing it at me. "Newspaper writers, maybe. They're here in town and taxpayers like to read them, and since the taxpayers have an unholy grip on my balls every budget time, I gotta keep them happy and amused. But not magazines from Boston. I don't owe you, I don't feel like wasting my time with you, and you can't hurt me."

Even without looking, I knew that the battle for the motel's timbers was almost over. The heat on my back from the flames was easing up. I said, "You're probably right in everything you said, and it's true I can't hurt you, but maybe I can help you."

His eyes narrowed at that, and he took another drag from his cigarette. I'm not sure why so many firefighters smoke. Maybe it's just fatalism.

Mike said, "Yeah? How? Free subscriptions?"

I shrugged. "Information. Let's just say I do a lot of research for my columns, and not all of my research appears in print."

That seemed to get his attention, and he looked away and said quietly, "This is the fourth major fire in as many weeks, and I'm getting mighty tired. A winter like this, you plan for maybe a couple of suspicious fires, when a guy who runs a restaurant decides to cut his losses and move to Orlando with an insurance check in his back pocket."

Then he looked at me, the light from the flames and the strobes from the fire trucks and police cars making his face look like it was shimmering with some emotion. "But not this time around. This time, it's crazy. No link. None of these guys who owned these hotels had a bad year. But here we are. With four hotels burned to the ground in a month. So far we've been lucky, with nobody getting hurt. They've all been closed for the winter and were empty. But next time?"

Mike stood up from his car and put his fire helmet back on, tugged at the chin strap. "Next time, we might need flatbed trucks here to pull away all the bodies, if our nut friend decides to try his or her hand at a motel with people in it. You say you can help? All right. We'll talk next week, when I catch my breath from this latest disaster."

After some fumbling on my part, I passed over my business card, which lists my name, home phone number and my post office box in Tyler, and my job at *Shoreline* magazine: columnist. I'm not sure if it's against the law to lie on business cards, but so far I've gotten away with it. The IRS and a few others think being a columnist is all I do, and I've never been one to discourage that fantasy.

Mike Ahern trudged across the snow to meet up with Diane Woods, and I gave her a half-wave as my own thermostat told me it was time to go. I silently wished her luck on her hot date, and then I began to walk away from the rubble that used to be a business that contributed something to this town. Maybe not a big deal as far as disasters went, and I knew that only the local papers might cover it, but for many lives, this was a big story. For those vacationers who came back to the Rocks Road Motel each summer, that place was now gone. For the chambermaids and clerks and short order cooks for its restaurant, their jobs at the Rocks Road Motel were gone. For the other businesses that supplied the motel with towels, soap, and food, one big customer had just been lost.

A lot of losses, all due to a man, woman, or a gang who was having too much fun with flammable liquids and incendiary devices this past month. As I walked to my Range Rover, parked skewed near a snow bank, I passed Sam and Amy Keller, still holding each other, still grieving at seeing so many years of work and effort being reduced to ashes.

FOR THE DRIVE home I took Atlantic Avenue—also known as Route l-A— and the road hugged the beaches of Tyler as it headed north. Driving here in winter is always disorienting. It's like going back to your childhood home and seeing a garage has been added and the familiar red paint has been replaced by ugly ivory siding. All along the beach road there were hundreds of empty parking spaces, and except for a set of taillights far ahead, I was the only one on the road.

Six months earlier I would have been in bumper-to-bumper traffic, at a time when fistfights sometimes break out over the privilege of parking near the sands. Instead of nearly a hundred thousand vacationers and moms and dads and kids and bathing beauties of both sexes, I had an empty road, flickering streetlights, closed-up motels, and beach sand and snow blowing across the pavement.

It was a cloudy night, promising more snow, and I saw not one star as I neared the border between Tyler and North Tyler. Near that dividing line is a resort motel that stays open year-round, the Lafayette House, and I pulled into the tiny parking lot across the way. A large sign at the entrance said

PRIVATE PARKING FOR LAFAYETTE HOUSE ONLY, and I turned into the lot and went to the north end, passing a few parked cars, BMWs and Volvos. The lot was plowed clean, which wasn't the case for my destination.

At the end of the lot was a low stone wall and an opening where some of the rocks had fallen free. There was a narrow, snow-covered path there, just wide enough for my Rover. The path went to the right past two home-made no-trespassing signs, and my house came into view. It's a two-story house that's one step above a cottage, that's never been painted, and that has a dirt crawl space for a cellar. The snow-covered lawn rises up to a steep rocky ledge that hides my home from Atlantic Avenue, and I parked in the sagging shed that serves as my garage. Just beyond my house is another outcropping of land called Samson Point, which used to be a Coast Artillery station, and which is now a state wildlife preserve.

I unlocked the front door and did the winter two-step, which is trying to remove heavy boots at the entrance without falling down or stripping off your socks. Before me was the rear landing of the stairway that led to the second floor. I shook off my coat and breathed in the cold air of my house. The building first served as quarters for the supervisor of a lifeboat station that was operating at Samson Point sometime in the middle part of the 1800s, and it has belonged to the government ever since. How it got from the U.S. government to my ownership is a depressing tale that I've not told anyone since I moved here some years back.

I padded across the hardwood living room floor, decorated in some parts by oriental rugs. There's a living room with a fireplace and big kitchen on the first floor, along with an outside deck. Upstairs is a bathroom, my study, and a bedroom. There are a lot of bookshelves, some antiques and historical memorabilia, and on this January night, not much heat. There's a lot to be said about living in a house that's almost a hundred and fifty years old, but its ability to retain heat is not one of them.

I sniffed as I went up the stairs. I smelled of smoke, and I knew it was shower time. In the bathroom I stripped off my clothes and jumped in the shower, suddenly feeling weary about having been out in the cold for hours, watching something as awful as a family's business burn to the ground. I stood under the hot water for some long minutes, feeling the cold seep from the bones and muscles. I stepped out and rubbed myself down with a white fluffy towel, and then started checking my skin, an activity that's almost a habit, but not quite. There's a scar at the small of my back, on my right knee, and two lengthy ones on my left side. The skin was smooth and supple, and I felt no bumps, lumps, or other disturbances, souvenirs from my previous career. I live in this wonderful house rent- and mortgage-free, but this shower routine is one payment that I make, almost every day.

Some days, I almost think it's worth it.

The bathroom is between the study and bedroom, and I went into the bedroom, still tingly and slightly wet from the shower. There's an old four-poster oak bed in the center of the room with matching bureaus and book-shelves, and a reflector telescope standing in one corner on a black tripod. A sliding glass door leads to a small deck on the south end of the house. I turned on a reading light and slid under the covers, shivering a bit, and then I picked up last month's issue of *Smithsonian* magazine. I hardly got past the letters page when my eyelids started drooping, and I switched off the light and let the magazine drop to the floor. My breathing started to slow and I listened to the wind and the whispering sounds of snow or sand striking the windows. The waves were there, always moving, never once letting up in their movement to my shore and my house.

And then I fell asleep on an evening that was to be my last quiet and peaceful night at home for many weeks.

2

When it happened, I had been dreaming, dreaming about my other life, the one before I came to Tyler. Back then I was a research analyst in an obscure section of the Department of Defense, and I was dreaming about one of the weekends we used to have, the ones called screamers. The screamers happened during crisis times, at a moment when the world's attention is focused on Kuwait, Bosnia, or a group of insignificant islands in the China Sea. Ships begin to move, aircraft begin to fly, surveillance satellites are moved in their orbits, the news media broadcasts a lot of loud words and threats, and a lot of late-night lights get burned in government buildings in DC. Sometimes a screamer meant working through the weekend, or catching a few hours' sleep at home, or napping whenever you could on cots brought into the office.

I had been dreaming about one of the latter screamers, a time when a heavy deadline was approaching, and I remember bells ringing and someone saying, "Holy Christ, we're bombing," and I sat up, breathing hard, sitting on a cot, a wool blanket falling off my trousers and stockinged feet, looking around at the cubicles and terminals and the other members of my section, from Cissy Manning to Carl Socha, and more bells were ringing and I gasped, closed my eyes and opened them again, and I was at my home.

I looked at the digital clock. It was just past two-thirty a.m. I shook my head and ran my fingers through my hair, and the ringing came back, seemingly louder.

It was the phone.

I swiveled off my bed and threw on a heavy terrycloth robe as I shambled out of my bedroom, yawning but feeling the adrenaline surge through me, making my heart roar along and my hands tingle. I took the steps downstairs rather quickly, not thinking of who was calling, only knowing that the damnable ringing was blasting through my head and I had to turn it off.

Grabbing the phone, I sat down on my couch, just across from the darkened brick fireplace, and I said, "Yeah?" and the static on the other line was loud. My caller was outside at a pay phone.

"Hello?" I said again, ready to hang up, and a tiny, strained voice said, "Lewis?"

My God. "Diane?" I asked. "Is that you?"

"Oh, Lewis," she said, sobbing, and I sat very straight and still, for in the few years I'd known Diane Woods, I could only remember seeing tears on her face twice.

"Diane," I said, trying to keep my voice level. "What's wrong?"

"Oh, Lewis," she repeated, trying to say words between the gasping sobs. "It's Kara. She's in the hospital."

"Diane—"

She interrupted me and it felt like a chunk of ice from the roof was now in my chest.

"Lewis, oh, shit, Lewis, she's been raped."

WITHIN FIVE MINUTES I was dressed and ready to go back outside. It had been hard, locating clean pants and a heavy shirt and sweater and socks while my hands were shaking and I was trying to keep focused on what I was doing and where I was going. Diane was at the Anna Jaques Hospital in Newburyport, Kara Miles's hometown, and she would meet me in the emergency room. About a hundred and one questions were swirling through my mind, but they would have to wait until I got there. I tossed on my coat, still smoky from the corpse of the Rocks Road Motel, and I stepped outside.

It was snowing, a light squall that wouldn't add much to the accumulation. I trudged through the packed snow trail that led to my garage and I clambered into the Rover. In another minute I was in the plowed parking lot of the Lafayette House, and in another minute I was heading south. I turned on the radio and then I just as quickly turned it off. What I had just learned was nothing that could be ignored through early a.m. talk radio or music. Instead of listening to imported noise, I listened to the noise inside my mind as I returned to the nearly empty roads of Tyler Beach.

A FEW YEARS ago I had gotten to know Diane, soon after I had moved into my home, newly liberated from the U.S. government. Though three new scars—on my side, back, and knee—were freshly healed, other wounds I had were proving to be stubborn indeed. I wasn't sleeping right or eating anything during the day, save for canned and take-out food. I was no longer working for the Department of Defense—officially, that is—and I had a new job as a columnist for a magazine based in Boston called *Shoreline*. I was responsible for the monthly "Granite Shores" column, which covered the eighteen miles of New Hampshire's coastline. The deal with the magazine was highly lucrative and highly unusual. Six hundred words a month, subject of my choosing—so long as it had to do with the seacoast—and if I submitted crap or submitted nothing, another column would appear under my name, and my substantial paychecks would continue. Some people might call that a hell of a deal. Others might call it a bribe to keep my mouth shut for what I had seen one horrible day in Nevada. Both would probably be right.

Earning this substantial salary meant researching and writing the column, which took about a week every month. This led to an increasingly fat bank account and an increasing amount of free time, which was quickly becoming a burden. There is only so much reading and cleaning you can do, and during the long and empty days, I was beginning to feel worthless, which was the first step on a slippery slope that would lead me to strike out for a swim to England one fine summer day and not turn around.

Instead, I began researching and writing other columns, on matters that interested me and that would never appear in the pages of *Shoreline*. The first was about a group of surfers at the North Beach who didn't seem to spend a lot of time in the ocean, but who were preoccupied with making furtive exchanges among hands, plastic bags and folded currency, with local passersby. This column took a couple weeks of work and some photographs, which I passed along to Diane Woods. I think she was surprised when I showed up with this information, and I know I was even more surprised when she didn't toss me out on my butt for interfering in a police matter. Since then our relationship—on a personal and professional basis—had grown.

After it had developed somewhat on the personal basis, she invited me out one day on her sailboat, *Miranda*, which she keeps in Tyler Harbor. We spent the day cruising up to the Isles of Shoals and back. It was a hot August day and Diane had on a skimpy pair of blue jean cutoffs and a white bathing suit top. She showed off an impressive amount of skin, and three or four times during the day she had asked me to rub suntan lotion on her light brown, muscular back. She had returned the favor, too, which is why I was feeling a bit slap happy when we got back to the harbor.

When the gear was stored and we went up to her condominium, she made us both frozen strawberry daiquiris and quite gently brought me back down to earth.

"Lewis," she said, sprawled out on her couch, "you've been a perfect gentleman all day, and I appreciate that."

I raised my glass to her in a salute, sitting on the floor, leaning against the couch near her feet. "Is this my only reward, or do you have something else in mind?"

When Diane is angry, her face would have caused Ted Bundy to shy away, but when she laughed, as she did then, it warmed something inside of me that I thought was dead. "Very good," she said, a wide smile on her face, "but there is something I have to tell you, just in case you're thinking about what's going to happen between you and me. Just so you know, my heart belongs to another."

Oh. "Well, I understand."

She was still smiling, and she shook her head. "No, you don't. Let me explain it to you. We're becoming friends, and I like that very much, but do know this about me. When I said my heart belongs to another, I didn't mean another person. I meant another gender. My gender. Understand?"

Oops. I took a swallow from the daiquiri, and it was a delicious cold slipperiness that traveled right down my throat and gave me a second or two to recover.

"Does that mean no date for this Saturday night?" I asked with some innocence.

She laughed and said, "Absolutely not. If you want to come here Saturday night, I'll cook you dinner, so long as you wash the dishes. Deal?"

"Deal," I said. "And I suppose I don't get to spend the night."

Diane winked. "If you want to, but it'll be on the couch."

"Best offer I've had all summer."

She kicked my hand. "How about another daiquiri?"

A pleasant nod. "Sure."

And we've been friends ever since.

THE ROADS WERE NEARLY EMPTY, and my mind was surprisingly clear as I drove south, heading to Newburyport. The shock of an early morning phone call can make you as alert as a deer smelling gunmetal during hunting season. The headlights made the snowflakes look thin and transparent as I drove over the sanded roads. There were only a few other cars on the road at this hour of the morning, and I wondered if we cold and numb drivers shared a common, dreary drive heading to some awful home or catastrophe during those few dark hours that remained of the night.

Newburyport was built right on the banks of the Merrimack River as it passes out to the Atlantic, and the city's hospital is on Rawson Street, which is just off High Street, a heavily traveled avenue that runs east to west through the city. The hospital building is tucked away near a warren of residential streets, and some of the homes still had the bright red and green lights of Christmas decorations in their windows. It was a cheery enough scene, but I couldn't imagine living there, on a street leading to the city's hospital, seeing the ambulances or police cruisers come by at all hours, emergency lights flickering into your bedroom or living room windows.

After parking I hurried across the slippery pavement, heading to the peaceful and shiny red letters of EMERGENCY ROOM, my hands moist in my coat pockets, thinking of what was going to happen in the next few moments. As I got closer to the entrance the doors slid open and Diane came out almost at a run, and I had guilty thoughts of how I should approach or touch her, or what should I do, and Diane took care of the matter by nearly slamming herself into my arms.

She was sobbing, great heaving cries that had no words or syllables, and I put my arms around her and let her burrow her face into my shoulder. I pulled her in tight with my arms, and her arms were across my shoulders, and I felt little thumps of her fists striking my back. I murmured into her hair and then she stepped back, tears rolling down her face, her mouth curled back, and she said, "What did you just say?"

"What?"

"Did you just say everything's going to be all right?"

I said, "No, no. I said go ahead, let it out, Diane."

She drew a hand across her face and started crying again, and I pulled her close and she said, "If you had said that, I swear to God I would have hit you. Nothing's right, nothing at all, and it's never ever going to be right," and the sobs came back.

"How's she doing?" I asked, and then quickly added, "I mean, I know—"

"Yeah, yeah," she said, her voice filled with anguish. "You mean besides the rape, how is she. Oh, Jesus." Diane took a deep, shuddering breath. "She's been beaten up some, around the face. Bruises and contusions, nothing that's going to last. Um, she's bruised elsewhere, too, the guy hurt her pretty bad down there..." Then she was back in my arms, keening, and I held her tight as the snow came down around the hospital.

WITHIN A FEW MINUTES we were on a couch inside the small waiting area, near a dirty coffee table that had magazines scattered around, most with their covers torn. The nurses' station was visible through the door and I could just barely make out the heads and shapes of the people there. Having spent some days in them on several occasions, I have mixed feelings about hospitals. On one hand, they have saved my life a couple of times, and the nurses and the doctors who took care of me during those occasions were straight professionals, compassionate and expert in what they were doing. On the other hand, I was in an unnamed hospital once in the Nevada desert, prevented from leaving by polite, bulky men wearing shoulder holsters. Not an occasion that left many happy memories.

Diane rubbed at her face with a wet towel I had brought from the men's restroom. A television set bolted to a frame from the ceiling was tuned to an all-sports channel, and the sound was off. Some men on the screen were playing soccer. There were two couches and four chairs, and a woman sat on the other couch, her head propped up by a hand, fast asleep. A girl of about three or four was stretched across the couch, dressed in a snowsuit, her head on the woman's lap.

Diane sighed and held the towel in her fists. "I should have been there, goddamn it. We were supposed to have gone out tonight, but that damn fire came up." She turned to me, fresh tears welling up in her red-rimmed eyes. "I should have been there, damn it. I could have prevented it, honest to God, I could have..."

I rubbed her shoulder. "Diane, it's not your fault. Don't torture yourself."

She nodded, chin trembling. "That's what I feel, that I should have been there."

"You were doing your job. It couldn't have been helped."

"Still, it doesn't make it feel any better. Oh, God, what he did to her..."

I spoke softly. "Do you want to tell me what happened? You don't have to if you don't want to. It can wait."

She twisted the towel, stared down at the floor. "No, it can't wait...This is what I know, and it isn't much. She wasn't too sure when I talked to her. Um, she said she was home in bed, sleeping, and then she heard a noise. A guy was in the bedroom door. She sat up and started to talk and then, um, the bastard was on top of her, said he would cut her if she made a noise. She started to struggle..."

Tears were rolling down her cheeks and she looked back up at me. "Kara. My Kara, who doesn't even raise her voice at anything, who's too shy to send back a bad meal, she started to fight this bastard...I don't know if she's the stupidest broad alive or the bravest...He could have killed her, Lewis. He could have killed her."

"Don't blame her for anything. She was just surviving."

Diane nodded. "I know, I know. So that was it." She took a deep, shuddering breath. "Um, he did... he did what he did, and then he left."

"Did she get a good look at him?"

A shake of the head. "No. It was dark. The whole apartment was dark. All she knows is that he was clean-shaven. She thinks he was wearing jeans, because she, um, she felt them on her legs. That's it. And after the bastard left, then Kara panicked."

"What do you mean?"

The towel was twisted again. "I mean she did the wrong thing, that's what I mean. She should have called the cops, she should have called me. Instead she panicked and took a shower and washed the sheets and then came here, and she destroyed the evidence, she destroyed practically every piece of evidence left behind there."

She started sobbing again, lowered her head into her hands.

"Stupid girl," she sobbed. "She should have known better, knowing me. Stupid girl."

I put my arm around her and let her cry for a while. Across from us the woman was still sleeping, and the little girl was now awake, staring at the two of us with the utter innocence and sense of wonderment of a child. I hoped that she would grow up fine and healthy and would never remember this winter night.

AFTER ABOUT ANOTHER TEN MINUTES, a doctor came through the door, clipboard in her hand. She looked to be in her late forties, with short red hair, her eyes heavy with exhaustion. A stethoscope hung around her neck and her nametag said her name was Morse. She reached out and held Diane's hand and sat down next to her.

"You're Diane, right?" Dr. Morse said. "Kara's asking for you. If you want, you can see her in a couple of minutes."

"How is she doing?" Diane asked, her voice trembling.

The doctor nodded. "Physically, she's doing all right, as best as we can expect. She's very scared, about a lot of things, and I think one of the things she's scared about is how you're going to react, if you will still love her, whether you're going to blame her for what happened. That's what she's talking about."

"Jesus Christ—" Diane started, and Dr. Morse held up a hand and said, "I'm not saying she's being rational. She's not. She's been through a very traumatic experience and she's acting human, that's all. Now. She needs to see you, and then a decision has to be made as to whether this will be reported to the police. It's up to her, Diane."

She nodded glumly. "You don't have to tell me that. I know."

The doctor looked at her clipboard. "We've collected what evidence we have, and the rape kit will go to the Newburyport Police Department, if she decides to report it. If not, it will go to the state crime lab for six months." She looked up. "It's her choice. We won't force her. Our primary goal is to take care of her."

Diane rubbed her hands through her hair. "Please. Can I see her again?"

"Certainly." The doctor stood up and I got up with Diane, wondering what I should do, when Diane grabbed my hand and said, "Walk in there with me. Please."

I squeezed back and followed her through the door. Before us was an area of doors and curtains, and I saw a drunk man sitting up on a stretcher, holding a white towel to his bloody head. He had a full mustache, a two- or three-day's growth of beard, and no shirt. Blood had matted on his chest hair and he said over and over again, "Pow. The bastard hit from nowhere. Pow. Jus' like that. The bastard hit from nowhere." A female nurse was next to him, talking in a soothing tone.

We came to a room with a large wooden door, and Dr. Morse knocked on the door and led Diane in. I hung back, not sure what to do, and my feet and hands seemed too large. The door was open and I noticed a shivering woman on an examining table, her head propped up by some pillows, and my first thought was, *They've taken us to the wrong room.* Who's this woman with the scared eyes, the tangled hair? Then Diane choked back a sob and moved into the room, and I realized just how terribly wrong I was. Kara Miles, Diane's best friend and lover, looked at us with bruised and battered eyes. Her right cheek was puffy and her bottom lip was swollen and split open, and there were scratches along her neck. A sheet was up about her bare shoulders, and a nurse was sitting on a stool next to her holding her trembling hand.

"Kara," Diane said, her voice strained, and as she moved forward to hold her. I stepped back, not wanting to be part of such a private scene. I felt out of place, out of time, like I didn't belong. I was out of the room, my stomach aching, my hands cold, and I felt like going outside and sitting in the snow. The staff in the emergency room looked over at me like I was a prisoner making an escape, and I walked back to the waiting area, and I waited. The little girl was still there, her head resting on the older woman's lap, though she was now sleeping again.

I took a cup of coffee I didn't want and sat back, and then I was reminded of something. It was a memory of an August a few years back, of walking along Tyler Beach. I had rested for a few minutes on an outcropping of granite boulders, watching the waves do their dance, seeing the hundreds of tourists stretched out before me, and then I watched a young girl, about nine or ten, playing in the sand. She was turning something in her hands, over and over, and was singing something. A young boy about a year or two older, who I presumed was her brother, was nearby, playing with bright yellow Tonka trucks. Mom was napping on a folding lawn chair. The girl stood up, holding something in her hands, and I saw it was a seashell, about the size of her small fist. I know next to nothing about seashells, but this one looked special. It was light purple and had complex curves that looked as if it had been sculpted in an artist's studio up in Porter.

I smiled at what I saw, but only for a second or two. Her brother had noticed what was going on and had come over, carrying a dump trunk in one hand. With no change in his expression, no words, nothing at all, he grabbed the shell from her hands and began walking away. She followed, shrieking. And then he turned and held the shell up, taunting her, and as she reached up he threw it at the rocks. I didn't hear a thing, but I saw how the shell was broken and destroyed, the pieces tumbling to the sand.

The girl kept on shrieking. Mom stirred herself up from the lawn chair and mumbled something about you kids behaving, and the young boy was looking up at me, defiant, not caring, for he knew I had seen it all and wasn't about to do a thing. His chin was jutting out and I felt a breathless chill, for I saw something dead in those eyes, and I hoped the trio had been visiting from a state far away, and that I would never have the chance to encounter this boy again, especially when he became an adult.

At his feet was something that only a few moments ago was a thing of beauty, a symbol of intricacy and life and peace, and now it rested on the dirty sands, broken and shattered, all because of some dark urges in that young man's mind. And all it took was a few seconds.

Shattered shell. It reminded me of a young woman, now someone completely different from the person she had been this morning, lying on a hospital examining table, being poked and prodded by strangers, in pieces, shivering from the fear.

I sipped at the coffee and burned my tongue and waited.

ABOUT FIFTEEN OR so minutes later, a man came through the emergency room entrance, tan trench coat flapping in the snow, and the way he carried himself instantly said "cop" to me. So the cops had been called in. He was about my height and his eyes looked intelligent enough behind round horn-rimmed glasses. He wore a checked driving cap and what I saw of his hair was black, and his eyes and expression dismissed me as he went to the counter and held his badge. The door to the emergency room quickly opened and just as quickly closed.

I waited some more. The man with the bloody head and mustache came out, coat draped across his bare shoulders, while the doctor—a man this time, not Dr. Morse—explained something to the now-awake woman across from me. The little girl was standing up, saying cheerfully, "Daddy, Daddy," as she hugged his legs. Quite a touching scene, except from the look of Mom's eyes. I gathered that little voice was about the only cheerful sound my mustached friend was going to hear for the next few days. They went out into the snow and in a few more minutes Diane came out.

Her lips were pressed together and the short scar on her chin was shiny white, and these warning signs made me sit right up and not feel tired anymore. Her eyes were red-rimmed and swollen, but her voice was steady as she said, "Can we go outside?"

"Sure," I said, tossing the half-empty cup of coffee into a wastebasket. I followed her through the sliding glass doors and out into the parking lot, and I drew my coat closer against me. The snow had grown heavier, and the cars and trucks in the hospital's parking lot were now odd-shaped mounds. I went to the Rover and climbed in, and Diane joined me, taking the passenger's seat as I started up the engine and switched on the heater.

Diane sighed and rested her head in her hands. I left the lights out and didn't bother to clean off the windshield, letting the snow cocoon us in. I reached over and gingerly rubbed at the back of her neck and she said, "Well, I let my cop instincts overtake everything else, and the Newburyport Police Department is now here."

"I know. I saw the detective roll in a few minutes ago."

"Yeah, you sure did. One Inspector Ron Dunbar, and already I don't like him."

I kept rubbing. "Why's that?"

She sighed and said, "I don't know. Nothing blatant or awful, like him asking her stupid questions about her sex life or sex partners or what she was wearing in bed, did she entice the guy, crap like that. No, he did an okay job, and maybe that's the problem."

"Because that's no standard case in there," I said. "That's Kara."

"You're so right." She turned to me, and her face was a gaunt shadow. "He did everything right and asked the right questions, and he and a squad are going over to her apartment right now, but I can tell. He's just doing it. He's just going through the motions. Call it cop sense, but I don't think he's going to bust his butt on this one, and I can't allow that, not for a moment."

I chose my words carefully. "Do you think he knows about you and Kara?"

I think she tried to smile. "You mean about our alternate lifestyle? No, I don't think so. I think he's just a guy cop a bit overwhelmed with his job and Kara's story so far... Well, she did everything wrong. She shouldn't have destroyed the evidence the way she did. She panicked, and I think this guy is going to hold it against her. I don't think he will make this case a priority, that's what."

Another sigh, and she put her head in her hands and said, "Shit, shit," over and over again, and then said, "We've been through some times, you and me, right?"

"Absolutely true," I said, remembering with a quick tinge of comfort the first time we had met, and how she had helped set me on the road to living again, after the worst months of my life. Although she was aware of what she did, those years back, I'm sure Diane doesn't know the extent of how much she had saved me.

"Then I can ask you for a favor, the biggest favor I've ever asked you."

I shifted some in my seat, the heat in the front just reaching the comfort zone. "You can ask and it's yours."

"You probably won't like it."

Uh-oh. "You're probably right, and I think it probably doesn't make a difference. What do you need?"

She sighed again. "I want your help, Lewis."

"You've got it. Just name it, Diane."

It seemed to take a few minutes as she raised herself up and sat back in the seat, and she reached across and grabbed my hand.

She said, "I want you to help me find him."

No need to ask who he was. "It'll be hard, and might take a lot of time, and the cops here might not like me sniffing around."

"I can handle that," she said. "Will you do it?"

I ran my fingers across the steering wheel. "So we can give him to the cops?"

A pause that seemed to stretch for quite a long time. "No," she finally said. "So I can kill him."

3

A snowplow grumbled by through the parking lot, its amber lights powerful enough to pierce the snow-covered windshield. I looked into Diane's eyes and saw a fierce determination there, a look highlighted by the plow's lights.

I said, "Diane—" and she just as quickly interrupted me.

"I'm absolutely serious," she said. "I know what you're thinking. You're thinking I'm distraught, I'm overwhelmed and a bit crazy, and all of that's true. But it doesn't change what I feel now, and what I know I'm going to feel tomorrow, and feel next week. I want that man dead. I want him gone. And I'm going to need your help."

"What makes you think I can do anything?"

She nailed me with her reply. "Don't give me any crap about being a simple magazine writer. You were once a Pentagon spook, and the fact I've never been able to learn anything about you from the Department of Defense tells me you were important. And if you were important, you were good, and you've got the talents to find this slug."

"You're asking a lot," I finally said, and it felt like the heating system had died.

"I know. But I'm sorry, I need you for this. If they're lucky, the cops may find a suspect. And that's a big maybe. And then my Kara will have to go into a room full of strangers and talk about the intimate details of her life, all while some smart sport from law school does his level best to destroy her on the stand, so his paying scum can slide away a free man. Do you think I'm going to allow that to happen to my woman?"

"Diane, think of what you're doing," I said, trying to keep my voice even. "You're asking me to get involved in something that could put the both of us away for a very long while, not to mention putting a serious crimp into your career—"

Again she interrupted, with an epithet of what I could do with her career. "I don't need lectures. I'm a cop, and I know the chances of anything happening to that bastard are slim. If he's arrested, if he goes to trial, and if he's convicted, then he ends up in the Massachusetts prison system. And excuse me for living, but I'm not too enthusiastic about a prison system that practically has a union for murderers. And if you think he'd serve out his full term in this lovely state, then you're nuttier than I think you are."

"I must be pretty nutty just for staying here and listening to you."

"Maybe so," she said with a sigh. "Remember, too, if he does get convicted, facing a ten- or fifteen-year sentence, then I have Kara facing life..." and her voice cracked. "Kara...she's been raped once, Lewis. I'm not about to let her get raped again by the judicial system. Believe me, I know," and the last four words were said particularly harshly. "That's why I'm going to do this, and I'm going to need your help."

Oh, my. I squeezed the steering wheel and looked over at her, recalling my first months at Tyler Beach, when I had arrived thin and jumpy, waking up at odd hours from dark and steaming dreams, sitting alone at my beach house, drinking and staring out at the ocean, feeling the acid of guilt dissolve me from the inside out, one bone and organ at a time. Then I began my involvement in those activities that skirted and sometimes crossed over the line of legality, and Diane had been there, as I clambered back to life. She had been there from the start, letting me do what I had to do, sometimes passing along help and information at crucial times, and always letting me get away with situations other police officers would have gladly arrested me for.

Diane.

I reached over and touched her face. "I'll do it."

I WALKED HER BACK, her arm looped through mine, and the snowflakes still fell and danced to their death on the ground. As we went up to the lit door I turned to her.

"I might need some other help for this, you know."

"Such as?"

"Such as Felix Tinios." I brushed some snow from my eyes as we stopped. "You and I both know I might have to go into some pretty dark rooms eventually. If that's the case, I want Felix with me, much as you don't like him."

She turned and held my hands in hers. "Last November, when we watched that documentary on Winston Churchill, the night I wanted to watch the ice skating, you said something funny about what Churchill did, back when Hitler invaded Russia. What was it?"

I nodded, impressed once again with Diane's cop memory.

"Churchill got in a load of trouble when he announced England would become allies with the Soviets, right after Hitler invaded. Some of his colleagues were shocked that a conservative anticommunist like Churchill would actually become an ally of Stalin. Some just wanted Hitler and Stalin to fight it out, to bleed each other."

"And didn't he say something about making a pact with the Devil in reply?"

I gave her hands a squeeze. "He said if Hitler invaded Hell, he would at least make a favorable reference to the Devil in the House of Commons."

Diane attempted another smile. "If Felix assists you, I will at least say nice things about him the next time his name comes up at a staff meeting. Do what you have to do but try to be discreet." She squeezed my hands back. "Talk to you tomorrow?"

"Absolutely." I hugged her and she choked, "Sweet God, I love her so much...."

"I know you do. Now go in there, because she needs you."

She gave me a quick peck on the cheek and walked into the emergency room, her shoulders slumped, and I looked around at the snow and lights and homes and wondered where the man was, the man that had brought me out into this night and had ruined two women's lives with less than an hour's effort on his part. Probably near here or in a neighboring town, resting. Was he sleeping? Did he feel guilt? Happiness? A satisfied glow? A lot of questions, and nothing but hard work and dismay ahead for me. I put my hands back into my coat pockets, shivered in the snow and walked back across the lot.

AT HOME, I boosted up the heat and saw from the kitchen clock that it was almost four in the morning. I made a cup of hot chocolate and went out to the living room, sitting on the rear of the couch. The ride home had been rugged enough, with the poorly plowed roads and the snowfall, and even though my vehicle is a nimble beast on bad roads, I was glad when I got her into the garage. I held the steaming cup of hot chocolate in my chilled hands and looked out the sliding glass doors after opening up the drapes.

With no lights on, I was looking out in the dark, watching the snowflakes rage down from the night sky. I felt a draft of cold air drift across my bare feet. Now that I was here, alone and in the dark, I had time to think, and some very loud voices were screaming at me. I tried to tell them to shut up, but I failed. Mostly the voices were saying the same thing, over and over: Are you insane?

"Maybe so," I said, speaking aloud, but it had also seemed so right, back in the parking lot, to help her in return for the many things she had done for me. But now, sitting alone in my house and watching the snow come down, my voices were demanding to know why I had just agreed to take part in something that could result in a murder, and could result in my being brought up on conspiracy charges, or could even end in my own injury and death if I wasn't careful. Marvelous. Ain't friendship a wonderful thing?

So I sat thinking, until the hot chocolate was gone, and I rubbed the still-warm mug against my cool face, and then I left the mug on the coffee table and went upstairs and crawled back into bed, listening to the wind. I thought some more and made a decision, one that I wasn't particularly proud about. Then I debated for a while on whether to turn on the light and do some reading, and while that debate was going on, I fell asleep.

I WOKE up and went back to sleep and repeated the pattern again, until it was nearly eleven a.m. when I stumbled out of bed. After getting dressed and a quick breakfast of tea and toast, I called Felix Tinios's house three times, and each time got a busy signal. The snow had finally stopped, and the sky was the deep blue that comes right after a good-sized storm. I then shrugged on my heavy coat, pulled on some boots, and did some work, shoveling a path from the front door of my house to the garage. The first winter I spent here I had ignored the shoveling and had just beaten down a path to the garage. That had worked well until the hard-packed snow had transmuted itself into slick ice and I fell on my butt. Now I take the time to shovel. I may not be bright, but I can be taught.

After two more unsuccessful calls to Felix, it was time for a drive. The boy must have had his phone off the hook, and I was aching for a visit. During the time I had been outside, I had been thinking with every toss of the shovel. Felix's help was critical, and without it, well, Diane was going to be even unhappier when I next saw her. I couldn't do this alone. I had paused for a moment, breathing hard, resting on the shovel. I looked out toward my tiny cove and looked at the waves and ice, and wondered if any beautiful shells were over there, covered by the snow. I closed my eyes and saw a scared, trembling woman with wounds I couldn't even imagine, and I shook my head and gave it up. I had said yes. I would see it through. And I went for a drive.

Felix lives in the next town over from Tyler, called, oddly enough, North Tyler. Atlantic Avenue was also mostly clean of the snow that had fallen overnight, and say what you will about New Hampshire and its tiny state government, at least they know how to plow roads. Away from the heavy traffic of the summer, everything looked clean and crisp. With the sharp January air, the Isles of Shoals some miles distant out on the Atlantic looked perfect enough to be Christmas decorations.

Felix lives on Rosemount Lane, which juts off Atlantic Avenue to the east and contains six houses, and his home sits alone on a small bluff, over-looking the ocean. Like me, Felix enjoys his privacy, but our living quarters have nothing in common. His is a low-slung ranch, only ten or twenty years old, and I was surprised at what I saw. There was another vehicle, parked next to Felix's own red Mercedes convertible. It was a black Trans Am with Massachusetts plates, its sides smeared white with old road salt. Oops. Looked like Felix had an overnight guest, which explained the busy signals. I was going to turn around and try again later when the door of the house opened up and Felix stepped out with a man. Oops again. Felix saw me and nodded, and I pulled to the side of the road.

The guy was talking to Felix and then shrugged, and Felix gave him a friendly tap on the shoulder and the guy walked down to the Trans Am. I checked him out through the rearview mirror. He was a few years younger than me, maybe in his late twenties, with a thick brown mustache, a day-old stubble of beard, thick, wide shoulders, and dark sunglasses. His brown hair was done up in a tiny ponytail, and he had on pale blue jeans, white hooded sweatshirt, and a dungaree vest. He looked up at Felix when he got to his car and gave a well-I-gave-it-my-best-shot shrug, and opened up the driver's door to his Trans Am. When his door slammed shut, I got out and went up the driveway, where Felix was standing outside.

"Friend of yours?" I asked, as Felix let me in. There was classical music playing—perhaps Haydn—that instantly cut us off from any outside sounds.

"More of an acquaintance than a friend," Felix said. "Here, let me take your coat." He had on pressed blue jeans, a heavy blue chamois shirt, and soft brown slippers, which on anybody else would have made me laugh. However, Felix is not one to accept unexplained laughter sent his way. He was built almost as solid as the man who had just left, with thick hair combed back and a blue-black stubble of beard.

I followed Felix into the living room, and he tossed my coat over an easy chair. Felix's living room has light, airy furniture, with a couple of maga-zines tastefully arranged on the coffee table and that day's copies of the *Boston Globe* and *New York Times*. Windows looked out to the ocean below, and there were no shrubberies, trees, or snow-covered lawn furniture out there to provide a hiding place for someone coming up to the house. Like me, Felix is a fairly recent immigrant to this resort seacoast, but his source was the North End of Boston, where he learned his trade. He once told me his income tax sheet lists his occupation as security consultant, and if you believe that, you probably believe we bombed Iraq to make Kuwait safe for democracy. Since my own tax sheet says I'm only a writer, I've never accused him of being a liar.

"Was that why your phone was off the hook?" I asked, sitting in a matching easy chair, which was done in a light eggshell blue. "Had some business to conduct?"

After turning down the volume on the CD, Felix sat across from me on the couch, grinning easily. "Sort of. When I'm dealing, I hate distractions. Did you try to call?"

"Yeah, which is why I'm here. You getting involved in anything interesting?"

Felix shook his head. "No, not this time. Old Nick is a neighbor from down south, and he has a shipment of, um, well, let's say some pharmaceutical items coming ashore in a few weeks. He wanted to know if I'd be interested in coming along as a chaperone."

"I'm sure. And what did you tell him?"

He rubbed at his pants leg. "Like I've told you before. Nothing to do with drugs. Nothing. The quality of people you get involved with import-export are rotten types, guys who'd turn you in or blow you away if they thought it would help them. That doesn't make for job security or an attractive career. So I said, nope, no thank you. And there were no hard feelings, all around."

"I can tell."

"So. You up to something?"

"That I am, and I'm stopping by to see if you'd be open to having your talents rented for a week or two."

Though the smile was still on his face, there was now an edge there, and I could tell he was getting just a bit uncomfortable. "Oh? For you, Lewis? What's the matter, someone steal a computer disk or something?"

I took a deep breath, knowing I wasn't going to enjoy the next ten or fifteen minutes. "No. An acquaintance of mine was raped last night. Her closest friend, one Diane Woods of the Tyler Police Department, wants help in tracking down the rapist. She knows me and I said yes. Now I'm here, asking for your expertise."

The smile was now gone. "You'll excuse me if I don't start responding enthusiastically, and please don't take offense, but are you out of your fucking mind?"

I sighed. "I've been wondering about that, and I have no choice. Diane's my friend, and I owe her. I can't say no to her, and I won't."

"Sure you can," Felix said. "Put an 'n' and an 'o' together, and take it from there. Look. This is a cop, of all people, asking you to get involved in something very heavy indeed because she can't afford to be so public and do the hunt herself. And knowing Diane, I'm sure once this guy is ID'd, she ain't going to send him a Valentine's Day card."

"You guessed right."

"Who's the acquaintance?"

"Kara Miles of Newburyport. A wonderful woman and close friend of Diane's. I know her some and it made me sick seeing her last night, what had happened to her."

"You say she's friends with Diane Woods?"

"I did."

"Care to elaborate?"

"No."

He shifted in the couch. "So you want my expertise. What do you think, I've got the entire North Shore section of Massachusetts wired, I can make a couple of calls and have this guy wrapped up for you by next Monday'?"

"No, but you have an eye for things, and I know you have good reflexes. That's what I need. We both can do a pretty good tracking job, but you're better when it comes to hands-on stuff. If I'm somewhere and something's going south on me in a hurry, I might hesitate, and hesitation might not be healthy. In the same situation, I think you'd be washing your hands while I'm still debating. Am I right?"

"Oh, quite right. And how do you think Detective Woods will feel, knowing you're asking someone of my character to join you in this little quest?"

I leaned forward, rested my elbows on my legs. "She sends her best. She wants this guy bad, and I know she'd be very happy if you helped me on this."

That seemed to make Felix think. "So it's that serious. Hmmm." He rubbed at the stubble on his chin and said, "If we're successful, then she'd be in our debt, right?"

I sat up. "Forget it. This is a straight hire. Don't think just because you're helping Diane, she's going to ignore you trying to rob the Tyler Cooperative Bank. This is a straight business proposition."

He slowly nodded. "All right. Glad that's spelled out, then."

He got up from the couch and disappeared into the kitchen, and then he came back out with two open bottles of Molson Golden Ale, and I was touched. Felix has never expressed a fondness for my favorite brand, but here he was, keeping a few of the green bottles on ice for me. I took the offering and clinked the bottleneck to his, and he sat back on the couch.

"If I'm in, then we're going to get some ground rules and understandings, right?"

"I wouldn't have it any other way," I said, and for once, I was telling the truth.

"Fine," he said. "If the job is to find this guy, then that's what we do. No side business. Nothing vigilante. We find him and present him to Miss Woods, and it's up to her to decide what happens next. You got me for the next couple of weeks, but if nothing comes up, no leads, no nibbles, not even a breath, then I'm out. I've got better things to do than to chase down ghosts. Either way, I get paid. Which reminds me," and he looked up at me with a grin. "Who gets the bill?"

"I'll take care of it. And another thing. If you're in and I'm paying, then I set the direction, I set the pace. If things get too weird and I decide it's over, then it's over."

He winked. "I'm in. And I wouldn't have it any other way," and I wished then I knew if he was telling the truth.

I STAYED FOR A BIT LONGER, nursing my beer, and we talked about the weather and we both wondered if the Red Sox were going to do anything this year, and I said that as much as I hated for it to happen, one almost wished for another Russian Revolution, because that's the only time the Red Sox ever win a World Series. Felix laughed and said, "You must know a lot about the Russians, considering your past job and all that."

"All what?" I innocently asked, and Felix laughed again and said, "One of these days, you old spy, I'll get you to talk," and I said not on this day, and then I refused a gracious offer to replace the empty beer bottle with a full one. Felix took the empty bottle away and he came back and sprawled out on the couch and his voice got quiet.

"You know this is going to be tough," he said. "I'm not bullshitting you. We're going to be spending some time rooting around in the mud, looking at bad things and talking to bad people that most citizens like to think don't exist. We're going on a trip to the dark side, because we're looking for one sick and nasty man, and I doubt he's going to be very happy when we start knocking on doors and start asking for him. You've got to be ready, because chances are, it's going to get a bit hairy along the way. You understand?"

I nodded. "I've known that ever since I said yes to Diane. I'm not happy about it, I'm not looking forward to it, but I don't see that I have much choice."

His arms were spread out on the rear of the couch, and I noticed the bulge of muscles, even with the thick shirt. "You thought yet how we're going to conduct this little investigation? You don't plan to pretend to be a cop, do you?"

"No, I don't, but I figure my *Shoreline* business card will help out. I'll just say that I'm doing a story about violent crime against women, and that I'm using Kara's case for research. You can be my trusted photographer and assistant. I assume you know which end of a thirty-five-millimeter camera is up, right?"

"I do." He brought his hands together in a sudden clap and said, "In a couple of weeks I'm off to the Cayman Islands on a courier job, but besides that, I'm your man. Give me a call in a few days, and try to get some leads from Diane. See if she can clear the way with the Newburyport cops. I'd hate to get rousted the first day on the case."

"Not a problem."

"Good. Let me walk you out."

I put on my coat and we went outside, the cold air wrapping itself around my face and hands. Felix talked as we went to my Rover. With my fingers on the door handle, I turned to him and said, "Who are we looking for, Felix? Any guesses?"

He shook his head. "Anybody and everybody, and the only requirement is that he can pee standing up. He can be a biker, a minister, a school-teacher, or a stockbroker. Only other requirement is that he has the need to hurt. That's it."

"Could be a lot of guys. With your record, somebody could say that you belong on the list. Criminals all."

If it's possible, Felix almost looked hurt. "That was a rude thing to say, and you know it. Whatever things illegal I get involved with, there's a reason for it. It may not be a good reason, but it's a reason. Enforcement. Courier jobs. Protection. I do it for the money and because I'm good at it, but there's no compulsion in there, nothing that makes me go out and hurt people. Especially women. Don't equate me with the creature that hurt your friend. That's a whole 'nother universe, and even the lowest of us out here know it. Look at prisons. Guys on the bottom of the totem pole are the rapists and child molesters. They usually don't last long."

"If we do what Diane wants, he might not last long, either."

He cocked his head at me. "You're really going to do this, aren't you?"

"What do you mean?" I said, finally opening up the door.

"I thought back there that you'd say we'd be doing this, but only going through the motions. Following empty leads. Wasting time and efforts. Hoping that the cops would eventually find this guy, or hoping that Diane would finally calm down and tell us to stop. I didn't think even you'd have the gumption to get along on a dirty ride like this."

I remembered the decision I made last night before falling asleep, and I said, "You're pretty close, but not on the mark. No, we're going to do what we can, make this as real as possible. But if we do come up with this bastard, I'm going to try my best to see that Diane doesn't do something she might regret."

"She might not let you."

"I know. But I'm going to try."

He gave me a slap on the shoulder. "Sometimes that's all we can do. Give me a call when you can, and you know what?"

"What?" I said, climbing into the front seat.

"As sick as it might sound, it's been a quiet winter, and I'm almost looking forward to getting back to work."

I gave him my best disgusted look as I started up the engine.

"You're right. It does sound sick."

Then I left North Tyler and went home, and eventually fell back to bed, the Molsons and the previous late night sending me back to sleep.

4

Sometime during my afternoon nap the phone rang again and I stumbled downstairs. It was Diane, and she sounded slightly better than she had the night before.

"I'm back home now, and Kara's with me," she said, her voice tired. "She's going to be staying here for a while and screw the town and the gossipers if that's a problem."

"How is she holding up?"

"Oh..." and the torment in that one syllable made me close my eyes, "she's holding up, but sometimes I think she's the one holding me up. Last night at the hospital I was scared and I was pissed, but right now, I'm just pissed." She stopped, and I could hear her breathing. "You haven't changed your mind about anything, have you?"

"Not a bit."

"Thanks," she said. "Look. Give me and Kara a day off tomorrow, all right? And then we can see each other on Monday, look at what we got, and start things rolling."

"That's fine," I said, secretly relieved I wouldn't have to start anything before then. "Will you have anything for me?"

"Oh, on Monday I'm going to try to chisel some stuff out of Inspector Dunbar," Diane said wearily. "Using professional courtesy and that crap, so at least you should be able to see his preliminary report. Tyler and Newburyport cops have a pretty good working relationship, so I should get copies of his case stuff without much of a hassle."

"Does it have a statement from Kara?"

"Yeah, I'm sure it will."

"Let's say I come over Monday afternoon to read the paperwork at your place. Will Kara be there?"

"Of course she will," Diane said. "Why do you want to know?"

"So I can talk to her after I read her statement."

Then it was like a sudden storm had attacked the telephone system, for the phone line was quite quiet and the receiver was like ice in my hand. No sound.

"Diane?"

"Look," and her voice was strained, "she's been through a hell of a lot, and I don't think having her re-interviewed is going to be that helpful. What's the problem?"

"There's no problem." I took a deep breath. "Look, you've asked me to do something. I'm trying to find this guy and I want to talk to Kara after I read the report, make sure that there's nothing there I've missed. Okay? I'm just trying to do the best I can, and I'm sorry if it's painful, but I need to talk to Kara."

A sigh across the phone lines. "I know, I know, you're right. Look. Can it be the end of the week, then? Give her some more time to rest up?"

There are the days when you feel like a shit, and I guess this Saturday afternoon was going to be one of those. "Diane," I said, as gently as possible. "You've told me before, on cases you've worked on, that each minute, each hour, each day counts. Do you really want me to delay this for almost another whole week?"

"No," she snapped back, and I tried to talk some more, and after a couple of one-syllable answers I gave up and we agreed to talk again on Monday.

I rubbed at my forehead after hanging up the phone, remembering again why I was doing something that was going to the very edge of criminality. Friendship. And I was beginning to get scared of what was happening to this one.

. . .

LATER THAT NIGHT I scraped off enough snow from the back deck so I could bring down my telescope. With the tripod it's one bulky piece of gear, and I took my time manhandling it from the upstairs bedroom. I had on a quilted winter jacket, wool cap, and wool gloves cut off at the fingertips, and I was chilled setting it up outside. Astronomy is always a venture of trade-offs, and this evening was no exception. The night was as clear and as crisp as only winter can bring, which meant that the stars shone hard and bright, but which also meant that my hands trembled with cold when setting up the lenses.

My target tonight was in the southeastern horizon: the constellation Orion, the hunter. It had risen above the horizon, and the light pollution was low enough that I could make out the three stars in his belt quite well, thank you. It was even so clear that the red star in his upper left shoulder shone bright indeed, and the star named hundreds of years ago by Arab astronomers, Betelgeuse, rose majestically up with the rest of the giant. At his right foot was the blue star Rigel, and the mighty hunter's sword and belt were also clear. Above him and over his shield is the constellation Taurus, the bull, and the two of them had been locked in combat for thousands of years, as long as the race called mankind looked up into the stars and thought and fantasized.

With some work I adjusted the scope and looked below the three stars of the belt. There is an odd, fuzzy patch of light that is visible there, especially on clear nights, and I could make it out just fine with the naked eye. It looked like part of the "sword" that was hanging down from Orion's belt. But when I aimed the telescope dead center at the patch, something glorious came into view: the Great Nebula of Orion, also known as M42. The faint green patch was a giant cloud of gas and dust, and I bet I was the only person on Tyler Beach looking at it this cold Saturday night.

Minutes dragged by as I kept watch on the Great Nebula, and I admit I was entranced by what I was seeing, and even the cold didn't seem to bother me. It's easy to lose oneself while stargazing, and this night was one of those times. I thought about these same stars, rising each winter, and how they had risen over thousands of years of history and horror on this little globe. Desert nomads, ancient Mayans, medieval Crusaders, Asian Cossacks—these stars had been over the heads of them all. The Mesopotamians, Egyptians, and Greeks all knew this constellation well, and whatever descendants still existed ten thousand years from now, they would still know that collection of stars, the fabled hunter, forever staving off a blow from the charging bull.

Then I heard something, off toward the beach, and the trance was broken.

I breathed, stamped my feet, looked up, and realized that my back was stiff and my fingers were numb. I cocked my head, pulled up my hat to unveil my ears, and listened again. The sound of sirens, far off. From an ambulance or a police cruiser, perhaps.

Or from fire engines.

I looked south, trying to see if there was a faint pink glow to the sky, marking another pyre, another set of dreams destroyed, another unsolved arson on Tyler Beach. Hard to believe, but the late night's phone call from Diane had packed up my fears about the arsonist and had placed them in the attic. I hadn't thought of the arsonist once this past day and a half, and it was easy to see why. Too many crises had shut down the brain. I waited for another few minutes, waiting to hear my phone ring, and I was pleased with the continued silence. Earlier I had made an arrangement with the night fire dispatcher to call me if any suspicious fires erupted, and I guess I was getting a night off.

"So who elected you defender of the faith?" I muttered, as I replaced the lens caps and prepared to go back in. I slid open the door and stripped off the heavy clothing, and then dragged the telescope back upstairs. From there I went into my office and switched on a couple of lights, and on my desk, next to my Apple computer, was a thick file. ARSONS was written on the tab. I blew air into my still-frigid hands and powered up the computer, and I started printing some files. As the files printed, I went back downstairs and made a phone call to Paula Quinn of the *Chronicle*. It was about nine o'clock.

Her answering machine picked up after the third ring, and I tried to make my voice sound cheerful when I left her a message, and then I let my frown come back when I hung up. Out on a Saturday night. Why not? Isn't that what most normal people did, instead of standing outside in the cold, looking at the ten-thousand-year-old light from a lump of gas and dust? She was probably out with her photographer friend, Jerry Croteau, maybe having dinner and seeing a movie, and why not?

"Knock it off," I muttered, and after another trip upstairs to shut down the computer and put the newly printed sheets of paper into the file folder, I came back to the living room. I knelt at the fireplace and reached in and opened the damper, and then crumpled up a few sheets of yesterday's *Globe*. A handful of sticks and a couple of logs and one match later, I had a fairly nice blaze building up in the fireplace, and the heat warmed my face and soothed me. I sat before the fire, feeding in another log, just watching the flames crackle up, seeing the red embers form and fall away, watching the entire magic of having something as dangerous and as awful as fire, trapped and tamed in my living room.

WELL, my phone message worked, which is why on Sunday morning I was with Paula, but instead of meeting for brunch as I had earlier offered, she wanted to pay a visit again to the burned bones of the Rocks Road Motel. I pulled in behind her Ford Escort and we both got out and she came over, smiling, her breath forming little clouds in the air. The day was clear and cold, and luckily, there was no wind.

"Thanks for meeting me here," she said, smiling, holding a reporter's notebook in her gloved hands. "I hate working on Sundays, but I figured if I got this taken care of first, I'd then take you up on your brunch offer."

"Hungry?" I asked, knowing the answer quite well. Paula has a much stronger appetite than I do, and her body is quite efficient at burning off calories, something I wish her body could teach mine.

"Starved," she said, still smiling, with a look that reached in and tickled me in a quiet way. "Let's go see what's up."

Last Friday night this street had been packed with fire gear, firefighters, and the typical crowd that always forms at a fire. Today I felt as if we were extras in a movie that took place in some winter apocalypse. Except for a red Chevette parked in front of the rubble that used to be the Rocks Road Motel, ours were the only vehicles on the street. The other motels had their windows and doorways boarded up with plywood. It was so quiet that the loudest sound was what our boots made, crunching through the snow.

Yet as we got closer to the Rocks Road Motel, there was the fumbling noise of an out-of-tune engine, and I saw gray tendrils of exhaust coming up from the Chevette's tailpipe. Mike Ahern was sitting in the front seat, smoking a cigarette and writing on a pad. He had on his yellow turnout gear and he looked up at us and then went back to his paperwork as we got closer.

"I needed to talk to Mike and he said this was the best and only time to see him," Paula explained. "I think the little bastard thought I wasn't going to come out here on a Sunday morning to interview him."

"I guess he doesn't know you as well as I do."

Paula smiled. "He should live so long," she said, and I had to smile at that.

Mike dropped the cigarette on the snow, looked over, and said, "So how come I'm so lucky I get two reporters bothering me at the same time?"

"Luck has nothing to do with it," I said. "Maybe poor timing, and the fact Paula and I are friends, but I wouldn't say it's luck."

He sighed, scratched at his unshaven face. "No, I guess not, the way my luck has been running. Well, Miss Quinn of the *Tyler Chronicle*, now that you've managed to corner me, what can I do for you?"

Paula had dug out her pad and pencil and then gracefully went into her work mode, a process I've always admired. "The usual stuff, Mike. When I was here Friday night, all you said was that it looked like arson. You got anything more firm?"

"Well, I could say that it's a probable arson. What else?"

"What makes you think that?"

"The normal signs," Mike said, smiling, as if he were enjoying this little give and take, and for all I know, he was.

"Such as?"

"Accelerant signs," Mike explained. "Look ... well, shit, let me show you. Come with me, if you've got the time."

"Oh, I think we can do that," Paula said.

Mike got out of the car, carrying a large black flashlight, his fire coat flapping in the breeze. He trudged across the snow-covered lot, packed down from the fire engine tires of two nights ago. The ruins of the motel were covered with snow, the blackened beams poking out like the skeleton of some huge beast. Most of the windows were broken and there were new NO TRESPASSING PER TYLER F.D. signs nailed to the walls. One of the signs was near a larger sign that said, THANKS FOR EVERYTHING SEE YOU NEXT SEASON! and we climbed through the open main door. Inside, the smell of burnt debris was still quite strong. Mike clicked on the flashlight as we entered the lobby, and we walked past sodden piles of brochures and pamphlets, each promising a wonderful time at sunny Tyler Beach.

"Watch yourself," he said. "It's pretty icy back here."

His flashlight lit the way through a dirty hallway, the carpet blackened and hardened in some areas with ice. At one point we had to do some fancy stepping over some crumpled beams and ceiling tiles, and Paula tripped and I grabbed her arm.

"You all right?" I asked, enjoying the sensation of holding her.

"Oh, I'm just fine, but I'm gonna hit up the paper for a cleaning bill later," she said. "I've got ashes on me and I know everything's going to reek when we're out of here."

After a few more yards we were in an area that looked like it might have been a storage room. It was almost impossible to make out what had been there earlier, for everything was a blackened mass of objects, some fused together. Part of the ceiling had collapsed, and Mike switched off the flashlight and stepped closer into the destroyed room.

"This is where I think it started, and the state fire marshal's office, God love 'em, is inclined to agree with me," Mike said. "Care to guess why?"

I spoke up. "This is where you found evidence of accelerants—something like kerosene, gasoline, or lighter fluid. The ignition point."

Mike nodded. "That's right. This was Mr. Keller's office, the owner, and he also used it for paper goods storage. Fire started here and went up through the walls, and by the time we got here ... well, our guys would have been hard-pressed to save the foundation."

"Did you take samples from here?" Paula asked, notebook stuck in her hand.

"We certainly did."

"And the samples told you that accelerants were present."

Mike grinned. "Nope. The report's not back from the state lab yet."

Paula looked up from her notebook, eyebrows furrowed. "So how do you know that gasoline or something else was used here?"

He tapped the flashlight against the side of his head, near the burned tissue. "I used my eyes. Here, let me show you something."

Mike squatted to the floor and ran his fingers across the scorched and blackened wood. "See this? Wooden floor, looks all burnt to hell. Right? Intense heat and flames. That's what you see on the surface, but I don't like to just look at the surface. Watch." From his coat pocket he took out a folding knife, which he undid, and then with the blade he dug at the floor. The knife looked tiny in his huge hands. He pulled up a couple of long slivers, and undamaged wood was exposed from under the charred covering.

"The damage doesn't go that deep," Paula said, holding her notebook in both hands.

"That's right," he said, as if pleased she had guessed right. "Intense heat, but fast heat. Whatever burned in here quickly burned off. That tells you the fuel was something that burned in a short period of time. And if you look at the floor joints... " He dug around some more, exposing an area between two boards. It was black all the way through.

"See that?" he said, tapping on the wood with his knife. "Let's say gasoline was spread over the floor. It runs down the cracks, so when the fire is lit, the fire reaches down through the soaked joists. Classic accelerant signature, and I knew what we had the minute things cooled down and we got in here."

"So you have gasoline or something similar poured in here. How did it start?"

He stood up, closed the knife, and put it back into his coat, grinning. "Now, now, Miss Quinn. You really can't expect me to give away any of our trade secrets, can you? So I'll have to say no comment."

She scribbled some more in her book, looked up, and smiled. "Outside you told us this was a probable arson. Care to change that to arson, with no probable attached?"

Mike nodded. "All right, I'll give you that. A definite answer. This was arson."

The hand with the pencil moved furiously. "And connected to the other three fires? All these arsons, are they connected in some way?"

Mike paused, rubbed at his chin. "The reporter from *The Porter Herald*, he might be pissed if I tell you that. It'll mean a scoop for you, won't it?"

"Unless he calls you between now and first thing Monday morning. Otherwise, yeah, then this will be an exclusive."

"Hmm..."

She brought her hands down to her waist, gloved fingers holding on to the pencil and notebook. "Look at it this way, Mike. I don't see him shivering in here on a Sunday morning. Do you? So who deserves the story?"

That made him laugh, and he kicked at the floor and said, "Sure, you can say that. All four fires were connected. And now, if you'll excuse me, I got a hell of a lot of work to do before this day is done. So you'll kindly get the hell off this fire scene, okay?"

MIKE WENT PAST US, and Paula caught my eye, and I knew she was proud of what she had just wormed out of Mike Ahern. And I also knew that she was overly talented for a newspaper like the *Tyler Chronicle*. We followed him out, Mike lumbering through the debris like a trained bear, shuffling and sniffing, and I blinked hard when we got outside, for the late morning sun was reflecting quite strongly off the snow. As we started back, Mike called out and said, "Lewis, a minute alone, if that's okay."

I looked at Paula and shrugged, and she said, "Men," in the same tone she uses when discussing editors, and I joined him at his Chevette. He tossed his flashlight on the seat, turned to me, and said, "You want to set up a time this week?"

"Do I?" I asked, not sure what he was saying.

He shook his head. "Last Friday night, remember?"

Oh. Last Friday night. He had agreed to see me about the arsons, and I had agreed to give him whatever information I had gathered in my research. Well, such a meeting seemed fairly useless considering what I was going to be involved with during the next few weeks, but then I remembered my upcoming brunch, and thought it wouldn't hurt.

"Sure, Mike. Sorry I forgot. What's a good day for you?"

"Let's shoot for some time on Friday. And is this going to be worthwhile?"

"I certainly hope so," I said, and then there was a creaking noise and a loud bang. We both turned in time to see a scorched beam at the motel, weighed down by the snow, fall into the mound of debris. I looked back at Mike and said, "What a waste."

"What do you mean?"

"Look at this," I said. "A guy builds a motel, runs a business that does fairly well, employs a bunch of people, and in one night some clown takes it all away."

Mike fished a cigarette from a pack hidden in a shirt pocket, lit it up, and shrugged. "Screw 'em. That's what insurance is for."

WE HAD brunch at practically the only open restaurant on Sunday morning in this part of Tyler Beach, which was the Portside Room, the in-house restaurant for the Ashburn House, located at the head of Ashburn Avenue. The Ashburn House is one of the more luxurious hotels on Tyler Beach, and also has a popular nightclub and the Portside Room, considered one of the finer restaurants on the seacoast. The maître d' sniffed at our smoky clothes and sat us in a corner, which was fine. I carried a Sunday *Boston Globe* and inside the newspaper I had secreted the file folder I had prepared last night.

I ordered the eggs Benedict, while Paula had three scrambled eggs, hash browns, and bacon. As we ate we passed sections of the *Globe* around, and I read the editorial page and tried to keep my chuckling down to a minimum, while Paula stuck with the comics and the arts pages. When the dishes had been cleared away and we were both working on our second glasses of orange juice, I said, "Congratulations on getting a scoop for Monday. Will it make the *Porter Herald* angry?"

Her eyes were glittering as she picked up her juice glass. "It sure will, and I can hardly wait. They're trying to beat us in a circulation war, but being idiots, they don't have the resources. You can't cover a town like Tyler by going to the weekly selectmen's meetings and calling the police station every morning to see what's in the log. That's what the *Herald* reporter does, and that's why I'm going to clean his clock tomorrow."

"Good for you," I said, and then I reached in past the advertising circulars and pulled out the file folder. "Here. This is for you. Maybe it will help in some clock cleaning next week."

She took the folder, gave a quick glance inside, and said, "Okay, I think I should thank you, but what's this all about?"

"It's stuff I've done research on for an article," I said, letting the old lie slip easily from my lips. "I've looked into the background of the people who had their motels burned these past weeks, trying to find a connection, patterns or something."

"And?"

"Didn't find a damn thing."

"So you're passing it along to me."

"Thought you could use it, maybe take a fresh look at it."

That brought a nice smile. "Such confidence you have in my abilities."

She opened the folder again, took a longer look, and read the names aloud. "Rob Olcott, owner of the SeaView. Been on the beach for five years. The first one, about mid-December. Then there was Karen Spooner. Remember her, that counterculture woman from Oregon? Ran the Snug Harbor Inn, right up to the first week in January. That was a sad one; saw her life savings go up in smoke. Then there was Frank Durant, owner of the Tyler Tower Motel. That burned down last week. Also runs a place up in North Tyler, and he told me that he sleeps there nights, with a shotgun at his side."

Paula looked up at me. "Not much here on Sam Keller."

"Well, that one was only a few days ago. Didn't have time to do some digging."

She ran her thumb across some of the papers. "Looks like you made up for it with the other three people. I recognize some of these documents, from the town and the Secretary of State. But where did you get this other stuff?"

I took a sip from my orange juice. "You'd be surprised what you can find out with a computer, modem, someone's birth date, and Social Security number."

She looked at me. "No, I'd be surprised why someone who claims to be a magazine writer goes to this length to find information about motels being burned down. What's the point?"

"Maybe he or they will start burning down houses for fun," I said. "Or maybe they'll pick a motel that isn't boarded up, that's filled with guests. Either way, I don't like what's going on in Tyler. This is winter, a time to take it slow and easy. Those poor firefighters have enough to worry about without a nut trying to burn down half the beach. Besides," I added, smiling, "all these fires cost a lot of overtime. Consider me just another concerned taxpayer."

"So you think it's a nut, do you?"

"If it's a nut, then there's nothing you or me or Mike Ahern or the cops can do about it, until he gets caught or surrenders. But I don't know. Consider it a gut feeling. This whole mess doesn't feel like it's a nut. The motels that have been burned, well, it feels like they were chosen for some reason, something that's not apparent."

Again, she held up the folder. "Something not in here?"

"That's right. I've talked some to Diane Woods, a little bit to Mike Ahern, and I've done all that research, and there's nothing there, no connection. I've looked to see if any of them were in financial difficulties. Nothing. Oh, they weren't rich, but all three were doing all right, and I'll bet you that Sam Keller and his wife were doing okay as well. I thought maybe that they each had a secret partner, or maybe a behind-the-scenes person who owned all of the places, but that didn't go anywhere, either."

"So why the gift?"

I stopped for a moment as our waitress dropped off the check, which I beat Paula in picking up. I left a hefty tip and Paula smiled. Winters are hard in New Hampshire, and especially hard for those workers dependent on people climbing out of a perfectly warm house and driving through freezing weather for an expensive breakfast.

I said, "The gift is for three reasons. First, I've got something coming up this week, and I can't spend as much time working on this."

"Oh, something interesting?"

I felt a queasiness at the back of my throat, knowing what I would be doing tomorrow.

"Something that has to be done," I said. "So I thought you might like some additional background, maybe some extra places you can poke around. Second, well, I may be good in digging up records, but Paula, you know the people here better than I do. I can't remember the last time I've been to a selectmen's or a planning board meeting. You know the people, and I think you might be able to find some connections there I've missed. Are these people related in some way? Go to the same church? Have feuds?"

She smiled and put the folder down on her coat, which was in the chair next to her. "You make me sound like Queen Gossip. And let me tell you, you haven't missed that much in going to town meetings. Most people who go are hardworking types, just trying to do their best for the town and themselves, but usually they're drowned out by small minds wrestling with even smaller issues. And what was the third reason?"

"The third reason is that I think you're a dear. That's why you got the gift."

I think she blushed, which made me happy. Nice to know I still had that ability. She finished off her juice and said, "You know I've been spending time with Jerry."

"I know. Is it nice?"

She shrugged. "Nice enough," and she looked up at me, something in her expression. "It's just that I think you're a dear, too. Don't you forget it."

"I won't."

As we got up and dragged on our winter coats, she said, "I'm impressed with what you got there." And then she giggled. "Is it because of your spy training?"

"Maybe it is, maybe it isn't."

We walked out and then we were in the cold sea air. She put her arm through mine and said, "In the time I've known you, I've tried practically everything, from threats to bribes, to get you to talk about what you did in the Pentagon, or to find out why when you're in a bathing suit, it looks like someone's used your skin for target practice. Why won't you talk?"

I squeezed her arm with mine. "It's not a matter of won't. It's a matter of can't."

"Was it dangerous?"

"Rarely. Mostly it was boring."

"But secretive."

"Very."

We reached her car and as she fumbled in her coat for her keys, she said, "So when can I expect you to tell me? When we have a new president? A new Congress?"

I touched her cheek. "The day people decide they don't want secrets anymore, and the spooks are all happily paid off to retirement, and we don't have to worry about demons who blow up airlines, shoot children in playgrounds, or burn down houses in the middle of the night, then give me a call, and I'll tell you everything."

She shook her head. "I won't hold my breath."

"Neither would I."

"Thanks for the gift. I'll let you know if I get anything," and she smiled one more time. "That will be a wonderful day, when I can get a scoop over *Shoreline* and the *Porter Herald* in one mouth."

I said that was fine and I gave her a quick kiss, which was nice enough, and then I walked back to my own vehicle, digging my hands in my pockets, boots crunching on the snow and ice, looking out at the empty sands of Tyler Beach and the cold waters of the demanding ocean, dreading the week that was ahead of me.

5

At about ten on Monday morning I went to a condominium complex called Tyler Harbor Meadows, which is on the northern end of Tyler Harbor where it narrows to meet the tidal flow of the Wonalancet River. It's made up of about a dozen townhouses, built near the water's edge and together in a horseshoe formation, and I pulled into an empty parking spot near number 14, Diane Woods's place.

There was a brisk wind coming off the harbor and I kept my hands in my coat as I walked across the parking lot, glancing back once. Out on the harbor was the normal complement of fishing boats, but all of the sailing boats—including Diane's *Miranda*—were gone, now in storage. I didn't like the view. I liked seeing Diane's boat out there, for I had been on a number of enjoyable day jaunts with her and sometimes with Kara as an extra passenger—and just seeing the empty cold waters was disturbing.

Diane answered the door on the first ring, and she tried to smile as she took my coat and failed. This wasn't going to be a smile-filled morning. I followed her up the carpeted stairs, which led to a kitchen on the left overlooking the parking lot and the harbor. On the right was a small living room with a low wooden counter holding up a television and stereo system, and a tan couch with matching chairs. There was another set of stairs that led upstairs to a bedroom and a study.

The kitchen had a white-tiled floor and a glass-topped table with white tubular chairs. On the refrigerator door were a number of photographs. Most either showed Diane with Kara or Kara alone, and there were a lot of smiles. I could not look at those happy pieces of paper for more than a few seconds before my throat started to ache. Diane draped my coat over one of the chairs and said, "Thanks for coming."

"You're welcome," I said, still holding a small tan notebook in my hand. "How's Kara doing? Is she eating all right?"

Diane shrugged, one hand on the back of the chair, leaning on it for support. "She's doing better, but she can only do soft foods, like scrambled eggs or soup. Her jaw's still pretty sore...And the bruises..."

She paused, gave a quick nod. "It's the nighttime when it's worse. She doesn't sleep that well, and she wants all the lights on, and, well, most of the time she has a bad dream about every couple of hours."

"She's upstairs?"

"Yeah, she was reading when you got here." She folded her arms. "Can't watch too much daytime TV. Ever watch daytime TV? All the goddamn talk shows, most of them have to do with violence against women or some sexual freak show, or shows that make us look like crazed, man-hating deviants, and shit like that Kara doesn't need to see right now."

I kept my voice gentle. "Is she ready to see me? Does she know what I'm up to?"

A curt shake of the head. "We've talked about it, and that hasn't been a wonderful topic to discuss, but yeah, she knows what you're here for, what's going to happen." Her eyes filled a bit, and she turned to look at the harbor. "Oh, Christ, this is so hard.... There's no way I can sleep at night, knowing he might get away with it, that he's laughing, telling his buddies about screwing Kara. I can't let him get away with it."

I rubbed at the notebook. "I know. And Felix and me, we're going to do our best."

She looked back at me, briefly rubbed at her eyes. "Felix Tinios is going work with you on this? Really? What was the jerk's price?"

"Nothing you have to worry about," I said. "Look, let's get started."

Diane nodded briskly, started walking around the kitchen table. "You're right. I have the incident report in my study. Do you want to look at that first?"

"No," I said, following her to the set of stairs that went up to the next floor of the condo. "Later, but right now I want to hear it fresh, and from Kara."

"I understand."

My legs were heavy as I went upstairs, and I tried to concentrate on what I would be doing over the next few minutes. At the top of the stairs a door to the right led to Diane's study, and the opposite door opened up to a bedroom that had a grand view of the harbor, the marshes, and the boxy buildings of the Falconer nuclear power plant a couple of miles away. I was trying to smile as I went into the bedroom. There was a set of bureaus, two rocking chairs, a television, and sitting in bed, up against the pillows, was Kara Miles, friend and lover of one of my best friends, a talented computer programmer who enjoyed Cajun music and mountain climbing, and who was now known simply as a rape victim.

And at that thought, I stopped pretending to smile.

Though Kara did do her best to smile at me as I came in. A blue down comforter was pulled up to her waist and she had on a green plaid flannel nightgown, buttoned to the neck with a little red bow, a romance novel folded over on her lap. On the nightstand next to her was a box of Kleenex, a reading lamp, a glass of water, and some medicine bottles. On the night-stand on the other side of the bed were some paperback books and a leather holster with Diane's .357 Ruger service revolver.

There was a chair near the foot of the bed, which I took, and Diane clambered up on the bed, outside of the comforter, and put her arm around Kara's shoulders. Kara blinked and reached up with a free hand and patted Diane's wrist. It was hard not to stare. Her eyes were still puffy, though the scratches on her neck looked like they were healing. Her right cheek was still swollen and her bottom lip looked awful, red and split open. Kara's light brown hair was done in a modified flattop with semi-shaved sides, and I guessed Diane must have washed her hair in bed, and I was touched by the thought.

"Well," I finally said.

Kara tried to smile again. "Here to save my soul, Lewis?"

I crossed my legs. "No, I'll leave that up to Diane. I'm just here for information, Kara, whatever you can tell me, and I'm sorry it's going to be so hard."

She moved her hand against Diane's, shifted some so that she was looking up at her. "I'm sorry, too. Why can't you just look at the police report? It's all there."

I made to answer, but Diane was faster. "Because he wants to hear it from you and doesn't want to read it from some official report."

Kara shook her head. "I'd rather just try to forget it all happened..."

Diane moved closer to her on the bed. "Hush, now. We've talked about this over and over again, hon. You know what we agreed. Please. Lewis is here to help—you, me, the two of us. I'll be right here. Every second."

Kara turned her head, looked out the window, and then she looked at me, her eyes filled with tears, but there was no fear or sadness there in those eyes. Just a flat anger.

"Go ahead," she said.

I looked down at the notepad, uncapped my black ink ballpoint. "Do you have a fairly good idea of what time it happened?"

"An exact time," she said, her tone bitter. "At one-fifteen in the morning, on Saturday. I heard someone opening the bedroom door and coming in and I woke up and looked at the clock. I checked the time, and I thought..." and her voice caught for a moment, "I thought it was Diane, coming in. We had made plans earlier, except that she called, 'cause of that fire. So I sat up and said something, and then ... then it happened."

"What do you remember happened first?"

She let out a breath, as Diane slowly rubbed her cheek. "Oh, shit, well, it all was a jumble, you know? Jesus, I was scared...the minute he jumped on the bed and grabbed me by the throat...I've never been so fucking scared in my life...I was rock climbing up on Cathedral Ledge last summer, and my harness came loose when I was a hundred feet up, and I started falling and I caught a ledge...I was so scared I peed myself, and that was nothing, not a damn thing, compared to what it was like that night..." She coughed and Diane looked at me, tears rolling down her cheeks, and I knew with absolute certainty that I would never back away from this one. Never.

"How long was he there for?" I asked, trying to keep my voice even.

"Oh, shit, when he left...shit, I checked the clock and it was almost two...but I knew I was just there, lying, not moving for the damn longest time after he left...He just jumped on the bed and grabbed my throat and said if I moved, if I screamed, then he'd cut me...Um, I just lay there for a bit, trying to pretend I was somewhere else, hoping that someone would rescue me, just like in these fucking romance novels..."

Diane winced and I knew that a spike of guilt had just gone through her heart. Kara continued, saying, "And he was just pounding me...Christ, it hurt so much...and I couldn't stand it and I tried to claw his eyes out...and then he started beating on me...Then I panicked after he left, I started cleaning myself up, cleaning up the room, 'cause I couldn't stand the thought of him still being there, his smell, his fluids, so I cleaned for a while...I don't remember much else, shit, I'm sorry," and the tears came back again and I so much wanted to stop talking and leave these two women alone.

Instead I asked, "Did you get a look at him at all? Any features, anything?"

"No, it was dark. I just know he was wearing jeans, and I think he was white, I'm not sure. It was all going so fast."

"Was he clean-shaven?"

"Hunh?"

"Did he have a beard? Mustache? Something you saw or felt?"

Kara's tone turned quickly. "Why?" she demanded. "Do you think he was kissing me? Do you think he was trying to seduce me after breaking into my apartment and jumping on my bed? Right? Kissing me tenderly on the lips and neck, so I could tell in the dark if the asshole had a mustache and beard?"

I swallowed, looked over at Diane, and she said, "Kara? Please. Could you tell if he had a beard or mustache?"

She looked away from us, burrowed into the comforter. "No. He was clean-shaven."

My hand was beginning to cramp from writing so fast, trying to get every word down exactly, and I said, "Just a couple of more questions, and then I'm finished. Kara, has anything odd been going on the past few weeks before this? Obscene phone calls? Problems with a neighbor or someone at work? Anybody odd hanging around the neighborhood that made you feel uncomfortable? Anything at all?"

One word. "No."

"Kara, did he say anything at all that might be helpful in tracking him?"

She looked incredulous. "Like what?"

"Like something that indicated he had been following you, or that he knew you at all. Did he say your name?"

Her tone was the same. "He said three things. At the start, he said if I fought or screamed, he'd cut me. At the end, he said if I went to the cops, he'd cut me. And in the middle, he said, shut up and take it, bitch, take a real man's cock."

"Oh."

Kara said, "Why, does that sound like one of your dates, or one of your fantasies?"

Diane started to say something and I shook my head and put the pen away and folded up the notebook, and as I left the room I said to Kara and Diane, "I'm sorry this all happened, and I'm sorry I had to do this."

Downstairs I poured myself a glass of orange juice and looked closer at the photographs plastered up on the refrigerator door. My heart was racing along from the past minutes I had spent upstairs, and I didn't feel particularly happy or proud to be a man. I know that sounds like the classic white male guilt, but tell me how many female rapists there are in prison and that'll give you an idea of what I was thinking about.

Diane came downstairs after a while, and I was sitting in a kitchen chair, looking out to the flat water of the harbor. A few gulls crisscrossed the sky, and the orange and yellow lights of the nuclear power plant were steady from across the marsh. Diane went to the sink and washed her hands and face and dried herself off with a towel, and then turned, leaning back against the counter.

"I'm sorry about what went on up there."

"No apologies needed. Whatever she said or did is fine. I don't take it to heart."

She shook her head. "No, I don't mean I'm sorry that she got upset with you. I'm sorry that you had to see Kara like that."

"I've seen Kara enough times before to know what she's like. She's just scared and hurting, and that's entirely understandable."

Both of her hands were grasping the counter. "You don't know what it's like."

"You're absolutely right."

"I mean, there she is, upstairs, and she's not the same person anymore, and neither am I. The Kara and Diane that were alive and breathing last Friday are dead. They were killed by an animal that broke into her apartment and raped her. Do you know what she's been going through, besides the trauma and the humiliation and fear? I mean, that asshole wasn't practicing safe sex, you know that? So when she was at the hospital she had to take a morning-after pill, which made her nauseous all this past weekend, and she had to have a shot of antibiotics in her butt, and she's going to have to get an AIDS test in a month, and every month for at least a year. Jesus."

Diane rubbed at her face, looked out toward the harbor, and her hands were shaking some. "You don't know what it's like."

This time, I didn't bother repeating myself. I just nodded in agreement.

After a bit she said, "Let me get you the Newburyport police file."

SHE WALKED ME OUT, her breath making little clouds in the cold air, and held on to my arm and said, "I've talked to Inspector Dunbar, told him that you'd be seeing him this week. I said you were doing research on a magazine article and were going to use Kara's case as a test example of how sex crimes are investigated in Massachusetts."

"I imagine he was thrilled by that," I said.

"You're right, and don't expect too much. Like I said back at the hospital, I don't think he's putting this case on the front burner. Just the way he talks tells me a lot."

I looked over at her and said, "Does he know about your relationship with Kara?"

"Oh, I don't know," she said, rubbing at her upper arms. The wind had picked up some and it had gotten colder. "Maybe he does and maybe that's why he's not hot to trot on the case, but I could give a shit. I'm not really counting on him, you know."

Boy, did I know. "I understand." I looked back up at the condo unit, and wondered if Kara could see the two of us down here, chatting. "So far I have a pretty good idea of how Kara is doing, but tell me this: How are you doing, Diane?"

A too quick nod. "I'm doing okay."

"The hell you are," I said. "How are you eating, and how are you sleeping?"

She looked away. "Here and there—when I can forget about it for a few minutes, which is tough—I sleep a little or get a bite to eat. I took today off and I'm going to take at least a couple of more days off this week, but it's going to be hard, especially with those goddamn arsons. But Jesus, Kara's always refused to learn how to use a weapon, and I get so frightened just leaving her by herself for an hour or two."

Then she turned and said, "I hate to admit, God I do, but I'm scared. I'm scared of what happened and I'm scared of that guy out there, whoever the hell he is, and I'm scared he might be stalking her, for whatever reason. I feel bad enough, not being there the night she was ... the night she was attacked. If anything else were to happen to her, I swear I'd take a dive off the Dow Memorial Bridge and not come up for air."

"I know," I said. "Look. Felix and I are going to do some work this week, see what happens. And I'll start tomorrow with that inspector."

"Okay," she said, and she pulled a key from her jeans pocket and passed it over. It was on a heart-shaped pink locket, and the sight of it damn near broke my heart.

"A spare key to Kara's place," she said. "I imagine you'll want to check it out."

I put the key away. "You imagined right."

"And promise you'll call if anything comes up?"

"Promise."

I unlocked the door to the Rover and reached out for a brief hug, and Diane hugged me back, but for the first time in the years I've known her, there was a slight hesitation there, a slight resistance that was probably something on a cellular level going on with her, for her woman was back up there hurting, and here she was, hugging the enemy.

I understood the hesitation. But that didn't mean I liked it.

I LIKE to think that I share some things with the young. A sense of wonderment about the night sky. A childish pride in our space program. And cooking skills that have never graduated much beyond boiling water. To get around endless meals of rice and soup, I've made an arrangement with the head chef of the Lafayette House across the way. The arrangement consists of clandestine meetings at the restaurant's back door, folding money on my part being passed to him, and some of the best dishes the Lafayette House has to offer, passed on to me.

So after a dinner of haddock stuffed with crab and lobster meat, along with a red potato dish and large salad, and washed down with a glass of Robert Mondavi red, I was stretched out on the couch, comforter across my lap, fire in the fireplace, and reading a thin file that described an evening of horror for a young woman not fifteen miles away from my peaceful room, the sounds of the wind, and the crackle of fire.

The preliminary incident report was fairly straightforward. It began with Inspector Dunbar being called from his home at two-thirty a.m. the past Saturday by the Newburyport dispatcher, and then arriving at the hospital about fifteen minutes later. There, the report said, he interviewed "one KARA MILES, age 29, of 64 B High Street, Newburyport," who claimed that earlier that evening that she had been raped by "u/k male who broke into her second-floor apartment." Dunbar wrote that "KARA MILES" had obviously suffered some trauma, and he went into some detail about the extent of her injuries, which—despite the fire and the warm comforter— chilled me. Some evidence of vaginal bruising, though any semen evidence (which I knew would be important for DNA testing) was not readily available due to Miles's taking a shower and performing a douche upon herself before stumbling down the street to the hospital. The standard Massachusetts Sexual Assault Kit had been collected and the chain of custody for this evidence was being maintained. An examination of Kara's apartment indicated that entry had been gained through the front door, and there were some signs of a struggle in the bedroom. There was no evidence, however, of any burglary being committed.

There were two other apartments in the building. Sixty-four C was empty. The bottom floor apartment, 64 A, was occupied by the building's owner, one "JASON HENRY, 67," who was home on the night of the assault and said that while he had heard some voices from upstairs, it was nothing so unusual that would cause him to be concerned.

And that was that.

I read and reread the report for a while, looking at the sparse language of Inspector Dunbar's, trying to think of what I was going to do if I was lucky enough to catch him tomorrow. One thing was for sure: I was going to pump him for more information, since the preliminary report was dated and timed for late Saturday afternoon. Some new information, some kind of progress, must have come up since he wrote his report.

And when I read the inspector's words for the last time before stoking the fire and going upstairs, I came back to the one thing that disturbed me at the outset and was still disturbing me as I got up from the couch. It was just a small thing, just one line in a multipage report, yet it was an inconsistency that I didn't like, not at all.

For when Inspector Dunbar asked Kara if the attacker had any facial hair, she had said she was sure the man had a mustache.

I knelt before the fireplace, jabbed at the dying embers with a poker, and just remembered, over and over again, what Kara had said to me earlier. The man had been clean-shaven, she had said.

It didn't make sense. And when I was finished with the fire and put up the grate and turned down the thermostat and shut off all the lights downstairs and checked the locks, it still didn't make sense.

So I went to bed.

6

The Newburyport Police Department is in a two-story brick building on Green Street near Merrimack Street in the heart of the downtown, which is an attractive collection of brick buildings that look like they've been there for hundreds of years. There are some touristy-type shops that butt right up to old hardware stores and lunch counters that are a haven for the natives. I parked in a municipal lot across the street and walked to the building, sloshing through rough half-frozen slush. The river and the marinas and the drawbridge spanning over into Salisbury were visible from the station, which had an old-fashioned blue and white sign at the entrance that said POLICE.

When I had called earlier, Inspector Dunbar hadn't seemed particularly cheerful over the phone, and he said he had a half-hour free in the afternoon. I went through the glass doors and into a reception area, and told the receptionist I was there to see the good inspector, and I was surprised that my hands were moist and my heart was racing right along, like I was seeing a prisoner instead of a cop, and then I walked down the hallway.

Inspector Ron Dunbar's office was the opposite of Diane Woods's, so I guess police detectives don't necessarily share furnishing tips. While Diane's office is organized chaos, with files piled on the desk and cardboard filing containers on the floor, and enclosed by green cinder-block walls, Dunbar's office was a study in neatness. The walls were a pleasant light blue with framed certificates and awards hanging up. A neat desk, with manila folders piled in some semblance of order. Diane's sole window is barred and has a view of the rear parking lot of the Tyler police station. Dunbar's view was much more pleasant, the busy downtown and the wide Merrimack River.

Dunbar had short-trimmed black hair, horn-rimmed glasses, and light blue eyes that disconcertingly almost never blinked, so it always looked as though he was gazing at you in surprise. He had on a blue button-down shirt and a Scottish tartan wool tie. He leaned back in a black leather chair and looked at me sideways, holding a water jug in his hand, the kind that runners use, with a long, flexible straw.

After I sat down, I handed over my business card, to which he shook his head and gave it right back, and then he started right off, without even pretending to be polite.

"Mind telling me what the hell you're looking for?" he asked.

"Information about the Kara Miles case," I said, opening up my reporter's notebook. "I'm considering doing a story about violent crime in tourist communities during the winter, when the money is tight and the tourists go home."

"And why this case? Just because Diane Woods is a friend of yours?"

"That and other things," I said, not wanting to get into a deep discussion of what I was up to. "It just seemed to be the type of case that would fit into the story."

"What kind of case might that be?"

"Violent rape, in the middle of the night, middle of winter," I said. "Not exactly the typical crime one would associate with a tourist city like Newburyport."

"So what makes you the expert?"

Boy, this was getting more fun with every minute. "I never said I was an expert. I'm a writer, one who's lived in the area for a while, I like to think I have a pretty good idea of what happens in the towns around here."

"So because of that, I should spill my guts about an open investigation?"

I doodled in my notebook. "Any information you gave me would be confidential. I'm just looking to see what progress you've made in the case."

Dunbar smiled, tapped the end of the straw against his perfect chin. "Let's wrap this up, shall we? Cops around here, we like to do favors for each other. It's just good sense. We exchange tips, information, and occasionally we help each other out. It's the kind of stuff that keeps us going. Now, when Detective Woods had her friend," and I could hear the sneer in his tone at that word, "get raped last weekend, I told her I'd let her in on what we were doing, as professional courtesy. But the silly bitch thinks that case is the only one I got here in a city of twenty thousand, and whatever I do for her, it's never enough. She wouldn't even be happy with hourly updates."

"Imagine that," I said.

"Yeah, imagine that," Dunbar said, and I gathered his sarcasm-detection equipment was not fully functional. "So one of the things I agreed to do for her is to have a little chat with a friend, a magazine writer who obviously has too much time on his hands. So here you are, and we're chatting, and my deal is complete. I agreed to talk to you. I didn't agree to give you info about this friggin' screwball case."

"And why's that? And why is this a screwball case?"

He swiveled around and put the drinking bottle down on the desk with a little more emphasis than necessary, and leaned forward, finger pointing. "Do you think I have nothing else better to do than to waste my time with a fool like you?" he demanded.

I closed my notebook. "My thoughts exactly," and I got up and I left.

I SPENT another hour in Newburyport, just decompressing, wondering why, of all the wonderful officers who no doubt wear the uniform of the Newburyport Police Department, one Ron Dunbar had made it to inspector, and was thereby complicating my life. I had lunch by myself at one of the old downtown restaurants, the Grog, and enjoyed a salad, cheeseburger, and that day's *Boston Globe*. I read through the paper, and by the time I put down the sports section, an hour had passed and I felt better about myself.

Leaving the Grog, I walked up Simpson Street a couple of blocks, bravely passing by an attractive-looking bookstore, and then I came upon High Street. Traffic was steady and I started walking west, doing fairly well on the slippery sidewalks. High Street is wide and the vast bulk of the homes there are large Colonials or Federals, painted white with black shutters. Most were built during the wonderful years when Newburyport was a busy shipping port and fortunes were made by sailing out to Hong Kong, Havana, or Madrid. But now most of the watercraft that leave are pleasure craft or fishing vessels, and many of the homes of rich merchants and sea captains belong to investment bankers or computer software designers, or are subdivided into apartments.

After about a twenty-minute walk I went across the street and stood before one of the Federal homes. It looked similar to any one of a half-dozen up and down this street, but this one was special. It had two stories, and birch trees, stripped by the winter of their leaves, framed both sides of the house.

The front door was painted black and there was a large brass knocker in the center, and an old wreath from last Christmas was still hanging on. Next to the door were three mailboxes and I knew that one of them said MILES. I shivered, stamped my feet. A driveway to the right led to a side parking area, bounded now by mounds of snow. There were homes on either side, about fifty feet distant in each direction. I knew from previous visits that there was one large apartment on the first floor and two smaller apartments on the second floor, one of which belonged to Kara.

I looked down the street at a sign that marked the road leading into the hospital. This is where it happened, where she stumbled out of here early that awful Saturday morning, walking to the hospital, hurting and in pain and terror and crying. What it must have been like, going out in this cold morning, wondering if you could make it, wondering if the man who did this awful thing to you was still out here, watching. Maybe even following you, looking for another excuse to hurt you. Or maybe even something worse...

I stamped my feet again and stared up at the empty windows.

What was it like for you then? I mused. I imagined a man, hunched over from the cold, perhaps standing on the other side of the street in the night. A man with cold eyes, a man who in any other life would have been a concentration camp guard or a sniper killing children in the Balkan mountains. Maybe he sees her, up there on the second floor of the apartment. Maybe the lights are on, the curtains are open, and he sees Kara, moving back and forth, maybe getting ready for bed, maybe stepping out of the shower. Maybe he's been out here, night after night, just staring up there, feeling the desire and the need and the drive to hurt and control just rise and rise, until it snaps. Something happens. A line is crossed, a decision is made, and instead of walking back to an empty home, the man walks across the street and through the open door and upstairs. And there he finds...

Finds what?

I slapped my gloved hands together and started walking back to where I had parked earlier, feeling a need to get someplace warm and strip off the heavy clothes and drink some tea and forget about things for a while, for in those past few seconds, I had gotten into the mind of a rapist, and I didn't like it one bit.

And I also didn't like knowing that I would probably have to do it again before this was all over.

7

The day after my visit to Newburyport and its grumpy police inspector, I returned to the small city in the company of Felix Tinios. I was a bit touched when Felix had joined me back in Tyler, for not only had he brought along a 35mm Canon, but he also had a camera bag with him as well, so he was quite up to playing his part. And I was also surprised when I noticed the shoulder holster and weapon as he clambered into the passenger seat, his long gray winter coat being unbuttoned.

"Carrying?" I had asked. "We're just looking over Kara's place today, maybe ask a few questions. Seems like a waste of firepower."

"Maybe so," he had said. "But we're going to visit a crime scene, and we're going to start asking questions that you and I hope will lead to some creature who gets his kicks out of raping women. I just like to be prepared in case he answers the second or third door we knock at today."

"And you have a concealed-weapon permit for Massachusetts?" I had asked. "Word is, they're hard to get in our sister state."

Felix grinned. "For the unconnected, you're right." And I had left him alone.

Now he looked over at me as we crossed the Merrimack River, and he said, "So, what was the point of talking to the police inspector? You figure he was going to roll over and give you everything, maybe even a suspect's name, maybe so you and I could finish this by the weekend?"

"Hardly," I said, taking the first exit off the bridge and maneuvering my way up to High Street. "It's just that it was something that had to be done, getting the first interview out of the way. I didn't expect total cooperation, but I was looking for an idea of where his head was at."

"And besides his shoulders, where is the inspector's head resting these days?"

"He said this is a screwball case, and he wouldn't tell me anything more than that, and I think he was about two minutes away from tossing me out of his office."

"Well, I can see you're glad you got that out of the way."

"You better believe it."

I pulled into the small parking lot belonging to Kara's apartment house. Her car was still parked there and was the only vehicle in the lot. A chest-high wooden fence and some brush surrounded most of the lot and a tiny backyard. We got out, Felix carrying his camera bag and me with my reporter's notebook, and we went around to the front door, and I pointed up to the second floor. "That's Kara's apartment up there."

"What room do those windows belong to?"

"Living room."

"Are there windows for the bedroom and bathroom?" Felix asked, his head tilted back, looking up at the windows and the surrounding homes with a practiced eye.

"We'll see once we get in."

We walked up a brick walk and through the front door, which was unlocked. Felix shook his head. "Easy and open access. Jesus. Anybody could come in here."

"Anybody did, last week."

I closed the door behind us. There was a small foyer, and a door to the left with a tiny brass knocker and a nameplate with a piece of white cardboard that said HENRY in careful block handwriting. Before us was a set of stairs and to the right, green trash cans with black covers. I reached up to knock and Felix held my hand back.

"Let's give it a while, why don't we," Felix said. "I want to look around firsthand, get some impressions, and then we can talk to the landlord."

"Sounds good," I said, and we went upstairs. There was a small landing and doors to the left and right. The nameplate on the left was empty and the one on the right said MILES. The area around the doorknob was dirty, and I recognized the light gray powder that cops use when they're looking for latent fingerprints. Felix turned away from the other door and gave me a quizzical look and I said, "Yeah, the apartment across the way is empty, has been for a couple of months. Kara's by herself up here."

"You got the key?" Felix asked.

"I do," I said.

"Then let's go in."

"Fine."

THE DOOR OPENED with no problem, and we stood there, just taking in the small apartment. There was a short hallway, leading into a kitchen and dining area. To the right was the living room, with couch, chairs, television and stereo, a couple of bookcases, and a large, woven tapestry hanging on the far wall, showing a mountain scene. We were in an entryway with a coat rack, open closet, step off pad for dirty boots, and a small table that held a collection of mail. On the floor by the table were a couple of small, square, black zippered bags that looked like carry-on luggage. To the left was a bathroom, and beyond that another door, which was open and led to the bedroom.

"Cozy," Felix said.

"That's right," I replied, and closed the door behind us. We both took off our coats and hung them up, and Felix dropped his camera bag on the floor. I noticed that as we went into the living room, we were talking with low voices, like we were both trying not to disturb anything, being in a sacred place that had been desecrated by some old horror.

But not too old. Only a few days old.

In the living room Felix knelt on the couch and looked outside the window, the curtains on either side already open. Without his coat I saw he was carrying his Smith & Wesson 9mm in his shoulder holster. "Clear view," he said. "Guy standing out there could get a good look in if he wanted to."

"I was thinking about that," I said. "And I think the same is true for the kitchen."

In the kitchen some dishes were still piled up in the sink, and I had an urge to wash and put them away. The kitchen was big with a square oak table and four chairs, and more mail piled up on the table, along with a candle-and-flower centerpiece. Felix opened up the refrigerator and closed it and I noticed him looking at the photographs taped up there. Most were similar to the ones back at Diane's condo, showing Diane and Kara together, arms around each other, and Felix looked at me and raised an eyebrow.

"They speak for themselves," I said. "Let's poke around some more."

We walked through the bathroom, quickly noting there was no window for the benefit of any Peeping Toms, and then we were into the bedroom, and something tugged at my throat. The bedroom door was also dusty, where the cops had looked for latents, and there was a wide bed in the center of the room, a short four-poster. The mattress was bare and some sheets and pillows had been tossed in the corner. The mattress was askew and I tried not to think of the awful violence that had been committed there. Again, just like in the kitchen, I had the urge to clean this place up, to ask Felix to help me haul away the bedding and burn it at some faraway place, and instead I kept my mouth shut. The two windows had their shades drawn and Felix and I went over and lined them up and saw that they looked out over the small yard. A couple of evergreens blocked any view.

"So much for someone from a neighboring house seeing Kara going to bed," I said. "Unless he had been up in one of those trees, and with the weather we've been having..."

Felix grunted. "Yeah. Good point. Tell me again what she said happened?"

"She said she was sleeping when someone came into the room. She sat up and a guy jumped on her, threatened to slit her throat. She fought back a bit and he beat her up some as...as he raped her."

"Did she see what he looked like?"

"Nope. Only thing she could tell is that he was wearing blue jeans. She said it was too dark in the room." And I was going to say something about the facial hair contradiction between Inspector Dunbar's report and what Kara had told me and decided it could wait. I wanted Felix to focus on the matter at hand.

"Did he say anything while he was in the room? Did it look like he knew her?"

"No, nothing like that. He said the usual and customary things a rapist says."

Felix had an impatient look about him. "Look, what did the son of a bitch say?"

I thought back to what Kara had told me, shrugged, and said, "The guy said he would cut her if she struggled or screamed, cut her if she went to the cops, and as she struggled, he said, quote, shut up and take it, bitch, take a real man's cock, unquote."

Felix's features darkened. "Such a charmer. I think I'll enjoy meeting him."

"Me, too."

We poked around the bedroom some more, and I was under no illusions we were going to find anything the police had overlooked. Felix and I were there just to get a sense, maybe even a scent, of what happened that night, something that would help us as we started our work. Felix went through the closets, and I examined the bureau. There was a portable CD player there with matching speakers, some jewelry boxes, hairbrushes, and the usual stuff. I looked again and said, "Is this odd, or is it just me?"

He closed the closet door. "What's that?"

"Here on the bureau," I said. "Look, I know that the guy who came in here was looking for a woman to rape, not to clean out her apartment. But it seems strange that when he was done, he didn't scoop this stuff up on his way out. He could have gotten some money for the CD and jewelry, at least a few hundred bucks."

"Maybe it was too dark to see," he said.

"Maybe."

I followed him out to the living room. The bookshelves contained mostly paperbacks, with a few hardcovers concerning computers and software. Most of the paperbacks were science fiction and fantasy, with a handful of romance novels tossed in, maybe for spice. The bookshelves flanked a fireplace that had been closed off. On the mantelpiece in the center was a framed photo of Kara and Diane. There were some knick-knacks near the photo. A Hummel sculpture of a young girl knitting, and three ceramic sculptures about the size of my fist. Two were pushed together, and showed a knight on horseback with a lance, bearing down on a creature that looked like a troll. The detail of the work was quite fine—this wasn't stuff knocked out at some evening ceramics course. The muscles on the horse were defined, and you could see the knight was dirty and worn, his chain mail not in good shape. The troll had on leather armor and had a matted beard, and he had a mace raised up to ward off the horseman.

The other ceramic sculpture stood by itself. Another knight, similar to the one on horseback, on one bended knee, sword outthrust and shield raised, like he was defending himself against something awful approaching him from the sky. Even the knight's eyes were half-closed, like he was fearful of what was coming toward him.

I looked at the books again and Felix said, "Going to borrow something?"

"Nope, not tonight."

We went back to the entrance foyer, and I saw the black bags there again. There were two of them, and I squatted down and zippered them open. They weren't luggage. They were portable computers—one a Macintosh and the other a Compaq. I shook my head and zippered them back up and looked around at the apartment, seeing another CD player, a collection of silver in a tiny display case built into a kitchen wall, a small Sony TV set on a kitchen counter, and another, larger set in the living room, and I looked at Felix, who leaned against the bathroom doorjamb, arms crossed.

I said, "There's a lot of stuff here, stuff that could be fenced in another city a couple of hours away, with not much chance of an easy trace, and it's still here. The computers, the CD sets, the silver..."

He shifted his weight, crossed his legs. "Which tells you what?"

I chose my words carefully. "It tells me that this guy wanted one thing, and one thing only, and wasn't interested in picking up some free and easy cash in the bargain."

He slowly nodded. "That's right. Which means this son of a bitch is one obsessed creep. He came in here intent on raping your friend, and he could care less if there was cash or jewelry or anything else laying around."

"True." I looked up at the kitchen wall clock. It was nearly four o'clock in the afternoon. "You about finished in here? Want to start knocking on some doors?"

He glanced up at the clock and said, "Sure, and we can start with the landlord. And I hope you're not feeling too sleepy, because I want to come back here later tonight, to see what things look like when it's dark outside."

I nodded in understanding. "So do I. Let's head out."

We gathered up our coats and went out the door, and I took my time closing and locking the door behind us. I looked into the brave little apartment and remembered some good times here, as the guest of Kara and Diane. There had been dinners here and Trivial Pursuit tournaments— with me versus the team of Kara and Diane, and me usually winning—and some long chats on the couch with the two of them, just talking and sipping glasses of wine, nothing earth-shattering or worth noting or remembering, except that it had all been so civilized, so beautiful, and just so damn peaceful, and I knew with a tinge of melancholy it would never be the same again.

I joined Felix downstairs.

JASON HENRY, landlord to Kara Miles, was not home. Felix knocked a few times and I said, "We'll try him again later," and Felix looked over and said, "You want to leave your business card, a note, or something?"

"No" I said, zipping up my coat. "Best to surprise your interview subjects, Felix, before they have a chance to practice their stories."

Felix granted me a small smile. "Sounds like your job gets to be more like mine, day after day."

"Maybe so," I said, heading out the foyer. "Let's get to work."

And so we did.

. . .

OUR PATTERN that night was simple and to the point. After each door was answered, I passed over my business card and identified Felix as a photographer who was working with me on the story. I said I was a friend of their neighbor, Kara Miles, and with her cooperation, I was doing a story for *Shoreline* magazine about violent crime in a tourist community, using her case (and a pseudonym) for the story's basis. I would quickly say that if it made them more comfortable, everything would be off the record, and Felix would keep his camera gear in the case. I asked general questions about the neighborhood, their lives, how long they had lived here, and among these questions I had a couple I considered vital: Did they know Kara, and if so, did they know if anybody nearby had been asking questions about her? Did they see or hear anything unusual on the night of the rape? Did they notice any strangers in the vicinity during the past few weeks? Was there anything out of the ordinary that had stuck in their minds?

And through it, Felix sat, arms crossed, and occasionally asked his own question.

There were four houses in the direct area around 64 High Street, and the one directly across the street was the easiest, for it was a two-story Colonial with every window darkened and a tilting Century 21 For-Sale sign on the snow-covered front lawn. Its neighbor was a smaller Colonial, and an older man answered the door, a *Newburyport Daily News* clasped in his hands. He wore half-rim glasses, was almost entirely bald, had on a white sweater and khaki slacks, and invited us into his living room. His name was Walter Doyle and his wife Melissa joined him on the couch.

We spent a half-hour there, and then went across the street to a light yellow Cape that belonged to a Reuben Cortez, his wife Maria and their three children. Reuben wore jeans and a New England Patriots sweatshirt, while his wife was still in a dark blue uniform, having gotten off work at the Salisbury Fire Department.

She made strong coffee for us while we talked around the kitchen table the two boys and girl underfoot, screaming and playing, and even Felix managed to smile.

When we were done there, we went to another white Federal, this one divided into two apartments, one upstairs and the other downstairs. Paul Vachon talked to us at the downstairs door without inviting us in, half-apologizing because his wife Carol was in bed with the flu, and their infant son Henry was napping on the couch. He worked at a service station, and his large hands were still stained with grease and oil.

Upstairs at the house were the building's owners, Art and Mary Allen. Both were retired from the Porter Naval Shipyard and felt lucky to have tenants like the Vachons. Felix and I went through another round of coffee, this time with cinnamon crumb cake that had been made that day, and at the end of about two hours, we were back in my four-wheeler, the engine rumbling, the heater quickly warming up the interior. Felix leaned against the door, arms folded, while I examined the notes under the dome light.

"What do you think?" Felix asked. "These people part of a conspiracy or what?"

"I know what you mean," I said, flipping through the pages.

"All of them knew Kara as the pretty young woman with odd hair who lived down the street. Reasonably friendly, but they weren't neighborly to the point of exchanging Christmas cards. Everyone was surprised about the rape—no one knew it had happened, which tells you about the level of newspaper reading in this neighborhood. And no one saw anything unusual that night, the night before, or even the month before."

Felix rubbed at his hair and looked out into the dark parking lot. My fingers were cold, holding the notepad. There were pages of notes, but there was one thing I hadn't written down yet I would always remember. It was the look in their faces, the widened eyes and slack jaws, when Felix and I told them about the terror that had slumped through their neighborhood last Friday. After the initial shocks and the standard first question—"How is she doing?"—I saw all of them look away for a moment, and I knew what they were thinking: It was no longer safe here. The territory had been invaded and their illusions of safety and peace on this part of High Street were now gone. One night, one man, and his influence was widening, like some awful plague.

Felix sighed. "Came up with squat."

"That we did. I didn't think we'd have much success tonight, but I thought we'd at least come up with something we could work with, but we don't have a thing. Not one lead, not one trace, nothing."

Felix shifted in his seat. "No, but we did what we had to do. We started the process of asking questions and poking around, and you can tell Diane that the next time you talk to her. We've had negative progress, but it's been progress just the same."

"I'm sure that will thrill her."

"Maybe not, but this might make it easier for you," he said.

"A couple more nights like tonight, and we're going to end up with thin air. You might have to go back to her and tell her to leave it up to the regular cops, that her friendly hires just couldn't do it. That would take care of some of your concerns, wouldn't it?"

I closed the notebook with disgust, thinking again about that apartment with its memories and mementos, and the horror that had been visited there a few nights ago. "I might feel better, but that wouldn't make me happy, Felix. Damn it, I'm beginning to want this guy very badly, and I don't like coming up blank."

"Who does?" he said. "You want to try the landlord again?"

"You see a light on back there?"

He swiveled in the seat. "Nope."

"All right. Then let's get some dinner."

"You buying?" I shifted into reverse.

"After making you trudge through snow and play Jimmy Olsen, how could I refuse?"

He laughed. "A deal, then."

WE HAD dinner at Michael's Harborside, a fine old seafood restaurant in the downtown and built right on the banks of the Merrimack River. Felix and I were in the main dining room. We were both fairly quiet during our meal, and when we were waiting for the check, Felix eyed my plate, which still was about a third full.

"No appetite?" he asked.

"Too much on the mind," I said. I looked over at his own empty plate. "I see nothing seems to be bothering you."

"Why should it? And why does it bother you?"

"Because it's something awful that we're looking into, something that happened to a friend of a close friend, and it's not very pleasant, and that always affects my appetite. Can't be helped. What's your excuse?"

"I don't let it bother me. It's just a job, nothing involving anything personal, and I try to stay above it. That's the only way to do it."

"Sounds pretty cold."

Felix shrugged. "I'm sure brain surgeons and pathologists maintain a hearty appetite, and so do I, Lewis. You should get used to it."

I pulled out some bills and left them on the check as we both got up to leave. "You're right, I should and probably will, but I'm still not looking forward to it."

WE HAD a few more hours to kill, so we went to a movie theater in the next town over, Salisbury, and saw the only film that hadn't yet begun playing. We spent the next one hundred and twelve minutes watching a horror film that must have been created with teenagers in mind, for Felix and I were easily the oldest viewers there by at least a decade.

Felix fell asleep almost instantly and I mechanically ate my popcorn, growing dismayed at what I was seeing up on the screen and in the audience. I'm no prude by any stretch of the imagination, but there was something coarse about the movie, which was one of those slasher films that involved a group of young college sorority women stuck in a snowbound cabin on a back lot somewhere. There was hardly any suspense, the dialogue was as wooden as my house's rear deck, and the only imagination exhibited in the entire film seemed to be on choosing the implements of death that the young ladies—most wearing nightclothes or tight spandex ski wear—suffered through. The characters in the film exhibited about as much group intelligence as a herd of water buffalo, as each (except for the obligatory sole survivor) was bloodily dispatched. That was the action up on the screen, and the action in the audience was almost as bad, and it made me wonder if the intruder to Kara's apartment was a fan of such movies.

There were some screams and giggles from the young girls in the audience, and there were mostly bellows of laughter and a few "all rights" from their male companions, and one imaginative fellow yelled out, "Give it to the bitch!" when one of the actresses was impaled by an ice auger. I'm also not a prude when it comes to cause and effect, and I believe evil and bad people exist because of choices made, not because of books read, TV programs or movies watched, or bathroom training missed. Yet my popcorn tasted like gravel as I looked around at the slack faces, the smiles, and the shiny eyes of the young men and women around me, and I couldn't help but believe that somehow these one hundred and twelve minutes were corroding that thin shell of civilization around their young souls, millimeter by millimeter. I wondered if that young boy I had seen on the beach that August, carelessly shattering a shell and hurting his sister, was now in the audience. If so, I feared for his date.

Right after the killer was identified and dispatched by the brave young survivor (the killer was the kindly old caretaker introduced in the first five minutes of the film, who obviously had a grudge against college girls from his days at old State U) the credits started rolling up and the rock music score boomed out. Felix stirred himself awake, yawned, and looked over at me.

"Whodunit?" he asked.

"We all did," I said, getting up and taking his empty popcorn container. "Let's get rolling."

THE DRIVE BACK WAS COLD, with our breath visible inside the Rover, and Felix quietly said, hands deep in his coat pockets, "It's nights like these that make you believe that winter does, in fact, suck."

Back at Kara's place there was an old blue Ford Escort parked in the lot, and a light was on in the downstairs apartment. The clock on the dashboard said it was almost midnight, and it didn't seem like we should wake up Mr. Jason Henry at such a late hour, so we didn't. We walked carefully and quietly up the main set of stairs, and I was carrying a tiny black flashlight that helped light the way, and even though it was probably fifty degrees or so inside the foyer, it was practically tropical compared to what we had just come in from.

As we went to the door, I pulled out the key and Felix gently held on to my arm and said, "Let's take a look at something, shall we?" And then he knelt down on the floor and held the flashlight close to the door. He ran his fingers along the doorjamb and near the lock, shining the light close, and then he looked up at me with a troubled glance and said, "See what I see?"

Something went *ka-chunk* inside my chest as I knelt down next to him and looked at the wood frame of the door, the lock, and the door jamb. I took my hands out of my gloves and repeated the same moves that Felix had just performed. The wood was smooth. No roughness. No splinters.

"I certainly do," I said. "Which is nothing."

Felix shook his head, got back up, and I joined him. "No scrape marks, no pry marks, nothing."

"Either the door was unlocked or he had a key."

"Does young Kara have a habit of leaving the door unlocked?" I thought back and said, "Not that I know of. And the police report did say that she indicated the guy broke in."

Felix said, "Maybe it's nothing. Maybe she just forgot to lock the door that night. Happens."

"Sure," I said, not believing a word that either of us was saying.

INSIDE THE APARTMENT something heavier was now rummaging around in my chest, and I had a quick wish that we had left the movie theater and had gone back to New Hampshire, for I didn't want to be here. Felix muttered something and I followed him through the bathroom and to the bedroom, and turned around, moving easily enough in the dark. Felix looked over at me and said, "Get on the bed, will you?"

And as queasy as it sounds, that's exactly what I did. I lay back on the bare mattress and looked up at the ceiling, noting the cracks and fissures in the plaster, trying not to smell the scent of blood or sweat, and then Felix came into the bedroom. I sat up and looked at him. His features were crisp and he still needed a shave, and his coat was open, and it was easy enough to count the five buttons on his coat.

"This is awful," I said.

"It sure is."

I followed him out of the bedroom and we stood back near the door to the apartment. Just outside the living room window was a utility pole, and hanging from the pole was a bright streetlight, and the steady beam from that light illuminated the entire living room, short hallway, bathroom, and bedroom. No curtains blocked the light.

"Nothing in the report about the guy closing the bedroom door behind him when he came in?" Felix asked, the tone of his voice resigned.

"No, nothing," I said, crossing my arms, just staring at the streetlamp, thinking, well, maybe it was burned out that night, and knowing that I would check it out tomorrow with the utility company and knowing my wish wouldn't come true.

How I hated what I saw.

"This doesn't look good at all, not at all," I finally said, not looking at Felix, just staring out at the living room. "Valuables still here, place untouched, no signs of a forced entry, and there's practically enough light here to read a newspaper."

"Maybe that's why your police inspector friend thinks this case is screwball," Felix said, the tone of his voice gentle. "Everything here is wrong. You just said it yourself. Kara's story doesn't make sense. Something else happened here that night, and she doesn't want to tell the cops, her friend Diane, or you."

"You don't think she was raped?"

"No, I didn't say that. I think something awful happened to her, no doubt about it. But it's not what's in the report. As a former spook, even you should see that."

My chest felt constricted, thinking of what was ahead, and I said quietly, "We were always taught, back then, not to let your emotions cloud your analysis, your work. No matter what you saw, no matter how bloody or awful. The work was your god and you didn't let anything else get in the way."

Felix said, "I think that's the most you've ever said about your time at the Pentagon."

In the light I tried to smile. "Then I've made a mistake."

"Perhaps you have." A pause, then, "I feel sorry for you, Lewis."

"And why's that?"

He reached over and gently slapped me on my shoulder. "Because you're going to have to tell Diane Woods that her Kara hasn't been telling the truth, and that's going to be painful for everybody involved."

I was trying to ease the tension in my gut by saying something bright in return, but I heard something odd, something loud, and Felix looked at me and we went across the living room, hearing the noise again, sounding almost like a radio. We both looked out and down at the street below, and parked right on the street, blue lights flashing, was a Newburyport police cruiser. Another one came roaring up the street, pulling behind, and as the doors flew open I looked over at Felix and said, "Right now, I'm feeling sorry for the both of us."

"I guess so," Felix said, and he opened his jacket and pulled out his 9mm, and I said, "Felix!" and he said, "Relax, I'm just ensuring there are no misunderstandings." He put the pistol down on a coffee table, on top of a *Boston Phoenix* newspaper, and I said, "We've got a few seconds, let's go sit at the kitchen table and act real polite."

"I'm there."

Which is where we were when the Newburyport cops came pounding up the stairs and into the apartment and arrested us both.

8

Well, it certainly seemed that the patrol unit of the Newburyport Police Department had gotten all of the charm and hospitality handouts that Inspector Dunbar had missed, for after we were arrested and taken to the police station, we were treated politely and professionally, and when a couple of phone calls established that we had permission to be in Kara Miles's apartment, we were set free with a cup of coffee and an offer of a ride back to the parking lot where my Rover was parked.

But before Felix and I left, we spent a few irritable minutes with the good inspector, who was not pleased to have been called out of bed to come down to the station on this chilly January night. He was wearing a down coat and University of Lowell sweatshirt and gray sweatpants, and his face was carpeted with gray-black stubble. We were in an interrogation room, Felix and I sitting in orange plastic chairs, Dunbar sitting perched on a table, looking like a sleep deprived football coach, confronting two of his charges who had been out drinking. The room smelled of stale tobacco.

"I've talked to the arresting officer, and I must say I'm impressed," Dunbar said.

"Why's that?" I asked. Felix sat next to me, a quiet smile on his face, one I'm sure he reserved only for officers of the law.

"Because that story was one sorry piece of bullshit, from start to finish," he said, arms folded. "Doing research for a magazine article. Bah. Do you expect me to believe that, that the two of you were crawling around that apartment at midnight for some friggin' magazine article?"

Felix spoke up. "Why not? It worked for the sergeant."

Dunbar shifted his ice-gaze to Felix. "And for you, who's supposed to be taking pictures for this article, mind telling me why you were there without your photo gear?"

Felix shrugged, still looking amused. "I guess the cold made me forgetful."

"Really? Well, don't forget this. I think you're up to something about this woman and her friend," and his voice dripped sarcasm at the word, "over in Tyler. I think you're sneaking around, maybe up to a little vigilante shit, trying to find out what happened. Well, get your asses back home and forget it. You talk to that Tyler detective and tell her to mind her own business, and if you clowns ever come back here and so much as race through a yellow light, your asses will be in jail for the weekend, with the phones out so you can't make any calls for bail money or a lawyer. Got it?"

I looked at Felix and said, "Gee, I've gotten it. How about you?"

"Oh, I got it a long time ago."

Dunbar swore one more time and then left, and we followed, and soon we were back outside and a female officer, dressed in a heavy leather jacket and whose nametag said CAROL APPEL, bundled us in the rear seat of a police cruiser and drove us back up to High Street. Along the way she said, "You guys rile up Dunbar back there?"

"That we did," I said.

"Good for you," she said, and Felix laughed.

At High Street she made a turn into the apartment building's parking lot, and she left the cruiser's engine running as she got out. Officer Appel opened up Felix's door—since it was a cruiser, the rear doors had no handles inside—and the two of us slid out into the frigid night air. Little breath clouds formed about her head as she said, "Next time, fellas, don't go visiting so late and make so much noise. You woke up the landlord."

Oops. "Thanks for the advice," I said.

"No problem." She ducked back into the cruiser and emerged with a 9mm in her hand. She handed it butt-first to Felix, and then passed along the full magazine. "Good for you that you had a carry permit, or you'd still be our guest," she said.

"With you as our hostess, it wouldn't have been that bad."

She grinned. "Don't be so sure. Now get the hell out, will you?" As the cruiser went back to High Street, Felix looked at me and said, "Now that's a woman I would like to meet someday out of uniform."

"Because she's a cop?"

"Because of the challenge."

THE DRIVE BACK WAS QUIET, with the road fairly empty and a half-moon at our rear lighting up the cold waves of the ocean. Faint drifts of snow covered the asphalt as I drove north, the radio station tuned to an all-news station, the volume turned down low. It was two a.m. on Thursday, and I was getting more tired with each passing mile. Felix was hunched over in his seat and said, "So, where do you want to take this?"

"A couple of options are open, and none of them are that attractive," I said. "My question to you: Are you still along for the ride?"

He yawned. "Oh, that I am. First, I still think something bad happened to your friend, and I'm still interested in meeting the guy who did it. And second, this gives me an opportunity to eventually raid your bank account, and I don't want to pass that up."

"Thanks for the good words," I said. "Why don't we get together in a day or two, look things over, see where we go from here?"

"Just so long as I get some sleep here and there, that's fine." I turned right onto Rosemount Lane and up the narrow road to his house. The road was bumpy with a layer of cracked and fissured ice. I stopped in front of his Mercedes and reached over and shook his hand, a gesture that seemed to surprise him.

"Thanks for being here, and thanks for not losing it with the cops."

Felix smiled. "Cops are part of the job, part of doing business. Nothing to worry about." And then his smile faltered a bit. "I'm worried about you and one special cop, though. Diane isn't going to like what you're going to tell her."

"I know," I said, "and I also know that I'm not going to talk to her tonight. Soon, but not tonight. You want me to walk you to the door or something?"

That made him laugh as he stepped out onto the snow. "The day you have to walk me to the front door must be the day I start collecting Social Security. Go to hell."

"Thanks, but not tonight," I said, and I turned the car around and drove home.

It was nearly Thursday afternoon before I was awake, showered, and shaved. With only another four hours of daylight left, I decided to take the rest of the day off, and not talk to Felix or Diane or Kara or Paula or even Inspector Dunbar. One of the few joys of being a magazine columnist, and of living secretly off the federal government's largesse, is the ability on some days to do what I damn please.

I dressed for the outdoors, gathered up my EMS day pack, and went to my tiny dirt cellar and the kitchen for some supplies. I took out my cross-country skis and waxed them up, and then outside I trudged through a rough path in the snow, heading north, carrying the skis and poles in my arms. The sky was bright blue, and the ocean was just as majestic, and the air was so crisp and clear that it looked like the Isles of Shoals were just hundreds of feet away. Snow and rime ice covered the rocks, and I moved slowly, trying to keep my balance while wearing cross-country ski boots, which have no traction, no tread, and look like miniature clown shoes.

After about fifteen minutes I passed over into state-owned land, into the Samson Point State Wildlife Preserve, and I strapped on the skis near a grove of birch trees. Half-covered by the snow was a concrete bunker, its iron door welded shut years ago when the early-warning radar system that had replaced the huge coast artillery pieces had itself been shut down. The whole of the state park had once been the Samson Point Coast Artillery Station, built when the Spaniards were considered a threat for those several months in 1898, and over the years the enemies had changed to Germans and then the Soviets.

I started skiing, moving in that graceful rhythm that only takes a day or two to learn, and that is a great exercise. There was a trail I was following, one broken by me some weeks ago. As I traveled through the quiet woods, breathing deeply, I met not a single other skier. The trails were probably empty for two reasons: It was the middle of a work week, and this part of the park was officially closed, due to the discovery a few years back of some hazardous waste and chemicals in some of the bunkers.

The trail went deep into the woods, and except for the salt tang in the air, you wouldn't know you were near the ocean's edge. Snow still clung to the branches of the pines and evergreens, and I savored the cool air and the quite *shush-shush* of the skis sliding though the snow. Along the side of the trail were the marks of animals in the snow, the deep trio of indentations that mark a rabbit, the tiny marks of a field mouse, and even once the sharp marks of a deer, and I saw where bark and branches had been gnawed on the trees. As I skied along in the quiet forest, I tried to forget my trip last night to Newburyport, what Felix and I had found in Kara's apartment, the memory of the fires that had been tearing apart Tyler this winter, and the bitter thoughts of what had happened to me once in the Nevada desert that had eventually brought me here.

The trail then came out into the open, to a narrow point of land that was one of my favorite places. There was a large, flat rock near the tide line of the water, and I brushed away some snow and sat down, undoing my pack, and had a late afternoon lunch. Having stopped skiing, I was a bit sweaty, and I started to cool off, but my meal soon warmed me back up. I had two Thermos bottles, one that contained tea and the other tomato soup, and a sandwich made of leftover steak from a previous Lafayette House meal, along with lettuce, cheddar cheese, and tomato. The cold air seemed to sharpen my appetite and I sat there and ate, and later sipped a cup of tea when I was finished eating, just listening to the wind whisper through the snow-covered limbs and the sounds of the waves moving against the icy shoreline.

I just sat, not thinking, just looking at the sharp blue of the ocean and the different shades of white among the snowdrifts on the park and the tall majesty of the evergreens. It was wonderful, feeling the minutes ooze by, and then the wind picked up and I shivered. It was time to leave. I repacked my belongings and tossed out a crust of bread for the benefit of the birds, and then I gathered up my ski poles and skis and started to move away from rock. I had to get back to my house and my work and the thoughts of Kara Miles and Diane Woods and even the mystery arsonist, for they would not wait.

I turned and looked back and saw something by the rock. I poked with my ski pole and uncovered some empty beer cans. I knelt down and pulled them out, placed them in my pack, and then started to ski south. I felt good. No one saw me pick up the old trash, but I knew, and that was what counted.

I pushed forward through the snow.

9

During winter, lunch can be a challenge at Tyler Beach. In the summer, the beach is famous for the dozens of restaurants, fast food booths, and snack joints on every block, but when the first snows fall, those shops are closed and shuttered tight, leaving one or two brave places open along the entire stretch of the Strip.

For Diane Woods and me this Friday afternoon, lunch was eaten from the front seat, parked at the town's tiny Bicentennial Park, up beyond Weymouth's Point and near North Beach. Diane had to prepare for a court appearance later that day and didn't have the time for a drive into town. We got take-out from Sal's Super Subs on Atlantic Avenue, and she had some clam chowder while I made do with a steak-and-cheese sub. The air in the Rover was stuffy and smelled of cooked food and grease, and paper napkins were scattered everywhere. A handful of other vehicles were parked sloppily in the poorly plowed parking lot of the town park.

Diane held a white container in her hands and spooned up the chowder, looking outside, and said, "By God, I hate this time of year, I really do."

It was overcast and there was a mix of snow and frozen rain scattering down, not enough for a serious accumulation, but enough so that I kept the engine running and the heater on so the water wouldn't freeze up the windows. There wasn't much to see—piles of snow, ice-covered boulders at the water's edge, and the incessant movement of the gray and cold Atlantic. Supposedly this park was where the Reverend Bonus Tyler—the town's founder—and his congregation landed in 1638, and I'm sure that if the weather had been like this on that special day, they would have turned around and headed back to England.

I had finished my sandwich and was working on a salad, and I looked over and said, "Is it really the weather, or is it just the circumstances?"

She spooned in some chowder, eating almost mechanically.

"Oh, you're probably right, but I can never really remember feeling that thrilled with January. With who I am and what I do, the holidays have always been a time to be endured, not enjoyed, and it's days like these that make you think winter's going to last right through to June."

Her face was drawn and her normally shiny brown hair looked dull. I put down my fork, reached over and stroked her poor hair, and said, "How are you doing?"

Diane's eyes filled up. "I know there's going to be a time out there, maybe next year, maybe in two years, when I won't feel so rotten, and by Jesus I wish I could be there right now. It seems like every hour of every day is just pure, grinding misery, and I even thought going to work would help, but it hasn't."

"The old keep-busy routine?"

"Yeah, that old keep-busy routine. You know, it does work. Keeping yourself busy does make the day go by and makes your problems manageable, but the problems are still there, still waiting to gnaw at your brain at two in the morning. And what work I do achieve isn't that much. I'm letting this arson case slip by, letting Mike Ahern and the state fire marshal's office take more and more of the case, and if that was going on a month ago, I'd scream and raise a fuss, but now I'm so tired and zoned out, some days I could give a shit. A crappy attitude, but I'm afraid it's the only one I have."

Another car joined us in the parking lot, its wheels spinning in the snow. "And how's Kara doing?" I asked.

Diane looked down at her lunch, moved the spoon around a bit. "She's doing all right physically, and her mouth doesn't hurt as much. But that's not the problem."

"Both of you getting on each other's nerves?"

She kept on stirring the chowder. "We've been fighting, and it's not pretty."

"Not that my ego is so healthy, but is the fighting over what I'm doing?"

"Oh, some, but there's other things as well. Like living arrangements." She took a deep breath. "We've been together for a while and I've made the suggestion, here and there, that she move in with me. Maybe we find some-place a bit secluded, maybe in North Tyler or Exonia. A few eyebrows would be raised, but we could just get by on smiles and lies about room-mates, and we'd do fine, and I'd be very happy." She looked at me, her eyes shiny. "I really do want her by my side, every day and night."

"But she's got other ideas."

"Yeah, and she's mentioned that eventually she's going to want to move out of High Street and find someplace new to live in. I've told her she should just stay here with me, and she says no, she needs to recover and stand on her own two feet again. She thinks moving in with me would just be a sign of weakness. She doesn't like being weak, and shit, I don't like her going into an empty apartment at night."

"And there's been other fights?"

"Well, yeah...it's just...well, she's told me a couple of times that she's trying to put everything behind her, and that I should do the same thing. That I should just let go and not let revenge run my life and try to move on."

I hoped I wasn't going to regret what I said next. "Those are valid points. And what do you say back to her?"

She picked up a spoonful of chowder and then let it fall back.

"Drop the lecturing tone. I know it makes sense, that we should grieve and mourn and get on with things. I know I shouldn't obsess on it, and if Kara wants to put it behind her, then I should just do what she wants. That makes sense."

"But..."

Her voice grew more harsh. "But then I close my eyes and think of what happened to her last week, think of that bastard who raped her...Then I can't just forget it. I just can't let bygones be bygones. I won't allow it. I won't allow him to live."

I finished my salad, put the plastic dish and fork away in a bag. "Well, you've just answered one question I had today."

"And what was that?"

"I wanted to make sure that you haven't changed your mind."

She took a deep breath. "No. Not at all. That hasn't changed. You still with me?"

"I'm still with you."

"So. What have you got?"

"You mean besides undying thanks that you and Kara managed to keep me and Felix out of jail for the night?"

That brought a slight smile to her face, and I felt a touch of victory at seeing that mouth move upwards. "Yes, I mean besides that. I've talked to Jason Henry. He feels bad about having gotten the two of you arrested, but he was just scared, hearing the two of you upstairs and not knowing who you were. And he also says he's going to be home tomorrow, if you still want to talk to him."

"I do."

She turned to me again. "Again, Lewis. So. What have you got for me?"

An answer that I've been practicing for a half-day, I felt like saying, but instead I said, "Not much, I'm afraid. We talked to her neighbors. They all knew Kara at some point or another, but I got the feeling that she didn't go out of her way to be best friends with them. A fair assessment?"

Diane nodded. "You're probably right. Kara worked so many hours at Digital and I know she liked to just relax when she got home. And whatever free time there was, we tried to spend as much of it together as possible. She likes to keep to herself, so yeah, I can see that her neighbors didn't know her that much. What else?"

"Well, they all pretty much had the same reaction when we told them what had happened. Sheer horror that such a crime could happen in their neighborhood. And I'm afraid nobody saw anything out of the ordinary. No strange cars or strange men in the neighborhood. No break-ins, nothing unusual to be noted."

"So what's your next step?"

My next step is to find out why in hell Kara's not being entirely open should have been my response, but I wanted to follow some other leads before dropping that live hand grenade in Diane's lap. Hoping against hope, I wanted there to be some solid answers out there instead of fuzzy questions, and I wasn't ready to give it up quite yet.

"We talk to the landlord tomorrow, maybe talk to the people where she works," I said. "Might do some checks on the neighbors and even spend a few more cuddly minutes with Inspector Dunbar. But we don't have much. Has Kara said anything more?"

"Why, do you think she's changing her story?" Her voice took on a sharper tone.

"No, it's just that sometimes things are remembered later, after some reflection. I might need to talk to her again, Diane."

She finally put the half-eaten chowder into the plastic trash bag we were sharing. "I might not want you to do that."

I looked out the window, seeing the frozen rain pelt against the wind-shield, and said, "That's Diane Woods talking to me, and not Detective Woods. A world of difference. And if Diane Woods doesn't want me to do things in a competent way, then she should have a talk with Detective Woods."

A soft tap on my shoulder. "Both Dianes are sorry," she said. "I know you're doing what you can. It's just...Lewis, it's just so hard."

"I know."

"No, you don't," she said, "and be glad you don't. Take me back to the station, will you?"

"Sure."

WHEN WE GOT to the Tyler police station, I followed Diane in so I could wash my hands and discreetly toss away our lunchtime trash in the station's receptacles. When I was done, I went down a tiled hallway to the rear office that was the detective's bureau, going by a kitchen area where a large, uniformed officer was sitting, his back to me, his neatly shaved head moving side to side with effort as he laboriously typed a report with two fingers on a manual typewriter. Diane's office was as cluttered as ever, and the sickly green paint on the cinder-block walls looked more faded. She was sitting at her paper-strewn desk, where a bong for smoking illegal substances was being used as a paperweight, and she looked up at me oddly, holding a telephone.

"It's for you," she said. "You can pick it up at the spare desk." Her odd gaze continued, and I shrugged and gave her my who-knows-I'm-here? look, then sat down and punched up the blinking light and said, "Hello?" and a familiar voice was there.

"Cole, it's Ahern, over at the fire department."

Right then a missing file popped into my memory. "We're supposed to meet today, right?"

"That's right, and you're late. Why don't you head on over?" I was going to politely decline but decided doing so would tick him off, and as I didn't know him that well, ticking him off didn't seem to be the right thing to do. Besides, whatever I did find out could get passed over to Paula Quinn, so I said, "I'll be over in five minutes," and he hung up.

Diane said, "Give the cheery fire inspector my best."

"Can't do that," I said. "I'm afraid he might hit me."

That earned me another smile and she said, "Thanks for lunch and keep in touch."

"You're welcome, and I'm yours to talk to, any minute of the day."

I think she blushed, and I didn't stick around to find out.

I DUCKED out the rear locker-room entrance and walked carefully across the ice- and snow-covered parking lot. The town of Tyler has two fire stations: one at the beach and the other uptown, near the town hall and library. The one uptown is fairly modern, made of brick and stone and bordered with a nice lawn and shade trees. The one at the beach is across the street from the police station, is wooden, and was built back in the 1880s. It was originally built for horse-drawn fire engines, and there's still a sliding door on the second story where hay had been stored. I've been told that in the spring, some hay still sprouts from seeds that had fallen into the cracks of the wide wooden planks years ago. A great story, if true, though I've never been able to check it out.

I went in through a side door and walked to the rear, past the silent and well-shined fire apparatus. The truck bay area smelled of smoke, soap, and rubber, and the floor was gray-painted concrete and shiny. At the rear, high up on the wall, were framed photos of old fire chiefs, beginning with one O.W. Oates in 1910. There was a short hallway and a couple of steps up, and I was into Mike Ahern's office, which was near the hose tower, where fire hose was hung to dry after being used. He stood up and shook my hand and hauled out an office chair for me to sit in. The chair had green vinyl upholstery and the seat had been repaired in a couple of places with duct tape.

"I see you got out of the police station in one piece," he said,

He sat back in his own chair, holding a handful of files in one large hand. He had on a white dress shirt with a gold fire inspector's badge and black necktie, and his closely cropped black hair looked like it had been in the hands of a barber a day or two ago. I tried not to stare at the shiny patch of burn tissue on his head, just above his left ear, wondering about what fire in what town had caused him that pain.

"Oh, I usually get out of the police station just fine."

He grinned, but he didn't look particularly friendly. "Then you must have a pretty good relationship with our lady police detective, eh?"

The room had one dusty window overlooking the parking lot. Standing up and holding hands, Mike and I could have stretched out and touched both walls of the office, but I doubted we would do that anytime soon. I decided I didn't like the tone of his voice.

"It's fine," I said. "What's next? Want to know our sleeping arrangements?"

He smirked. "From what I hear, that's nothing you need to worry about," he said, and I was tired and felt like walking out on him, but I just put on my impatient look and he moved around the files some and said, "Last week, you were hot to talk to me. What's the matter? No longer interested in the story?"

There was a whiteboard on the wall nearest me, and listed on the board in black marker were the names and dates of the four motels, beginning with the SeaView last December and ending just this week with the Rocks Road Motel. On the other walls were certificates of achievement and some photos, mostly color shots of fires here in Tyler, and I paused for a moment, looking above his head at a couple of framed items, and I forced myself to answer him, not wanting him to see any change in my expression.

"Oh, I'm still interested," I said, feeling warm and unzipping my coat. "But I'm sorry about forgetting it was today."

He shrugged. "No problem. So, do you have something for me or what?"

I waited, still intrigued by the items above his head. Mike had been fire inspector for only a few months, and this was the first time I had been in his office.

"Look, when I told you that I had some information on these fires, it was more like negative information," I finally said. "I did some research, mostly by tapping into data banks, looking at records at the town hall and the county courthouse in Exonia, contacting the Secretary of State's office, and whatever I have, I'll send you. But what I have is probably something you already know. Right?"

He swiveled a bit in his chair. "Which is what, Mr. Cole?"

"Not one of the hotels that burned was owned by people with money problems," I said. "None of the owners had a history of suspicious fires, they were the sole owners of their buildings, and they had no business dealings with each other. None were over insured. That's what I have. Which tells me we have someone who enjoys what he's doing."

"Firebug, right?"

"Right."

He nodded. "I'd be interested in seeing that paperwork, but I'm surprised you're passing it along. Any newspaper reporter, especially that young girl from the *Chronicle*, they'd tell me to go piss up a rope if I asked for any stuff."

"I'm a different kind of writer. I don't have deadlines that newspaper reporters have. And besides, I live in Tyler, too. I don't like the idea of some nut going around burning down buildings for fun. I think I want him caught just as much as you do."

His face seemed to darken. "Well, you're wrong there, my friend. I want this guy so bad I think I can smell him sometimes, out there walking around and torching buildings. Arson is the easiest crime to commit and the hardest to prove. You think every building out there is doubly locked and alarmed? Please. Especially in winter, when most beach buildings are empty for three months. Just get in and do your dirty business, and five minutes later the building's burning merrily along. And if you think it's easy proving arson, then I got the word for you. It ain't."

"I can believe that," I said. "Most of your evidence goes up in smoke, and what you have left can be blasted by water and then left open to the air. Hard to get good evidence from a crime scene like that."

A firm nod. "Absolutely goddamn true. Let's say the slug business owner, let's say he's up to his ears in debt. Bill collectors are camped out on his front lawn and his phone's ringing off the hook from banks and vendors, and he's over insured his ratty motel for a half million dollars, and then it burns down. Then let's say I'm in there rooting around, working with the fire marshal's office and whatever nitwit detective manages to string along, and then we have signs of an accelerant. Fine. Arson. Then what? You think an arrest is right around the corner?"

The room seemed to be getting warm. "Based on what I know, probably no."

Mike cocked his head. "You seem to know a lot."

"I like to read."

"Unh-hunh. Well, you're right. Unless I have six witnesses, swearing that Joe Schmoe, business owner, was seen entering the basement of his hotel with a gasoline can and box of matches, there's not much we can do. And if you think there's six spare witnesses out there looking at what's going on with their neighbors, go for a walk on the beach right now and tell me how many people you run into."

There was the sound of a garage door opening, some slapping footsteps on concrete, and then the sudden and sharp rumbling of diesel engines firing up. A voice came over a speaker in the building, loud and distorted.

"Tyler engine four. Tyler ambulance one. Respond to intersection of Marshwood Avenue and Atlantic Avenue. Motor vehicle accident, personal injury."

The engines roared louder and there was the raucous wail of the sirens, very loud and then dimming as the fire truck and ambulance went out on Ashburn Avenue, heading for one of the side streets that would get them heading north. I looked over at Mike and his hands were clasped together, knuckles quite white. He noticed me looking at him.

"Sometimes I'm like an old fire horse," he quietly said. "Those sounds just get me going and I feel like jumping up on the truck. Hard to remember I'm in this desk job."

"How did you get here then?"

Something odd happened to his face, and it was like I was looking at two or three Mike Aherns as expressions changed and melted into another, and then into a blank look and flat voice that said, "Things change, that's all. You have to use your talents where you can."

I said, "And your talents tell you that the nut is still out there?"

"Oh, yes, he is," he said, looking down at his desk. "For some reason he's chosen Tyler for his work, and I'm going to track him down, whoever he is. And then his fun will be over and mine will begin." He looked up. "You may think your stuff may be redundant but do send it along. It might answer some questions I have."

"All right," I said, wondering why I was going to make this next promise, but also knowing it was the right thing to do. "I'll pass along the stuff I've learned, but here's a suggestion. You get to the point you think you know who the arsonist is, that you've got a good case built, but something happens and you can't make an arrest, give me a call."

A quiet pause, quiet enough so I could make out the sirens of the fire truck and ambulance, heading north for whoever was up there, scared and bleeding and hurt.

Mike stared at me. "Are you suggesting something illegal?"

I shook my head. "No. I'm suggesting something creative."

A thin smile. "Some magazine writer. I've heard some things about you, Cole. That you showed up here a few years back, thin and scary-looking, and you managed to move into the prettiest little beach house on this coast, once owned by the government. And I also heard that you used to work at the Pentagon, but you didn't just shuffle papers. Some people have told me that you were a spook, and since you've moved here, you've been involved in a couple of spooky things. Maybe even a death or two. That right?"

"I'm not sure," I said. "Sometimes I'm scared of the dark. What kind of spook does that make me?"

He slowly swiveled in his chair, pointed up to three framed objects on the wall near his head. "You ever get a chance to play in the sandbox?"

The room seemed warmer still. "No, I was stuck back at the puzzle palace, probably making your lives miserable with out-of-date reports and intelligence estimates. Were you regular or reserve?"

His eyes were still on the wall. Framed there were two black-and-white photos. One was an aerial photo and showed a few oil wells, burning hard, their black clouds of smoke nearly filling the photo. The other framed photo showed a group of four men standing in front of a Humvee, arms around each other, grinning. Their faces were filthy, and goggles were pulled up over their helmets. All four wore the "chocolate chip" camouflage gear for the desert. I recognized Mike as the third soldier from the left.

In the middle of the two framed photos was another, larger frame that didn't contain a photo. It contained what appeared to be a folded-over Iraqi flag.

Mike swiveled back in his chair, blinked his eyes. "Reserves. Combat engineers. I was in the regular Army after getting out of high school, and once I learned enough to get around on my own, I got out and joined the fire service. But I stayed in the reserves, for that extra income and because I liked the guys I drilled with. Not a bad deal, until that shitty summer when Saddam invaded Kuwait and Poppy called us up."

He looked back up at the photos again. "Oh, some of us bitched about getting taken away from our families and our jobs, but I went overseas, all right. I knew when I signed up there was always the chance I'd get called up and sent into harm's way. That was the deal. And it pissed me and other guys off how so many of our fellow sunshine patriots got deferment conversions when the call-up order went out, or suddenly found out after months of service that they were really pacifists after all. I remember reading about one little nitwit, in the Marines, I think, who was shocked to find out that yes, indeed, he might be asked to report for duty and get sent overseas to kill people, and he sued the government to get discharged. I mean, how dumb can you get? Jesus. And what did you do back then?"

"Pretty boring stuff, though the hours were long. Read a lot and wrote a bunch of reports and did some analysis work."

"Did you learn a lot?"

"More than I wanted to," I said.

"Like what?"

"Like I signed an agreement when I left never to talk about it," I said.

Nor anything else, I thought.

"And you," I added. "What did you learn?"

Then his mood went somber, and he looked up again at the photos. "Learned things about myself, about handling pressure. Learned that the government does some things good, but freeze drying food isn't one of them." He started to rub at the bum tissue at the side of his head. "I also learned that some people don't belong in difficult places, no matter how many laws you pass, no matter how many congresswomen think otherwise."

"Oh?"

He nodded, and his face reddened as he said, "Women, Mr. Cole. Sorry if I'm not correct enough, but they shouldn't be cops, they shouldn't be firefighters, and they don't belong on a battlefield. They can't handle the pressure, they can't handle the stress, and too many things can go wrong."

"Like what?"

His eyes were aiming straight at me, and his fingers were practically stroking the burn tissue at the side of his head. "Like killing their own soldiers. Understand?"

I didn't understand, but I wasn't in the mood for an explanation. So I nodded in a few more places, and when the conversation dribbled away, I got out of there and back in the cool air, closed up my coat, and headed for home.

As I drove, I thought about the cheery fire inspector, and wondered just how deep his dislike for women in general and one woman in particular really went.

10

On Saturday morning I was in Newburyport, and the man I was meeting had a bright red face, whether from embarrassment or the cold, I wasn't sure. He had on a thick green cardigan over a plaid shirt, black pants, and slippers, and his hands were gnarled. What little hair he had was white and parted over one side, and his face had the wrinkles and splotches that told of years out in the sun. Jason Henry, landlord to Kara Miles, opened his door and invited me in.

"Jeez, so you're Mr. Cole, listen, I'm still sorry about the other night," he said, his voice low and moving quick. "It's just that I know nobody's 'spose to be up there, and when I heard all the footsteps and talking, I felt like I had to call the cops."

As he shut the door behind me, I said, "I'm sorry we barged in without telling you first. You were right to call. I'm just glad you're not into making citizen's arrests."

"Excuse me?" he said. "You might have to speak a bit louder—my ears aren't as young as they used to be."

So I repeated what I said with a louder voice, and also added the comment about making a citizen's arrest, and he laughed and waved his hand. "Christ, maybe when I was younger, but not now. Listen, can I get you something to drink? Coffee? Tea?"

"Tea would be fine," I said, and I took off my winter parka and tossed it over one end of the couch while he went into the adjoining kitchen. The room was big, but it felt cramped because of the furniture—large, black antique dressers and bureaus with ornate columns and mirrors. Built into one corner and with clear glass shelves was a floor-to-ceiling display case. Each shelf was jammed with figurines, shot glasses, statuettes, and other stuff that looked like it could be sold at Tyler Beach in the summer. I could see Jason as he moved around in the kitchen, a steaming kettle in his hand.

"You're in luck, you know," he said. "I just had the water on when you knocked. I was about ready for my morning routine."

"Sorry about disturbing the routine."

He laughed. "No problem. Guy like me, sometimes I need to knock the dust out. I'll be there in a sec."

On the walls were framed photographs of ships, but they weren't old clipper ships or modern war vessels. They showed working craft, cargo vessels, and container ships. Nothing sexy about them, except many millions would starve if they were all to sink overnight. Jason came out of the kitchen, carrying a wooden tray, which he set down on a coffee table. I took my mug of tea and added a spoonful of sugar, and he took his own steaming mug and sat across from me. On the tray was a blue dish, cracked on one corner, and carefully laid out were a handful of Pepperidge Farm cookies.

"Well," he said, settling himself in. "Let me tell you about last week, it was—"

I held up a hand. "Please," I said. "I appreciate that, but let's just sit for a bit, all right? Let's enjoy the tea and chat, and then let's get to the topic."

"All right, whatever you say," he said, and I smiled and said, "So, what morning routine am I disturbing?"

He crossed his legs, laughed again. "Oh, nothing major. It's just that I like to have a leisurely cup of tea and midmorning snack while I go through the day's papers. When I was younger and working, I never had the time just to saunter through a morning. I was always on watch somewhere, working."

"Merchant marine?"

"Yep, the same," Jason said, blowing some air over his cup. "'Damn near forty years of my life, from Hong Kong to Sydney to the Panama Canal and Durban and every place in between and around the world a dozen or so times, and you know what?"

"What's that?"

He shook his head ruefully. "I didn't get much chance to see anything. Worked a lot below, in the engines, and you don't get topside much when you're on duty, and when you're not on duty, there's always sleep to catch up on. And then one wonderful side effect is that with all that engine noise, you don't hear as well as you used to."

I nodded over to the display case. "You managed to come home with some souvenirs, though."

He looked over and said, "Yeah, and I'm glad I did. Some guys thought stuff like that was a waste of time, but I bet you as they got older, they wish they had something except some thin memories and a bad bladder. Other guys took so many pictures and movies they didn't do much 'cept wander around with a camera plugged to their head, and what kind of fun is that? Me, I found that if I picked something up like a glass or little statue, man, I can remember things. I can remember what I was doing and what cargo we was shipping, and where I bought the damn little trinket. Almost like magic."

"Sounds like it," I said, enjoying a sip of the tea. "And then you came home."

He nodded. "Right. Saved most of my money and invested some and bought this house and another one in Salisbury that I rent out, and I do all right." He held the cup in both of his large hands. "Not like some of the guys I was with, they whored and drank all of their paychecks. I was raised right, and so here I am, homeowner and landlord."

"Tenant problems?"

"Hah," he said, slurping loudly. "I tell 'em they have one shot with me, and that's it, out they go. Word gets around. I don't have many problems."

"How is Kara Miles as a tenant?"

"Just fine, just fine," he said, moving the cup down to his large lap. "Never any problems, rent on time, always something nice to say to me whenever I saw her."

I picked up one of the butter cookies and decided my cholesterol level could take a hit this morning. "Many visitors?"

He cocked his head. "You said you're a friend of hers, right?"

"That's right," I said, munching on the cookie. "And I'm also friends with Diane Woods."

A quick nod. "Just checking. It's none of my business who Kara is and what kind of friends she brings in. She and her lady friend are damn nice people."

"Other friends you can remember? Other people who came by for a visit who might not have been so nice?"

"Nope, not really," he said. "Her parents might have been by once or twice, and her brother, but that's about it."

"They from around here?"

"Her parents live in town. I don't know about her brother."

"And nothing's been out of the ordinary the past few weeks?"

"Like what?"

I finished off the last Pepperidge Farm product. "Like phone calls where the other party hangs up. Attempted break-ins. Odd guys, hanging around. Kara saying her mail is missing, or someone's been bugging her at work."

He seemed to think for a moment, staring at the far wall, and slurped again at his cup of tea. "Nope, nothing. Nothing at all."

"All right, then. What happened last week?"

He nodded, gave me an exaggerated wink. "My, you're a slick one. You start way back there and work your way up and get your questions answered, nice and smooth, and then you go right to the core. Not bad."

"I was once trained well. Were you here that night?"

He looked down. "You know, I wish I had been more awake. I could have felt something was wrong, something wasn't right, and I might have stopped it."

"Were you sleeping?"

"Oh, I was in bed and I had dozed off, watching my TV in there. Then I had woken up and heard some sounds, and I was in that half-awake state, you know, when you're not sure what you're listening to? And then the voices got loud and there was some, well," and I think he blushed, "the sound of the bed, you know how it is..."

I gave him a smile. "Something you've probably heard before, right?"

He nodded a bit too eagerly, like he was pleased to be talking to another man of the world or something. "That's right," he said. "I mean, Kara's a healthy young woman, there's nothing wrong with what goes on up there..."

"I see," I said, suddenly curious about something. I made a motion of rubbing my fingers together. "Mind if I take a moment to wash my hands? Those cookies tasted great but my fingers got sticky all of a sudden."

"Sure," he said, gesturing over to one side of the house. "Go over to the kitchen, take a right, and it's the door on the left, right by my bedroom."

"Thanks." I got up and went through the kitchen. It was neat and orderly and quite small. The hallway was narrow and the door to the bathroom was on the left, as promised, and I went in and turned on the spigots and then went back out into the hallway and ducked into the bedroom. I had a minute, maybe more, and I half-remembered the old exercises I had to do when I had joined up with the DoD, when you had ten seconds to stare at a photograph and ten minutes to tell an examiner what you saw.

Right now I saw a bedroom with a large single bed. Magazines on the floor, bookshelf on one side, windows that overlooked the yard. Near as I could figure it, this room was right below Kara's bedroom. There was a bureau near the foot of the bed, with a small TV on top. The bureau was filled with knickknacks and coins. I looked up at the ceiling. It was white plaster, cracked in some places. A faint black smudge about the size of my hand was near the center of the ceiling. Two doors that looked like closets. A chair near a nightstand, with a large mirror. I went over to the chair. Two shiny spots in the center of the chair, where the red fabric in the seat had been worn away.

Then, like a little click inside my head. Time was up.

I went back to the bathroom and splashed water on my hands, and then, as an afterthought, I sprinkled a few drops on my pants leg. I wiped my hands down with a towel and walked quickly back out to the living room, where Jason nodded as I came in and said, "Ready to hear the rest of the story?"

I settled back down in the couch, hoping he couldn't tell that my heart was thumping along with the exciting, scary feeling of almost getting caught. I picked up my cup and took another sip of the tea.

"Sure," I said. "What happened after you heard the sounds in the bedroom?"

Another gaze back in the cup, like he was looking for tea leaves to tell his fortune. "Like I said, I heard sounds from upstairs. And then I woke up a bit more, startled I guess, 'cause something didn't sound right. There was sobbing."

He looked at me, his expression bleak. "Sobbing. And then it stopped. And then I heard the footsteps on the stairs coming down, and the laughter and voices."

"Then what?"

"Then the door slammed, and a car from the side parking lot started up," he said. "Sounded like one of those muscle cars the young guys like to drive, the rough-sounding ones that sound like they have a bad muffler. Then a while later, I don't know how long, I guess I heard her take a shower. Then the door up at Kara's place opened up and she ran downstairs and, well, that's when I guess she went to the hospital."

"The car that you—" and then I stopped, the teacup halfway up to my mouth. "Hold on. You said voices on the stairs. What did you mean by that?"

"What?"

"What kind of voices were on the stairs?"

"Just like I told the cops," Jason said, and what he said next damn near made me drop my teacup.

"There were two men coming out of her place."

BACK AT HOME I had a fire going and I just stared at the flames and tried to bounce around what I had learned. It was a little past three o'clock in the afternoon and already the shadows were lengthening through the windows of my home. It was days like this when I wished winter was only a month long.

Years ago I had done well in my own little world in the Marginal Issues section of the Department of Defense, but in many ways it was like any other workplace. You had your routine, your boring meetings, and your own set of code words. A "fire drill" was when we were busy responding to a threat that never materialized. A "rocket report" was a document that we prepared that was sent right to the top, either with the SecDef or to the White House. And being "knee-deep in rodents" was our own fond expression, a way of saying we were being overwhelmed with squirrels—meaning a case that was too squirrelly for its own good.

With what I was now doing, the damn furry creatures were up to my waist.

First there was the discrepancy between what Kara had told the police and what she had told me about the rapist being clean-shaven. Then there was her apartment—signs of a struggle in the bedroom, but no sign of a break-in. No broken lock, no splintered doorjamb. And then there was the little tactical nuke that Jason Henry had tossed my way. Voices. More than one man was in the apartment that night, maybe helping or looking, but definitely there. That was something that even Inspector Dunbar had failed to mention in his preliminary report.

I tossed another chunk of wood onto the fire. What had happened to Kara that night, and what was happening with her now?

Then there's the landlord. Something about him didn't seem right, not right at all, and I thought about that as I picked up the phone and dialed Felix's number.

He was home, which was a surprise, and I got to the point.

"Want to get together tomorrow, get a sense of where we're going with things?"

"Sure," he said. "How about breakfast at the Ashburn House?"

I said that sounded fine and hung up, then stared again at the flames, watching their little dance as the shadows grew longer in my house.

11

When the breakfast dishes had been cleared away and we were left with our second cups of coffee, Felix looked at me and said, "So where do we stand?"

"Right now, it feels like we're standing on quicksand," I said. "Nothing is making sense, and nothing is fitting together."

The Ashburn House on this Sunday was doing reasonably well, and the post church crowd had arrived, men and women and kids dressed in their goin'-to-meetin' clothes. Felix and I were sitting against a table at the south wall, the windows freshly washed, the beach a fresh white, and the ocean bright blue.

"Knew the minute we saw the bedroom was lit up like noon that things weren't right," Felix said. "And let's face it. We both looked at the door. Either she knew her attacker and let him in or the son of a bitch had a key to the place."

I nodded. "Yeah, I knew that, too. Just didn't want to admit it. Plus, I went to see the landlord yesterday, and he told me what he heard the night of the rape."

"Which was what?"

"Which was two guys, coming down the stairs, laughing and talking Then they get into a car parked behind the house and drive away. You think a random rapist is going to park in a small lot like that, where he sticks out like a bass drum in a bathtub?"

Felix folded his hands before him. "What the hell are we involved with?"

"I don't rightly know," I said.

His voice was flat. "You think she faked the whole thing?"

A memory, of a broken shell, and then of a bruised face and shaking body in a hospital examining room. "No, not at all," I said. "I saw her that night, and she was hurt bad. Somebody—whether one guy or two or even six—hurt her that night."

Our waiter dropped off the bill and Felix opened up his wallet. "Maybe our Kara has a secret life, something she doesn't want our police detective to find out."

"Maybe so," I said.

"So what do you intend to do about it?"

"I'm going to see Diane today, tell her what we've learned, and then go on from there."

Felix smiled, shaking his head. "You make it sound like you're getting your teeth cleaned. Listen, my friend, you're about to tell a woman that someone dear to her may be lying about a rape or something equally awful. If you think she's going to shake your hand and say thanks for passing that along, then you've gone into orbit."

"I know."

"From what I know of the lovely Detective Woods, she is going to explode, and it's not going to be nice."

I gathered up my coat. "I also know that, and I don't need you to remind me. Diane and I will be just fine. We've known each other for years."

Felix still looked bemused. "You want to get together again later this week, see what we do next?"

"Sure, but are you going to be around this afternoon?"

"Yeah, I will. Why? You want to talk again later?"

I got up and put on my coat. "No," I said, trying to put some humor into my voice. "If Diane gets really mad, she might put me in a cell this afternoon, and I might need to be bailed out. Can you do it?"

"Absolutely," Felix said, and there was no smile when he said it.

So much for humor.

. . .

I HAD CALLED Diane earlier and we were to meet in the police station parking lot in about a half-hour, since she was going to drop off some paperwork she had been doing at home. Instead of driving home and then turning around and driving right back, I stayed at the beach and walked to the Tyler Point Market, where I bought a bouquet of flowers.

Most of the sidewalks weren't plowed—with so few people living at the beach, what was the point?—but traffic was so light that walking along the side of the road posed no problem. A few cars grumbled by, their sides whitened by the road salt that New Hampshire uses so lavishly on its winter roads, and seagulls flew overhead in the empty sky, no doubt wishing for the summer and the tons of food scraps to return. I walked past the empty and shuttered shops, yet there was some sign of life. On D Street, there were some yelps, and two children bundled in snow gear played among the snowbanks with a shovel and a broken chair. Their faces were alive with the reddish glow of those who are young and at play, and utterly innocent of where they are.

There was an odd quality about the air and light as I went past the empty and closed stores. I felt like I was trespassing in an amusement park condemned and prepared for destruction. With the piles of snow and ice and the empty shops, it seemed hard to believe that anything or anybody would come back to this place. But it happened, every spring, like the return of the migratory birds—these stores and hotels and shops would open up again, and the tourists would return. You could guarantee it.

I stopped for a moment, catching my breath, looking over at the blackened hulk that used to be the Rocks Road Motel. But some businesses weren't coming back. I kept on walking, stopping only when I reached the crest of the Felch Memorial Bridge, which crosses over into Falconer, spanning the channel that connects Tyler Harbor with the ocean. I undid the plastic wrapping of the flowers and tossed them into the cold salt water. I didn't bother with a prayer. Those words would do nothing to bring them back or to punish the guilty. Instead I gave myself over to memories for a moment, recalling the members of my dead group back at the Pentagon, especially a very special woman with a bright smile, reddish hair, and a laughing look that seemed able to seize me for whatever ransom she desired.

The wind picked up, scattering the flowers on the water. Old scars under my clothes began to ache, and I turned around and started walking back to Tyler Beach.

WE WERE PARKED between two pickup trucks, which were the unofficial off-duty vehicles of choice for most Tyler cops. There was a clear view across the unplowed lot to the chilly marshlands and the squat buildings of the Falconer nuclear power plant. Diane had a cup of coffee in her hands and said, "Heard on the news yesterday that the nuke has shut down for refueling. Going to be off-line for a couple of months."

"Feel any safer?"

She shook her head. "Not really. Every time they're down for refueling, that place brings in a couple of hundred contractors. That means two or three hundred lonely guys here in the middle of winter with paychecks in their pockets. Sometimes that means more work for me and the other cops, just when I need it easy."

My coat felt tight around my chest. "Anything happen yet with those workers?"

She looked right through me. "Stop dicking around, will you? What's going on?"

Here we go. I took a deep breath. "Diane, things aren't making sense."

"What do you mean?" Calm voice.

"I mean we're finding discrepancies in what Kara has told me and the cops. And they're not minor problems, not at all."

She looked through the windshield. "What kind of problems?"

I pressed on. "Kara said the man broke into her place that night. Diane, either the door was unlocked or she let him in or he had a key, for there was no sign of a break-in. Lock looked fine and the door hadn't been jimmied. She also said she couldn't get a good look at his face. You know that street-light across the way lights up the entire bedroom and hallway. If someone had come into her room, she would have seen his face."

Her gaze hadn't shifted. "What else?"

"Other things that don't make sense. She's been with you for a while, and she must know how important evidence is—yet she destroyed every piece of evidence she could before she went to the hospital. Her apartment has computer gear and jewelry and other stuff that's easy to pick up and fence, but nothing had been touched. Nothing."

A sip from her coffee cup. "You've been busy. Is that all?"

This wasn't going where I expected. "Just one more piece, and it's the hardest one to figure. She said there was just one guy there that night. The landlord said he heard two guys come down the stairs. Not one. Two. And then they got in a car parked behind the house and drove away. That didn't make sense, either, that a rapist would park in such a small lot where he would stand out and be remembered."

"Is that all?" she asked, voice still calm.

"That's it for now."

She turned to me and said, "No, that's going to be it. Period." Her chin scar was white and prominent, a blatant danger signal coming from Diane, but the calmness of her voice didn't match the whiteness of the old scar tissue.

"Listen, will you?" she said, looking out at the quiet marsh. "Don't think that I'm finally going off the deep end, but I need to say this. Look, I grew up in Porter, all right? Oldest of three girls. Mom worked as a beautician and Dad was at the shipyard. He drank, which was no big deal, but he could be a mean drunk, especially when times were tough, when there were layoffs. So he'd drink and, like most cowards, he was afraid, and he took his fear out on Mom. You know, until I was in high school, I didn't realize normal families didn't have mothers who wore sunglasses in the kitchen in the middle of the day, or who wore long-sleeve shirts during the hottest days of the summer."

A glance my way. "I'm sure that a psychologist or a psychiatrist would have a lot of fun with me, trying to determine why I love who I love is because of my father. Big deal. I just knew one day enough was enough, that no one would be around to protect my mom or my sisters, or even myself. The parish priest didn't care, our neighbors didn't care, and my guidance counselor didn't care."

A long, shuddering breath. "One of my uncles was on the Porter police force, and maybe that's why I always wanted to be a cop. Uncle Ray was a good guy, but even he couldn't be around all the time. So one night, at some family get-together, I went to his gun collection and took one of his .38 revolvers. A week later, when the news from the shipyard was bad, ol' Dad started hitting the sauce, and then he started hitting Mom. And when Mom was in the bathroom and he was in the living room opening up another cold one, his oldest and dearest daughter came in and surprised him. Oldest daughter put the barrel of that .38 into her father's mouth and cocked the hammer and said that if he ever touched Mom or her sisters ever again, she would blow the back of his fucking head out."

She looked bleak, her eyes pale. "Oldest daughter was sixteen at the time. The beatings stopped right there and never started again, and oldest daughter learned a very important lesson that night: When it comes to protecting loved ones, you can only count on yourself. No one else will do it. No one."

"Diane—" I began, and she cut me off quick.

"Forget it, Lewis," she said, her tone sharp. "That's what I learned and that's what I should have remembered. I shouldn't have asked you to do anything."

"Diane, look, let me talk to Kara again and—"

No!" She turned fully in the seat. "You're not talking to her again, not today, not ever. You just don't get it, do you? God, I hate to sound like a man-hating shrew, another goddamn stereotype, but you just don't get it. You assume the woman's lying or making things up. Damn it, for everything you said, there's another explanation. You ever wonder how well that landlord keeps his spare keys? You ever think that maybe Kara was so terrified of what was going on, she kept her eyes closed through the whole thing? And that instead of acting coolly and logically after being raped, she panicked and washed everything? You ever think that your typical sex offender might not be a burglar at heart? Ever think that maybe the rapist brought someone along, someone to stand outside and keep an eye on things, and that Kara might not have seen or heard him? Jesus H. Christ, I thought you knew something about finding things out, you with the big spook background, but you came up with squat. Not a useful goddamn thing."

"Look—" and another interruption.

"No, you look," she said, her jaw set, her scar still an angry white. "Forget I even asked you to do a thing, all right? Just drop it and go back to your safe house and your books and your telescope and just leave me and Kara alone. You just keep on blaming the victim and playing your idiot games, but don't you dare talk to Kara and don't you dare cross me. Understood?"

Before I could say a word, she was out the door, tears streaming down her face, and she turned and tossed the empty coffee cup at me. Cold wind blew through the interior and she slammed the door. By the time I got out she was in her own car, speeding out of the lot. I stood there for just a moment in the cold and empty lot, and then got back behind the wheel and folded my hands in my lap, for they were shaking so.

LATER I CALLED FELIX, and he was to the point: "Are you calling me from jail?"

"No."

"The Exonia Hospital?"

"No, I'm at home, Felix," and I wondered if he could tell how tired I was.

He said, "Well, it couldn't have been that bad. You're not wounded and you're not in jail."

I recalled the fury in her face. "No, it was pretty bad. I told her about the discrepancies we learned, and she had an explanation for each problem. She also said that as men we, quote, didn't get it, unquote. She didn't take it well, and she basically told me to stay away from her and Kara."

"For a while, or forever?"

"I'm not sure," I said, realizing that Felix had asked an important question. "I really don't know what she meant."

"And what are you going to do about it?"

"Short-term, I'm going to take a shower and open a beer. Long-term, I don't know. I'll probably give her a call in a few days or so, give her a chance to calm down some."

"Do you think she has a point?" Felix asked. "About the discrepancies we learned about Kara's story. Is Diane right?"

I took a breath. "I want to believe her, I really do, but there's something wrong about this whole mess. I just wish we knew more, but now, damn it, I don't know."

"What do you mean by that? You intend to give up on this?"

"If Diane has her way, I think she'd want that very much."

"I know what she wants you to do. The question is, is that what you want to do?"

Outside it was growing darker, the ocean free of any lights, save for the steady glow from the Isles of Shoals. "That's a question for later," I said. "Right now I'm tired and want to take that shower, read the Sunday papers and have a beer."

"Well, football is on if you're interested," Felix said. "Come on over."

"Who's playing?"

"What difference does it make?" he said, laughing, and I thanked him for his offer and declined graciously and hung up the phone.

AN HOUR later I was back on the couch, tingly and warm after a shower, wearing a terrycloth robe. I made some popcorn and, with a bottle of Molson Golden Ale, I was working my way through the *Sunday Globe* when the phone rang.

I almost spilled the beer, reaching across for the phone.

Might be Diane.

"Hello?"

No Diane, but I wasn't disappointed. "Lewis. It's Paula. How's it going?"

"Oh, it's going. And with you?"

There was something in her voice. "Well, I think I might have something."

"Something...oh, something about the hotel arsons?"

"Yep," and she giggled, an expression that still made me smile. "And so sorry, it didn't come from anything you provided me."

I sat up, putting down the Molson bottle. "So where did it come from?"

Another bit of laughter. "From my bottom desk drawer at work. Look, let's get together to go over this, all right? How about dinner at my place tomorrow night?"

How about that? I thought. "That sounds fine. Six?"

"Six it is," she said, and then, "Lewis?"

"Yes?"

"Thanks anyway for the info you gave me last week. It got me thinking, and that's what counts, and that's what paid off. You'll see."

"All right." After she hung up, I went back to my paper, finally smiling after such a long day.

12

After helping Paula Quinn wash the dinner dishes, coffee cups in hand we went into the living room of her second-floor apartment on High Street in Tyler. She lives near the beach, and within easy walking distance are a half-dozen motels and condos. It was a cold night, and Paula's apartment was chilly. The heating system for the building was creaking and groaning, and Paula confessed to me that her first winter here, she slept with socks, long underwear, and a hat, and I told her to stop talking dirty and she laughed and punched me. The living room had a boarded-up fireplace on the far wall, and the usual bookshelves, used furniture, and piles of newspapers. The eastern windows had a good view of the beach and a few motels. On the wall were some framed poster art and a metal front-page plate from the *Tyler Chronicle,* an issue that had been published two years back. It was one of Paula's proudest accomplishments: Due to the breaking news in Tyler and the sickness of another reporter, she had written all of the six stories on the front page.

"Not a bad record, eh?" she had told me once.

"Pretty impressive," I had said, peering at the plate, which was used to print the actual newspaper page. "But why do two of the stories have no bylines?"

Her mouth had become a thin line. "My editor Rollie took my name off.

Thought it would make the paper look silly, to have one person responsible for all the day's stories. So much for pride in your staff."

Tonight we sat on a couch that was covered with a red and black-checked blanket, and she opened up a thick manila folder that was filled with documents, newspaper clippings, and photocopied legal pages. She started going through the piles of paper, balancing them on her lap. She had on jeans and a shapeless dark green wool sweater, and I tried to stay warm with pleasant thoughts of what she looked like in summer, when she usually wore shorts and a comfortable top.

"Here we go," she said. "Rocks Road Motel. The Seaview. The Tyler Tower Motel. The Snug Harbor Inn. Four motels burned down the last four weeks. According to everything you and I and Mike Ahern and even Diane Woods have checked out so far, there's no connection, right? They weren't owned by the same company, the owners were all in good financial shape, and the owners had no real enemies. So. Just random arsons. Nothing you could connect. But something bugged me about these buildings."

"Like what?"

She shrugged, a triumphant smile on her face. "That's what drove me crazy. I just had the feeling that I had seen those names before. I dug through the clip files and morgue at work, and there was nothing, but I had this funny little memory of seeing at least two of the names on a piece of paper, and I kept on rooting around my desk."

I looked around the cluttered apartment. "If it's anything like this place, I'm sure it took a while."

She kicked me, but her pretty smile was still there. "Beast. It took some time, but I found it. Care to guess where?"

I thought for a moment and looked at the pile of papers and said, "Town board of some kind. Zoning board?"

Her face fell. "How did you guess?"

I motioned to the pile of papers. "Looks like some town documents are there, that's why. Photocopies of meeting minutes. You go to so many select-men's meetings, I didn't think it would be something that would come up there. Your memory is too good. So that doesn't leave too many choices. Which is why I guessed zoning board."

"You guessed wrong," she said, her voice flat.

"Oh?"

She then wiggled her nose. "Bastard. It was the planning board. That's where."

"All of these places were mentioned at a planning board meeting?"

Paula nodded, passed over a thick pile of paper. "Here's your copy of the meeting minutes for the past six months. I try to be the best reporter I can, but it's impossible to make every board meeting each week. So Dawn Duncan, she's the recording secretary, she drops off a set of minutes a day or two after each meeting. I run through them, see if there's anything worth writing a story about. It's a great time-saver."

I weighed the papers in my hand. "So what's with our destroyed hotels?"

"They all came before the board at one time or another the past few months, looking to get plans approved for construction work of some kind. An addition. A new restaurant. And the Tyler Tower Motel, the owner wanted to convert to condos."

A faint little tingling started at the base of my skull, a feeling that was quite familiar to me from my times at the Department of Defense, when you spent months working on a problem, "walking the dog backward" as it was called, and then had something fall in your lap that was a big, beautiful key to the whole mess.

"You did well."

Her face blushed, but her smile grew wider. "It was just dumb luck, that's all."

"No," I said. "You remembered. You had a voice telling you something and you didn't give up, and you dug and found out. Good for you. Your editor underestimates you."

She shrugged, "All men seem to do that. And don't you forget it."

"Have you started doing something with this?"

"That I have," she said. "Look, it's too much of a coincidence to have all four of those places burn down, and then to see that they were mentioned in the planning board. There's got to be a connection. A bank, a mortgage company, an architect firm, a law firm. Hell, even the members of the planning board." She added firmly, "And I intend to find it. And I intend to break that story and scoop everybody and everything in Wentworth County."

Remembering a promise I had made earlier, I asked, "Agree to something first?"

"Like what?"

"Like going to Mike Ahern, the fire inspector, the day before you go to press?"

She looked at me quizzically. "Why in the hell do you want to do that?"

"Because I promised him I would, if I found out any good leads on the arsonist."

Paula's face colored and she said, "Just because you made a promise to the fire inspector, I have to jump through hoops, too? I don't remember signing on to any particular promise, Lewis. I got a problem with that, a real problem."

"I don't mean that—"

"Look," she interrupted, "I don't mean to sound like a First Amendment queen, but I don't get that many good stories here in the wintertime. This place is dead, and if I get a chance to blow this story open, I don't intend to play footsie with the local public safety officials. It's my story, not theirs."

I was going to jump in and then I looked at her, and the color of her face, and I said, "You have a run-in with Mike Ahern since we last saw him?"

She opened her mouth as if to argue with me, and then closed it and nodded.

"Yeah. A couple of days ago. I made the mistake of phoning him at home. Ouch."

"Was it late?"

"I didn't think it was late. It was just before nine o'clock, and I was trying to get a jump on the next day's story, see if anything had come back from the state crime lab."

"And what happened?"

"Well, I think he was drunk, or maybe just in a pissy mood," she said. "I've always thought anyone who gets paid by tax dollars should be open to answering questions at reasonable hours, and I didn't think I was that unreasonable. I said sorry for calling so late, and then I asked my questions, and then he just nailed me with one of his own."

"Which was what?"

She smiled, but her face was flushed—from the memory, I suppose. "He asked me again to ID myself. Which I did. Then he asked me what time it was. Which I told him. And then he said something to the effect, that, quote, I was at work until six p.m., and my responsibility to you, the *Tyler Chronicle*, and every other nosy asshole was finished at six-oh-one p.m., unquote. Then he hung up."

"Well," I said. "And what did you do next?"

She shrugged. "I waited until nine the next morning, asked him the same question, he gave me a reasonable answer, and things were fine. But it struck me strange. The man just lost it."

"I guess he did."

"Well, he did, but he didn't. It was odd. His voice wasn't raised, his words weren't slurred like he was drunk It was just...it was just like he was being himself."

"Like when he's at work as a fire inspector, he's not himself?"

She rubbed her arms and said, "I know it sounds weird, but that' s exactly it. During the day, I was dealing with the daytime Mike Ahern. After hours, I was dealing with the nighttime Mike Ahern. Like he was a freaking vampire or something."

I slowly moved my fingers across the pile of papers she had just handed over. "So. Let me rephrase the question. If you manage to find out something about who just might be behind these fires, would you mind going to the fire inspector—in the daytime—and our local police detective, and tell them what's going on?"

Paula moved her legs up under herself. "Oh, just so that it's one minute before the *Chronicle* goes to press. I don't want to give the Porter or Dover papers any favors."

"Absolutely. The only favor I'm looking for is putting one very bad person away for a long time, before he burns down half the town."

"Fine. Any other questions?"

"Yeah," I said. "You moved the bathroom lately, or is it still in the same place?"

"Same place," she said, and then an exaggerated wink, "And so's the bedroom."

"Hah," I said, and a warm feeling settled nicely into my chest, and lasted until I went past her bedroom. Just inside by the wall was a bureau, complete with large mirror. A picture was in the side of the mirror, and I stepped into the bedroom for a moment and touched it. The photograph showed Paula. Her smile was wide and even, and her eyes were crinkling in that festive mood I've seen many times. Her ears were sticking through her blond hair—a physical trait that she hates, but that I find adorable—and she was wearing a black cocktail party type of dress. I had never seen that dress before. Around her delicate neck was a string of pearls. Paula looked like a knockout, and I wish I was able to tell her that.

She wasn't alone in the photo. Standing beside her, an arm flung around the bare skin of her shoulder, was Jerry Croteau, her photographer friend. He wore a suit and tie and his beard was bushy and his eyes were quite bright. I gently traced the outline of her face on the photo and then went to the bathroom. Later I washed my hands and looked at myself in the mirror and grimaced. Choices. For a brief moment, months ago, Paula and I had been together and had shared some wonderful times. Then we made choices. I made a choice to draw back, and so did she, and now she had made another one, with another man. So what is to be done?

"Time to head out," I murmured aloud, and I went back out to the living room.

Paula was on the couch and as I went to her, there was something in the air.

"Is your oil furnace acting up again?" I asked, taking a sniff. "Mmm? she asked, flipping through a copy of that week's *Time*. "What's up?"

"Oh, I don't know," I said. "I thought I smelled something. Is the stove still on?"

"Damn, I think you're right," she said, getting off the couch. "I'll be right back."

She went out to the kitchen and just as quickly came back.

"Everything's off. You know, I'm smelling something, too. Let me look down the hallway. Mrs. Wilson from downstairs, sometimes she has the habit of burning her evening meal."

Something was tingling along my legs. I couldn't stay still. I went to the windows as Paula went out. The smell was stronger. I looked out at the winter landscape, saw the streetlights and the dark stretch of ocean, and the houses, and the motels—

Paula came back and I said, "Quick. The name of the motel next door here."

"The what?"

"Paula, damn it, the name of the motel right here. What is it?"

She clasped her hands in front of her. "The Crescent House. Why?"

I moved over to her, racing for my coat. "Call the fire department," I said, fiercely proud that my voice was calm and not shaking. "The Crescent House is on fire."

She went to the phone, and I ran downstairs and then out, breathing in the cold air, gasping for a moment. I ran across the poorly plowed parking lot, almost falling down once, and got to my Range Rover and into the glove box and came out with a flashlight. From the parking lot I ran down High Street, about fifty feet or so, the light bobbing ahead of me, showing me the cold pavement and the frozen ice puddles and banks of snow. The Crescent House was on the left side of the street and built in a U-shape, with two stories. Smoke was billowing out of a set of downstairs windows. The parking lot was unplowed and the lower windows were boarded with plywood.

There were no lights on at the motel, but that didn't stop me from going to the front door and banging on it several times, yelling, "Fire! Get out now!" over and over again. An underreported story but a true one: Many homeless in this part of the state take up illegal winter residence in the closed motels and cottages of Tyler Beach.

There was no answer. The smoke was getting thicker. I moved around again, shining the light into the second-floor windows, hoping that no one was in there slumbering through a day's worth of booze or drugs. I could now hear the crackling of flames devouring wood, plastic, and plaster.

To the side of the motel now. There was shrubbery and some trees, masking the rear end of the motel from its neighbors. The pool was surrounded by a fence and the snow was quite deep. I shone the light closer to the snow, my breathing harsh, my chest burning with a cold stiffness. No footsteps in the snow. I moved the light around. No arsonists skulking in the shadows. Not a soul. The smoke was still billowing out, the orange light from the fire now making odd silhouettes on the snow. It seemed to be alive, seemed to be bent on consuming itself and everything surrounding it.

"Lewis!"

I turned and Paula was coming down the road, coat flapping behind her, slippers still on her feet. "I made the call," she said, stopping and gasping. "They're on their way."

She looked over at the hotel, hugging herself. "Jesus Christ, not this one..."

"You know the owners?"

She nodded. "Retired couple. Old Greeks, came here years ago. Used to let me and the neighbors use the pool. The Kostens. Oh, Lewis, this will kill them, I know it will."

I couldn't think of anything to say. Paula was trembling from the cold, and in her gloveless hands she held a reporter's notebook and a Canon camera. She brought up the camera and started snapping off the pictures. A true professional. Cars started to slow down, pull over on the street, the occupants getting out, gaping at the sight of an untended fire.

"Where are they?" she said, almost talking through clenched teeth. "I called them minutes and minutes ago. They should be here now, damn it."

I put my arm around her shoulder. "They'll be here," I said. "Time's just playing tricks with you, that's all. They'll be here."

But even as I said that, it was hard to ignore the gnawing discomfort I felt at seeing the motel merrily burn, with no firefighters or fire trucks in sight. In my mind I knew that they were moving as fast as possible, that they were racing to their trucks, starting them up, maneuvering the heavy vehicles out of the station house, setting off the lights and sirens, and beating their way up here. But something was tugging at my heart, wondering if Paula had in fact made the call, if in fact had she given them the wrong address, because, God, it had been so long since we'd been out there.

Tricks, that's all. They would get here. It just seemed so long because of the fire right in front of us, and in crisis situations, seconds and minutes pass like hours.

A window on the second floor shattered with a loud bang, the shards of glass tumbling to the snow below, and Paula yelped. "Lewis, is somebody trying to get out?"

I aimed the light up to the window, where dark smoke billowed out, rolling up into the winter sky. "No, I think it's just the heat. That's all."

And with that, I began to feel the warmth from the flames on my face. Two more cars pulled to the side of the road, and just as I was going to ask Paula if she was sure she had called the Tyler Fire Department, and not the North Tyler Fire Department by mistake, there came the far-off sounds of sirens.

"They're coming," Paula said. "Christ, I hope they get here in time to save it."

Again, I didn't know what to say. Fire had broken through to the roof in two places and it didn't look good.

More sirens from up the street. She turned and said, "They must have called mutual aid."

"Or it might be trucks from the uptown station. But I think the beach station is going to beat them."

Then the sirens became louder as a corner was turned to the east, and I saw the flashing red lights and bright red strobes of the fire trucks coming up High Street. The sound of the engine and the sirens mixed in a loud clamor that seemed to rattle my bones. A fire engine was first, followed by a ladder truck, and at about fifty feet away the fire engine stopped. Paula said, "What the hell?" and I said, "Just look. They're laying out the hose," which is exactly what happened.

One of the firefighters leaped from a side jump seat as the truck started up again, and hose spewed out like thick spaghetti from a pasta machine. He made his way to a shoveled-out hydrant and went to work, as the pumper truck screeched to a halt in front of the motel with a hiss of air brakes. The ladder truck pulled in closer, and seeing the firefighters at work was amazing, how they moved and worked with a minimum of yells and calls to each other. It looked like a very complex, choreographed, masculine ballet. A fire lieutenant came out of the truck's cab, dressed out in bunker gear, helmet, air pack, boots, and white helmet, and moved purposefully over to Paula and me.

"Anybody in there that you know of?" he asked. Like most firefighters in this state, he had a thick mustache.

"Not a one," I said. "Place is closed up for the winter."

"Yeah, that's for sure," he said, turning with a weariness, pulling on his gloves. "You know, I'm getting too old for this shit."

As he went back to his crew, there was another sound of sirens, and I turned to see two more fire engines coming down High Street, racing from the uptown fire station of the Tyler Fire Department. It soon became very crowded, with people streaming out of the neighboring houses, draping on coats and blankets, coming out to see this midwinter disaster in motion. Paula mentioned something about getting some more pictures and blended in with the crowd of people, and I stood by myself, watching the firefighters at work. The aerial ladder had maneuvered over the roof of the motel and was drenching water from a deluge gun, and a crew had broken in through the front door, carrying a hose line, and there was a burst of steam and gray smoke when the water hit.

Tyler police cruisers had blocked off both ends of High Street and uniformed cops in winter jackets got some sort of crowd control going, moving us away from the crumbling building. I looked around but didn't see Diane, and I felt guilty at feeling relieved. It had only been a day since we last talked, that disastrous time in the parking lot of the police station, but it seemed like weeks.

But then I did see something that bothered me, that shouldn't have concerned me, but that still stung.

Paula Quinn, standing at the edge of the parking lot, reaching over to kiss a bearded man, burdened by his camera bag and gear. Jerry Croteau. Looked like a nice couple, and I shouldn't have been bothered, but I still didn't like the sight. I looked over again, and they broke free from an embrace, and Paula went over and talked to a fire captain from Tyler.

Then Jerry got to work, taking photographs of the burning building, the crowd of people straining to see what they could, and the hunched-over forms of the firefighters, hauling in hose lines, moving deliberately and forcefully, as the flames began to get beaten down and the smoke continued to billow out. With each picture he took, there was a brief flash of light, freezing everyone and everything in their spots, and I marveled for a moment at the directness of what he was doing. In my so-called job as a columnist for *Shoreline*, I had to look at things and fight with words to come up with a meaning of what I was seeing. But with his foreign tool in his cold hands, the images were there, waiting to be captured, waiting for someone with skill and drive.

Sounded like a hell of a job, but it still didn't mean I had to like him.

I looked for Paula and couldn't find her in the crowd of people and not liking being with so many of my fellow residents, I started heading out. A small red Chevette sputtered to a stop and Mike Ahern came out, shrugging on a fire jacket over his thick shoulders. He saw me and said, "Hell of a night, ain't it?"

"Sure is," I said. He shook his head and opened up the hatchback of the Chevette and said over his shoulder, "You'll excuse me if I don't stop to speak, but it looks like I have a goddamn fire on my hands."

I nodded and headed back to the parking lot, when there was a tap at my shoulder and I turned, seeing Paula waving some paperwork.

"Here's the files I gave you earlier," she said. "And I'll save you some time."

I took the papers from her cold hands, a little voice telling me that I should offer to warm her chilled fingers, and instead I said, "The Crescent House. It's on the list."

A nod. "Dear God, it certainly is. A proposal to turn it into elderly housing, six months ago. Look, I've got things to do. We'll talk later this week."

"We certainly will," I said, and I watched her for a moment, walking back to Jerry and the crowd and the firefighters, her slim figure silhouetted from the death of another dream and business, and I trudged back to the parking lot in the snow, the grumbling of the fire engines echoing among the buildings.

13

On Thursday, just a few days after the Crescent House burned down into a pile of rubble, Felix Tinios called and suggested a drink and mid-afternoon snack. I said that was fine and met him at the Lady Victoria House, a pleasant bed and breakfast with attached restaurant and bar near the North Tyler harbor. In summer the French doors at the Lady Victoria are opened to the sights and sounds of the harbor, but on this day a bank of snow prevented the doors from being opened by anyone with fresh air on his mind.

We sat in wicker chairs, me with a cup of coffee and cheesecake, Felix with Irish coffee and some strawberry dessert that looked designed to clog arteries.

As we ate, Felix said, "Haven't heard from you since your meet with Diane, and I was just wondering. Are we finished with this rape matter, or are we going ahead?"

"Diane doesn't want anything to do with us and doesn't want us to have anything to do with Kara."

Felix scooped a bit of his dessert up in a spoon, winked, and swallowed. "Nice answer, but not the answer to my question. Are we done?"

I had my hands clasped around the warm coffee mug, looking out the windows at the snow-covered landscape. The restaurant was doing fairly well and most of the people at the bar or tables were cross-country skiers, having spent the day across the road at a golf course. But I couldn't focus on the happy skiers in their bright colors or warm woolen clothes. I just saw a frightened woman, lying on a hospital examining table, eyes wide and teary, holding the hand of someone who loved her dearly.

"No," I finally said. "Not by a long shot."

"So where do you want to go next?"

"Eventually, we might have to go to her family," I said. "But first, there's two places to start. First up is Kara's landlord. He's the only other witness so far as to what happened that night, and I think he deserves another round of questions."

"Deserves?" Felix asked. "What do you mean by that?"

"A couple of things," I said. "Things that don't add up. Jason Henry is retired merchant marine, and I had to raise my voice for him to hear me when I talked to him."

"So there's a problem with that?"

"Yeah, there is." I looked around the room, which was filled with laughing and rosy-cheeked people, and I was quite envious of them, thank you. "The problem is, he told me that he was in his bed when he heard the sounds upstairs."

"Those sounds being..."

"Those sounds being a bed being used rather vigorously, and heard the voices of two men, laughing and talking on the stairway outside."

Another scoop of the dessert from Felix. "But he's got a hearing problem. You think he made it up? Do you think he was in on whatever happened that night to Kara?"

I played a bit with the empty packets of sugar. "Tell you what I do think. I think he did hear something that night, and he probably heard it from his bedroom, but I don't think he was lying in bed, dozing off. I poked around his bedroom just for a second and saw a couple of things that made me think."

"A collection of slasher movies?"

"No, a chair and a dirty ceiling," I said. "The chair was near the night-stand, and it was worn in a funny way. There were two impressions there, like someone had been standing on it. And right above it, on the ceiling, was a smudge of something dark. Like newsprint. The smudge was about the size of someone's hand."

Felix nodded, tossed the spoon into the empty dish. "So you think Jason likes to listen in to what's going on upstairs, and standing on the chair and balancing himself by keeping a hand on the ceiling helps him along."

"That's right," I said. "Maybe he heard more than he wants me or the cops to know, something that's going to embarrass him. Which is why he deserves another visit."

"All right," he said, nodding in satisfaction. "That takes care of one visit. What's the other visit you've been considering?"

"We've talked to Kara, her neighbors, and her landlord, but we haven't talked to her place of work. If Kara did know her attacker and did let him in, then it might be someone from her company. God knows everything else so far has been a bust."

"So what would you like?"

I rewarded him with a half-smile. "My, aren't we being considerate today?"

He waved a hand. "Being considerate has nothing to do with it. You're paying for my time, which means you can give me polite suggestions on what to do next."

"Okay, here's the suggestion," I said. "I'll do the employer interview, and I'd like you to go back to the landlord. I played the good cop with him, and you can play the bad cop. Get him upset, get him concerned, do something to scam him into telling you more."

"Like what?" Felix asked.

"I'll leave it up to you," I said. "I don't want to be accused of micro-managing."

"Bah. Thank you very much. And what do you intend to do?"

"I plan to head over to her job tomorrow and talk to whoever will listen to me, but first, I've got something else to do."

"Which is what?"

The waitress came by, dropped off the check. I smiled and picked it up and handed it over to Felix. "I've got to arrange a peace treaty."

. . .

LATER THAT NIGHT it was quite cold, dropping into the teens, and I was parked at the Tyler Harbor Meadows, up against a snowbank, waiting for someone to come home. There was a broken yardstick and a piece of cloth at my side. I didn't want to draw attention by leaving the engine rumbling, so I was bundled up in a coat and hat. While the engine was off, the key was switched on, and to pass the time I played around the stations, listening to AM talk radio from Boston, then some of the local FM music stations, and then bouncing over to the National Public Radio outlet from New Hampshire, up at WEVO in Concord. A nice mix that kept me awake, though the grumbling in my stomach was certainly not helping things. It had been many hours since that cheesecake and coffee. But I didn't want to leave, not after having gotten the courage to get here in the first place.

Lights were on up at the condo unit numbered fourteen but there was an empty parking space out front. There had been movements up there by the window, so I knew that someone was home. But it wasn't the someone I wanted to talk to.

I flipped through the radio dial again, and then there was the fanning beam of headlights, coming up the condominium driveway. I sat up, conscious that it had gotten so cold that my breath could be seen inside. A green Volkswagen Rabbit burbled into the parking lot, and as it came to a stop, I gathered up my possessions and stepped outside.

Diane Woods was stepping out, also bundled up from the cold, carrying a soft leather briefcase. She turned and saw me standing there.

"Lewis? And what the hell is that you're carrying?"

I shook out the cloth that had been tied to the broken yardstick, and waved the piece of white fabric back and forth.

"Truce?" I asked. "Please?"

It seemed like her face was struggling with a variety of emotions, from being standoffish to being merely curious, and the slight humor of the scene seemed to take control and she smiled.

"Why? Afraid I was going to shoot you down on my doorstep?"

I smiled back. "Well, I'd be lying if I said the thought hadn't entered my mind."

"You really think I'm still that mad at you?"

I waved the stick and white flag. "That's why I brought this."

Another smile. "Men. Always looking for the grand gesture. Look, the both of us have a lot of history and times between us." She gestured up to her condo, where I thought I saw a shape, looking down. "That's something important to me, up there."

"And for me, as well."

She seemed small there, bundled in winter clothing, standing in the snow by the door. "I felt bad, the way we last saw each other."

"I do, too," I said. "I'm sorry for acting like I knew it all. Even in my old job, I should have known better. I don't know it all, especially about you and Kara."

"I'm sorry, too. I'm sorry about tossing that male-bashing nonsense your way. You're not perfect, but you sure as hell get it more often than any other guy I know."

"So?" I asked, and I waved the white flag again. "Truce?"

A laugh, this time. "Yes, a truce. Is that all?"

"No, just one more thing."

Diane motioned again. "You sure you don't want to come up?"

I shook my head. "This won't take long. Look. It's entirely up to you, but I want to close the circle, Diane. I want to finish this matter for you, as best as I can. It won't mean talking to Kara again, but it'll mean talking to her neighbors again, her landlord, and where she works. After that, if there's nothing there, I'll write it up and give it to you, and it's over. Done. Unless you have something else for me to do."

"Why do you want to do that?" she asked, her voice quiet and neutral.

I shrugged again. "I promised, that's why. Because you asked me, that's why. And because you're my best friend, Diane. That's why."

I think she was biting her lip. "Those are pretty good reasons." She looked up at her condo. "Kara's doing a bit better. She's starting counseling and I've even agreed to come in with her. She's eating and sleeping more, but, my friend, I still want to know who he was. So, yes, continue. But I'll hold you to your word. Don't come talking to Kara. She's beginning to smile again, and that's very important to me."

"A deal," I said. "Felix and I will do some more digging, and I'll pass it along when we've reached the end."

"Thanks. What have you got planned?"

"Felix is talking to the landlord again, and I was planning on going to Digital tomorrow."

"Let me call for you," she said. "Otherwise they won't tell you what time it is."

I finally put the white flag down. "How are you doing, otherwise?"

She hefted up her briefcase. "Goddamn Crescent House burned down earlier this week, in case you haven't noticed."

"Oh, I noticed, all right."

"Same damn thing. Nothing makes sense. No money problems, no threats, no connection with the other fires. But still the damn thing burned, and it was arson again."

I thought of what Paula had found out, about the planning board and the motels, and decided to keep quiet. That had been a promise to Paula. Damn hard to keep track of one's promises, sometimes. "You working any better with the fire inspector?"

"Hardly." She shivered and said, "I often don't think this way, especially in the summer when it's busy and I get to sleep every night about one minute after I get to bed, but all that's gone on these past few weeks has made me think about evil."

I could tell she was in no joking mood, so I kept my expression straight. "One would usually think about evil in the hot months. Not necessarily the winter."

"No, not for me. I think about bad things and evil in the winter. Everything around here shuts down, everything's boarded up, and there's not enough light in the day. People leave home in the morning and it's dark, and when they get home, it's still dark. It's cold and windy and the ocean seems that much wider, and the nights are very long, Lewis. Long enough for minds to be at work, for minds to urge people on to do evil things. Like burning down motels. Like raping young women."

"And where does it come from?"

"From the sick ones," she said. "Not the ones with bedwetting problems when they were younger, or who caught Mommy and Daddy bouncing in bed. I mean the real sick ones, the ones who enjoy torturing small animals when they're kids and who move on to bigger animals when they get older. I think they're born that way. Just born evil."

I said, "Some local clergy might not like my opinion but I'm with you on this one."

"Good. An ally. Tough to be the good guys nowadays, we're so unfashionable."

"And probably freezing, too," I said. "You should get inside. Kara's probably wondering what the hell we're doing."

"Fair enough," she said. "And...thanks for coming by."

"My pleasure." I turned to walk away and she called out, "Wait!"

"What's that?"

She stepped up to me. "Fool," she said. "What makes you think I was going to let you leave without a hug?"

She grasped me around the waist and I returned the favor, and something seemed to catch in my throat when I said, "I'll do the best I can, Diane. Promise."

A firm squeeze, a kiss on the cheek. "I know you will. Now get going, before my woman sees us in action."

THE NEXT DAY I was driving through a remote part of Newburyport, near the town line of Newbury and just a few minutes off I-95. This part of Massachusetts is known as the North Shore, and the Merrimack River cuts through a lot of the towns on its way to the ocean. Parts of it are still fairly rural, and the road I was on curved gently among the snow-covered fields and bare forests.

Eventually I turned right at a driveway that was marked by a blue-and-white sign saying DIGITAL and quickly found a spot in the visitors' section. About half of the parking lot was empty, and the lot was poorly plowed. This Digital plant was a distant cousin of the big and brawling company that had roared through the early and mid-1980s, making its mark in the world and also causing giddy headline writers, who should have known better, to compare the North Shore with Silicon Valley. The fall from favor and profitability had been a long one, and Digital had shorn off plants and employees like desperate Russian sleighers being pursued by wolves in a Siberian winter, tossing off passengers to lighten the load. It was still surviving, though it had gone through two or three additional rough years.

The reception area was tiny, with vinyl-covered couches and chairs, a scuffed metal coffee table that had a copy of its annual report, and issues of *Money* and *Fortune*. The receptionist sat behind a glass window arrangement that looked like it belonged in a bus station in the Bronx, and after announcing who I was and passing over my New Hampshire driver's license, I was privileged to get a green plastic badge that said VISITOR. I clipped the badge to my shirt collar, took off my coat, and sat down, watching the snow melt from my boots.

I didn't wait long. The door was buzzed open, and a man poked his head through.

"Mr. Cole?" he asked.

"The same," I said, getting up.

"Scott Weber," he said, extending his hand, which I shook.

"I don't have much time, so let's see if we can get things squared away."

The head of security for the Digital plant wore a two-piece dark blue suit, white shirt, and light red tie. He had on black-rimmed glasses, and while his features were delicate, his eyes were hard blue and unmoving.

"That'll be fine," I said. "I don't think it should take that long."

I followed him through, and the security door slammed shut, bringing back some memories of my old job, and I followed him down a tiled corridor. Off to both sides were cubicles and the sounds of phones ringing and the incessant tapping of computer keyboards. There was a banner taped to the side of one cubicle that said SCREW HEWLETT-PACKARD, with an illustration that showed a long screw protruding through a circuit board that bore the Hewlett-Packard logo. Weber saw that I noticed the banner and said with a thin smile, "Bit of corporate cheerleading, I'm afraid."

"Does it work?"

"It better."

The hallway opened up on the right-hand side with large windows overlooking an assembly area. People were hunched over on long tables, working with power tools of some sort, slapping together circuit boards and cathode-ray tubes and other electrical devices. Most of them wore earphones of some sort, and all were working with heads bowed, staring at what was before them. There were no windows to the outside.

Inside, we went to a conference room, and another man stood up, and again repeated the centuries-old ritual of shaking hands as Weber introduced me to him. He was about my age, wearing a light blue polo shirt and stonewashed jeans. His black hair was quite short and his tanned face sported a black goatee.

"I'm Rick Kiper," he said, sitting down as Weber sat down next to him. "I'm Kara's supervisor. Listen, before we start, can you'll tell me how she's doing?"

I sat down, putting my coat on the polished wood of the table, "She's doing better, but I think it's going to be a while before she comes back to work."

Rick shook his head, looked over at Weber. "All of us were stunned when we heard what happened. First that something awful like that could happen in Newburyport, and then to hear that it happened to a lovely woman like Kara...My God. Makes you wonder if anyone's safe."

Weber crossed his arms. "Well, I'm concerned about Kara, but I'm also concerned about the company and its liability in speaking with you, Mr. Cole. The only reason I arranged this session is because a law enforcement official from Tyler asked that it happen, and because Rick here insisted on speaking with you. I also want to tell you that I don't intend for this meeting to be a fishing expedition. Not to be a prick about the matter, but I would like you to ask your questions, get your answers, and then leave."

Rick looked over at me, smiled. "Such a charmer, eh? You ought to see how he acts when me or some of my people come in and forget our access badges."

I decided that I didn't like Weber's attitude, as much as I could understand it, but I also knew my presence here was on shaky ground indeed. They had no official reason to allow me here in the first place, and only because of Diane's insistence and the kindness of Kara's boss was this interview even going forward.

I picked up my pen and notebook and said, "I know this is highly irregular, but I'm doing some inquiries about Kara Miles and what happened to her. It may end up as a story one of these days in my magazine, but more likely than not, nothing will come out of it. However, there's a chance that in preparing for this story I might find out something that will help the police."

Weber's look was grim, but Rick seemed intrigued. "Really? Are you also a private investigator?"

"Nope," I said. "Just a private citizen who wants to see what I can learn."

"What might that be, Mr. Cole?" Weber asked.

I ignored him and looked at Kara's boss. "Tell me about Kara, her job history, how she got along with co-workers. That's good for a start."

"Well, Kara's one of our best," Rick said, crossing one leg over, holding the knee with both hands. "She runs one of our customer support groups and she does a wonderful job. It can be a stressful job, but she knows how important it is."

"What exactly does it entail?"

Rick looked over at Scott and smiled. "It means keeping us out of trouble, that's what it means. It means holding on to our customers and taking care of their needs. It's taken a while for this company and others to realize it, but the customer calls the shots. There's a lot of competition out there, and if you get a reputation of screwing over your customers and not taking care of them, then you're dead. That's it."

"Does she work alone?"

"No, she had a crew with her, and the number fluctuated, depending on the problems they were working with."

"Any problems with co-workers? Someone not liking her, not getting along?"

A quick move of the head. "No. Absolutely not. She's a joy to work with, someone who really likes what she does. Lot of people, they're content to spend a good chunk of their time bitching and moaning about their job or their co-workers or the company's personnel policies. Not Kara. Always the first one here in the morning, and usually one of the last to leave the place. Wish I had two or three more like her."

I made a few quick notes in my notepad, none of which was probably going to be helpful. "Customers, then. Anything come up with customers? Vendors hitting on her? Customers feeling like they were getting a runaround from the company?"

Rick looked at me with an odd expression. "You mean, someone who would get so pissed at the company that they would do something to Kara? Is that what you're saying?"

"No," I said, aware that Weber's expression was slipping from studied boredom to annoyance. "I'm just looking for something that might give me an idea of what to do next. You ask a lot of questions. You get some answers. Sometimes those answers lead you to other people, other places. Most times, they don't do much. But you have to ask them."

Rick didn't look convinced. "I'm afraid I can't help you there."

I shifted my position and looked over at Weber. "Anything you can offer?"

"Like what?"

"Like security incidents at the plant. Hate mail. Odd men hanging around the parking lot, the bars where your people go after work, harassing women or following them. Anything like that at all?"

"No. Any more questions?"

Time to go, I supposed. I closed up my notepad and said, "One more thing. I'd like to see Kara's office."

Rick smiled, relaxing a bit. "You mean her cubicle. Sure."

"Wait a minute—" Weber started.

"Oh, don't worry," Rick said. "I'll make sure that he doesn't see any secret plans. Look, you go back to doing your security work and I'll take Mr. Cole here out to Kara's office and then escort him back out."

Weber didn't look too pleased, but he stood up, and after a brief hand-shake he left the conference room, and Rick said, "Brrr, nice to have him leave the place. Helps raise up the room temperature a few degrees. Ready for a quick tour?"

"Sure," I said, and I followed Rick out to the hallway. Other people were there, moving fast, carrying reams of printouts or legal-size notepads.

"How's business?" I asked.

"Is this for publication?" he tossed back.

"It's for polite conversation," I said.

"If that's the case, Mr. Cole, then we're struggling," he said, looking to me and raising an eyebrow. "But then again, everybody's struggling. A few years back, when I was out in California in Los Gatos things were quite different."

"Where was that?"

"Near San Jose. The original Silicon Valley. My friend, back then if you were smart and knew your stuff, it was a dream. Money was great, working conditions were even better, and if your boss was a twit, you literally could quit on a Friday and start work somewhere else on a Monday morning."

I said, "What happened then?"

Rick stopped at a locked door and took out a keycard, swiping it through the bulky lock. A green light flashed and in we went.

"Like most dreams, this one ended, and everyone woke up, and a lot of people woke up unemployed. Recession, higher taxes, increased competition, especially from overseas. Some people saw it coming, others didn't."

"And what did you see, Rick?"

The door closed behind us. Before us was a warren of cubicles and corridors. Rick said, "I saw that it was a dream, right from the start. While my friends out there were spending money on houses, cars, and skiing trips up to British Columbia, I stayed in a quiet little apartment and rode my bicycle to work and put everything else into mutual funds and T-bills. When the great collapse happened, I decided it was time to come back home to New England, and here I am. And here's Kara's office."

He had led me through a maze of corridors, and I was outside of a cubicle, about twelve feet square. There were metal bookshelves built into the walls, overflowing with books and technical manuals. A whiteboard filled with blue marker writing—most of which were in acronyms and symbols —was on another wall. Her desk was fairly clear of clutter, and there was a computer terminal at one side. Alongside the phone was a headset. There was a calendar of Shaker art over the computer terminal, and there were a couple of framed photographs on top of the terminal. A nameplate outside the cubicle said KARA MILES.

"For someone you said is a great worker, this isn't much of an office," I said.

"Unless you're a director here, this is all the office you get," Rick said. "This is the newer, leaner Digital. Not much time for fancy offices or executive parking spaces."

I walked into the cubicle, looked at the computer screen, "You said she's good?"

"One of the best. Once she was hooked up to the phone and the terminal, she'd be kicking along so well that she'd often skip lunch. There's a rush out there for the really good ones, about cutting through bureaucracy and the engineering crap, getting the answers you need. It's a big puzzle game, every day, and Kara is one to solve puzzles."

I looked at the photographs on top of the terminal. There were three. One of Diane out on her boat, and another of Diane and Kara mountain climbing. The third photo was black-and-white and older. "Anything you want to tell me, now that the friendly security presence isn't here?"

"Like what?"

"Like anything you might not have felt comfortable with." I picked up the black-and-white photo. It looked like a family shot, taken in the 1970s. Mom and Dad, plus a daughter and son. They were on a picnic table in a wooded area somewhere. Only Kara seemed to be smiling. The looks on the other faces were hesitant, as if they were concerned about the photographer's intentions.

Rick crossed his arms. "Care to be more specific?"

I put the photo down and turned to him. "Kara's sexual preference. Did it matter to anybody here? Anybody around here think it was his God-given duty to convert lesbians by any means necessary?"

He frowned and his features darkened. "That's a hell of a shot."

"No, that's a hell of a question. You got an answer?"

He motioned with his head. "This may be a leaner place, but it still has a heart, as weak as it is."

"That so?"

He looked directly at me. "That's so, Mr. Cole. I know from experience."

"How's that?"

The same steady gaze. "Let's just say that Kara and I have similar lifestyles, and that it's no big secret, and it's never been a factor here. You got a problem with that?"

"Not at all." I returned the photo and said, "Look, I know my questions aren't always so polite, but I'm trying to do something here. I'm trying to find out who hurt Kara. Sometimes that means being a bit hurtful to people I just meet. That's the process, and I apologize for interrupting your day."

He seemed to relax and said, "No problem. Anything else?" I looked around the cubicle, thought about how long it might be before a young and confident woman was back at work here, feeling that her life was at last back in order, at last made sense, at last was no longer hurtful.

"One more. What do you think?"

"Hmmm?"

"Anything I haven't asked that I should have? Any loose ends? Anything that went through your mind the moment you found out that Kara had been raped?"

He leaned back against the cubicle's doorjamb. "Not a damn thing, and I'm very sorry for that. I really wish I could help. I really do."

I gave the cubicle one more glance. Something bothered me, like the faint breath of someone at the back of my neck, someone standing too close. What was it? I wanted to spend another hour in this little office, toss the papers, go through the drawers, and talk to some other coworkers, but I knew I was right at the edge of overstaying whatever welcome I had here.

"Thanks," I finally said. "Mind walking me back out?"

"Not a problem."

Rick led me back through the cubicles and hallways, past workers scurrying about, and through the locked door. In another minute I had given back my visitor's badge and Rick walked me out to the door, where the late afternoon sun was already setting beyond the fields and woodscapes of Newburyport. He came out in the parking lot, coatless, and shook my hand and said, "I have one question for you, if you don't mind."

"Go right ahead."

A confident smile. "Mind me asking what side of the tracks you like to play on?"

I smiled back. "The one recommended by nine out of ten registered Republicans."

A short laugh and he headed back to his work. "Such a pity."

WHEN I GOT BACK HOME Felix Tinios was waiting for me in his red Mercedes convertible, dirty gray exhaust smoke tendriling up into the cold air. I pulled into the nicely plowed parking lot of the Lafayette House and Felix stepped out and came over. I rolled down the window and he said, "Thought I'd come over for a visit. You got time?"

"Sure do. Learn anything at the landlord's house?"

His face was dark, and I think it was from the cold. "Sure. Learned a lot. I'll tell you the whole story when I follow you down."

"Hop in," I said. "I'll give you a ride."

"Nope. Prefer to walk. See you in a sec."

After I was done in the garage I walked out and Felix was trudging along the rutted snow path that my four-wheel drive has made for me on my poor dirt driveway. Felix followed me into the house, stamping his feet clear of the snow and shrugging off his long black leather coat. He was carrying a thick envelope in his hands.

"Feel like a beer, if you don't mind," he said, and after grabbing two Molsons from the fridge, I joined him out in the living room. He stood by the couch, looking out through the sliding doors at my snow-covered deck and the ocean view.

Felix took the beer I offered and swallowed almost half of it in one move. "Ah, I needed that," he said.

Something was not right. "How was it?"

He turned and said, "You ever been up to the mall in Lewington lately?"

"Um, a couple of weeks ago," I said. "At the bookstore there."

"You see anything there, anything new that struck you as fantastic?"

Lewington is north of Tyler, almost an hour from Newburyport. I had no idea what was going on.

"No, I can't say that I did."

"Well, I did. There's a kiosk in the center of the mall where you can do your own photo developing. Take a roll of film, plug it into the machine, and come back an hour later, your prints are waiting for you. Everything in a nice little package, untouched by human hands, unseen by human eyes. Even takes three kinds of credit cards."

I took a sip from my own bottle. "This going anywhere, Felix?"

A hint of a smile. "Oh, it's going places you probably can't imagine. You know what's wonderful about that kiosk, besides its simplicity? You can develop embarrassing photos and have as many prints made as you like, and no one will ever know. Candid shots of your wife in the shower. More candid shots of you and your wife in bed. Or pictures like these, which might be of interest to Massachusetts law enforcement officials."

He handed over his package and I put the beer bottle down on an end table, knowing what I was about to see, and yet still unprepared for what was hidden behind those flaps of paper and plastic. The beer inside me seemed to roll around a bit as I looked at the garish colors and the slickness of the paper. It seemed fake, unreal, as if Felix and I had been taken in by a very clever hoax.

"That was pretty wild of you, chancing to take these photos," I said, conscious that my hands were shaking.

Another defiant gulp of beer. "Well, I was pissed, I guess. Getting in there and seeing what was waiting for me. I wanted to take something back, show you what I faced, tell you that things have changed, and have changed to the very weird."

I looked back at the photo. There were three others, all similar. It showed Kara Miles's landlord, Jason Henry, sitting on his couch. His eyes were closed, head resting back on the couch. He was wearing a cardigan sweater similar to the one I had seen during my visit, and his weatherworn hands were empty. He was wearing a shirt underneath the sweater, but it was impossible to tell what color it was, or had been.

The entire front of his shirt was a reddish brown, where the gush of blood had soaked in.

And his throat was raw and bloodied and not nice to look at, where someone had drawn a knife across it.

14

Later that night, after seeing Felix's photographs, I got us dinner from the Lafayette House, stored nice and warm in Styrofoam containers. By the time dinner was finished and I had a fire in the fireplace, we were starting to calm down from seeing those photos. Jason Henry, who had been around the world and was proud of his collection of souvenirs, dead on his couch, throat slit. I'm sure it wasn't an ending to his life that he would have predicted. Drowned by a sinking ship or swept overseas in a gale, but not taken away by some bit of evil that had slumped into his home.

In the firelight Felix's dark skin looked shadowy. "When I got there, the only car in the lot was his own. I got to the house and saw that his door was open. I knocked and went in, and there he was on the couch, just like the pictures."

"Strong thinking on your part, to take those photos," I said.

"Well, the poor bastard was obviously dead, and there wasn't anything I was going to do about it. The camera was in my hand and I took a couple of pictures, and then I got the hell out. Walked quick and calm to my car, got in, and drove out."

"Anyone see you?"

"If they did, they were in their homes, looking out their windows. The sidewalk was empty and I got on High Street, and in less than ten minutes I was back in New Hampshire, thank you very much."

"Did you think about making a call to the Newburyport cops?"

He glanced over, a look of disbelief about his face. "Do you think I'm stupid?"

"No, but someone killed Jason Henry. The cops should know about it."

"They will, but in due time. Look. The poor guy's dead. I had nothing to do with it. But I was at the crime scene and might be considered a suspect by our new friend, Inspector Dunbar. So the longer it takes for the cops to get there and start their investigation, the less likely I'll be brought in. If the cops had started this afternoon, one of the neighbors might remember a red Mercedes with New Hampshire plates. A day later, they might remember only that it was a red car. That makes my life easier."

Felix was right, of course, but that didn't make me feel any better. There was something obscene about letting the body of Jason Henry grow colder with each passing minute, alone in his apartment, but Felix was right. He had to be protected.

A spark popped out from the burning logs, and Felix sipped from his wineglass and said, "I'm still in your hire, so here's the question. What's next?"

I sat back against the couch. I should have been enjoying the warm feeling of the fire on my skin and the glow from the wine, but it was impossible. The rape of Kara Miles was one thing. The murder of her landlord was in another universe.

But there had to be a connection. Had to be.

"What's next is that we tell Diane, and keep things quiet," I said. "She's got to know that someone has just knifed Kara's landlord. I find it hard to believe that the landlord of an apartment where a rape has occurred got his throat slit because of something else. Hell of a coincidence."

"Agreed," Felix said. "So what's the connection? Anything come to mind?"

"Connections," I repeated. "Could be a number of things. Maybe Jason remembered something more about that night, and the rapist finds out and eliminates a witness. Maybe he was in on it."

"How so?"

Something seemed to gently stroke my forehead. "Kara's place wasn't broken into, that's for sure. So either the door was unlocked—unlikely, from what we know—or somebody had the key, like a landlord, who always keeps spare keys about."

"Arranging the rape of your tenant isn't high on the list of ways to keep your tenants happy."

"That's true, in a logical world. Since when is rape logical?"

"Never said it was," Felix said. "So there's a connection. You want to look into the background of this landlord, see where that leads us?"

Another ember popped and shot out. "No, not really. Too dangerous, to have us poking around and asking questions about Jason Henry the same time the Newburyport cops are looking into his death. You and I have managed to mightily tick off those cops. I don't think we should take another sharp stick and poke them some more."

"Maybe not, but there's one thing I intend to do, and that's to get my story straight," Felix said, draining the last of his wine.

"And what story is that?"

"The story of where I was this morning, which wasn't Newburyport. Give me an hour and I'll be set, and unless the cops have got a videotape of me walking into that apartment building, then I'll be fine."

I got up and joined him as we went into the kitchen, the air feeling cooler away from the fireplace's heat. "Just an hour? How did you do that?"

He gave me a look that might have been a smile, and I remembered again never to underestimate Felix or his background.

"Let's just say there are people in this state who owe me. I call them up, and in an hour they're ready to go to a grand jury, if necessary, to swear that I was over at their house, having brunch and playing Monopoly."

He started washing his wineglass and I passed mine over and said, "You still in for the ride?"

"Right to the end," he said, wiping one glass dry. "Now my professional curiosity is beginning to sniff up and take notice, and I want to know what went on and what happened in that apartment building. I've got a personal stake in it."

"Does this mean you're forgoing any compensation?"

"Said I was interested, not stupid." He finished drying off the second glass and said, "Well, without looking into the background of our dead landlord, and with you having struck out at her place of work, where do you want to go now?"

I remembered a faded picture, sitting on top of a computer terminal. "One more place," I said. "One more very important place."

THE NEXT DAY it was late afternoon by the time we got started, and we returned south, a bit concerned at traveling through Newburyport. Jason Henry's death had been reported on the local radio stations this morning, and I'm sure Diane Woods had something to do with that. I had called her the night before, right after Felix had left, and she had immediately asked me if Felix had reported it.

"No."

"Why the hell not?" she asked.

"Because he doesn't want to spend the next few weeks of his life worrying if he's going to be charged with murder, that's why," I said.

"Jesus," she had said, her voice wavering. "I'm a cop, Lewis, You're asking me to hinder an investigation into a capital crime,"

"No. I'm asking for some time, that's all."

"Then why in hell did you call me in the first place?"

"For you and Kara. You should know that Jason Henry was killed. Listen, maybe the two of you ought to go on a skiing trip into the Whites for a few days, get away—"

"Oh, damn, I wish I could, but not with these goddamn fires..." I thought I heard her choking back some tears.

"Diane?" I asked.

"Look," she said, voice more brisk. "I'll be okay. Thanks for giving us the heads-up. Jesus. Now, instead of a rapist, we have to worry about a murderer."

"Seems to me the two are pretty closely related."

"You are so right. Look. I have to go. I...I have to go tell Kara, and I know this is going to upset her. She really liked the man. But, Lewis?"

"Yes?"

"I can't keep this secret forever."

"I understand."

So it was on the next day that the radio stations had news about Jason Henry's murder, and with the Newburyport cops not telling the reporters how his body was discovered, it was a good guess that either Diane or Kara had made the call. Anonymously, I'm sure, with Diane struggling against her oath of duty, and with Kara struggling against her oath of friendship.

But I still wondered if that friendship was just one-way. I was certain the landlord had been up to something. No man with hearing that bad could have listened into what he claimed had happened, unless he had been standing on that chair, listening in, as he had listened in before.

And whatever else he might have heard would never be learned.

We were on I-95, heading south to Boston, and about a third of the way there we took a right off to Topsfield, one of the suburban communities that houses the moneyed class and professionals who don't mind making money in Boston, but who aren't thrilled with the idea of living there. Once off the highway, you were immersed in a rural world of the wealthy, homes off of the narrow roads with twisting driveways that went back into the woods or up into the fields. House numbers were hard to come by, and some of the homes were content with names: Idlewood. Repose. Blake Arms.

But no factories, strip malls, or mobile home parks. Big money equals heavy zoning, and while God may be on the side with the heaviest artillery, He's also often on the side with the best lawyers.

"Quiet places," Felix observed, as I maneuvered along the narrow lane. High banks of snow and ice lined each side of the road where the plows had tossed them up.

"Someplace you'd like to retire to?"

"Like hell," he said, looking out at the passing scenery. "If the quiet didn't kill me, the cold would. Nope, when the time comes when I'm too slow to be making a living, I'm moving south, and I'll be very happy to only find ice in my drinks."

"No sense of adventure."

"Maybe not, but a lot of common sense, thank you."

About ten minutes away from I-95 the road curved to the east, and there was a stone gate with a plaque that said Thornwood. The metal gate was open, and I turned into the well-plowed driveway.

"They know we're coming?" Felix asked.

"No, they don't. I figure surprise might work best."

"Maybe, and it might also piss them off as well."

"Guess we're going to find out." The driveway went on for about a quarter mile, curved up and around. There was a circular driveway and a three-car garage, and two cars were parked out front: his and hers silver Audis. How domestic. The house looked like fake Tudor, with exposed stonework and beams and narrow windows. The snow-covered shrubbery was well-groomed, and I caught a glimpse of a large and open yard to the rear as we halted.

I looked over at Felix and said, "For this one, why don't you stay behind?"

"Why's that?"

I gathered up my reporter's notebook. "Two people might be too intimidating, and while that might work on the next go around, I want to try to be quiet here."

"Hmph," Felix said. "Well, leave the car keys so I can at least listen to the radio."

"Sure," and when that was done, I went outside.

A short walk up the brick walkway I came to a polished black door, and set under the brass knocker was a little brass plaque that said MILES. I rang the doorbell, and heard a loud gong echo from inside.

I stamped my feet. It was damn cold.

The door opened and a slim, older man with a glowing tan answered. He wore black slacks and a lime-green sweater, and his thin white hair was perfectly combed. In one hand he had a leatherbound book, and in the other a pair of reading glasses.

"Mr. Miles?" I asked.

"Yes?"

"My name is Lewis Cole," I said. I passed over my business card. "I'm a writer for a magazine called *Shoreline*, and I'd just like to take a minute or two of your time to talk about your daughter, Kara."

"Well..." he said, peering at my card, and before he could say anything else I walked in, saying, "Thank you, this won't take long."

FROM THE ENTRANCEWAY we went to the right, to a sitting room, where a fire was crackling along in the fireplace. There were bookshelves with glass doors, a marble mantelpiece over the fireplace, and paintings and wood paneling and oriental rugs and soft classical music playing from hidden speakers.

A woman came into the room, carrying a half-filled cocktail glass in her hand. She was about the same age as the man—sixties—and wore tartan slacks (Black Watch tartan, it looked like) and a dark blue sweater with a single strand of pearls. Her hair was dark brown and coiffed in something that looked like Jackie Kennedy Onassis was trying in the late sixties, and she got right to the point: "Henry, who is this?"

"A Mr. Cole, Louise," he said, his voice wavering. He held up my card, like he was trying to ward off something. "He's a magazine writer and wants to talk about Kara."

She looked right at me, eyes flashing. "What makes you think we have anything to say? And what do you mean by barging in here without even the courtesy of calling first?"

I had my coat off, hanging on my arm. When conducting an interview in hostile territory, you play some little tricks to stay in and do your business. One is to assume that you'll be invited in and act as if you were, walking by before an objection is raised. Another is to take off your coat. With your coat on, it's easier for someone to toss you out. Useful tricks, ones they never teach you in journalism class.

"I apologize, Mrs. Miles," I said. "I should have called earlier, but I was in the area and hoped that I'd be able to impose for just a few moments. I'm also hoping that I can just ask a few quick questions, and then I'll leave."

"Why are you even here?" she demanded. "What are you up to?"

"I'm doing an article about violent crime in tourist communities," I said, the lie once again coming easily to me. "Along with the general nature of the story, I'm also doing what we call a sideline piece, an article on what happened to Kara, as an example of the types of crime that take place—"

Her skin seemed to pale, as if the valves inside her blood vessels had suddenly clicked shut. She slapped the cocktail glass down on a nearby table and said, her chin quavering, "Do you mean to say that our name is going to be in your magazine, in a despicable story about what happened to Kara? Henry, did you hear that? Our name, in his magazine, for everyone to read about our daughter."

"Now, look here," Henry Miles began, his tone getting livelier, and I interrupted, saying, "Excuse me, no, the story was going to use a fictional name. No one would know. It would just be—"

"But of course they'll know!" Louise Miles protested, her tone furious. "How many crimes like that happen in Newburyport each winter, do you think? My God, Henry, think of the scandal if the neighbors found out. Especially if that rag mentions..."

She paused and Henry took a step forward and said, "I think you should leave. We have nothing to say to you. Nothing."

"Yes," his wife said, "and Henry, get Ross Tremblay on the phone. Within the hour, Mr. Cole, our lawyers will be contacting you, and if anything—anything at all—appears in your magazine, you can bet you'll be on the receiving end of a hefty lawsuit."

I started to slowly put on my coat, trying to salvage whatever I could. "It wasn't going to be a part of the story, but you sound more upset about Kara's private life than about what happened to her."

Henry Miles's lips tightened and his wife repeated, "Within the hour, Mr. Cole, within the hour."

"Fair enough," I said, coat fully on. "But when he does call, it'll be a short conversation. I'll just mention a certain amendment that begins with the words, 'Congress shall make no law', and then I'll hang up. And just so there are no more surprises, Mrs. Miles, I also intend to talk to Kara's brother."

"Good luck finding him," she snapped. "I haven't seen him in years, and I have no idea where he is. Now. Head for that door or our first call will be to the police."

The door sounded pleasant enough, shutting behind me, and I walked out, pausing to look back at the house. Everything seemed wrong, out of kilter. I was trying to reconcile the Kara Miles I knew—the laughing woman with odd taste in jewelry, the outdoor adventurer who rock-climbed, and the woman who was also deeply in love with my best friend—with what I had just seen, and it didn't make sense. There are enough stereotypes about the type of woman Kara is to fill a CD-ROM disk, and I hadn't been too sure what to expect about the kind of family she came from. But it was nothing like the expensive North Shore home and twin Audis and wealthy parents I encountered, who were more concerned about scandal than their daughter.

I got to the Rover and opened the door. Felix looked over at me, arms crossed. "Must've had a lot of fun in there, time passing by as quickly as it did."

"Not really."

"What did you learn?"

I turned the key and started up the engine. "Not a hell of a lot." We went down the driveway and at the stone gate I stopped and looked over.

"All this money, all this privilege, all these expensive homes and toys, and up there are two old and angry people in a lot of empty rooms. Is this what they mean by the good life?"

"I guess upward mobility ain't what it used to be."

"I guess so." And then we left, heading back north.

As I DROVE BACK into Newburyport, I made it a point to stay on the back roads. "One thing for sure, the Mileses don't have much of an imagination or much curiosity," I said.

"Why's that?" Felix asked.

"Mrs. Miles said that she had no idea where her son lived. But I do."

"Oh?"

"Yeah. Took me all of five minutes this morning, looking in the phone book."

He shrugged. "Some people like to stay lost. Other people prefer not to go looking. Sounds like a fun family."

"Not sure if 'fun' is the word I'd use."

. . .

IT WAS GETTING near four o'clock in the afternoon and already I had the headlights on. The depths of winter in New England have always tugged at the dark parts of my soul. In the summer it can be light until nine o'clock at night, but when the weather turns cold, it can be as dark as midnight before the five o'clock news. Nothing I can do except cope, but sometimes the cold weather saps my coping skills.

We were in the western and rural part of the city, on Deering Road, and only by counting mailboxes and looking at house numbers with the aid of a flashlight were we able to find Doug Miles's home. It was a sagging structure with peeling paint, and it looked like a two-car garage that had earlier been converted into a residence. Snow and ice and frozen dog turds dotted the lawn, and the lights were off. A dog was barking at the house nearby, which was up on a hill, visible through the bare branches of some maple trees. The driveway was hard going. It was dirt and frozen solid with ice and snow.

Felix wasn't impressed.

"Are you sure this is it?" he asked.

"Sure as I can be," I said. "Diane told me that Kara's brother lived in Newburyport, and this is the only Doug Miles in the book."

"Can't believe it," Felix said, shaking his head. "This guy's parents look like they start their fireplace by burning worn-out dollar bills, and he lives in a shack."

"Maybe he's a free spirit who doesn't want to get entangled in this oppressive, capitalist society of ours."

"You believe that?"

"No, but it was a better answer than just grunting." Outside, the wind had picked up some and I held my coat close. I could make out the steady hum of traffic on I-95, out beyond the woods. Felix came over to me and said, "What do you want to do here?"

"Honestly?" I asked.

"Yeah."

"Truth is, I want to fill in all the blanks and go back to Diane and say we've done our best. Cops, neighbors, landlord, co-workers, her family, I want to tell her that we talked to everybody out there."

"Then what?"

"Then maybe she's satisfied that we've done as much as we can. Then maybe you get paid and we all get to stay out of the cold for a while. Come on, let's see if he's home."

There were no lights on inside. There was a shaded window and door to the left, and a closed garage door to the right. Sometime in the past, a dormer had been built on the left side of the residence, and what was probably a bedroom window was also dark. I knocked and there was no answer. Felix had a flashlight and played it over the house.

"Doorbell?" he asked.

"Sure," I said, pointing to a painted-over doorbell. "But I don't think it's going to ring much."

A couple more unanswered knocks and Felix went around to the front window, shining the light inside. "Whatever Doug does for work and however he earns his money, I can tell you that he doesn't spend it on housekeeping."

"That bad?" I asked.

"Pretty foul. Clothes and magazines and shopping bags jumbled up in a mess. Look, I'm hungry and it's getting cold. Are we finished here?"

"That we are," I said, and as I turned, I stopped stock-still.

Felix kept on looking into the house. "So we can leave."

"Nope," I said.

"Why the hell not?"

"Because he might not want us to."

"Who?" Felix said, turning around.

"Him," I said, "and don't ask me his name. We haven't quite been introduced yet."

Before us was a Doberman pinscher, sitting quite attentively, ears cocked forward. Felix lowered his flashlight, and the dog growled a greeting.

"Well," Felix said.

"My thoughts exactly."

The wind whipped up and I shivered, and the dog kept its steady gaze on the both of us.

"You wouldn't happen to have a doggy treat with you," I said.

"Nope. The treats I usually have aren't for dogs. You know any dog commands?"

"Like 'run away and leave us alone'? No, I don't. You got any other suggestions?"

"One of us could run at the dog, while the other goes to the Rover."

"Sure," I said. "Was that a suggestion, or an offer to volunteer?"

"Well, what do you think?"

"I've got the keys. So. Ready to run at the dog?"

Felix said, "You could always toss the keys to me, and you could run at the dog."

"I'm a bad thrower. I might miss and the keys would drop in the snow."

Another growl from the Doberman, and he came forward a few steps, then sat back down on the snow.

"I don't think he likes us talking," Felix said.

"I think you're right. Why don't we wait for a bit, see if his master shows up?"

"Then what?"

"Well, at least we'll be able to talk to someone who can talk back."

Felix clasped his arms around his chest. "That will be an improvement, but if I get any colder, then I will volunteer to take the dog on, understood?

"Understood."

"All right."

The Doberman growled again. "Oh, shut up," Felix said.

15

Thankfully, we didn't have to wait long. My toes were starting to tingle with the cold, and I was going to ask Felix if he was ready to make that run to the dog when I heard a woman's voice and saw the bobbing light of a flashlight approach. The Doberman's head canted to the side and the woman called out, "Krypton! Krypton, come here, boy!"

The dog ambled over to her, short stub of a tail wagging, and Felix said, "Jesus, at least I can move." The woman came over, her booted feet crunching in the snow. She was heavyset, wearing a thick down jacket that was patched at the elbows, and she had long brown hair that cascaded down the back of the jacket. Her blue jeans were tucked into the leather boots, and I blinked as she played the flashlight around my face and Felix's.

"You looking for Dougie?" she asked, voice rasping a bit.

"That we are," Felix said.

"You friends of his?"

"No, we're not," I said.

"Oh." She came closer. "You guys cops?" There was a hopeful tone in her voice.

"No," I said. "Should we be the cops?"

"Hah." She lowered the light and said, "I was just hoping, that's all. Dougie is a kind you always expect will be found in the back seat of a police cruiser, and I was kinda hoping this would be his night. Well, if you're not cops, who are you, then?"

I gave her my name and Felix's and passed over my business card. "We work for a magazine. We want to talk to him about a story we're doing. Are you his neighbor?"

"Sort of, though I don't like it," she said. "The name is McPurdy, and this is my land and my house here. Dougie is just a tenant, and I'm just waiting to tell him that it's time he be moving on. I don't like his kind."

Felix spoke up. "Is he in trouble, is that why?"

"Not that I know of," Meg said, patting the head of her dog.

"But I don't like his attitude, and I don't like the kind of fellas he's been hanging around. That's why I sent Krypton down here when I saw your lights. I thought it was Dougie coming home, or some of his friends. Work for a magazine, eh? What kind of story?"

I looked over at Felix and looked back at Meg. "It's kind or confidential, but we're working on a magazine article involving a member of his family. We just want to talk to him, try to get some background information. Do you know when he might be back?"

"Dunno. He's been keeping odd hours, leaving in the middle of the day, coming back real late at night or early in the morning."

"Does he have a job?" Felix asked.

"So he says, and he tells me he works down at the docks in Boston, but I don't know of any job that he can keep such crazy hours. But he pays his rent every month—mostly on time and with a money order—so he does have some money coming in. I just don't see how he gets it, that's all."

I put my hands back in my coat jacket. "Is there a chance he'll be back tonight?"

"He could be," Meg said. "If he does come in, best thing for you to do is to come back real late tonight or real early tomorrow morning. That is, if it's important enough to bother him. Or you could just keep on trying to phone him, though I've seen times when I've called him and I know he's there, and he's just ignored the calls."

Felix nodded at me, and I said, "I appreciate your time, and I'm sorry we made you come out here in the cold."

She waved a hand. "Not a problem, but do me one thing, will you?"

"Sure," Felix said.

"You chat with Dougie, you tell him I need to talk to him. I want him out of here."

"It's a deal," Felix said.

As she turned to walk back up to her house, I said, "Meg? Where did you get the name Krypton?"

She whispered something to the dog and the animal turned and stared at Felix and me, muscles trembling, lips pulled back, growling.

"That's why," she said. "I figure any superman type me or the dog runs into, Krypton will take care of him, real quick."

"Nice name," Felix said, and I couldn't disagree.

BACK IN MY four-wheeler I had the heater on full and we stayed in the driveway for a few minutes, waiting for Doug Miles to show up, just talking. Funny thing about sitting like that—the minutes seem to drag on as you wait for the heater to kick in, ready for the interior to fill up with warm air, certain that you'll never be comfortable again. And in the space of a few minutes, you're nice and toasty and you forget you were ever cold, and you move on to other subjects.

Like Doug Miles.

"Well," I said. "What do you think?"

"Two things," Felix said. "First, I don't know if my feet will ever get warm again. Second, I don't know. Doug seems like an interesting character, and I'll leave it at that. I'm not going to get riled about anything until I talk to him. But if you'd like, I can poke around, see what I can find out. He's sure making his landlord nervous."

"You want to wait for a while longer, see if he shows up?"

"Yeah, but only for a bit," Felix said. "I need to get some food before I faint."

Long minutes drifted on by and I switched on the radio and listened to some classical music, and then I said, "To hell with it. Maybe he's out partying or something, but I need to find a bathroom, and fast."

"You could always go behind the house," Felix offered.

"Sure," I said, backing up on the bumpy driveway. "Meeting Krypton with my pants around my knees sounds like a wonderful idea."

On the drive back we didn't say much of anything, just listening to the music and feeling our body parts thaw out. It was starting to snow and the news breaks within the music warned of a major storm heading up the coast. As we made our way up to Route I-A, looking at all the empty houses and cottages, and with me wondering which motel might go up in flames over the next few weeks, Felix said something that poked me, just a bit.

"What was that?" I asked, as we headed up past Weymouth's Point.

"Hunh?" Felix turned to me. "I said something like I bet you Diane will want to hear from us soon, one way or another, so she can get back to her life."

"I thought so," I said.

"Is there a problem?" he asked, just as we went by the intersection of High Street, where a few nights ago, a motel had burned to the ground. And Diane Woods had not been there, not for a while.

"Not yet," I said, slowing down behind a grumbling town plow, its amber lights flashing, working to widen the roadway. "Not yet."

WHEN I GOT to Felix's house at North Tyler, I took him up on his offer to use his bath facilities, and I admired a new piece of artwork framed and hanging right next to the porcelain goddess: a sheet of U.S. currency, twenty-dollar bills, uncut and untrimmed. I wondered if it was his mad money.

Afterward he was in the kitchen, coat off and wearing jeans and a black sweater, working on the stove, whipping something up, and he looked at me and said, "Okay, give."

"What's that?"

He undid a wine bottle, poured me a glass of white wine, and passed it across the counter. "I said, what gives? About halfway through the trip you shut right up and didn't say another word. Something's on your mind."

I sat on a stool and held the glass in both hands. Unlike my usually unused kitchen, Felix's place always contains an earthy scent of old spices and dishes, and the polished wooden cabinets contain dishes and cooking utensils that look like they belong on a home cooking show. He's an accomplished chef and sometimes that's enough to temporarily forget what he does for a living.

I said, "It's something you said, about Diane and getting back to work."

Felix was by the stove, switching on a burner. "All right. I said something about her getting back to work. Was that it?"

"Yep." I traced a finger around the rim of the wineglass. "I'm just hoping that you and I haven't been wasting our time looking in the wrong direction."

He looked a bit put back. "What do you mean? We've done everything right to the T. Started with the victim, talked to the landlord, neighbors, place where she works, and now we're wrapping it up with family members. How else could we have done it?"

The wine looked nice and cold. I looked up. "But we never talked to Diane."

He stood still by the stove, stirring spoon in his hand, looking steady at my face.

"I'll be damned," Felix said. "You're right."

LATER WE WERE at the dinner table, eating pasta with a light tomato sauce and a type of garlic bread made with goat's cheese that seemed to melt and ooze around in one's mouth. Felix said, "Talk to me some more. What do you think is up?"

"Nothing I can prove, but something we should look at," I said. "It's also going to be something that might be dangerous to do."

"Dangerous for you, or dangerous for the both of us?"

"Just for me," I said, twirling some of the pasta on a fork.

"Diane is a very private woman, and she won't be thrilled if questions start being asked about her."

"So tell me again, why would we be asking questions?"

I ate and swallowed and said, "Without getting into any of the details, let's just say Diane and Kara share a special friendship. Let's also say that what has happened to Kara has upset Diane tremendously, has almost ruined her life, and is also in the process of ruining her job as the sole police detective for Tyler."

"All right, those are all givens," Felix said. "What's next?"

"What's been going on around the same time Kara was raped and assaulted?"

He held his fork quite still. "The arsons."

"Right. Someone is merrily burning down Tyler Beach, and at the same time, the detective handling the case has her private life shattered. Her work has suffered, she can't concentrate, and some days she doesn't care who's burning down what."

"So an arsonist is also a rapist?" Felix asked. "That's a hell of a stretch."

"Right," I said. "But something...I don't know. Something just seems odd there. I think it's worth a look. Tell you what, I'll take care of that, and in a day or two we chat with Doug Miles, and then it's a wrap, unless we come up with something new. Agreed?"

"Oh, I agree, but be careful. I'm going to leave that side of the house entirely up to you. Based on my background, I don't think the local police detective would be very happy with me looking into her personal life."

"Nice way of getting yourself out of that one," I said.

Felix nodded. "Thanks."

WHEN I GOT up the next morning something was rattling the glass in my bedroom windows, and I sat up and saw only white. After putting on a bathrobe I stepped across the cold floor and observed that the local weather people were having a hell of a year. There was nothing to see except for flying flakes of snow. I showered and shaved and, after getting dressed, went downstairs. The snow was so thick and furious I could barely make out my private cove and the heaving gray waters of the Atlantic. At least six or eight inches were already piled up on my rear deck, and I knew I would have to go out soon to shovel that mess away. I shivered, looking at that marsh and the unforgiving water, and imagined what it must have been like, years ago, coming across this ocean in a ship of wood and sails of canvas. No weather-tight cabins with central heating or hot water or TV. Just the unforgiving wind and cold.

I was deciding if it was worth going outside when the phone rang.

"Lewis? It's Paula. Surviving another lovely day of New Hampshire's finest weather?"

"I'm trying," I said. "Where are you? Still at home?"

"Are you kidding?" she asked. "This sucker is becoming a blizzard, and a blizzard is news, and so I'm at work. Listen, I've got some other news for you, and it isn't good."

"Go ahead."

She sighed. "I've spent hours looking into everything about those motels, and I didn't find a single connection. Not a one. I started by looking at each set of minutes, to find out what motels were up for discussion. The first step was easy, because each owner was represented by a lawyer, and that's mentioned right up front. But nobody was sharing the same law firm. Then I went to the town hall and got copies of their construction applications, and still not a thing. They all used different bankers, different architects, different contractors. The only connection I could find is the basic thing, that they were up for a planning board review for some type of work, either renovation or conversion to condos. But they didn't share banks, lawyers, architects, or even landscapers. Zero."

"Any other leads out there that you see?"

Another sigh. "Not a one. Look, do you realize how many hours I spent chasing down this information? And do you think Rollie is going to be happy if he ever finds out the time I wasted doing research for a story that's never going to come together?"

A stronger gust of wind rattled the sliding glass doors to the rear deck. "You didn't waste time, Paula. You were tracking down leads and you were able to eliminate some possible motives, some possible areas of inquiry. I don't call that wasted."

"How nice of you to say that," she said, with exaggerated politeness. "Glad I made your job easier with all my hours of work."

I walked over to the sliding glass doors, trailing the phone in my hand. "Last I remembered, you and I were having dinner at your place, just before the Crescent House burned down, and you said you were going to break this story. I don't remember you saying that you were going to give it to the local columnist for *Shoreline*."

A bit of a pause. "You're right. Sorry. I've got stories backed up and I'm stuck at a drafty newspaper office in the middle of a blizzard, and I really wanted that arson story wrapped up. Something about a corrupt contractor burning down buildings or the like. Would put a nice shine to this lousy winter, and it fell through. Not your fault."

"Not a problem."

"Well, maybe the son of a bitch will come in here tomorrow and confess to me, but I'm not going to hold my breath."

"You never know."

"Yeah, right," she said. "Well, time to get going. I've got to go outside and walk downtown and do the traditional local-businesses-adjust-to-blizzard-conditions story."

"Sounds like fun."

"After you've done four or five, they can usually write themselves. Keep in touch, all right?"

"Sure," I said, and I hung up the phone and watched the snow fly for a bit.

ABOUT TEN MINUTES LATER, I got bundled up and went outside, carrying a pair of snowshoes I had purchased last month as a Christmas present for myself. I squatted down on my stone steps and buckled them on, and then strode across the yard and up the snow-covered dirt path that pretended to be a driveway.

Even though I was wearing a Navy wool cap, thick gloves, insulated pants, and a down parka that went down to my thigh, the blustery wind instantly cut through me, chilling my skin and making me shiver after only a few yards. The area around my house was a wild and horrible beauty of snowdrifts and icicles. I stood for moment, drinking it all in. My house and the nearby garage were blanketed with wet snow, and pounding surf roared up and over the ice-covered rocks, making a booming sound that seemed loud. The ocean was a churning dark gray mass of whitecaps and waves, the waves driving into the shoreline with the fury of a train being tossed off the tracks, and I wondered for a moment if my house would be there when I got back.

Across the parking lot I went over onto Atlantic Avenue, and from here I had the first real sign of the blizzard's magnitude. Usually the town plows manage to keep the roadways clear, and it's a big storm when you can just make out bare pavement under the tracks where the cars and trucks drive by. Here, the roadway was solid white with compressed snow and blowing drifts. This was a big one. I peered down the road. Great sheets of snow blew across, was slipping into drifts, scattering across the road. I could barely make out the condos and stores just down the way. There were a few lights on the road from souls either brave enough or stupid enough to drive in such weather.

I made my way across the street and to the Victorian splendor of the Lafayette House, and at the doorway I took off my snowshoes and went in. The interior of the lobby was potted plants and fine paintings and well-dressed women and men, staring out at the snow, wondering where their midwinter vacation had gone. A few looked my way, their expressions saying it all, as if I were an Arctic explorer, lost on some doomed mission. I just gave them all a polite smile and went to the gift shop and left a minute later, with the day's *Globe* and *New York Times*. I lucked out, for the newspaper trucks must have made their deliveries before the full brunt of the storm had struck. They felt nice, tucked into my coat as I went back outside, put on my snowshoes, and tramped back home.

Breakfast for me is usually something light, but the falling snow seemed to trigger a food switch in my brain, and so this morning I had a couple of scrambled eggs, toast, bacon, and coffee. I read the papers, savoring the feel of newsprint, enjoying reading what was going on in the world as I ate. An odd habit, one I've always had, is the need to read the morning papers before I start my day. Of the few women who have entered my life, only one really shared my need, back in my previous life in the DoD. Sunday morning breakfasts would mean buying two copies of the *Post* and the *Times* so we wouldn't fight over the sections, but would leave enough energy for other, more pleasant morning exertions.

I washed the dishes, smiling with melancholy at the memory of my dear Cissy, dead all these years.

· · ·

AFTER READING through the morning papers, I got bundled up again and went out to the rear deck, where I shoveled away the accumulation of snow. The tide was coming up and soon I was being drenched with frozen spray, and that was another clear sign that this was not the typical winter storm. It was quite rare that spray from the waves striking my private cove ever reached up to the house, and to have it drenching me was disturbing. I paused, breathing heavily, leaning against the shovel, looking at the white caps and dark ocean moving toward me and my home. Even the icicles from the roof were growing in lengths I had never seen before, and when I was done shoveling, I reached out with the shovel and broke them clear. They fell like spears, burrowing themselves into the snow banked up against the rear wall of the house.

A change of clothes later, I made some tomato soup and a roast beef sandwich, and watched the noon news out of Manchester and Boston from my living room couch. If this wasn't turning out to be the storm of the century, it was definitely becoming the storm of the decade, and was going to last another half-day. Airports were closed, most highways were clogged, and businesses and schools were also shuttered tight. As I ate and watched the television reporters doing their live remotes out in the roaring wind and snow, I thought of Paula Quinn and how nice it would be to have her here with me, instead of outside in the blizzard, feeling chilled and wet, and no doubt in the company of her photographer friend.

Another round of dishwashing later, I was up in the office, organizing some computer files, wondering what I would write for my next *Shoreline* column. I would be writing for the June issue and I found it was hard to get ideas for a summer piece when I was sitting in the middle of a blizzard. The rattling noise against the windows was louder, and it sounded like sleet or frozen rain was mixing with the snow. I had left the television set on downstairs, and I poked my head down occasionally to check the news.

A couple of hours dragged by in front of the computer screen, and later in the afternoon I decided to give Felix a call, to see how he was surviving the storm, etcetera, and when I picked up the receiver, there was no dial tone. No hum, no buzz, nothing.

Just then the lights in my office went out and my computer went black.

16

Well. Things were quite dark, and the quiet hum of the computer was now gone, and it seemed like the wind had picked up some, shaking the house and the windows with regular gusts. I got up and peeked out the window, which looked out to the west. At this time of the day, with the heavy clouds and no sun, I should have been able to see the glow from the lights of the Lafayette House.

Nothing. Just darkness and the flailing flakes of snow, and it would be getting even darker, and with no power that meant no furnace, and it would be getting colder. My house is old and has lots of history, but it doesn't have much in the way of insulation.

"Time to get down to basics," I said to no one in particular, and I got to work.

I went down the hallway and into my bedroom, and pulled out a flashlight from a nightstand. Even that little cone of light was comforting as I went downstairs, the shadows crazy upon the walls, hearing the wind roaring outside and the crash of waves. In the living room I knelt at the fireplace and in a few minutes had a nice fire going. Then I went into the kitchen and dug out some old plumber's candles, and within a few minutes the downstairs was lit up with the soft and pleasant light of the centuries.

I went down to the cellar and in a couple of trips I brought up a few more lengths of firewood, my propane camp stove, and a down sleeping bag. In the kitchen I got the stove up and running, making sure it would work later, and I checked the time on a battery-operated clock near the toaster. Not even five o'clock. It seemed much later.

I decided to wait to start dinner and I went back upstairs, flashlight in hand, to turn off my computer. As I switched off the equipment, I spotted an unfamiliar manila folder. I picked it up and turned to the papers inside. TYLER PLANNING BOARD MINUTES, it said, with a date from last summer, and it was the collection that Paula Quinn had given me, about a dozen sets. I brought the folder back downstairs and, with the aid of nearby candles, I sat on the couch and started to read, pulling a down comforter over my legs. Pretty dry stuff. Convoluted arguments over site plans, perc tests, rights of way, Zone 4-a, light industry. You never learned in grammar school that democracy could be so complicated or so dry.

I flipped through each set, seeing how the minutes were set up. Each cover sheet listed the members of the board, as well as the agenda for that night. There were an average of about a half dozen building proposals for each night, and the board met every other week. Each proposal was identified either by address or by business name: FOURTEEN KING'S HIGHWAY or CRESCENT HOUSE HOTEL. With each identification there was a listing of who was there, representing the project. So something like a proposal to build a new restaurant up on Weymouth's Point would be listed like so:

BOAR'S HEAD INN, 6 Weymouth Lane

IN ATTENDANCE: JEREMY GRAY, owner
    ATTORNEY STEPHEN TWOMBLEY
    GUS BALDACCI, Baldacci Construction

                         .   .   .

THE MINUTES WEREN'T VERBATIM, either. Just a brief identification of the speaker and the issue, and a thumbnail sketch of what was going on. Like this:

CHAIRMAN KNOWLES ASKED MR. GRAY if he thought parking might be a problem, since there are already so few spaces on Weymouth's Point. MR. GRAY said he intended to use a valet system of parking, and that he already had a leased parking agreement set up with the Point Hope Motel, which is across the street. CHAIRMAN KNOWLES said that if he were to vote for the proposal, he would want to ensure that some sort of permanent valet parking arrangement be agreed upon by all parties as a condition of his approval. CHAIRMAN KNOWLES reminded everyone that parking at Tyler Beach was a yearly problem, and that new projects shouldn't add to the mess. After a brief discussion, ATTORNEY TWOMBLEY said that his client would not object to such a condition.

Democracy in action. There were almost two hundred pages worth of material, and in flipping through it quickly, I saw how Paula had worked it. She went to the front of each minutes and highlighted the motel being discussed, as well as the attorney and the contracting firm. A few afternoons on the phone and it wouldn't have taken long to find what, if any, connection existed among all the destroyed motels.

And sure enough, it hadn't taken long at all. No connection. After apologizing in advance to town board members everywhere, I yawned a few times and put the packet aside, feeling the onset of hunger pains. I tossed aside the comforter, shivered in the air, and tossed another log on the fire. I went back upstairs and put on a heavier sweater, and in poking around my set of bureaus, I found my battery-operated shortwave radio receiver.

Back downstairs, I set up the radio on the counter as I lit up the stove. On good nights I can pick up Radio Moscow and Radio Beijing and a lot of countries in between, but on this not-so-good night, I wanted to see what was going on closer to home. I picked up a Dover station, and learned the storm of the decade was still packing a punch. The governors in New Hampshire and Massachusetts were declaring states of emergency. A couple of fishing boats from Gloucester and one from Tyler were missing.

A few dozen shoppers were stuck inside the Lewington Mall. Power was out along the north shore of Massachusetts and southern New Hampshire, and probably would be out for most people tomorrow due to the scope of repairs.

While listening to the chaos outside, I made a quick and dirty dinner. Working swiftly in and out of the dark and silent refrigerator, I managed to get the fixings for a weak salad, heavy on lettuce, light on everything else. The appetizer was tomato soup with saltine crackers crumbled over the top and a few chunks of cheddar cheese tossed in for flavoring, and the main course was corned beef hash, heated in an old cast-iron skillet. It was comforting to cook in the candlelight, listening to the confident hiss of the propane tank, knowing I had enough food to last even if the storm lasted a week. I ate standing up at the counter, looking out the windows at the dark ocean. The wind was still howling, buffeting the house and windows.

When I was finished, the demon of sloth almost made me crawl back onto the couch, but I didn't listen to the demon, and I heated up water on the camp stove and did a fair job of dishwashing. When I was done, I could see my breath in the kitchen, and I left the kitchen faucet open a bit, dribbling. I then went upstairs and did the same in the bathroom, and already the cold air was thick up on the second floor. The water dripped and dribbled out of the sink, and I also opened the faucet to the tub and shower. No frozen pipes tonight, thank you. I brushed my teeth and washed my face in the cold water.

Back downstairs I was drawn to the fire and stood there, letting the trapped flames warm me. I thought of my ancestors who were here in the first hundred years or so of settlement. A fire like this was the only thing that kept them alive during those long winters. In many of the homes, the entire family would share a single room, huddled under the covers, staying warm and praying to God they would live to see spring. Food was whatever could be stored for the winter, and the days were cold and short. Some life. It was a wonder any of them survived.

Another two pieces of wood on the fire, and I went around blowing out most of the candles. Quite lovely and romantic, but quite dangerous if one of the shaking gusts of wind made them tip over when I was sleeping. I went back to the couch, bringing the radio with me, and I unzipped the sleeping bag and quickly stripped down, shivering, and crawled in, radio earphones on my head. The power outages had spread. The fishermen were still missing. Plows were losing the battle to keep the roads and highways open. The shoppers trapped at the mall were spending the night at Sears, sleeping on beds and other furniture. The high tide due later at night would probably flood out most of the low-lying homes and businesses along Falconer, Tyler, North Tyler, Wallis, and Foss Island. (My home, thankfully, is not low-lying.) Off-duty police and fire personnel were being called in. Schools were being used as evacuation centers. The New Hampshire governor was activating the National Guard.

The wind continued to howl, and in my lap the radio and antenna trembled as the house shook. I thought of how Paula was doing. I hoped that she was done with her stories and was back home. And poor Diane. She was no doubt at work in foul-weather gear, helping evacuate people from the beachfront cottages and motels, setting up cots and such, not doing any detective work but serving her town. And what of her lover, Kara? Huddled in a dark home with a candle flickering, probably nervous and scared.

After listening to the radio for a while I switched it off, tiring of the reports of ongoing doom and gloom. It was time to read a little and then blow out the candles about me and go to sleep, and then I realized something: I was trapped. One of my many faults is that I have to read before I go to sleep. Something about reading the printed page—even if it's only a few paragraphs on a night when I'm exhausted—manages to shift my mind into another gear, and it allows me to doze off. But there were no books or magazines in easy reach. I was undressed in my sleeping bag on the couch, warm and comfortable, and I could feel that even with the fire burning merrily away just a few feet from me, the room was beginning to get quite cold.

Trapped.

I reached down with my fingers, looking again for an old *Newsweek* or *Astronomy*, and I found the manila folder. I stifled a yawn. This would definitely do the trick. I opened up the folder, and in the uneven light from the fire and the candles I began to read, vowing to start right at the beginning and end when my eyelids couldn't stay open.

Nice plan, but it didn't work.

.   .   .

FIVE MINUTES into the planning board documents, I was sitting straight up, looking at a name on the pages that was quite familiar, one that I didn't expect to see: Fire Inspector Mike Ahern. Speaking out against the conversion of the Snug Harbor Inn into condominiums. One of the motels that had burned down.

I flipped through the rest of the pages with cold and trembling fingers. Each motel that had been up for review and which had later burned down —the Crescent House, the Rocks Road Motel, the SeaView, the Tyler Tower Motel, and the Snug Harbor Inn—was the subject of some condemning language, and all from the same person.

Mike Ahern.

His comments were at the very end of each set of minutes, for the time set aside for general citizen comments. Most of them were quite similar, like this one:

SPEAKING on behalf of himself and not as a member of the Tyler Fire Department, MICHAEL AHERN said he was opposed to the conversion of the Rocks Road Motel into condominiums. MR. AHERN said it was time that the Board stop approving every single renovation or construction proposal that came before it. The purpose of the Board, MR. AHERN said, was not to protect and promote big business, but to protect the general welfare of the citizens of Tyler. Adding to the growth and putting a strain on water and sewer and other town resources was hurting the town. It was time for the Board, MR. AHERN said, to change its philosophy, to stop shilling for big business.

THE ROCKS ROAD MOTEL, the same place where Mike Ahern had flippantly dismissed the concerns of the business owners. Something about "screw 'em, that's what insurance is for," Mike had said, when Paula and I had visited the burnt ruins.

I held the sheets of paper close to my chest. A lot of questions wore racing around in my mind, and I could not, would not allow myself to start leaping ahead. I had to start somewhere, and I had to start at the beginning, and right now, the beginning meant trying to get some sleep. I put the papers back into the folder, blew out the nearby candles, and burrowed farther into my sleeping bag. I lay awake, listening to the wind and the noise of the snow and frozen rain racing against the house, sounding like sand being tossed down from above, and also listening to the contented crackle and hiss of the fire.

I stared at the fire, thinking of what I had just read, trying to remember what I could about Mike Ahern, and knowing I would have to do some serious digging, and soon. Maybe there was nothing there at all. Maybe just coincidence. But I didn't like the tone of his voice when he talked about Diane, I didn't like that flip comment when looking at the destroyed dream of a Tyler Beach family, and I didn't like his words in the Planning Board minutes. For each motel he spoke against had eventually burned down.

Some coincidence.

Then the investigation kicks into high gear, and something awful happens to the lover of the chief police investigator on the case, a woman who's not well-liked by the preachy fire inspector.

Some coincidence number two.

I needed to learn more, but most of all, I needed to sleep. Eventually I closed my eyes, feeling the heat from the flames upon my face.

I WOKE up in the middle of the night, throat so dry that my tongue was sticking to the roof of my mouth. I tried to ignore the sensation, tried to get some saliva going by chewing on my tongue, but my mouth still felt sticky and awful. I shifted on the couch and looked out to the living room. There was a steady glow coming from the orange coals in the fireplace. My nose and cheeks were quite cold, and about then I realized that my bladder was in need of some relief.

Damn. Time to get out of my warm cocoon.

I zipped open and tossed aside the sleeping bag and yelped as I swung to the floor. I slipped on a pair of socks and raced upstairs to the bathroom, where I quickly took care of task number one, knowing that I looked quite ridiculous in just a pair of socks, but also knowing with a firm sense of righteousness that no one would see me.

As I came back downstairs, shivering, I stopped at the closet and pulled on my down jacket, and shook and shivered some more. I went over to the fireplace and opened up the chain grate and I tossed in four more chunks of wood, and I stoked the embers with a poker until the flames came back. Next stop was the kitchen, where the lemonade I always keep in the refrigerator was cool to my lips, and I gratefully chugged down a few swallows, feeling the wonderful acid taste of the lemonade scour my night mouth clean.

Then something odd came to me, as I put the lemonade jug away.

It was quiet.

No, not silent, but there was no howling of wind, no shaking of the house, no sandpapery sound of snow slamming into the windows. I leaned over the sink and looked outside. I could see stars. I went back to the closet and put on a pair of boots, and then slumped my way back to the rear sliding glass doors. I tried to open the door. It was stuck. I put my feet against the kitchen counter and leaned into it, pushing hard with both hands, and the frozen door literally popped open, and then slid a few inches. Cold wind blew through the opening, swirling around my exposed legs. I pushed a few more times, until it was wide enough to slide through, and then I was outside, standing on my deck.

I stood in at least a foot of snow, and I tilted my head back and looked up. The storm clouds had finally blown free and the night sky was dark and crisp with the cold air. To the west Orion was still there, shield and club always at the ready. Out over the ocean was the familiar Big Dipper and at its rear, Bootes, son of Jupiter and Callisto. Off to the southeast, Venus was so bright it almost hurt to stare at it, and hanging below it, bright enough in its own glory, was the king of the planets, Jupiter. The night sky was magnificent and was made even more so by the darkness below.

I lowered my head and looked up and down the coast and shivered. Not a light to be seen. The power was still out. Usually the lights of Tyler and the beaches and the North Shore sprawl of Massachusetts set up a steady glow to the south, and to the north you could always count on the lights from the city of Porter. But there was none of that on this night, just the shadow shapes of the hills and land.

Another shiver, this time on the back of my neck. I was seeing something I would never forget, and that I would probably never see again: the New Hampshire coastline at night, looking as it did four hundred years ago when the land belonged to the Micmacs, Algonquins, and Pennacooks, before men and women with fire and iron landed here in leaky boats to begin their conquest of a continent. I looked up and down the coastline again, willing myself to remember everything I saw. In a way I was privileged to be a time traveler, being put in a spot to see what it had been, what it had looked like, and how it had sounded.

After a few minutes the practical part of my nature took over, and I got to work, shoveling off the accumulation of snow from the rear deck. But even with this exertion, I would stop and rest every few minutes, just to look at the awe-inspiring sight of darkness fallen upon a settled land that was home to thousands, and that now had been transported back to the sixteenth century.

When I was done, I gave the stars and planets and the cold and quiet coastline one more look, and then I went back inside and went back to sleep.

THE NEXT MORNING, I trod along in my snowshoes, heading north into the woods of the Samson Point State Wildlife Preserve. As I moved, I felt tired and soiled. The power was still out, and I had built up the fire again in the fireplace, which had warmed up the first floor of the house. No shower, of course, and while I was hungry for a nice big breakfast, I didn't like the idea of washing those dishes one by one through heated hot water, and I made do with hot oatmeal and half-burnt toast cooked in the fireplace.

The radio reports I listened to as I ate were slightly less hysterical than last night. The storm was now making trouble for upstate Maine. New Hampshire and Massachusetts were digging out. The fishing boat from Tyler had been located, and the search was still on for the fishermen out of Gloucester. People evacuated overnight from the beaches were returning home. Roads were slowly returning to normal. The president was considering officially declaring the region a disaster area.

And I was outside, not enjoying being cooped up in a cold and powerless house.

I moved through the woods, snow from the overhanging branches trembling and falling as I went deeper into the silence, and then came the sound of the ocean, as I reached my favorite sitting spot. The rock was covered with snow, and I waited, knowing that I should be enjoying these few minutes of solitude. No power, no phone, and no way of leaving the house and dealing with the arsons, Kara, Mike Ahern, or anything else.

I should have enjoyed the solitude, but instead I was conscious that it was cold, I needed a shave, and my skin felt dirty. The air was clean and cold, and the snow was a white, virginal blanket over everything, but the beauty of the winter landscape was wasted on me, and I turned and trudged back home.

When I got back and walked through the front door, I froze, hearing voices. Someone had broken in, and I was ready to back out and try to assess what the hell was going on when I started to hear music.

Music?

I walked into the living room and smiled goofily at what I had been panicked over. The television was on, that's all. I must have left it on yesterday afternoon when the power went out. Now the power was back.

Power.

I dropped everything in a bundle on the floor and went to the thermostat and clicked it up, and I was rewarded with the gruff grumble of the oil heater starting up. I turned on the faucet in the kitchen and was rewarded with steaming hot water, and then I raced upstairs, stripping off my sweaty and snow-sodden clothes, leaving drips and puddles of water on the wooden risers. In the bathroom I started trembling from the cold, because the second floor was still frigid, but there was a welcome blast of warm air coming from the register set in the floor.

A minute later I was under the hot streams of water, washing away more than two days' worth of dirt and grime, and for no reason at all, I started singing what little I remembered of a song I had learned way back in high school, when I had been a bashful member of the chorus, but a proud member of the crew of the *H.M.S Pinafore*.

Silly, yes, but cleanliness and hot water can sometimes do strange things to you.

An hour later I was on my couch, the oil heater still plugging away, dressed in clean clothes and before a small, crackling fire, which was now there more for atmosphere than warmth, and I had a cup of tea in one hand and my phone in the other. It took a couple of tries, but I managed to connect with Paula at her office just before noon.

"How's it going with you?" I asked.

"Hellish but improving," she said. "Me and Jerry, we spent the night at an evacuation center set up at the junior high school. We spent most of the day getting stories and pictures from the downtown yesterday, and when we were finished at the junior high, the cops strongly advised us about going out."

"Really?"

"Really," she said. "One of those cops happened to be your detective friend, and I was going to make a fuss until Diane told me that even if I wanted to, I couldn't get home—the part of High Street where my apartment building is located was covered in two feet of water. That plus the snow and ice...well, me and Jerry bunked for the night."

"In separate bunks?" I asked, trying to put an innocent inquiring tone to my voice, which Paula threw back at me.

"Spare me the jealous talk, Lewis. We were stuck in a gym with about fifty or so people, complete with crying kids, people snoring, and people coughing, trying to sleep on bunks that must have been designed back when Civil Defense was first set up. Still, it made for a great first-person story that AP in Concord bought from me. How did you do?"

"Lost power and phone yesterday afternoon, and I thought the tide might carry the homestead away with a couple of good waves, but the house is high enough off the beach. I'm just glad the fireplace still worked. Up to getting together for lunch tomorrow?"

"I don't know about tomorrow, but—"

"It's about the arson case."

"Oh, anything you want to tell me over the phone?"

"No, not really. Something I want to tell you face-to-face," I said.

"Oh," she repeated. "Sounds intriguing."

"Actually, it sounds pretty nutty, which is why I want to see you in person."

"You got it."

We talked for a few minutes more and after we both hung lip, I sat on my couch, quite content, cup of tea warm in my hand. I felt clean and refreshed, the house was warm, and the electric lights were bright indeed. I still remembered that sense of awe last night in seeing the darkened miles of seacoast, but that had been a temporary adventure, and just as well.

Time travel had been fun, but as one Kansas girl once said, there's no place like home.

17

By the time I got to the *Chronicle* on Tuesday, I was sweaty, irritable, and late. It had taken me longer than I expected to shovel a path from my house to the garage. Then, getting out was also a challenge, even with the Rover's four-wheel drive, and I clawed up the unplowed driveway until I reached the Lafayette House parking lot, where I found the expert plowers had stripped the lot of snow nearly down to bare pavement. However, they had also created a mound of snow and ice that blocked my way and was damn near as tall as me. At first I had attacked the mound with the folding shovel that's always in the back, but after several long and sweaty minutes, it became quite clear that if I continued, I would make it to the *Chronicle* in time for dinner. So I trudged back down to the house—falling down once in the process—and trudged back up with a larger shovel. Another dreary set of minutes later, I was able to plow through the parking lot by using the vehicle as a battering ram, and I left the parking lot a mess of snow and ice, and by then I didn't care.

The drive along the beach was educational, seeing what had happened when the low-lying areas had been swept over by the storm tide. The snow-banks were peppered with rocks, some the size of my fist, and a little cool sensation went along the back of my hands when I realized that the rocks had been thrown up here from the beach and over the concrete seawall.

Several cottages had been stove in, like a giant hand had crumpled them with the ease of crushing cardboard, and along one portion of the road, abandoned cars were off to the side, fenders and doors crumpled in, as the plows last night had pushed them to the side to keep the roadway clear.

The ride uptown was almost as educational, with huge mounds of snow and my Tyler neighbors, busy at work, shoveling or snowblowing their way clear. A few trees had tumbled over and I could hear the incessant chattering of chain saws at work.

The downtown traffic light was still on blinking yellow. I parked near the rear of the Tyler Professional Building, which houses the *Chronicle*, and carrying a manila envelope, I went through the rear door. Inside it was a wet and cluttered chaos, with ringing phones and the green industrial-strength carpet soiled and puddled with melted snow. There were metal desks jammed together and mounds of newspapers and blue-and-white plastic mailboxes for the *Chronicle*. Rollie Grandmaison, the editor, was at his desk by the far wall, and there were three or four others at other workstations. Paula was at her desk, talking to her photographer friend Jerry as I went over.

"Sorry I'm late," I said. "Even with four-wheel drive, it was tough getting out."

She looked up at a clock. "Then we're stuck here for lunch. The governor's press secretary is supposed to be calling me back, and I have to stick around."

I held up the envelope. "We're going to be hungry, because this is all I brought."

She smiled at me and then at Jerry, who was sitting in a chair by her desk, holding some photos and contact sheets. "That's all right, I've got it covered. Hey, Frank?"

At that a young man at a far desk looked up and came over. He looked to be in his early twenties, with hair in a bit of a ponytail and wearing patched jeans and a rag sweater. "What do you need, Paula?"

"Lunch for two," she said, pulling a menu out from her desk and handing it over to me. "Lewis, is there something here you like?"

I scanned the menu—which was from the High Street Cafe, a short walk away—and said sure, and after the two of us had given the uncomplaining Frank our lunch orders, he put on a winter coat and went out, and I said, "What was that all about?"

She had a wicked smile on her face. "Frank's our college intern for the spring term from UNH. Call me cruel, call me unfair, but I remember when I was an intern, I had to do the same thing. So just consider this passing on a tradition."

"All right," I said, "I won't call you unfair."

She wiggled her nose at me and said, "I'll go clean up the conference room. We can eat in there. Jerry, show Lewis your stuff from the storm."

Paula got up and walked out to the paper's conference room. Phones were ringing and computer keyboards were being tapped, and I took off my own coat and draped it across an empty desk, and then sat down in Paula's chair. It was pleasingly warm, and I saw something that made me smile. On her desk was a photo of Paula and Jerry in the audience at some news conference, but taped to a filing cabinet drawer—and only visible from her seat—was a picture of me, snapped last summer on the rear deck of my house. I didn't try to read anything into it, anything deep or philosophical. It was just nice.

Jerry spoke up, saying, "Make it through the storm all right?" I turned. He had on a thick brown sweater and jeans and his brown hair and beard were neat and trimmed. Maybe this budding romance was helping his grooming habits.

"I did pretty fine, but I hear that you and Paula had some adventures."

"Sure did. Look at this stuff," he said, passing over some eight-by-ten black-and-white prints. I was going to give them a quick courtesy glance, but I slowed down in an instant. I looked at him and said, "Jerry, these are really good."

I think he blushed. "Thanks."

"No, I really mean it," I said. "These are great."

An embarrassed nod. "Well, the AP Concord Bureau did pick up the last shot, so that's on the wires. I'll be happy to see where it ends up."

I went through each print. There were two of the beach, showing the waves exploding over the seawall, a couple of cars and a plow being inundated. Another showed a wide-eyed elderly woman being carried by two Tyler cops to a National Guard truck, the cops knee-deep in water and slush. And another showed an older man bent over a shovel, a snowbank near him that was over his head, and a small dog on top of the mound looking down quizzically at his master. In each photo, he had framed it so you were looking at the faces of the people, their expressions, their fears, their exhaustion.

The last photo was the best of the bunch. It was taken from a height and showed the center of Tyler Beach, the Strip. Jammed with thousands of tourists every summer night, in this picture there were just two men in the foreground, tugging at a canvas awning in front of a closed-up building, trying to prevent it from blowing away. They were staring up at the awning, hands tense, struggling. Behind them a snowplow was approaching, and a wave of snow was being tossed up, and you knew that in a matter of seconds those two men were going to get covered with the snow.

"Did they save the awning?" I asked.

"Nope," Jerry said. "They got socked by the snow and fell, and the wind just took that awning and whipped it away. The guys were all right, but the last I saw that awning, it was heading toward Falconer. Here, you can see the series."

He handed over a contact sheet, which was an eight-by-ten sheet of strips of negatives, each photo just a bit larger than a postage stamp. I saw what he meant and saw that there were about a half dozen shots in the series, starting with the guys working, the plow approaching, the guys getting knocked down and then standing up, cursing at the plow. Out of all the shots, Jerry had picked the best.

"Nice vantage point," I said. "Where were you to get these pictures?"

He looked sheepish. "I was on top of the Chamber of Commerce building."

I stared at him. "How in hell did you get up there?"

Jerry shrugged. "The Tyler cops were in there, getting some gear from the state. I let myself in and went up, and there was an access hatch to the roof. I figured I might get some good stuff up there. The hatch was frozen shut, but I managed to beat my way through it, and when I got up on the roof, you wouldn't believe the view I had."

Oh, I could believe it. Last summer I was up on the same roof with Diane, as she was tailing some drug dealers that were working on the Strip.

We both lay flat on the roof, and even there, with no wind, no snow, and no slippery conditions, I was uncomfortable. The roof was built at a sharp angle, and I dug in with elbows and heels to keep position, and I was never happier that evening than when we both climbed back down.

"How did you stay in one place?" I asked.

"Just stubbornness, I guess."

"You could have fallen and broken your neck."

Another shrug, a bearded smile. "I got the shot, didn't I?"

"But you could have fallen."

The smile remained as he picked up the photos and contact sheet, and then quickly turned his head. "But I got the shot. Looks like someone's waiting for you."

I looked up and Paula was beckoning to me, and Jerry got up and walked to the stairway that went down to the cellar, which held the paper's morgue and darkroom. I went forward, past Rollie Grandmaison, who was pencil-whipping his way through a press release from the Friends of the Tyler Harbor. His tan sweater was wearing through the elbows and his strands of light brown hair were flattened atop his freckled skull.

"How's the editor biz, Rollie?" I asked as I went by.

He didn't lift his head and the eyes behind his black-rimmed glasses didn't move as he said, "Still sucks, Lewis."

I followed Paula into a conference room, again admiring the way she filled out her blue jeans. Her ears were still poking through her hair, but I was too polite to mention it. I raised my eyebrows and she sighed and went up to the door and closed it.

"Well," she said, sitting down, legal pad in hand. "Got something good, I hope."

"You tell me," I said, passing over the envelope. She pulled out the planning board minutes, and I looked up at the paneled walls. There were some framed photos there, of the governor with Rollie and a few of some senators and congressmen, passing their way through here on that bumpy and detour-filled road to the White House.

She looked up after a couple of minutes, face set. "You must think I'm an idiot."

"No. I think you're overworked, and I think you looked at the obvious paths. Nothing stupid about that."

Paula looked back down at the minutes, where I had highlighted where Mike Ahern had made his points. "This is insane. Do you really think Mike's behind these arsons?"

I folded my hands. "I don't know. On the surface it does sound crazy, that Mike would be involved and leave such a paper trail. But in your line of work you know what crazy things people do, every day. Murderers who videotape their own exploits. Mothers who kill their children and blame it on witchcraft or mysterious black men. Sex offenders who call their victims later, looking for a date. It happens."

"All right, it happens," she said. "Plus, I don't think he's the most balanced person I've ever met. So. What's next?"

"Research," I said. "I'd like to find out more about our town's fire inspector. He's been here, what, a year? Would like to know more about where he's been, what he did before he came to Tyler, what other towns he worked in."

She flipped through the pages again. "You think he's done this before?"

"I don't know what to think. All I do know is that if we're going to believe that the town's fire inspector is burning down businesses in Tyler because of some grudge, we better have some good information to start with. So far," I pointed at the minutes collection, "this is all we've got."

Paula's reporter's face was now firmly on. She has a number of faces, from ones that make me smile to others that give me the heebie-jeebies, and her reporter's face was creepy. She looked like a mother bear who's just found someone shaving her cubs.

"I think I can help you with that," Paula said. "Kristie Graham. She roomed with me for a semester back at UNH. She's now the secretary at the fire department."

"You think she'll let you see Mike's personnel file?"

"See it?" Paula said. "Hell, I helped her pass English two semesters in a row. She damn well better let me make a copy of it."

"If she does, pass it along."

"The hell I will, this is my story."

"The hell you won't," I said. "This isn't just a story. This is some very strange stuff. If you start digging around and Mike Ahern finds out what you've been up to, then your job will become even more hellish. All of the firefighters, most of the cops, and a good chunk of the townspeople will be quite upset with you."

She sounded glum. "But nothing bad will happen to you, right? Sounds pretty macho to me."

"No, it sounds right, and you know it. I can still write the column, even if the entire town boycotts *Shoreline*. I don't have much to lose. You do. And I promise, if anything comes up, it's yours. Your story, top to bottom. Deal?"

"Oh, it's a deal, damn you."

Then the door opened up and Frank the intern came in with two paper bags containing a veggie sub for Paula and a pastrami and cheese on rye for me, and iced tea for both of us. As Frank went out Paula said, "Frank, can you go down to the police station this afternoon to check on the log for me?"

His face brightened. "Sure. That'd be great."

When he closed the door behind us and I started unwrapping my sandwich, I said, "You hate going to the police station for the log in the winter, don't you?"

"Unh-hunh," she said, taking a big bite from her sandwich "It's cold and I have to park in that lot that never gets plowed, and there's hardly anything there anyway."

"So you sent the intern."

Paula looked up and smiled. "I sure did. Payback can be fun, can't it?"

AFTER A BRIEF STOP at the post office, I drove back home, seeing that the roads hadn't improved much since my drive into town. There were still cars stranded in snowdrifts and people shoveling and snowblowing as I made my way back to Atlantic Avenue. When I got in and took off my coat and tossed away most of the mail, I saw the blinking green light on my answering machine, and found that I had a call from Meg Purdy, the landlord for Doug Miles. She was quick and to the point:

"Call me back, will you?" she had said. "Dougie will be home tonight."

So I did, and she answered the phone and told me, "One of Dougie's friends stopped by, asked me to give him this envelope. He says Dougie will be by just before eleven."

"He wants you to hand deliver it?"

"Yeah, can you believe that?" she said. "I made a fuss, and he gave me twenty bucks for my trouble."

"What kind of envelope is it?"

"Nine-by-twelve, the brown kind. Nice and sealed shut with tape, so don't go asking me to open it."

"I won't," I said. "But thanks for the call."

"You're welcome. So. Are you and your friend coming by tonight?"

"I imagine we will."

"Well, you imagine yourselves nice and careful," she said. "You two look like a couple of strong young men, but you be prepared. And tell you what, you manage to get Dougie out, I'll give you something, and I don't mean twenty bucks."

"Thanks for the offer," I said.

"Don't bother, and don't mind me if I stay in my bedroom with the *Tonight Show* on and Krypton sharing my bed," she said with a laugh. "I don't think I want to know what's going on down there."

I nodded to myself. "I think you're right."

WE WERE HAVING a cup of coffee and some late-night dessert at the Grog in Newburyport, and I asked Felix how he had made it through the blizzard.

"Made it through, nice and fine."

"Even with the power out?"

He took up another forkful of cheesecake. "Who said I was at home? I had a business appointment in Boston."

"North End?" I asked blandly, and he gave me a look as he continued, "and I knew the storm was just going to get worse, so a friend of mine, we ended up in the Parker House. Nice place to ride out a blizzard. Big bed, big tub, and wonderful room service."

"Sounds like fun," I said. "Any chance I'll be meeting this friend anytime soon?"

"Not a chance," he said.

"Fine," I said. "How did your background check go on young Mr. Miles?"

"Our young Mr. Miles has been a busy boy, but nothing too outrageous," Felix said. "A few driving offenses and two burglary charges. A couple of barroom brawls, a marijuana possession, and one armed robbery charge that never went anywhere."

"Nice fellow. No wonder his landlord wants him out."

"Oh, I've seen nicer," Felix said, which I didn't doubt.

Later we went outside, walking carefully along the ice-covered sidewalk. It was about eleven o'clock and the hot coffee, along with the thoughts of our evening's work, had wired me up. Everything seemed crisp and clear, from the brickwork of the buildings and the sharp light from the streetlamps, to the crunch of ice and sand under our feet. After we got into my four-wheeler and waited for the engine to warm up, Felix rubbed his hands together and said, "A few more days, I'm going to be so warm, and you're going to be so jealous."

"Run that by me one more time?" I asked.

He turned and smiled. "Courier job coming up very soon. Sun, sand, and fun in the Cayman Islands, thank you very much."

"Plus bruises, broken bones, and a little blood to go along with it, right?"

"Only if I screw up, which I promise I won't."

"What are you bringing in?" I asked, as I drove out of downtown Newburyport.

Felix shrugged. "Maybe I'm taking something out."

"Maybe I'm stupid in asking you."

"No argument here."

We drove out to the western part of the city, where Doug Miles and his odd landlord lived. Felix reached behind him and pulled out a small black bag, which he zippered open. Taking out his 9mm Smith & Wesson, he opened up his winter jacket and placed it in a shoulder holster. He left his coat open and tossed the bag back into the rear seat, saying, "And you?"

"Underneath the front seat."

"Good."

He pulled the coat closed around him and said, "What do you think the landlord meant with her little statement?"

"Exactly what she said. We should be careful."

Felix crossed his arms around his chest. "Well, others might disagree, but I feel more careful when I'm carrying."

"Glad to hear it."

IN NEW HAMPSHIRE, carrying a concealed weapon means getting a permit from the local police chief, which was easy for me, considering my relationship with a member of the Tyler Police Department. In Massachusetts, getting such a permit as a resident was very difficult, and getting one as an out-of-state resident, like me, was damn near impossible.

So tonight Felix and I would be breaking the law in the fair Commonwealth save for one thing: Some time ago he had secured permits for the both of us as representatives of a security firm that probably exists only from a mail drop somewhere in Boston. While I'm sure the way Felix managed to pull that scam off was an interesting story, I was content to have the permit and also content not to ask too many questions.

"Coming up in a minute or two," Felix said.

The banks of snow along the road were quite high, and the pavement was still covered with a hard pack of snow and sand. "Here it is," Felix said. "Slow it down."

Which I did, and which I kept on doing as we slid past Doug Miles's home. Nothing in the driveway, no lights on, no sign of anyone.

"Damn," Felix said.

"Exactly."

We drove by twice more and then, thinking we would arouse the suspicions of anyone awake, I drove back to town and we stayed in a shopping plaza parking lot, listening to some late-night music. The sodium-vapor lamps made everything look orange, and at the far end of the lot, plows and earthmovers were widening the lot, dumping the snow into huge mounds that looked to be almost fifty feel tall.

"You got a grand plan after tonight?" Felix asked, resting his head in his hand.

"Nothing too grand about it," I said. "We talk to the young master Miles, and see what he tells us. If it's nothing worthwhile, then that's it, we're wrapped up and I talk to Diane later this week. I give her a full report of everywhere we've been and everything we've done and admit defeat."

"Nice."

"No, it's not nice, but it's all we can do. But if Doug offers us something, even something as small as knowing somebody that might not have liked Kara, or something Kara might have done to someone that she wouldn't admit to Diane, then we keep on going until this road reaches a dead end."

"Then?"

I thought of Mike Ahern and the fires, and his dislike for one police detective. Another road to travel for a while, but nothing yet to get Felix involved with. Not yet.

"Then I think of something else."

"Couple of days ago, you said you might be taking a look at Diane and what might be going on with her. Still true?"

"Still true, but later," I said. "You ready for another trip back?"

"I suppose I don't have a choice."

"You suppose right."

THIS TIME, there were lights.

"All right," Felix said, zipping up his coat. "Slow down and let me out, and then come back in about five minutes. Head up to the driveway and knock on the door and I'll wait out back, and let's see what kind of mischief we can get into."

"See you soon," and I slowed down, and Felix opened the door, a cold blast of wind coming through the interior, and he slid out and onto his feet and I sped up. I drove up the street, thinking again of why I was out here on a cold January night in a state not my own, with an automatic pistol under my seat and soon to be in my coat, and going in harm's way. I went about a quarter of a mile, enough time for Felix to settle himself in, and then I turned around and headed back, knowing full well the answer: For my friend. That's it. No deep philosophy, no heavy questions, no turgid debate. I was doing this for Diane, and for no one else.

The lights were still on at the shuttered and cold-looking house as I pulled into the driveway, making no attempt to quiet my approach. Parked in front of the house was an old Dodge Colt, its blue paint whitened with road salt, and I pulled up behind and switched off the engine. I reached under the seat and pulled out my own 9mm Beretta, unzipping it from its case, putting it in my own shoulder holster.

With flashlight in hand I got out and crunched my way across the frozen lawn, cold air on my face, not seeing Felix but knowing he was out there just the same. A comforting thought.

I went up to the front door, making a quick look around to ensure that Krypton or any friends of his weren't sniffing around, and I knocked a few times.

No answer.

"Doug? Doug Miles?"

I rapped on the door with my flashlight, and I thought I heard something moving around inside, and then there was a loud thump. I moved off the doorstep and was going to move around to the side of the house when the door suddenly opened, and standing in the light, breathing heavily but smiling, was Felix, pistol in hand.

"Selling something, young boy?" he asked.

"Depends on what you're buying, I guess."

I walked in and suddenly started breathing through my mouth. We were in a walkway that led off to the garage at our right, and to a living room to the left. A sour-looking man who looked to be Doug Miles was sitting on a couch, rubbing at his jaw. He had on jeans and a thick blue sweatshirt and had one sneaker on. The room looked like someone had taken a Salvation Army drop-off bin and had tumbled it inside. Clothes were strewn around and were flowing out of torn green garbage bags. The room was thick with the smell of old grease and unwashed clothes. There were some newspapers crumpled up and some torn magazines, and a leaning bookshelf that held some paperbacks and a couple of souvenir sculptures or something. I looked quickly and saw one of the little statues was of a busty woman, holding up a beer stein, and on the base of the sculpture was "Beer and Broads: The Way Life Was Meant To Be." Toward the rear, an open door led to the back yard, and next to the door was a counter that had a mini-fridge and two-burner hotplate. The walls were cheap paneling, bowing out from the wall studs, and a clock on the near wall was off by an hour.

"What the hell is this?" Doug asked, looking sullenly up at us. His hair was brown and thick and combed back, and he had a two- or three-day-old growth of beard. His nose was red and runny, and his eyes were weepy.

I said nothing and Felix poked through another door, which led to a bathroom that had a toilet and stand-up shower, and another thick mass of clothes on the floor. I walked through the mounds of trash and clothes to the rear door, which I closed, and Felix came back and stood next to me.

"Any other rooms?" I asked.

"This is it," Felix said, holstering his pistol. "Man must have to sleep on the couch, which must be damn uncomfortable unless it's a fold-out. Is that what it is?"

"Who are you guys?" Doug demanded, his voice quavering, I looked around the room again. No other chairs. Oh, well, I opened up my coat, making sure that Doug could see my own 9mm, and I reached into a side pocket and took out a thin piece of cardboard. I smiled at him as I tossed my business card into his lap.

"We're your worst nightmare, Doug," I said.

"Hunh?"

I motioned to the card. "We're magazine writers, and we're here to talk."

18

He didn't seem impressed. Doug picked up the card and examined both sides and tossed it to the floor.

"The hell you're from some freakin' magazine," he said. "What do you want?"

Felix moved around so we were flanking him, and Felix had this odd little smile I've seen before on a few occasions, when he's in his working mode. Doug was looking at me, and I wished he was looking at Felix. He would definitely be more impressed.

"Information," I said. "We're looking for some information."

He sat back. "You should get the hell out of here, 'fore you get into trouble."

"What kind of trouble?" I asked. "Word is, you're not friendly with the cops."

By now he was smirking. "I didn't say anything about cops now, did I? But you still can get into the shits if you don't watch yourself. So why don't you get out?"

"We sure will," Felix said, and Doug turned and looked at him and the smirk wavered. "But after you tell us what we need. We want information about your sister."

"Hunh?" and he looked back to me. "All this action, coming in here, wearing metal, and pulling me around, and you want to talk about Kara?"

"That's right," I said. "Kara, you know what happened to her a couple of weeks ago, right? Well, we're working on an article about the whole matter. We've interviewed her, the cops, her neighbors, her landlord, the place where she works, and even your parents. You're the last one on the list, Doug, so tell us what you know."

He rubbed at his nose, sniffled some. "You're whacked. I haven't seen her in months, and the only thing I know is something my dad said, about her being attacked or something." He smiled up at us. "Why don't you go talk to a detective up in Tyler? She probably knows a lot about Sis."

"You said your dad told you about Kara?"

He nodded. "Yeah, a week or two ago, when I was over there for a visit."

"Funny thing," I said. "I saw your parents last week and your mother says she hasn't seen you in years."

"That's right," he said. "Can't say you can blame her. Look at her two kids. One's a freak and the other turns out like me. So I stay away, but dear old Dad, he feels guilty. So we have a beer about once a month, and he slips me a Ben Franklin note, and that holds him for another month until he starts feeling guilty and he calls me up again." He shrugged. "No matter. I stay and talk and listen to him whine for an hour about his empty life, and I get a couple of free beers and a hundred bucks. Not a bad deal."

Such a sport. I looked around the cluttered room and said, "So that's all you know, that she was attacked. Did you call her, write a note or something?"

He laughed. "Man, Kara is a lot different from all of us, but she and the old lady share a common gene, one that has an intense dislike of males. Nope, haven't seen nor spoken to her in ages. Dad told me she was doing fine, and I said that was good, and then he got weepy about all the Red Sox games we took in when I was a kid and left it at that."

Felix spoke up. "How are you keeping busy, Doug? Job market all right?"

He crossed his arms. "I'm doing okay. I got a setup in Boston, working in the harbor. Off the books but the pay is all right."

"Really?" Felix asked. "How's the pay in your extracurricular activities? Broken into any cottages on Plum Island or Tyler Beach lately?"

Another gaze, back and forth. "You guys are from a magazine. The hell you say."

"Let's just say we're thorough researchers," I said. "So, how's your career path? Staying on the straight and narrow?"

"Piss off. And while you're at it, get the hell out before I call my lawyer."

Felix said, "Gee, now I'm trembling."

"Okay, piss off and get the hell out before I call some friends of mine, some friends that can put you two in a world of hurt."

"These good friends of yours?" I asked.

Another smirk. "No, not good, but tough."

I looked over at Felix, and he gave me a half-shrug. Not much to go on. We could stay longer and beat up on Mr. Miles and see what else happened, but it didn't seem like much. I nodded to Felix and he surprised me by sticking out his hand, and Doug, surprised, too, I guess, shook Felix's outstretched hand.

"Sorry to waste your time," Felix said. He motioned in my direction, "Lewis, there, he gets worked up on a story and he tends to go in pretty tough. Sorry again."

He looked over at me and said, "Time to leave, right?"

"Sure, why not?" I turned to leave, and then, for one searing moment, I wished I had done a better job of looking around earlier. I had missed something important, very important indeed, resting on the bookshelf with the paperbacks and souvenirs.

It was a ceramic dragon, rearing up, talons extended and mouth opened, looking like it was seconds away from spewing death upon a knight.

A knight, kneeling in terror and holding up his shield, in an apartment on the other side of the city.

WE WERE PARKED in the same store lot again, watching the plows do their night work, scraping and moving tons of snow into piles that were beginning to dwarf the surrounding buildings. I had the heater on and we had cups of coffee, taken from a drive-up window at a Dunkin' Donuts. The coffee tasted fine, but I was in a foul mood.

"Well, we learned a lot tonight," Felix said, and I grunted in reply. He went on. "See the little scam I pulled with him, just before we left, when I shook his hand?"

"Sure. What were you trying to do, see if he belonged to the same lodge?"

"Hardly. The man says he has a job at the docks in Boston, working under the table. Those guys work hard in all weather, and even if you wear gloves, it does a number to your hands. The guy's hands are soft, soft as a virgin's butt. There's no way he does outside work. And did you notice the other thing about him?"

Amber lights flashed from the growling plows. "No, what was that?"

"Jesus, Lewis," Felix said. "The guy was coked up to the gills. Sniffling like that, his hands shaky, eyes watery. I bet you that's where his business interest lies, not with the docks. Our Doug was seriously strung out. Couldn't you see that?"

I turned and looked over at him. He was being polite, but he could tell he was chiding me, and I said in return, "No, but I saw something else."

"Oh? Like what? Like Doug doesn't do laundry?"

I raised up my coffee cup. "No. Our Doug was lying. He's been to Kara's place."

Felix shifted in his seat to get a better look at me. "Say again?"

"Doug's been there, and probably recently. When you and I were at Kara's, do you remember her living room? What was there, besides furniture and books?"

He thought for a moment. "Tapestry hanging from one wall. Coffee table and such. Closed-off fireplace, some junk on the mantelpiece."

"That junk was three ceramic sculptures, showing a fantasy world. Knights and trolls and horses. Two of the sculptures were a matched set. The other showed a knight, kneeling in fear, waiting to be attacked. But there was nothing attacking him. Nothing."

"You saw it at Doug's place," he said, no more chiding in his voice.

"That I did. A sculpture of a dragon, waiting to move down to kill something, and a perfect match to the knight sculpture. It belongs at Kara's place, but it's at her brother's dump. He says he doesn't know where she lives, and he says he's never talked to her. Felix, the man's lying about the first and I'm sure he's lying about the second."

Felix's voice sounded bleak. "Are you saying he raped his sister?"

The coffee seemed to back up my throat. "I don't know. I do know he's been to her place. Look, we've tracked this one down pretty far. We talked to Kara, cops, neighbors, parents, employers, and the landlord, who later gets his throat slit. He was the closest thing we had to a witness, someone who said he heard two sets of voices that night. Now he's dead and, as someone once said, that's a hell of a coincidence."

"That it is. Go on."

"Now, here's another coincidence. Kara's brother has a record, and as you've pointed out, he's probably working something illegal with pharmaceuticals. I'm not saying he's a suspect. I just think for the first time in a long time, we've got someone we want to talk with again, someone with an interesting background."

"Tonight? We could be back there again in ten minutes."

A plow rumbled by, the driver up in his cab looking down at us, probably wondering what in hell we were doing out here on a cold January night.

"No, not tonight," I said. "I want him to think about things, maybe get him nervous. If you got the time, maybe I can convince you to do some surveillance."

"More money involved?"

"Yes."

"Then I can get convinced, until it's travel time. Then what?"

"Then we come back and ask him some more questions. Play good cop, bad cop."

Felix yawned, rubbed at his face. "I don't know if I like that."

"Why?"

"Because I always have to play bad cop, that's why."

I finished my coffee and shifted the Rover into drive, and we ambled out of the parking lot. "That's the curse you have, Felix. You have a gift. You should be proud."

Felix muttered something about what I could do with the gift, and I drove us both home. When I got back into my house I had a message on my answering machine, and it was from Paula Quinn, and she sounded out of breath.

"Lewis? It's Paula. I have to see you tomorrow. I've got Mike Ahern's personnel file and there's something in there I've got to show you. Something very important."

THE NEXT DAY Paula and I shared sandwiches in the front seat of my Rover, parked next to a crowded sub shop in Falconer on Route 286, looking out across the marsh and the snow and ice, leading all the way up to the concrete and steel structures of the Falconer nuclear power plant. As we ate she nodded in the direction of the plant.

"Story I'm working on now involves that place," she said, munching on a vegetarian sub. "Something about the siren poles."

"What about them?" I said, picking out onions from a plain steak and cheese.

"There's over a hundred utility poles set up around a ten-mile radius of the plant, each with a siren that can blast your eardrums if you're standing underneath them. Part of the emergency evacuation plan. Thing is, some radical anti-nuke group that no one's heard of before—called the Nuclear Liberation Front—they've started taking potshots at the poles, chopping them down."

"Let me guess," I said, giving up on my now-cold sub. "They figure if they take out the poles, the federal government will say the emergency plan is flawed, and that the plant's operating license will be pulled. Right?"

"Yep," she said, taking a swig of iced tea. "But our radical geniuses either don't know or don't care that each pole has been wired. You knock out the siren mechanism, the plant automatically gets notified by a radio signal, and they call the cops and roll a repair truck, and in about a half-hour, the pole's either back in business or they drive in a truck-mounted siren to fill the gap if the pole's been cut."

"Demonstrating yet again the power of big business to over-come every obstacle in order to maintain operations," I said. "Look, enough of the nuke. What do you have?"

She picked up a slim leather case and zipped it open, pulling out some documents.

"You would not believe the heat I went through to get into his file," Paula said. "I had to remind Kristie how I saved her butt back in college. Still, she was scared, and I don't blame her. She could have gotten fired, letting me look at a personnel file."

"But still you asked her, right?"

She looked at me. "You feel so guilty about it, why don't you hand it back?"

"I don't feel that guilty," I said, beginning to flip through the sheets. "At least not yet. Tell me, what am I looking for?"

She leaned in a bit, a stray hair tickling my ear, which I enjoyed. "Our Mike Ahern has had an interesting career. Originally from Dover, up the coast. Joined the Army after high school and served his time, and then joined the Porter Fire Department. Also stayed with the Army Reserves. Stayed in Porter a couple of years, and from there went to Nashua, and stayed there a few years more. Then interesting things happen."

"He gets called up and serves during the Persian Gulf War."

Paula moved away, and so did the tickle of her hair. "How did you know that?"

"He told me, week before last. All right, then what happens?"

Her reporter's face then came up, one part joy at finding something out, one part determination in learning more. "That's the funny thing. Nothing happens, according to his file. He gets sent home when the war is over and then there's a blank spot of nearly two years. No employment record at all. Then he comes to Tyler, working as a fire inspector. When he left to go overseas, he was a lieutenant in Nashua, and when he gets another fire-fighter job, he's an inspector."

"That's important?"

She nodded. "Damn important. Look, all of the firefighters I know, they consider themselves macho guys who eat smoke and save lives for a living. They try to get jobs in busy cities, like Nashua or Manchester, and they hate sitting around the station house, polishing brass and doing drills. They love to go out and fight fires. And sitting behind a desk or becoming a fire inspector is something the real tough guys despise."

I glanced through the file, confirming what Paula had said, seeing the odd two-year blank space between his Nashua and his Tyler jobs. "So our tough fire lieutenant leaves to go overseas, comes back and stays out of the line for two years, and when he does get work, it's doing something that some guys would consider a demotion."

Her eyes were glittering. "That's not all. Kristie only photocopied the parts of the file that showed his job history. There was other paperwork she didn't copy, which I managed to poke through, I saw something that made me sit up and take notice. It was an insurance statement, from an outfit in Canterbury called Allied Health Services, for services rendered for Mike Ahern. And the dates of service were in that two-year gap, Lewis."

She looked so proud of herself that I pretty much knew the answer to my next question. "I suppose you've found out more about Allied Health Services?"

"I have," she said, smiling widely.

"So," I said. "What do you know?"

"They're a hospital, Lewis. A hospital for mental patients. And Mike Ahern was a patient there, right after he came back from the Gulf War."

LATER IN THE afternoon I was up in my office, leaning back in my chair, looking at the bookshelves, just thinking about what I was going to do. In some circles it's called lying, bearing false witness, or being a slime. In my own odd circle, I call it scamming. I try to make it quick and painless, and there's no malice on my part. Just the knowledge that this was the only way of getting information from people who have it and who otherwise wouldn't give it to me. I know in my heart of hearts that it's wrong, but I try to convince myself that I'm not seeking the information for purposes illegal or immoral. Most of the time, that takes care of my guilty feeling.

Most of the time.

The phone was in hand and a legal-size notepad was in my lap. I got to work.

First visit was to directory assistance, for the number of Allied Health Services in Canterbury. With that number, my first call was quick and to the point.

"Allied Health," came the reply from a chipper young man.

"Good afternoon," I said. "Craig Sher calling from the Department of Health and Human Services down in Concord. Updating our patient records directory. Whose name should I list as the contact for Allied?"

"Um, that would be Rita Dexter."

"Thanks."

"You're welcome."

I hung up and leaned back in the chair and reached over and picked up a pencil. I waited ten minutes or so and then called back, but this time, I had the pencil firmly clenched in my teeth as I talked to the helpful young man and asked for Rita Dexter. Try it sometimes, you'll see how your voice changes.

A *click-click*, and then, "Rita Dexter. How can I help you?"

"Good afternoon, Rita," I said, pencil now out of my mouth. "Carl Solomon, from Mutual Casualty Insurance. We're the new insurance carrier for the town of Tyler, and I'm trying to clear up a billing matter for one of their employees."

"Unh-hunh. And what would that be?"

"Mike Ahern," I said. "He's on the fire department in Tyler, and our records show he was a patient there sometime..." and I shuffled some papers near the phone and told her the time period. "Correct?"

"Hold on for a moment," she said, tapping a keyboard. "Yes, I have him here. He was admitted here for about eleven months, and then we saw him for another six months on an outpatient basis. What seems to be the problem you folks have?"

"We have a billing here from a physician in Porter, and we're trying to determine if he was seen for a preexisting condition. Who do you have as his doctor?"

"That would be..." *tappity-tappity-tap-tap*, "Dr. Sweeney."

"I see," I said, scribbling on my notepad. "Is he there?"

"Yes, but his office is in Concord."

"Thank you, you've been a great help."

"Wait, what do you—"

I hung up on her, silently apologizing for being so rude. I looked down at my notepad and saw that the white sheets were smudged with my sweaty hands.

But it was still clear enough.

I looked over at the clock on my credenza. It was just before four p.m. I leaned back again, thinking of what I was going to say, who I was going to talk to. I made another phone call to directory assistance, for a doctor's office in Concord, and then looked at the clock again. Four-fifteen. Still not they're yet. I gazed out the window.

Another clock check. Four-twenty. Almost there.

Outside it was getting dark, and I thought about my telescope in my bedroom just a few feet away. Hadn't taken it out lately. Maybe it was time to upgrade to a larger scope. Lord knows I could afford it.

Four twenty-five. Time. I picked up the phone and dialed, and after two rings, a quick woman's voice said, "Dr. Sweeney's office."

"Patient records, please."

"One moment."

I tapped my pen against the pad. Almost four-thirty. Time for the people in this office to be digging out their winter coats, changing their shoes for boots, putting on hats and gloves...and quickly getting rid of any last-minute phone calls that came their way.

"Patient Records, this is Mrs. Glen," came another quick voice.

"Good afternoon, Mrs. Glen," I said, trying to put a cheery note in my voice, "I'm calling from Dr. Kimball's office, down here in Porter. We have a patient here who used to be a patient of Doctor Sweeney's. One Mike Ahern, of Tyler."

"Yes?" The tone was sharp and to the point.

"Look, I know it's late, and I'm getting ready to leave, too," I said. "I have here that he was a patient of Dr. Sweeney's from..." and I read off the dates. "Tell me, has he seen Dr. Sweeney since then?"

"Hold on," and the phone was thunked down. I could hear a file drawer open and the rustle of papers and then she came back.

"No, his last visit was over a year ago."

"Unh-hunh. And his treatment?"

"Excuse me?"

"What was he being treated for?"

"Oh." A flip of a page, rustling over the phone line. "PTS."

"I'm sorry, what was that?"

"PTS," she repeated. "Post-traumatic stress. I'm surprised you don't have that."

"Me, too," I said, and I was rude again in the space of that hour. I hung up.

19

I woke up in the middle of the night, shivering. I must have dreamed, for the down comforter was kicked off, and my bedroom in the middle of winter is a cold place indeed. Instead of pulling the comforter back up, I got out of bed. Sweat was drying on my body and I went to the bathroom, making my way through starlight, and I got a glass of water and wiped down my skin with a towel. I checked my skin and my old scars, and there were no bumps or swellings. Very nice. Back in my bedroom I went to the door that led out to the smaller, second-floor deck. There was a clear view of Weymouth's Point and the lights of the houses up there, and I watched some clouds pass by, blacking out the stars, darkening the sky. I went back to bed and thought about the previous day's work.

Mike Ahern. Post-traumatic stress disorder, right after he came back from the Gulf War. Thankfully that war had not created the host of "crazy vet" stories the news media loved to spread around after Vietnam, and I wasn't about to do that with Mike. Still, there were questions. Something had scarred him, had made him into something different. Before the war, a fire lieutenant in a busy city in New Hampshire. After the war, months at a mental health institution and then a job as a small-town fire inspector.

And a year after he arrives, he takes on the locals during the planning board meetings, and motels begin to burn down. He also doesn't hide his distaste for Diane, and just about the same time the arsons begin, her dear one is attacked.

Connections?

Maybe.

Connections.

And just before I fell asleep, I thought I heard a phone ring, and I think I was dreaming again.

ON THURSDAY AFTERNOON Felix called me and said, "Well, you didn't miss much. I sat on the little bastard for most of the day, and he stayed cooped up in that shack."

"Where did you watch him from?"

"Took a while, but I found a nice place, a little knoll that looks down with good views. To get there, you go past Doug's about a half-mile, take a right. It's a dirt road that's plowed out for a couple of houses. I managed to park there and hoof it over to the knoll. Brought along some thermal underwear and a stool and blanket, and still froze my ass off. I'm going to be looking at a bonus when this little adventure is through."

"You'll get it," I said. "Tell you what, I'll do some work this afternoon, then get over there and watch him during the dinner hour. See what I can find."

"Go ahead," Felix said. "I'm still shivering."

I then called Diane, and we met an hour later, with me picking her up at the station. With cups of coffee we got from a sandwich shop, we parked in one of the hundreds of empty parking spaces along the deserted beach. As we talked, I felt something had changed. There was more of the old Diane, with a slight smile and a few choice words about the weather, though she seemed to move more slowly, as if deciding what phrase or word to say.

She held her coffee cup in her hands and said, "Usually when summer comes, I'm torn. Half of me is looking forward to the warm weather, the long nights, and being able to walk out of my house without worrying about a coat or a sweater."

"And the cop half, she isn't too happy?"

"Nope," she said. "The cop part means busy nights and dealing with lowlifes who see this place as their own private playground, and there are some young men and women out there right now, walking and talking and living, whose lives are going to be changed for the worse because of a night with the wrong people at Tyler Beach."

I sipped from my own coffee. It was early afternoon and the shadows were lengthening, and the sky over the beach and waves was a hard, polished light blue. "I gather, then, you're feeling differently about this summer that's coming up."

"Oh, yes, my dear friend, I am. Summer means I'm six months away from this point in time, and that thought makes me quite happy indeed." She looked over to me, an odd mix of cop and friendship in her eyes, and she said, "What do you have? Anything?"

I chose my words carefully. "A slight lead, that's all. Nothing solid."

Her eyes were now locked right onto me, pure cop. "Go on. Tell me more."

"Kara's brother, Doug. What do you know about him?"

Her gaze didn't waver. "Not a lot. Kara's not one to talk about her family. Go on."

"He doesn't have a pretty past and not much of a present. He's got a record of some drug dealing, breaking and entering. It looks like he's still busy with other things illegal. Felix and I want to find out about his friends, who he hangs out with. That's what we're up to. No names, no faces, nothing. And we've come up empty everywhere else. Kara's brother being involved with things criminal, well, that's the best we can do."

I didn't like what I had just done. I hadn't mentioned the piece of sculpture that had gone from Kara's apartment to Doug's place, and for a reason. I didn't know enough, and if I told Diane just that tiny bit of information, she would demand more. And if I couldn't provide it, then she might be tempted to go out looking on her own.

"I could help," she said. "Let me—"

"No, Diane," I interrupted. "Not wise. You start making phone calls and doing record checks, you'll be leaving a trail that you really don't want to leave. Right?"

The look was still there, and then she nodded and said, "Good point.

But the minute you've got anything, anything at all, I want it, and I want it yesterday."

"All right," I said, draining the last of my cold coffee. "What else is going on?"

She looked out at the empty sands and the long line of cold waves. "Kara talked the other day to Inspector Dunbar from Newburyport, about the murder of her landlord, Jason Henry. She told him what she could, and he didn't say anything useful in return. Just that the matter's under investigation, but you and I know that's a crock."

"Hell of a coincidence, a rape and a murder happening there in less than a week."

"Oh, I agree, all right, and from his tone of voice, I do believe the inspector may believe that it was just a coincidence. Of course, that didn't stop him from asking her if poor old Jason had done it to her, and if her, um, friends hadn't gotten their revenge."

"That's a hell of a reach."

"Yeah, well, I talked to Dunbar and he didn't have much else to offer." She looked over at me again. "You'll do good, won't you?"

"The best I can."

A pause. "I have an odd favor to ask."

"Go ahead."

"Put your arm around me, will you?"

"Excuse me?"

Diane said, "You heard me. Not a very hard request to fill now, is it?"

"Not at all."

I let my empty cup fall to the floor and I reached over with my right arm and pulled her close. Diane snuggled up to me and said, "Squeeze a little harder, will you?"

"Sure."

Diane seemed to sink down a bit and her head ducked onto my shoulder. Both of her hands were clasped together in her lap. Her brown hair tickled my face and smelled of clean soap, and she sighed and said, "Don't get any ideas."

"Nary a one."

"I just felt a need to be held, and you were there."

"Glad to be of help."

"I know I've got this image thing," she said, her voice quiet. "At work I'm the tough, no-nonsense detective who's not afraid to talk to anybody or chase down leads or fight with the selectmen over my budget. With Kara, I'm the take-charge type who's promised to be with her and protect her and help her."

"That's a lot to carry."

"Sure is," she said. "Sometimes..." and her voice was almost a whisper, "sometimes I just need to be hugged and told everything will work out, by and by."

I cleared my throat. "Diane, things will work out, by and by."

"You're a lousy liar."

"Just part of trying to be a good friend."

She shifted some more, her fine hair stroking my cheek. "You and I have been through some odd times, haven't we?"

"That we have."

"And I'm sure some odd ones are coming down the pike, that we can't even think about."

"True enough."

"You know, when you came here, a few years back, I didn't know what the hell to make of you. You started living in that old government house and you had an odd job and lots of money. I thought you were in the witness protection program, of all things."

"A good guess, based on what you know," I said.

"Then I got to know you, and you started doing those odd little stories of yours that never go anywhere and, well, there's still some things that don't make sense. I know you used to work at the Pentagon, and that's it. I guess you left there on a bad note."

Well, this wouldn't breach the agreement. "Absolutely right."

She moved her head against my shoulder. "You had a woman then, didn't you?"

Oh, my Cissy. "Yes."

"Something bad happened back there, didn't it?"

Out there in the desert with her and the others in my section, the high blue sky, and the helicopters coming by, our mistake of being in the wrong place at the wrong time, out there during a biowarfare experiment. And I the sole survivor, pensioned off to this town with the bad memories and the worse medical history, waiting for those odd bumps and swellings in the skin that meant the old bio agent had bit me yet again.

"Something quite bad," I said.

"She's dead, isn't she?"

I cleared my throat again. It was quite dry. "How did you guess?"

"Because you never talk about her, that's why. Because there's no regular woman in your life, except for me and whatever the hell is going on with you and Paula Quinn, that's why. You're still mourning her, aren't you?"

I was glad she couldn't see my face or my eyes, as I stared out at the darkening ocean. "Some days, yes."

Her voice, almost a whisper. "Let her go, Lewis. Let that time slip by. Believe me, I know. You keep on mourning for what was there, for what can never come back, it will eat you and change you into a not-so-nice person, and I don't want that to happen."

"Thanks," I said, and it was the only word I could say.

We watched the ocean for a while in silence, the quiet gulls skimming across the foam and sands. Diane moved a bit and said, "I've never been a follower. I went my own way and did what I wanted and loved who I wanted. I didn't dress to make a statement or march or be political, and unlike a few I know, I don't have a hatred of all men."

"Speaking as a male, I'd like to say thanks."

"You're welcome," and I sensed her smile. "And I'm glad I didn't have that blind hatred, for I might not have met you, and I can't imagine not knowing you."

Something seemed to be in my eyes. "The same, Diane. The same."

We were quiet for a while longer, until she gently moved from my grasp and said, "Please take me back to the station, will you?" And another, gentler smile. "Before someone sees us out here and gets all confused."

"I wouldn't mind."

"Neither would I, but I do have work to do."

Which I did, too, due south. "You've got it," and as I drove her back to the station, Diane held my hand, every yard of the way.

. . .

AN HOUR later I was on my own camp stool, shivering. I had found the turnoff just as Felix had described it, about a half mile from Doug's house. It was a dirt road that had been plowed out and rose up the slight hill. There was a cleared area off to the right, probably used by a snowplow for a turnaround. There were also tire marks, left by Felix's car. I had backed in as far as I could and then trudged through the snow, following his tracks and setting up a watching spot that he had so thoughtfully scouted out for me.

I lifted up the binoculars in my gloved hands and scanned the crumbling structure that was Doug's home. His car was in the driveway, and on a couple of occasions I made out movement behind the front window. It was cold. I had on my heavy winter coat, lined pants, long johns, and a shirt and sweater and wool hat, and I still shivered and stamped my feet. At my side I had a small rucksack with a Thermos full of hot tea, a couple of chocolate bars, and an apple. I was going to stay for a while, but not the entire night. Freezing to death in these woods wasn't part of the deal.

A couple of chickadees skittered through the limbs and then moved on. A car or two traveled by on the road. If Doug were to leave, I figured I had a good few minutes to get the hell back to my Rover, supplies in hand, and get down to the road in another minute or two. With the poor condition of Doug's car and the lack of side streets on this particular stretch of road, I knew I would have little problem in catching up with him.

Another shiver. I ate one of the chocolate bars and sipped from a cup of tea that quickly cooled. It was getting colder. The flesh on my face was getting numb. I fell into a routine of sitting, with hands in pockets, and then every few minutes lifting up the binoculars for another dull scan of the house. The minutes seemed to ooze by as it grew darker. The cars going by had their headlight on now. The birds went away. A light went on from inside Dougie's house and I kept it in view, seeing him move around, seeing him with a bottle of beer in one hand, and a slice of pizza in another. I wondered what he would do if I were to visit him. I wondered how the pizza tasted. And I also wondered how and why that sculpture from Kara's ended up on his bookshelf.

It was time for the apple, and the tea was now cold. My feet were getting stiff and I tried wiggling my toes. No luck. I tilted my head back and tried to look at the stars, and all I saw was a tangle of tree branches. Another pass with the binoculars. There was a flickering blue light coming from the house. Doug was watching television, now munching on pretzels. How nice. I wondered if his lips moved as he watched his favorite shows, whatever they were.

I lost track of the time, though my stomach's clock was grumbling and quite active. I finished the last of the chocolate and wished I had been bright enough to pack my portable shortwave radio. At least I could have had something to listen to while watching Dougie watch television and eat pretzels from a bag. Another loud grumble from my stomach, competing with the sound from the highway. Almost time to go home.

Almost. Up with the binoculars again. There was a seductive feeling here, of watching someone without him knowing it, but after a while that feeling was replaced by boredom. I yawned and looked up at the branches again, trying to see if there were any stars.

Nothing. Then the wind sighed past me, and a chunk of snow fell on my face.

After sputtering and wiping my face, I decided the wayward chunk of snow was a sign from someone, and I packed up and slowly walked back through the snow, wondering how Antarctic explorers could put up with this every day. My hands trembled as I unlocked the door, and I got in the Rover and let the engine and heater run for a few minutes before I began to feel warm again, before I started to feel human.

When I got back to Tyler, I stopped off at a Sunoco gas station near the center of town. As I pumped the gas I was shivering again, and I also knew that I would be in bed soon enough, comfortable and cozy and deliciously asleep. After paying the attendant I went back outside and a red Taurus drove up next to me, the window rolling down.

"Hey," came a male voice. "Lewis." I looked over, quite surprised. Fire Inspector Mike looking up at me from inside his personal car, out of uniform. I tried to keep a poker face, knowing what I did about his history and his opinions of businesspeople, but still, here he was.

I nodded over at him. "Hello, Mike. Pretty late to be up, isn't it?"

He shrugged. "Had some night business to catch up on. Hey, I've got some information to pass along. Interested?"

I came over closer to the car. "Arson information?"

A quick and friendly nod. "The same. Climb on in, I'll give you an update, and maybe you'll have something you can help with."

I looked longingly back at my Range Rover, which was to take me home, and then looked back at the expectant face of Mike and said, "Give me a minute just to move my wheels from the pumps."

When I was done, I climbed into the warm interior of' the Taurus. I snapped on the seatbelt and Mike drove out onto Route One and headed south. Traffic was light. The interior of the car was comfortable and had a pleasant scent of old tobacco and that new car smell. I undid my coat and checked the dashboard clock. Well past eleven p.m. A late night for me. I was hoping this would only take a few minutes. I really needed the sleep.

Mike turned right down Drakeside Road, and I was pushed back into my seat by the acceleration. He was moving fast.

"Hey, Mike," I said, trying to keep my tone light. "Slow it down some. You don't know where the cops might be hiding tonight."

He didn't look at me, but he shifted the car up into fifth. "Yes, but I do know. Here's a little secret. These small towns around here, after eleven o'clock, maybe there's one or two cruisers out here. That leaves a lot of open miles that you can pretty much do what you want on. And there are a lot of back roads out here in Wentworth County."

The road was empty, but it was a narrow country blacktop with high banks of snow. Farmhouses and the occasional trailers could be seen through the trees, the lights from the windows and porch lights illuminating the snow and ice around the buildings. Another sharp curve and there was the fierce squeal of the tires.

"Mike, this is ridiculous," I said. "Slow it down."

He glanced over at me. The look wasn't too friendly. "Looks like I'm the driver here, doesn't it?"

"I don't care. Slow it down or bring me back."

We went up a slight hill and crested, and the road tipped down and to the side. Mike downshifted and I could feel the rear wheels of the car sway as we hit a patch of ice, and I grabbed on to the door handle.

"Mike, that's it. Take me back."

He wasn't looking at me. "Thought you wanted to know more about the arsons."

"Right now I don't care. You're making—Jesus!"

I blurted that out just as we rounded another corner. A pickup truck was in front of us, moving at least twenty miles or so slower, and Mike swore and downshifted, and then passed the truck. There was a loud scrape and a banging noise as the car bounced off a snowbank. Another swerve and a screech of brakes and the blaring of horns behind us, and I was grabbing the door handle even tighter, my hand slippery with sweat.

He took a deep breath. "Well, I care about the arsons, probably more than you do. Here, listen to this."

"What?" I asked, and his hand went forward to punch out something on the dashboard. The volume was up loud, and the sound was filled through with static, but I could make out the voices just fine. A male and a female.

Her: "It was an insurance statement, from an outfit in Canterbury called Allied Health Services, for services rendered for Mike Ahern. And the dates of service were in that two-year gap, Lewis."

Him: "I suppose you've found out more about Allied Health Services?"

Her: "I have."

"So. What do you know?"

And Paula's voice, one more time: "They're a hospital, Lewis. A hospital for mental patients. And Mike Ahern was a patient there, right after he came back from the Gulf War."

The acceleration increased. I had both hands on the door handle. We screamed through another tight corner, and Mike spared me another quick look.

"Well?" he demanded.

I didn't say a word as we sped through the night.

20

As terrifying as it was, I was also admiring Mike's skills. He was adding at least twenty to thirty miles per hour to the speed limit, which is fine for dry pavement in the middle of a July day. Nearing midnight in January on roads that were neither well-plowed nor well-sanded, in the backlands of Wentworth County, keeping in control and keeping that level of speed going was an amazing feat of driving ability.

But I was still terrified. "Mike—"

"Hold on," he said, and he braked and downshifted as we went down another hill. Another patch of ice, and again, that sickening feeling in your gut when you realize you are about a foot or so away from an accident.

"How does it feel, Lewis?" he asked, furiously shifting gears. "How does it feel to be sitting beside a crazy man, hurtling through space like this? Pretty scary, right?"

Another corner, and I reflexively closed my eyes, and my right foot tamped at the phantom brake pedal, wondering just how good the seatbelt was. "Yeah, it's pretty scary. Look, no one's calling you crazy."

"Oh, but you were, you and that little snot reporter. Can't figure out what's going on so it must be the loony fire inspector. Right? It's not fun to pick on Vietnam vets anymore—most of them are getting too old. But us

Gulf vets, we're fair game. We're pretty fresh. So check out the loony vet, he must be burning Tyler Beach."

Thankfully, a relatively straight stretch of winter road. "We were looking at every possibility, Mike. That's all. We never thought of you as a loony vet."

"No, just an arsonist." He turned to me, his face mottled. "You have any idea how insulting that is, to have you two...you two civilians," and he made that word sound like an epithet, "think that I would put my brothers in danger? Do you? Do you have any concept of loyalty, of brotherhood, of taking care of one another. Of course not!"

The road deteriorated into a series of S-turns, and he flipped the steering wheel back and forth, speaking through each fierce motion. "No, you got a reporter who makes her living off misery and you got an ex-DoD weasel who's spent his entire life behind desk. You don't know what it's like to depend on your buddy for your goddamn life, whether it's in a burning building or in a desert with someone shooting at you."

Then he made a sharp corner and went down another side road. There were more homes here, more lights, and then we burst out into a small parking lot, into a shopping plaza that had about four or five stores, all of them closed. Mike made a wide looping turn and said in a quiet tone, "You might want to hang on."

"What—" and then we were spinning, heading for a snowbank, and I closed my eyes again and there was a *thump!* as we struck something, followed almost immediately by another solid sound as my head snapped to the side and struck the passenger window.

I WASN'T UNCONSCIOUS, just disorientated for a few moments. I blinked a few times and swallowed, and Mike was calmly smoking a cigarette. "Look there," he said, motioning with his hand. "I've got you butt-up against a snowbank." I saw he was right. He had slid the car into the snowbank, so my door was solid against the snow.

"Nice driving."

"Thanks. Learned how to do that when I was younger, racing up north on frozen lakes. Now. I put you in there for a reason. We're gonna chat. The only way you're getting out of this car is by talking to me. Nothing else will work. You can't get out that door, and the only way through my door is through me. Think you can do that?"

I rubbed my head. "No, but I might try, just for the hell of it. I don't appreciate the driving demo. One mistake could have put us into a tree instead of a snowbank."

"I wanted to get your attention."

"Good job. What are you going to do next, start tugging at my finger-nails? We could have talked anytime. I didn't need this macho demonstra-tion to do it."

Another puff of the cigarette. "Figured if I got your attention, might set a foundation for an interesting talk. About why you and your reporter friend think I'm burning down the beach."

I touched my head again. Still sore. "The hell with you, then. After that little drive, I owe you nothing."

He tapped the ash into an open ashtray. "Feel like another drive?"

"Go ahead. Unless you've got rope in your back pocket to tie me up, the minute you move away from this bank this door's open and I'm out, and after a couple of phone calls, I'm home and you're hearing from your chief about this little excursion."

A puff of the cigarette. "You're doing better than I thought. Anybody else would be blubbering and begging to be let out. You sure you've never served?"

"Never in any places you've heard of."

"All right, then, let's work something else out. Question to question. I'll answer anything you give me, and then you return the favor. How's that?"

My head was starting to feel better. "Sounds okay, under the circum-stances."

"Fine. Show you how agreeable I am, I'll let you have the first question."

I suppose I should have asked him the logical question, but my head was still a little fuzzy. "That taped conversation. How did you get it?"

His look was direct. "Through illegal means, which doesn't bother me. I got a nut out there, and some night, he's going to burn a hotel that's full of people. Our investigation is stuck. It's not going anywhere. But before we get to dozens of bodies in the snow from another hotel fire, I decided to bend a few things."

"Like surveillance," I said. "Shotgun mike, maybe? There were a couple of cars in the parking lot that day."

"Good guess," Mike said. "I've got a private investigator friend of mine, up in Concord. He owes me a couple of favors and he agreed to follow that Paula Quinn around. I wanted to see who she was talking to, what kind of leads she might be tracking down."

He tapped out a little more ash again. "My turn. You and that reporter come up with anything besides me?"

"No, nothing. She went pretty deep and couldn't find a single connection. No relations among the motel owners. Nobody shared a bank, law firm, or contractor."

"Except for me," he said, his tone fairly even.

"Except for you."

"How did I come up, then? Someone drop a dime on the nutty fire inspector?"

Except for a lonely pickup truck at the other side of the lot we were alone in the plaza. It looked like we were in Bretton, maybe East Warren.

"No," I said. "Something unusual, that's all. I saw in the planning board minutes how you spoke against the Crescent Hill, the Rocks Road Motel, SeaView, Tyler Tower Motel, and the Still Harbor Inn. All of them were up for some sort of planning board approval. You spoke out against all of them. They all burned down."

He was smiling. "Little hobby of mine, and I can't tell how much fun it is, pissing people off like that."

"But no fires, right?"

"Nope." He took a drag, the ember giving his face a ruddy glow. "Look, I do my job and I do it well, but I'm also a taxpayer. There's too much damn construction going on and pretty soon everyone in Tyler will be selling each other motel rooms or T-shirts. Hell of a way to run a town. So I do what I can. I go to these meetings and raise objections and nothing happens, but at least I can sleep at night."

"Still, it's a hell of a coincidence."

"Sure it is," Mike said. "And here's another amazing coincidence. Go back in the records even more. Like a year or two ago. This is nothing new. I speak out against all types of construction work, not just motels, and not just the past few months."

Ouch. Right then my head and ego were both aching, and it was hard to tell which one was more painful. "But there's got to be something there," I said. "What are the chances of all of those places coming before the planning board, and then burning down?"

"Pretty slim," he said, and his voice grew in frustration as he twisted the cigarette butt into the ashtray. "Damn it, we've looked at everything. Just like you did. Even looked into the planning board members' backgrounds, and I'll thank you in advance for keeping that bit of information confidential. But there's nothing there. Nothing."

He swore and said, "Let's get back to town," and he started up the engine, and we moved away from the snowbank. Mike drove through the parking lot until he came to the road, and then came to a complete stop. He looked both ways before making a right-hand turn and heading back to Tyler, a few miles under the posted speed limit.

Later I said to him, "There's more to what drives you, isn't there?"

"Hunh?"

"Your explanation of why you go to the meetings. You do talk about too much growth and protecting the town. But you also talked about big business, and how the board should stop cozying up to them. Hell, even at the Rocks Road Motel, you said something about 'screw 'em, that's why they got insurance.' So. What else is there?"

He was quiet for a moment. "Let's say I had a bad firsthand experience, then."

A thought. "The Gulf War?"

"The same," he said. "Remember how we talked earlier, how I said it was a learning experience? Man, the things I learned over there is stuff that's still with me." He spared me a glance. "You were in the puzzle palace back then, right?"

"Yes."

"What did you do?"

"Read and write."

"For who?"

Ah, that same question. "Can't say. Sorry."

He shrugged. "Not trying to pry. Just establishing that you were there. So tell me. Were we fighting for freedom, for democracy, for human rights?"

I looked out again at the lights. "No, we weren't."

"That's right. We weren't. We were fighting to keep the oil fields and oil lanes open, open to the people who were our friends. Maybe they're real sons of bitches, but they're our sons of bitches. And those oil fields were pumped and produced and refined and sold by businesses. You come right down to it, me and my buddies and everybody else out there, we weren't fighting for Old Glory, we were fighting for Old Boardrooms."

"Some people might say you're simplifying things," I said, knowing from my own times at my old job that there was sometimes more than just one answer. "Some people might say that keeping that oil flowing was in the national interest."

"Maybe so, but I don't particularly care about listening to what those people have to say, unless they were over there. That's probably not fair, but that's what counts."

"So what happened?"

He was silent for just a brief moment, and then he let the car slow down until we pulled over in a wide portion of the road. He switched on the hazard lights and Mike started to talk, and his words were low and intense and full of weight, and I knew why he had pulled off. He couldn't drive and tell the story at the same time.

"It was just near the end, when my unit got into Kuwait," he said, looking out the windshield. "The war was over, and we were still on edge. We had been stuck in that desert for months, training and preparing and just being terrified. A lot of crazy stories were being tossed around, about what we could expect. Remember?"

I remembered, all too well. "Sure. Bio and chemical warfare. Tens of thousands of allied casualties. Maybe even a wider war if Israel was brought in."

"Yeah," Mike said. "That's right. Then the air war started and I waited and then the Scuds started dropping in. Ever try to sleep at night with your chem suit at your feet, waiting for the alarm to sound? Ever get woken up with that damn air-raid siren howling at you? If there's a scarier sound that's been invented, that's guaranteed to make your hands shake and your bowels turn to soup, it's those damn sirens."

"You were in the military engineers?"

"That I was," he said. "Supposedly not front line troops, but with Scuds coming in every night, where was the front line? It was everywhere. Then we moved up when the ground war started, and in less than a week that part was done. But not for us."

"Oil wells, right?"

He took a deep breath. "Never in my life had I ever seen such utter and complete devastation. Not ever. I still have nightmares about it. It was like we were on a different planet. Just sand and dead things at your feet. Burned-out personnel carriers and Russian-made tanks. Some parts of the sand crusty with oil. And everywhere you looked, the oil wells on fire, like tremendous torches out of the ground, roaring and screaming. The sky just black, black, black, even at high noon. Some ways, it was worse than when we were back at Saudi, waiting for the Scuds to start dropping. It was hard to breathe and your eyes stung and your skin was filthy, and we had to work there."

"What kind of work?"

He still stared out at the winter landscape, though I knew in his mind's eye he was thousands of miles away, in a hot and destroyed land. "We shouldn't have been there. Man, we had done our tour and had put in our time. It was somebody else's turn. We were tired and beat and we weren't as sharp. The major shouldn't have pushed us, but there was a schedule to be met, a plan to be worked on." He turned and looked at me, his face troubled. "Don't you agree? We shouldn't have been there. We were tired."

I looked right at him. "You're absolutely right. You shouldn't have been there."

He wiped at his face and looked back through the windshield, voice a bit lower. "Good guys in our squads, all of us reservists. None of us had to be there. We were all volunteers. Patriots, maybe, if you can believe it. We were more than friends. You spend months in the desert with a bunch of guys, you become...brothers. I know that's a cliché, but it's true. Maybe we were patriots, maybe we were a little naive, being there and thinking we were fighting on the side of the good guys. But we also did our job, no matter how dirty and dangerous it was, no matter how stupid the orders."

He rubbed at his face. "I mean, what was the rush? The war was over. We had kicked some serious butt. But the word came down to start taking care of those oil wells. They had to be capped and put out. Looked bad on the evening news, and besides, we had to get those oil fields producing so our grateful sons of bitches could start making money again, both for our businesses and to pay us back for this little adventure. So we got to work, tired as we were, and the damn major kept on pushing us."

"You weren't doing the actual capping work, were you?"

"No, we were doing prep work. Besides the burning wells, everything else there, the support buildings and pumping mechanisms, had been sabotaged or booby-trapped. We had to clear the way, make the place safe for the goddamn businesses."

Another hand-wipe of his face, another brief pause.

"Mark Fletcher was from Northern California. Retired surfer, we called him. An old beach bum who said he loved sand, no matter what kind. Worked as one of those legal aid lawyers. We always teased him about being such a leftie and being a soldier at the same time. Contradiction in terms. And his buddy was Scott Flannery. A blue-collar guy, someplace in Kentucky. Ran a grocery store. Don't ask me how those two got to become such good friends. It just happened. Fletch and Flatch, we called them."

By now I was getting cold, but I dared not make a sound. "We had been working for twelve straight days, no break at all, couple of us went to the major, but the major wouldn't hear about it. There was a schedule to be met, goals to be reached. We had to keep going. End of the day, Fletch and Flatch, they were working at some small pump house, an idiot little place. But it had to be checked out, so in they went."

Mike cleared his throat, his voice wavering slightly. "It didn't even make much of a noise when it happened, like a little burp. We all looked back. The door of that shed flew open and Fletch came straight out, yelling, and then he stopped. Can you believe that, the man stopped. Here he was, a lawyer from California, wife and kids and everything ahead of him, and he stopped and went back in after Flatch. Just like that. Just like that."

We waited for a while, and I said quietly, "What happened after that, Mike?"

His voice didn't waver again. "The door blew open again and Fletch and Flatch come out, fire all around them. About a second or two after Fletch went back in. No time at all. They came out in flames and the heat was so strong, none of us could reach them. Seconds, seconds was all it took and they were on the ground, almost touching each other, like they knew they weren't going to make it and they were going to be together, right there...God, it was horrid...Ever see a man burn to death?"

A simple answer. "No."

"Ghastly, simply ghastly. The clothes go real quick and then the arms and legs draw up, like they were in an oven or something. Like maybe their body is remembering what it was like, back when it was a fetus. Skin cracks and pops and in a minute or two, what was a great guy, a buddy who stole your hot sauce and shared his socks, someone who lived and breathed next to you, had dreams and loved ones, this great guy is now a chunk of charcoal."

Another look over in my direction. "Two of the best guys I've ever known, guys who were there to watch out for my back, these guys were snuffed cause we had to keep those businesses going, and there was a schedule to meet. Do you understand now?"

"I do."

"So do I," he said, briefly touching the burn tissue on his head. "Every goddamn time I look in the mirror in the morning, I remember, and I'm always going to remember. So you can see why I don't often have fond thoughts of businesses."

He switched off the hazard lights and shifted the car into first and we were back on this snowy lane in New Hampshire, and he said, "When I came back I went back to Nashua, like nothing had happened. But the first time I went into a burning building, I freaked. I couldn't be there, couldn't bear the thought of seeing another buddy of mine get killed because some idiot landlord skimped on smoke detectors, or some sleaze business owner burned down his furniture store for the insurance money. That's why I ended up in the hospital, and when I got out, some of my friend in the fire service, well, they understood. Which is why I'm in Tyler."

I saw the lights of Tyler up ahead, and I thought of something and said, "Mike?"

"Yeah?"

"One question."

"Go ahead."

"The major," I said. "The major was a woman, right?"

"That she was," he said. "Major Grace Kimball, a nice enough woman under any circumstances, but who didn't belong on the battlefield. But diversity being such a brave and noble goal nowadays, quotas had to be met. You tell me if it's fair. One woman on the battlefield and two corpses. Hell of a quota, don't you think?"

I suppose I could have made the argument, but it was late and I was tired and my head ached. I said nothing more as he drove me into the Sunoco parking lot. The station was closed and the lights were off, and as I made to open the door Mike said, "You might want to check one thing."

"What's that?"

"You and your reporter friend might want to check the *Tyler Chronicle* issue the day after the third place burned down. The Tyler Tower Motel."

By now I was outside, looking back in. "What's there?"

"You're both so smart, I'm sure you'll figure it out. Thanks for a hell of an evening."

"You're welcome," I said, but I think he missed the sarcasm in my voice as I slammed the door and walked over to my Range Rover. For some reason—maybe it was the reflection from the streetlights—the grill and headlights seemed to be mocking me.

For good reason, no doubt.

21

When I had worked for the DoD we used to call them Mental Health Days, and the day after my wild night ride with Mike Ahern certainly met the threshold. At the DoD, those days usually came after budget time, or after we helped prepare some assistant SecDef for some congressional testimony, or after some crisis blew over that rarely made the papers. Mental Health Days meant coming in late and leaving early and catching up on paperwork or reading the Style section of the *Washington Post*.

For the civilian version, my Mental Health Day began after I got home and pulled the plug on my phones. I went straight to bed, and I slept late and woke up stiff and sore. After I got the papers from across the way I had a big breakfast, eggs and sausage and toast. I was very hungry, for last night's dinner had been snacks outside of Doug Miles's house, and dessert had been that ride with Mike Ahern.

As I cleaned the dishes, I remembered what he had said last night. I spent most of the morning reading on the couch, feet stretched out and with a couple of mugs of tea to keep me company. Just before noon I reconnected my phones and called Paula Quinn.

"You got any back issues of the *Chronicle* there?" I asked.

"You know we do," she said. "What are you looking for?"

"Something. I'm not sure what. Pull out the issue earlier this month, right after the Tyler Tower Motel burned down. The issue the day after the fire."

"Hold on."

There was a clunk as she put the receiver down. A minute or two passed and then there was a clatter as Paula picked up the receiver, and the rustle of newsprint.

"Okay, I've got it. What should I be looking for?"

A little too obvious, but let's give it a try. "Look for something on Mike Ahern."

"Hmm," she said. "All right."

A few more rustling noises. "Well, I'll be. There's a photo of some firefighters, taken down in Boston. Some guy was retiring and Mike was there, representing the state. Nice photo, he's all dolled up in his dress uniform. In fact, he looks like...Oh, shit."

Now I knew what he had meant. "He was in Boston, the night of the fire at the Tyler Tower, wasn't he?"

The faint rustle again, like dead leaves crushed in your hand, "Doesn't mean anything, Lewis. He could have set it up with a timer or something. Or maybe he was working with somebody. Or maybe we've got a copycat, and Mike is the real one. Or—"

"Or maybe we're wrong," I said. "That's as good an excuse as any. I had a chat with him last night. I don't like to say it, but my gut tells me that he's not involved."

She swore, using some choice words that I'm sure the Tyler Garden Club would be horrified to hear, and said, "Damn it, where in hell do we go from here, then?"

My head was still achy and my stomach was beginning to grumble. "Actually, I was thinking of lunch. You interested?"

A brief, oh-so-important pause. "No, can't do it," she said. "Maybe tomorrow?"

"Sure," I said, looking out at the gray waters of the Atlantic. "Maybe tomorrow."

Lunch was take-out scrod and during the afternoon I puttered around the house, taking a couple of aspirin for my head, cleaning up my office, and dumping some old computer files. I kept busy because I didn't want to think about Mike Ahern, fearful of going into a burning building, or of Kara Miles, terrified of shadows and the touch of a stranger, or of Paula Quinn, who was having lunch with a workmate who was admiring her smile and her laugh and the funny way her ears poked through her hair.

When I was all puttered out, I gave Felix a call and he started right into it. "Met an old friend of ours this morning," he said.

"Who was that?"

"Inspector Dunbar of Newburyport. He pulled me over right after I had spent a couple of hours at Doug's, looking at snow melting and seeing his car in the driveway."

"And what did the friendly police inspector have to say?"

"Not much, and it wasn't pleasant. He told me again about me being in the fair city of Newburyport, and also mentioned something about harassing the citizens therein."

"Interesting."

"Yeah. Makes me wonder if Doug and his oddball job have any connection with our nice policeman."

"Maybe so," I said. "Maybe it's Doug. Then again, maybe we've ticked off the neighbors by driving up and down their driveway without their permission."

"Could be. God knows I'm sick of being up there."

"Anything else happen? Did he just let you drive away?"

Felix laughed. "Funny you should say that, yeah, there was something else there. He had this little edge to him, you know? Kept on pushing me and pushing me, making little insinuations about my heritage and manhood. Trying to rattle my cage."

"Being provocative?"

"Yeah, that's the word," Felix said. "It's like he wanted me to lose my cool, maybe punch him out, so he'd have an excuse to haul me in. That's the feeling I got."

"So you acted nice and sweet?"

Another laugh. "Believe me, one thing I do know is how to be polite to cops when the time comes. I kissed butt so much that I got lint on my lips from his pants, and then he sent me on my way. So—your turn tonight keeping an eye on young Doug?"

I shifted the phone to another ear as I made my way to the kitchen to get a drink of water. "I suppose it is, and you know, Felix, I'm getting tired, too."

"You are? What do you have in mind?"

I was smiling in anticipation. "I think it's time Doug knows we're out there."

ANOTHER FIVE HOURS later I was back at my previous perch, better dressed and with better provisions, watching the lights from Doug's home. The minutes dragged on like before and I listened to my shortwave radio for a while before I got tired of the cheery voices from warm studios thousands of miles away. So I sat and stared and played little mental games to keep myself alert and to prevent me from nodding off.

I was on the third or fourth of my little mind adventures—trying to name every novel written by Robert Heinlein—when Doug opened the front door and stepped out. I raised my binoculars and my hands trembled with anticipation as I saw him enter his car. I leaped up and gathered my belongings, and by the time I was at the Rover I could make out the sound from his car as he backed down his driveway.

I tossed everything in, and after turning the key I steered down to the road. I braked a bit too quickly at the end and skidded out into the main road, but I still saw the brake lights of Doug's Dodge Colt, heading into Newburyport.

It only took a minute or so to catch up with him and soon we were on High Street, back toward the center of town. Traffic had built up and I let another car get between us. As we got into the city proper, a little twinge crept up my back as we passed Kara's apartment. Something was there with Doug, though I wasn't sure what. I just knew that the sculpture at his home didn't walk from Kara's place.

A couple of turns later and we were on the waterfront, going down Merrimack Street. In the center of the city it was all rebuilt brick and wooden buildings, with ice-cream shops and antique stores mixed in with restaurants. In another mile or so the rebuilt portion of the city dribbled away, and we were in a part of the town that looked like an older, shabbier brother of the downtown. There were apartment buildings and old stores, and a couple of marine shops, and small dark homes that were built new, maybe about two hundred years ago. A small brick building with a chain-link fence around it marked the Merrimack River Station of the U.S. Coast Guard. Off to the left was the wide expanse of the Merrimack River, and the lights of moored boats in the marinas, and on the far shore, the dimmer lights of Salisbury. Out beyond the mouth of the river, the breakwater and the waters of the Atlantic.

Up ahead, Doug's car braked and pulled into a parking lot, and I pulled ahead for a couple hundred feet before turning around and going back toward the lot, seeing him walk into a building. I slowed and found a space a few car lengths down from Doug's Colt.

On both sides of the parking lot were apartment buildings, and one building had a flickering neon sign that said ROOMS TO RENT. Across the street was a two-story building with peeling paint and a few torn-off shingles. The upstairs looked like apartments and the downstairs boasted a well-lit Budweiser sign, and underneath that, a smaller sign that said BRICK YARD PUB. Doug was out for a drink, that's all.

"Well," I said aloud. "Maybe we're getting a bit thirsty, too."

I stepped outside and nearly fell on my butt. The lot wasn't well-plowed, and there was no sand or salt on the ice-covered pavement. I walked across the street and went up to the pub, navigating my way across a snowbank. The windows were darkened, and I could make out the noise of some rock music from inside. I opened the door and the noise battered at my ears, and the smoke was thick, thick enough to almost make me gasp.

The lights were dim, and the place was filled with men and women who probably would be listed as "blue-collar" on some sociologist's check-off sheet. There was a square bar set in the center, and off to the right, a couple of pool tables. A jukebox was playing some old Rolling Stones tune. Other tables and chairs were scattered across the dirty wooden floor, and the blue haze of cigarette smoke dimmed the overhead lights. I unbuttoned my coat and made my way to the bar, where an older woman with a beehive hairdo and a cigarette dangling from her lips held court. She was joshing with some of the customers, and I worked my way onto a barstool. At first I thought she didn't see me, but she had great peripheral vision and slapped down a napkin at my elbow. She had on a pink polo shirt and ANGELA was stitched in a heavier pink thread.

I could just make out her voice and I guessed what she was asking me, and, keeping it simple, I ordered a Budweiser. It came a minute or two later in a long-necked bottle, and I tossed a five-dollar bill on the counter and looked around the pub, taking a casual sip from the beer.

Then I looked again, closer. Doug wasn't here.

WELL. I sipped from the beer and pretended to be waiting for someone, and then I ordered another beer when Angela was looking at me expectantly. No Doug. I had seen him come in and he wasn't at one of the tables or playing pool. I headed to the end of the bar, where there was an alcove that had a pay phone and two restrooms. At the rear of the alcove was another door. I tried the handle. It was locked.

"Hey!" I turned and there was a man at the alcove's entrance, holding a few cases of beer. He had on a black T-shirt and leather vest, and his beard and shoulder-length hair were black and streaked with gray.

"What are you doing back there?" he demanded. "That's off limits."

The muscles holding those cases of beer looked pretty impressive, and I gave him my friendliest, slightly sloppy drunk smile. "Sorry," I said. "I gotta take a leak and the men's room smelled something awful. Thought there might be another toilet back here."

He just stared. "Then go piss in the snow. That's for employees only."

I shrugged and went past him, and I could tell his eyes were with me every step back to the bar. I retrieved my stool and took a swig from the bottle, and then the guy came back and came over and whispered something to Angela, who then stared at me and went back to work, wiping some glasses dry and hanging them overhead. Damn. Made so quickly. Maybe it was time to go home. I took a smaller sip and then saw Doug come out of the alcove, followed by two other guys.

Maybe not.

The three sat down at a comer table, and in a quick moment Angela was over there, placing down two mixed drinks and a bottle of beer on the table. She walked away without the usual tussle of payment or tips. Interesting. Very quick service for some very special customers, it looked like. Doug was sitting with his back to the rear wall, talking animatedly to his co-drinkers who flanked him. They looked like they came out of Central Casting: jeans, work boots, beards, and leather winter coats. They laughed a lot and seemed to defer to Doug, which struck me as odd, based on what I knew of him.

I made eye contact with Angela, and she took my empty and she shook her head.

"Excuse me?" I said, raising my voice to be heard over the music. Another Rolling Stones tune, though I wouldn't have thought this crowd was into classic rock.

She leaned over the bar, her voice raspy. "Sorry, pal. You're cut off. No more."

"I'm what?" I asked. "I've only had two."

She motioned with her thumb to the rear of the bar, where my earlier friend was walking over with another load of beer cases. "You got a problem, you want to talk to Harry over there. Or do you just want to go home?"

Message received, loud and clear. I got up and said, "You know what they say."

"What's that?" she asked, her face not friendly at all.

"Home," I said. "There's no place like it."

I guess she missed the subtle humor, because she stalked her way back to the other end of the bar. As I got my coat I looked over to the corner and saw Doug staring right at me. I smiled and gave him a little kid's wave, complete with fluttering fingers. His two companions were sitting up straight, looking over at him and then looking over at me. For a moment I thought of going over to talk, but a little part of me that's called common sense went into general quarters. I was in a strange place with no friends, no back-up, and no weapons. The staff of the Brick Yard Pub were already not too friendly, and going up and getting in the faces of Doug and his two burly friends made about as much sense as trying to sell Malcolm X T-shirts at an Aryan Nation rally.

So instead I blew Doug a kiss. He scowled and whispered something to one of his buddies. I headed for the door before Doug or his friends could catch up with me. Outside, the night air quickly cleared my head, and as I walked to the parking lot, I thought about what had just happened. Old Doug Miles, instead of being the jumpy loser that Felix and I had determined, actually had some pull. He was somebody, at least in this pub. He had respect and he had friends, and I wanted to know more. The curse of a curious mind, I suppose. I wanted to know why he was there and who his friends were, and what might have happened to Kara Miles because of what Doug was doing,

I was also aware of a couple of other things. My clothes reeked of cigarette smoke and I was quite hungry.

FIRST THINGS FIRST. Time to eat. I drove past my home and went into North Tyler for another hundred yards before stopping at the side of the road at a little restaurant called Sally's Clam Shack, built right on the beach. Sally's been dead for some years, but her two sons have kept the place going ever since. In the summertime they hire a dozen or so high school students, and their parking lot was always full. In the winter it's only the two brothers— Neil and Patrick—who keep the place going, along with another relative or two. All they do is take-out seafood and other fried delights, and they keep going in the winter because of a small contingent of loyal customers who keep enough money flowing in to make it worthwhile.

On this night the three spaces in the plowed-out lot were full so I parked against a snowbank, just barely off the road. The oldest brother, Neil, gave me a shout as I walked in. There was loud country music playing and the clattering sound of food being prepared. Most of the restaurant is closed off and there's a waiting area with folding chairs and menus to look at while waiting. Neil, who is about my age but who has wrists the size of telephone poles, took my order (fried shrimp and fried onion rings—sorry, no dieting tonight) and whispered to me, "It'll be right up."

I looked over at the half-dozen customers waiting for their orders and said, "Neil, you don't have to."

He waved a hand in the general direction of the far wall and said, "Hey, don't worry. It's our business, so to hell with them."

I gave up and leaned up against the wall. All of the chairs were taken. Near my head was something that always embarrassed me when I saw it.

Last year one of my columns had mentioned the old traditional family restaurants of the New Hampshire seacoast, and I had listed about a dozen. Sally's Clam Shack was one of those, and for the reaction I got from Neil and Patrick, you'd have thought that *Shoreline* had made them the cover story. They made me autograph a copy of the column and it was now framed—with their four sentences of fame highlighted in yellow—and hanging on the wall.

In a couple of minutes I was leaving the Clam Shack with a promise to come back real soon, now, carrying my quite deadly dinner in one hand, the smells making my stomach grumble. In the still night air steam was rising up from the bag, and it was when I reached the Rover that I heard the car approach.

I turned. It was a four-door sedan, coming up on the road, moving pretty quickly, with all of its windows down and—

I tossed the food down and threw myself on the ground, rolling underneath the Range Rover as the first shots came bursting out. The gunfire was loud and raucous and hurt my ears as I scrambled my way underneath, snow and ice and metal undercarriage scraping and pulling at me. I made it through as the gunfire continued, the sound of the exploding rounds impossibly loud, almost drowning out the metallic *pangs* and *pings* as the slugs ripped through the aluminum body of my four-wheeler.

I clambered through to the other side, knowing if I stayed under the Rover, I'd make a damn perfect target for anyone bothering to stoop over. I got on my hands and knees and moved through the ice and snow, propelling myself up and over the snowbank, causing another round of fire to come racing my way. In movies and television, the hero always manages to look back and memorize the faces of his attempted killers, the make of their car, and the license plate.

This particular hero rolled down the other side of the snowbank and yelled when his knee popped against a rock. I got up and moved farther down the snow-covered boulders that edge up against the ocean. I crouched behind a large rock and then spared another quick glance. There were two or three figures up at the snowbank, all carrying something in their hands that certainly weren't snow shovels. The beam of a flashlight came down and I crouched again, breathing heavily, snow melting down the back of my neck, my throat dry and raspy. Some raised voices up on the crest of the bank, and then came the slamming sound of car door and the squeal of tires.

They were gone. I was alone.

Alive, but cold, wet, hungry, and terrified.

ALTHOUGH MY COMMON sense told me in a casual voice that the men in the car were probably miles away by now, my not-so common sense was screaming at me to stay low. So I stayed among the snow- and ice-covered rocks, slipping and sliding my way south, making my way back to Tyler Beach. I suppose I should have been thinking great thoughts about what had just happened, wondering if Doug had the capacity to order a hit on me less than a half-hour after I had shown up at his favorite pub, but instead I focused on the matter at hand. Which, no pun intended, included my two very cold hands. Back in my vehicle—and I refused to think of how bullet-ridden it must be—were a pair of heavy gloves and a wool hat, all three of which I could have been using with great enthusiasm. My hands were numb and I tried to walk with them stuffed inside my coat, but I was slipping and sliding so much that I had to use them for balance. A couple of times I jammed them against the cold and harsh stone as I tried not to fall.

Once I didn't succeed. I slipped on a chunk of ice and tumbled down another set of rocks, and ended up knee-deep in the water. I yelped from the cold and slogged my way out onto the shore, shivering, my teeth beginning to chatter. The wind was cutting through me, and I reached down to touch my bruised knee, and winced at the torn fabric and the sticky feeling from the blood oozing out. I rested for a couple of minutes, sitting on the rocks, hunched over with my coat collar turned up and my aching hands buried in my pockets. I looked up at the stars and the elegant figure of Orion, the hunter, almost mocking me here on the ground. Some mighty hunter I was. I tease and poke at my prey, and then turn my back and damn near get my head torn off in the process.

The wind seemed to increase some and I was shivering all over, my knees trembling from the cold. I was sure that I was starting to slip into shock as my body temperature began to plummet. I looked up at the stars and saw the faint lights of Tyler Beach, and I made my way again over the rocks and stones.

"Damn it, Sally," I whispered. "Why in hell didn't you build your goddamn shack at North Tyler Beach? At least it's just sand there.

I tripped again and fell on the snow and rocks, and there was no answer from Sally's ghost or anyone else. Just the wind and waves and the damnable cold.

The way was slow going, tripping and falling and sliding, my teeth chattering. I saw the bulk of land ahead of me that jutted out to the ocean and marked the promontory of Samson Point. At night and in the silence of the state park, there were no lights. I stood for only a moment, taking stock of the situation. I could stay along the shoreline and hug the coast and be perfectly safe, but I knew that the cold would make me lie down and fall into that deadly grip of exposure.

The best route would be to get out to Atlantic Avenue, and to a warm building and a phone, and that meant cutting across the grounds of the park. There were no streetlights or lampposts here at night—just the quiet trees and the silent concrete bunkers, and out near the road, the parking lot and park buildings. Everything would be cold and snow-covered, but as I clambered up over the hills and onto the land of the Samson Point State Wildlife Preserve, I was gambling on something.

I finally stood on snow-covered land, breathing hard, my numb and shaking hands stuck into the soaking-wet pockets. I looked around and started walking, getting knee-deep in snow. The faint starlight made everything glow with an eerie light, and then I stumbled across another bank of snow and allowed myself to relax, if only for a moment.

Before me was a trail leading into the woods. A cross-country ski trail. And all of the trails led back to the parking lot. I jumped up and down a few times to get the blood moving in my lower legs and then I started jogging across the hard-packed snow. My throat was burning with thirst and my teeth were still chattering, and I was sure that with each step I was destroying the carefully groomed ski trails, but if the skiers were to complain, they would have talk to me tomorrow.

. . .

IT SEEMED like hours had passed, but I was back on Atlantic Avenue, seeing the lights of the Lafayette House. I stood in the shadow of a closed-up cottage and looked across the way. No four-door sedan. No mysterious grouping of men huddling around the entrance. Nothing. I turned and looked longingly in the direction of the hotel's parking lot, which led to my house, but I knew I wasn't going home alone tonight. Not in a single moment.

I scampered across the street, the relief at seeing the lights of the Lafayette House almost warming me. I went up the front stairs and a well-dressed couple coming out looked at me and looked at me again in horror. I'm sure I presented a wonderful sight, and I'm also sure that there'd be stories told later, about the winter vacation at Tyler Beach and the drunken, wet bum who stumbled into the lobby.

Inside, I began rubbing my hands in the warm air and unbuttoned my coat. I went over to the left, near the gift shop, where there was a pay phone. A portly man in his fifties, wearing khaki slacks and a monogrammed lime-green sweater, was on the phone talking loudly to someone named Albert. Along the walls here were polished insets of marble, and I felt queasy, staring at my reflection. My face was puffy and scraped, and my hair was matted down. Everything I had on was soaked, and I looked down at my pants legs and winced at the bloody knee. My hands were red and scraped raw, and I looked over at the man on the phone and just stared. I stepped closer, close enough to smell his cologne, and I continued to stare, unblinkingly.

He looked over at me. "Is there a problem?"

I said nothing. I continued to stare, and I continued to drip onto the expensive carpeting in the lobby.

"Um, gotta go," the man said, and he hung up the phone and walked away, muttering something about the lack of respect shown to paying guests.

I got to the phone and started to dial. I had to dial three times for my swollen fingers kept on slipping off the keypad. The phone rang twice and was picked up, and then I was suddenly tired, and I had to rest my head against the cool marble, tears trickling down my cheeks.

"Yes?" came the voice.

"Felix?"

"Lewis, is that you? Do you know what time it is?"

I took a deep breath and looked around at the comfort and warmth and good taste of this lobby, about a couple of hundred yards away from a place where I had almost been shot down.

"Lewis?" he said, his voice sharp and quizzical.

"Felix," I said, my throat still aching. "Felix, I am in a world of hurt."

His voice snapped down one level. "Where are you?"

"Lobby of the Lafayette House."

"You hurt bad?"

"Bumps, scrapes, and bruises. Plus I'm freezing to death."

"Someone out there looking for you?"

"Several someones, all of them armed, in a car."

His quick voice warmed me. "Stay there, right in public. Don't go anywhere. I'll be there right away."

Then he hung up.

I closed my eyes again, not caring who was watching me as I leaned against the marble, breathing in ragged gasps, just waiting and shivering.

22

I kept peeking out of the main doorway, ignoring the guests staring at me, until Felix came by about ten minutes later. He drove up to the entrance and I stumbled my way outside, knees and legs aching. Inside, the car was warm, with a faint smell of leather and cologne and Felix looked over, one hand on the steering wheel, his other holding his automatic pistol.

"Where do you want to go?" he said.

"Home."

"Not wise," he said.

"I don't care if it is or isn't," I said. "That's where I want to go."

He shrugged. "All right, it's your call." He made the short drive over to the parking lot. "By the way, you look like hell. Mind telling me what happened?"

"Not at all, but later. I've got to get out of these clothes."

"Fine."

He pulled into an empty spot and I joined him outside. I shivered, cold again and losing that wonderful warmed-up feeling. Felix went to the rear of his Mercedes and opened the trunk, removing a long, brown-zippered bag, which he unzipped. A twelve-gauge shotgun slid out and Felix handed his automatic pistol over to me.

"You know what the bad guys were driving?"

"Four-door sedan. Couldn't tell you make or model. Too dark and too scary."

He slammed down the trunk. "They usually are. Is it here in the lot?"

I looked around. These cars were either too new or too foreign to hold the guys that had ambushed me, and I told Felix that. He said, "Fine. Let's get you home."

I suppose I should have been frightened, walking down to my house at night after such a horrible event. My mind should have been creating ambush sites and guns and bad guys by the dozens in the shadows among the rocks and few trees near my home, but I felt oddly at ease. I was now armed and at my side was Felix, and the casual yet sharp way he walked with the shotgun in his hands helped make the racing noise in my ears slow down.

At the house some lights were on. "Anyone supposed to be here?" Felix asked.

"No. I've got the lights set on a timer."

"All right," he said. "You stand right here and I'll make a quick circle around, see if there's anybody inside."

He walked to the house and I stood there in the cold, listening to the waves, his weapon heavy in my hands, and then he was back. "Looks fine. Ready to go in?"

"Ready for that and a hot shower and clean clothes," I said.

"I'm sure you are, but let's make sure you don't get shot in the process. Tell you how it's going to be done. You snap open the door and I'm in, covering the left side of the first floor. You come in after me, keep watch toward the kitchen. Then I'll go upstairs first and you come along, and then a quick cellar check and we should be fine."

"Let's do it," I said, and that's what we did.

Watching Felix at work can either be disturbing or enlightening and this night it was the latter. It was like watching a Cy Young pitcher close out the ninth inning with three strikeouts, or a star quarterback march his team downfield with two minutes to spare, to seize the winning touchdown. He's that good. He moved through my house with quick, sharp, and economical moves, and in a fistful of minutes we were back on the first floor.

"You intend to spend the night here?"

"Yes." I noticed that my hands were beginning to shake.

"Again, not too smart. You should—"

"Stop with the lectures, will you? I'm not letting those creatures chase me from my home. Not tonight and not ever."

Felix stared at me. "All right, I need to make a phone call."

"Go ahead."

He picked up my phone and dialed, and when his call answered, Felix said, "Manny? Felix here. I've got a job." A pause. "Like right now, Manny. Security detail. A home on Atlantic Avenue on Tyler Beach, across the way from the Lafayette House."

He looked at me, raised his eyebrows. "Payment will be fair, you know that. Thing is, I need the house sealed. You got it? No one comes within fifty yards."

Another pause, and Felix put his hand over the phone. "Think the Lafayette House will mind a van parked in their lot?"

"No, I don't think so."

Felix returned to the phone and said, "You can set someone up in the parking lot, have them keep watch. Manny, make sure they're pros, okay? All right then, I'll—"

"Hold it," I said.

Felix looked up. "What's up?"

"I need something else done."

"What's that?"

My throat clenched up again, and damn, my hands were still shaking. "Need something cleaned up. North of here, by Sally's place, my Rover is parked. Felix, it's pretty well shot up. I don't want a state trooper or North Tyler cop poking around."

He nodded slowly. "Sorry to hear that." Back to the phone "Your lucky night, Manny. I need a tow job, too. Part of a clean-up. A dark green Range Rover's parked up on Atlantic Avenue by North Tyler, near Sally's Clam Shack. Get rid of it and store it somewhere."

I could make out the voice on the other end of the line. "Of course it's got to be towed, you idiot, it's full of bullet holes. Call me at this number..." and he gave Manny my home number, "when you've got everything set up."

Felix hung up and said, "You want to tell me what happened tonight?"

"Yes, but after a shower and some dry clothes."

His nose wrinkled a bit. "Thanks. I think that's for the best."

I managed a smile. "You're so gallant, Tinios, it makes my heart sing."

He said something not very gallant in return, and I made my way upstairs.

AFTER CLEANING up in the bathroom I started working on my knee. As I dug through the medicine cabinet, Felix's 9mm pistol was on the counter. My knee injuries were mostly scrapes, with one deep cut that was taken care of by a gauze bandage and some tape, and I when left the bathroom I got the willies again about what had happened, remembering the gut-clenching sound of weapons being fired at me, hearing the metal-jacketed rounds that were meant for my flesh go tearing through my Rover, and then I was on my knees. I threw up in a series of painful spasms, my gut twisting at nothing there, only bringing up bile, and my sore knee on the tile floor made the pain that much more exquisite. I washed up with some with cold water, got into my bedroom, and got dressed. In the top drawer of my oak dresser I retrieved my own 9mm Beretta, and I went downstairs and handed over Felix's piece.

"Thanks for the loaner."

"You're welcome. How about a beer?"

"After tonight, I'd brew you a beer if I knew how to do such a damn thing."

I got Felix a Molson Golden and poured myself some ice water, and as he sat on the couch with the shotgun across his lap and I sat with my Beretta, I told him about my trip south and my encounter with Doug and his friends at the Brick Yard Pub, and about the take-out meal on the ground that was probably now being picked over by seagulls.

Felix said, "Lewis, it looks like you have mightily pissed somebody off."

"I would guess you're right. I didn't think Doug was that much of anybody. But less than an hour after I was rattling his cage, there's a car full of goons waiting for me in North Tyler, waiting to cut me to pieces."

"Don't think it was just Doug. It might be his boss or a worker. Look, ever since I moved here, I've focused my attention on points north, like here and Maine. Too many people are fighting over the turf down south. Hell, I probably don't know half the players on the North Shore. But I do know this. That pub is a neutral place where deals get struck and agreements are made. You going in there and stirring the pot had to trigger a response. Only surprise is, that was one hell of a quick reaction."

"Someone with a temper, or someone who moves fast." The water tasted cold and sweet indeed, and my stomach rumbled hunger.

"Or both. Question is, what's next?"

"I suppose a good night's sleep and a hearty breakfast is what you mean."

"No, it's not. Question is, are you going to tell Diane about your little misadventure tonight, or are you—"

Just then, the phone rang. Felix picked up the receiver and said, "Yeah, Manny, it's about—Oh."

Felix had a strained look on his face as he handed it over to me. "It's for you."

I'm sure my face was full of questions, but I took the phone and said, "Yes?"

"Lewis Cole?" came a male voice I didn't recognize.

"The same."

"Sorry to hear about your misadventure in North Tyler tonight," the quiet and polite voice said. "Would you care to talk about it?"

Felix was staring at me, and I was staring right back. "I would love to," I said.

I scooted over to the couch and sat next to Felix, and I moved the phone receiver away a bit so he could make out both ends of the conversation. "Who is this?" I asked.

A bit of a laugh. "Please, Mr. Cole. You really weren't expecting an answer, were you?"

"One can always hope."

"Maybe so, but not tonight. There are things to discuss. Shall I start?"

"Go right ahead."

"About the...activity up in North Tyler," he said. "Were you injured at all?"

"A bump or two, but I'll survive," I said. "Were those...gentlemen who came to me in North Tyler, are they in your hire?"

Quiet on the other end for a moment. "On some nights they are. Tonight, they were working a little freelance. Something that I didn't sanction."

"Is that supposed to make me feel better?"

"I don't know what will make you feel better, Mr. Cole. I do know we must settle something before it gets too complicated. You're looking for someone, correct?"

Felix looked at me and I looked back and shrugged, "I am. How do you know?"

"I know you are looking for the man who raped a friend of yours. One Kara Miles of High Street. Would you be interested in knowing that I am aware of this man?"

I leaned forward, forcing Felix to keep up with me. "I would be very interested."

"Very good," the same voice said. "The fact that I know who you're looking for and why, that should be adequate enough to prove my bona fides, would it not?"

"You're doing pretty well so far," I said. "So what was the point of the gunplay earlier on, or is that something else you're not prepared to discuss?"

"Oh, it was nothing out of the ordinary," he said. "I'll explain, if you don't mind."

"I haven't said no yet, now, have I?"

Another laugh. I decided he was a bit too affected and pompous, and wondered how he'd feel if someone shot up his car. "Yes, you've been quite agreeable. Listen, there are business negotiations going on here in the North Shore that are nearing completion between two, um, rival groups. Nothing too fancy, nothing large enough to merit interest for the news media or most cops. They're too busy sniffing around Boston."

Felix made a face and I said, "Go on."

"These negotiations are almost completed, and when they are

completed, a number of people are going to get very wealthy, very quickly. So you can see there is a lot of interest from many people in these parts that these agreements conclude without a hitch."

"I've been called many things before, but never a hitch."

"Well, there you are. One group has a primitive young man who has a taste for...for the kind of thing that happened to your friend. Sometimes he acts alone and other times, like with Miss Miles, he has assistance. This man, unfortunately, has connection and is important to the members of his group. The incident—"

"Rape, you mean," I said, finally tiring of his smooth patter.

"Yes, rape," he agreed, without missing a beat. "That man's action would have made no difference to the final outcome of the deal. If you excuse the expression, these things do happen. But then you came along, Mr. Cole."

Felix nodded and I understood, as well. "Asking questions and poking my nose in, and getting people nervous."

"Exactly. So tonight someone's patience limit was reached, and you were paid a visit. Quite stupid on their part, for I'm sure you know what happens next."

"Two things," I said. "Either I go to the cops or I come back with some friends of my own, with some equivalent firepower."

"So true."

"And the deal or whatever the hell you're doing is in jeopardy."

A deep breath from the other side of the phone. "Again, you are quite right. So after I found out what happened, I decided to make this little call and make you an offer."

I looked over at Felix, who had a very studious look on his face. "An offer I'm sure I won't be able to refuse, right?"

A slight laugh. "An offer I think you'll find attractive. Sometime this week, I'll turn over this man to you. No questions asked. In return, you stay out of Massachusetts for the rest of the month. Stop asking questions, stop following people, stop showing up in public drinking facilities where you're not welcome."

"That sounds pretty generous," I said. "Why don't you give me his name and address right now, and we'll call it even. No need for a formal exchange."

I could still make out the nameless man's measured breathing. "But a formal exchange will serve a purpose. I want the word to get out to his colleagues that nothing will threaten this arrangement. Nothing. A public turnover will do just that."

"And when and how do you propose to do this?"

A faint rustle of papers. Checking his schedule, perhaps?

"Day after tomorrow. Eight p.m. At the old airport outside of Newburyport, the far south hangar. I'll be there, along with the man you want. You and whomever can show up and take him away, and whatever you do then is up to you. I don't care. Just stay out of my state for the rest of the month."

My stomach was still doing dips and wheels and I swallowed a few times from the excessive saliva, and I said, "This man we've been discussing. Does he have a taste for knives, and did he visit Kara's landlord not so long ago?"

A longer pause, and the voice, maybe not as sure, said, "I believe so, though I don't have direct evidence. It sounds logical, although, does it not? In either event, he's yours for the asking, and I'll be showing up in two days."

"Sounds too good to be true."

"I don't care how it sounds. I do care if we have a deal. Do we?"

Felix nodded vigorously and I said, "All right, then. We have an agreement. One rapist in exchange for me staying home and away from your charming home state."

"Good," said the voice, "See you then." And then he hung up.

I replaced my own receiver and looked up at Felix and said, "It's a trap, isn't it?"

"About as blatant a one as I've ever seen."

"They think I'm that stupid?"

"Maybe they think you're that desperate."

I jumped about a half-mile when the phone rang again, and I answered and a quiet, meek voice said, "Felix?"

"Hold on," and I passed it over and he smiled and said, "All set, Manny? Pickets set up? Rover towed away? Well, hell, I told you it got shot up. Not my fault you have to cover it with a tarp. I'll check with you tomorrow."

Felix hung up and we sat there, then I got up, made a fire, went into the kitchen, and got another Molson for Felix and a tall glass of water and a bag of saltine crackers for myself. I was tired and hungry and sore, but the fire felt nice and I liked having Felix in my house and his associates outside.

Felix drank from his beer and I tried to quiet the trembling tension in my gut, and I said, "So it's a trap. Do we ignore it, or do we go in, knowing it's a trap?"

"We ignore it, it's not going away."

"So we go in."

He cocked an eyebrow. "Not what I said. It's up to you, my friend, since you're paying the freight on this little adventure. I was just pointing out the options, as miserable as they may be."

"I know what you're doing, and I also meant what I said. We go in."

Another eyebrow movement. "Diane might be ticked off with what you're doing."

"Diane has asked me to do something. That's what I'm going to do, and I don't think I can accomplish it by going to her or any other cops."

"Fair enough," Felix said, finishing off his beer. "And here's another thing you're going to do. You're going upstairs and you're going to bed."

I almost laughed. "You really expect me to sleep?"

"Maybe, and you won't know until you try. Look, you're upstairs and the downstairs will be locked. Someone gets in the house, he's gonna have to go by Manny and his friends. Manny may not be too bright but he's a good subcontractor; he does his job. So. Even if they do get by Manny, they'll have to get by me. And if they get by both of us, then I hope to hell you're awake, 'cause there'll be a hell of a noise. All right?"

"All right," I said, and I went to the kitchen and put away the empty beer bottle, and then I went upstairs for spare sheets and blankets. Back downstairs, the fold-out couch was undone and most of the lights were turned off. Felix stood by the couch for a moment, after having taken off his sweater and shirt. His upper body was tanned and well-muscled, with ridges and pockmarks of scar tissue nestled among the fine black hairs. His clothes were in one hand and his pistol was in another.

He turned to me and said, "First time I've ever spent the night here."

"First time for everything, as they say."

"Maybe so." He looked around the downstairs, at the oriental rugs, bookshelves, and furniture, and out the glass doors to the deck, out to the faint lights on the ocean. "Now I think I know why you came back here tonight."

"It's my home," I said.

He looked out again. "No, more than that."

"Oh?"

He turned to me, a reflective look on his face, a look I wouldn't normally associate with Felix Tinios. "You came back here to heal, didn't you?"

I tossed him a pillow. "You must be tired, to be so philosophical. Good night, Felix."

"Night, Lewis."

UPSTAIRS I DRAGGED out the twelve-gauge Remington shotgun that I keep on a foam-rubber mattress underneath my bed and placed my 9 mm Beretta next to it, both weapons now within easy grabbing reach. I huddled among the cool sheets and blankets, listening to the wind and the waves, and also hearing those awful tearing sounds of metal ripping through metal, the sharp reports of the gunfire, and then I also began feeling the cold and the wet again as I ran along the icy rocks of the shoreline. Another shiver, and I hugged myself in a ball, and tried to will myself to sleep. I thought of Felix downstairs and the heavy locks on the front door, and the mysterious Manny, keeping an eye on things outside. I thought and tried to distance myself from what had happened outside Sally's Clam Shack, and I must have succeeded, for eventually I fell asleep.

IN THE MORNING I woke to the smells of something cooking, and after getting dressed, I limped downstairs to the kitchen, my joints aching, especially my knee. Felix was there at my stove, wearing jeans and a white T-shirt, with a holster and pistol hanging from his shoulders. There was the smell of coffee, and I sat down, unaccustomed to the sight of Felix cooking breakfast in my own home.

"Figured this would get you up, if nothing else," Felix said, pouring me a cup of coffee. "Bacon and cheddar cheese omelet sound all right to you?"

"Sounds perfect," I said. "How did you sleep?"

He winked. "Slept well. Trick is to convince your mind that everything is just fine. You keep on telling your brain that everything is fine, that there's nothing to worry about, and next thing you know, you're dreaming. How about you?"

"My brain is a bit more stubborn," I said, reaching over to retrieve a breakfast plate. "I slept all right, but not deeply. Kept waiting to hear something blow up."

"Don't we all."

I took a bite of the omelet, savoring the taste of the eggs, bacon, and cheese, and feeling my stomach grumble with pleasure. It had been a long time between meals. I turned and saw that he had put the couch back to its proper position, and that the bedsheets and blankets were carefully folded. All that and breakfast, too. Felix was becoming the perfect houseguest, if one could overlook his means of employment.

I certainly could, and I continued eating.

"Today," he said, wiping down the counter, "I'm going to do some recon work. Want to see the scope of the land, try to figure out how we're going to avoid the trap at the airport. I'll give you a call later, and I suggest you keep the next day pretty free."

"Then what?"

"Then we talk, and then we go in. If it all works out, which is a possibility, then you'll have a nice package for Diane. If not, well, we'll see what else we learn. At least we know we're dealing with the right people. But there's one important matter."

"What's that?"

He rinsed off the washcloth. "That courier job is coming right up soon. I can join you on this meet, but everything else for a week or two, you're on your own. Remember that, in case you decide there are places we need to go. I'm not going to be around."

"Any idea when you'll be back?"

"Depends," he said. "I'll let you know."

I said that was fine, and after washing my own dishes I walked him out to the front door. Felix stepped out onto the shoveled path and looked over at me.

"You were pretty lucky last night," he said.

"I sure was."

He smiled. "Let's just hope your lucky streak keeps on going, all right?"

"With you in my hire, how could anything else happen?" He waved and started walking, and I was going to thank him again for what he did, and then he was far enough along the path so that I decided not to. I closed the door, knowing that he knew, knowing that Felix always knew, and that was good enough.

LATER IN THE MORNING, I was cleaning my 8mm FN assault rifle and securing the cartridges I needed for it when the phone rang.

"Mr. Cole?" came the voice, and it was not my friend from last night.

"Yes?"

"Mr. Cole, this is Manny, up here in the parking lot, the guy that Felix hired?" he said, his voice rising. "There's a woman here who wants to see you."

"Is she a cop?" I asked.

"Nope," he said. "Just a cute little thing, no weapon on her at all. You want I should send her down?"

"Sure," I said, hanging up the phone, conscious that my house smelled of both bacon and gun oil. A not-unpleasant combination. I tidied up some, throwing newspapers and magazines into a reasonable pile, and when someone started knocking at my door. I walked over, wondering what news Paula Quinn might have for me. I opened the door and froze, the brilliant midmorning sunlight hurting my eyes.

"Well?" she asked. "Are you going to let me in?"

"Sure," I said, and I stepped aside as Kara Miles came into my home.

23

Kara came in and sat down on my couch, unbuttoning her short leather jacket and taking off a pair of black gloves. She looked good, with only a slight discoloration on her cheek and a puffy lower lip to mark what had happened to her in the outside world.

I made the usual offers of a befuddled host, and in a few minutes we were sipping tall glasses of orange juice. Kara smiled and looked around. "It's been a while since I've been here. Still such a beautiful place. You know, Diane once told me that if she were single and hetero, she'd be moving in here so quick it would make your head spin."

"Really?" I said. "Would I be allowed to live here?"

"Probably, but don't ask me if you'd be her lover or her roommate."

We both laughed, and after some forced discussion on the weather and the last big storm we had, she put the glass down on the coffee table and looked up, her face somber. I couldn't begin to imagine how different she was, and how she had changed in these past days. A shattered shell is damn hard to put back together again.

"I want to start by saying two things, okay?"

"Go right ahead."

"The last time we talked was awful. I know you're just trying to help. I was—"

I raised a hand. "Kara, please. You don't have to say a thing."

A firm nod. "Yes, I do. It wasn't right and I've felt bad. You were just trying to help us and you didn't deserve to get a flamethrower in the face. So I'm sorry."

"It's okay."

She sighed and crossed her arms. "That was the easy part. Here comes topic number two. Please stop."

No need to ask what she wanted me to stop. "I'm not sure I can do that."

"Yes, you can," she said. "Just go back to Diane and tell her that you're done, that there's nothing out there, nothing more you can do. Just stop it. Please."

I looked at her, seeing the tension in her face. "Protecting your brother Doug?"

She looked away from me. "I can't say anything about that."

"Kara," I said, trying to keep my voice even. "What happened that night? Is your brother connected? And your landlord died a couple of days later. What's going on?"

Her eyes were welling up. "I'm not going to appeal to our friendship. You're more Diane's friend. But please, for God's sake, will you stop asking questions and bothering people? You're going to get hurt, and if Diane ever..." Her voice trailed off.

"You're afraid of what Diane might do to your brother, is that it?"

She rubbed at her chin with a clenched fist. "I can't say any more, I'm sorry."

"What's your brother involved with? Why did your landlord get murdered?"

Kara still looked away. I went on and said, "Yesterday afternoon I saw Doug at the Brick Yard Pub. He didn't seem happy to see me. A couple of hours later, I'm getting shot at in North Tyler. So what's he involved with?"

She sighed. "Doug was my first friend. We could talk about things and play together and go hiding when my parents were on the warpath. Doug wasn't too bright, and I helped him with his schoolwork, though I'm not sure how much I accomplished. She smiled faintly and looked back at me. "You've met my parents, right?"

"We had a brief visit that seemed to last about a year."

"Good description," she said. "Mother and Father—I could really never call them Mom and Dad—felt like they had responsibilities. So they labored to have the required two children and were quite pleased that they received a male and a female. As we got older, we were just props, props for them to show that they were committed parents. We were also expected to do well in school, be active in the required school events—sports for Doug and music for me—and then join the right crowd. Which always turned out to be the children of my parents' friends."

"Somehow I don't think your parents are too pleased about what happened."

She was still smiling but in an odd way. I could see a note of anger play across her face. "That's so true. The true-blue son who was supposed to do well and go to Harvard and join the old man's business, well, he turns out to be a college dropout with a taste for potato chips and soap operas. The dutiful daughter who is supposed to marry the up-and-coming lad in Father's business and have two point-nine children, well, she turns out to be a dyke. After all these years, still quite a shock to both of them."

I leaned forward a bit. "After all these years, are you still protecting Doug? Even if it means something connected to your landlord getting murdered?"

She looked right at me. "Will you stop what you're doing?"

Everything felt heavy about me as I answered her. "I made a promise to Diane, one I take seriously. I can't lie to her. I have to see it through."

Her voice was clear and to the point. "If you do that, I'll never speak to you again, Lewis, and I can tell you, as much as Diane is fond of you, she loves me more. If I shut you out, she'll follow me. She might not like it, but she'll follow me, and you'll never see her again. Are you prepared to do that?"

"I'm prepared to keep my promise."

She nodded and said, "Don't get up," but of course I did, walking her to the door, and she trudged up the snow-covered path and my mind was racing, trying out the phrase or combination of phrases I could use to call her back and try to make it right with her, but nothing came to me, nothing at all, as she went over the rise.

I slammed the door and went back into the living room, and picking up the two juice glasses, I went into the kitchen and in one quick motion threw them down into the sink, the glass shattering so loud it almost hurt my ears.

FELIX CALLED me later that day. "I've finished my snooping. They did well, picking that place. The airfield's been abandoned, but someone keeps plowing it out. The access road is a couple of hundred yards in, and then you come to a grove of trees. Past the trees is the hangar. Nice and remote and wide open. Some old pieces of machinery in the yard, and a couple of outbuildings. You could hide a platoon of assassins in there with no problem. There's another access road, leading out back to the highway."

"So we get there early, and then what?"

"Then we wait for them. If it's not a trap—a slight possibility—then they're surprised to see us there and we apologize, saying we misread the time or something. If it is a trap—a much larger possibility—then we've spoiled their plans. We've confused them, then maybe we get a good look at who's been shooting at you. Or maybe everything works out for the best and we end up with the package. Do you believe that?"

"I don't know what to believe."

He laughed. "Who does? I'll be by tomorrow, about nine o'clock. You plan on bringing along some...um, supplies?"

"Wouldn't leave home without being supplied, not these days."

"Good. I'll see you tomorrow."

I hung up and went to wash my hands. The house smelled of cooking, gun oil, and a faint scent from Kara's visit. There was also another odor there, of fear and terror and apprehension, and I opened the kitchen window to the January air, hoping it would help.

AT FIVE MINUTES before five o'clock on the next day, my phone rang. It was Felix. "I'm up in the parking lot. Are you ready?"

"That I am," I said. "I'll be right up."

I hung up the phone, and by the front door I gathered up my belongings and looked back. I guess I should have been thinking great thoughts about what lay ahead for us this winter night, or at least I should have had melancholy feelings about leaving my safe house for a possible bloody encounter, but no, I was just ready to get on with it.

Felix stood at the parking lot's border, hands in pockets, the engine of his car rumbling and gray exhaust clouds eddying around the open trunk. He nodded at me as I placed two long zippered bags inside.

"What do you have there?" he asked.

"Twelve-gauge shotgun," I said. "And an eight-millimeter assault rifle."

He whistled. "Anything else?"

"Just my Beretta, under my coat."

"Expecting trouble, I see."

"No, expecting to be alive when this evening is over," I said. "And you?"

He grinned as he slammed down the trunk. "Let's just say you and I have parity."

I climbed in and Felix joined me. On the rear seat of the car was a collection of black zippered bags. We got out of the parking lot and I said to Felix, "Do we have time?"

"Time for what?"

"A quick favor." And when I asked him, he agreed and we headed north.

FIFTEEN MINUTES later I was standing on cold concrete in a garage in Bretton, hands in pockets, just looking. Before me, on three flat tires, was my Range Rover. The driver's side was stitched with bullet holes and most of the windows had been shattered. Fluid was still dripping from the engine. I wanted to touch the scarred metal, and I forced myself to stand there and look, feeling the memories come back to me, back when I had first moved into Tyler Beach and had bought this four-wheeler. Many good miles had passed with this vehicle, far from its home in England, and now it lay dead and hidden.

What an ending. I rubbed at my eyes and turned to Felix. "Let's get out of here."

.   .   .

WE HEADED SOUTH, to Newburyport and its neighbor Plum Island, a barrier island off the East Coast. It's a community made of loners, fishermen, malcontents, and other people who believe the mainland doesn't understand them, and they're probably right. It's connected to the coast by a drawbridge, and the north end is a cozy community of winterized cottages and shops, and the entire south is a national wildlife preserve.

As Felix drove, I looked around at his car. It was a rented black Toyota Camry. The fact that we were driving a rented car was another sign of what we were getting into.

I looked out at the lights and said, "Where do you get your vehicles?"

"Trade secret," Felix said. "And a pretty expensive one. The deal I have, I'm all set, no matter what dents, dings, or odd bullet hole might be in it when I bring it back. The only real no-no is blood. I can't bring back a car with bloody seats or trunk."

"How do you get around that?"

"Plastic sheets."

"I'd like to have you connect me with that someone," I said. "I need a vehicle, and I'd like to have it by tomorrow."

"Deal."

After another hundred yards or so, Felix pulled over to the side, letting the engine run, switching on an overhead light. He pulled a folded sheet of paper from the glove compartment and unfolded it. It was a hand-drawn— and quite nicely done—map of the airport and the surrounding buildings.

"Pre-job briefing," he said. "We drive in there, nice and slow, like we're lost or something. We'll both have windows down and weapons in our laps. We're about two hours early, so either we're going to catch them by surprise or it'll be empty. Then we'll sit, engine running, keeping an eye on things."

"They don't show up at eight, then what?"

"We give them a few more minutes and then we scram. We'll be waiting and getting nervous and wondering what's going wrong. To hell with that. I don't care what your caller said, we're running this show."

I looked down at the piece of paper, with the straight lines marking the buildings, and the two wavy lines outlining the access roads. "What should we be looking for?"

"They drive down and we all start acting like gentlemen, then it's fine.

They should have our rapist friend secured somehow. I'll handle the exchange, and it should go real quick. Anything longer than a minute or two, we're gone. This isn't a debating society. The deal is straightforward. We get the bad guy, and you stop bothering them."

"All right," I said. "We run into talkative folks and then we'll leave. What else?"

"You see a bunch of guys with weapons coming at us with no talking or talking it real rough, then it's going to the shits real quick and we're outta there. In fact, you get a bad feeling about anything, Lewis, we're driving out and we try something different."

"I'm getting a bad feeling right about now."

He grinned. "That's normal. Nothing to worry about. Come on, let's get dressed."

From the rear seat he pulled forward a larger bag, which he unzipped and from which he emptied two Kevlar bulletproof vests. We helped each other on and instantly the inside of the car started getting fifteen degrees warmer. Felix switched off the overhead light and I noticed that I was wiping my hands a lot on my pants leg.

"Okay, let's get to it," he said, and we pulled out into the road.

About a mile toward Plum Island Felix started whistling a quiet tune that I couldn't place, and he pressed a switch that lowered both windows. He kicked the heater up a notch and then I joined him in pulling out our pistols, resting them in our laps. Even with the heavy vest and the heater running at full tilt, I was shivering even harder as we went down the access road, which was bumpy and roughly plowed.

Felix clicked on the headlight's high beams. There were snow-covered fields stretching away to either side of us, glowing stark white. Bare trees spotted the landscape, their gnarled branches looking sharp and awful. Off in the distance to the right were some lights and low buildings, and Felix saw that I was looking that way.

"New airport, started last year. Place we're going to is just down the road."

We passed through a gentle corner and there were two small buildings and a large hangar. The doors were open and snow had drifted inside. Snow-covered hunks of rusted machinery were outside. Felix drove up and the headlights lit up the interior. Toward the rear were workbenches and the bare carcass of a Piper Cub and some doors. No one was in the building. Felix backed up the Camry until we were facing the access road. Off to my side the road curved, and I pointed that out and Felix said, "She curves around and reconnects to the main road. It's more rough than what we came in on."

He put the car into park and switched off the headlights, leaving on the parking lights. The engine still rumbled softly and the heater was on. Felix reached behind the seat and pulled a dark duffel bag toward him, which he unzipped.

"Little toy for the both of us, give us a little advantage," he said, taking out two hard plastic cases from inside the bag. The cases opened with a sharp *pop*! and he took out what looked like a pair of bulky binoculars, which I recognized instantly.

"Night-vision scopes," I said. "Very nice."

I could sense his smile rather than see it. "I suppose you might have had experience with these. Do you need a lesson, or do you plan to give me a lesson?"

I hefted the bulky instrument in my hand, found the power switch, and turned it on. "Oh, you might want to give me a few pointers. One does tend to get rusty."

"So they say."

Ten minutes later I had the night-vision scope up to my eyes. It worked by gathering all the available light—starlight, moonlight, whatever—and concentrating it to make the night visible. Everything was in a ghostly green glow, and I brought the scope up to my eyes every few minutes for a quick scan. Though I was with Felix and we were well-armed, I still had disquieting thoughts of men in white snowsuits, creeping across the fields, reaching into the open car windows and slitting our throats.

Felix coughed and said, "Pretty strange night for you, isn't it."

"The same could be said for you."

"True, my friend, but there's a big difference. This is a part of my life, a part of who I am. I expect this kind of work. Hell, sometimes I even look forward to it. But not you. You're a quiet bookish type who used to do something spooky for the Pentagon, and I'll be damned if I can quite figure out why you now do this. It doesn't figure. This is my turf, not yours. What happened to you out there with the feds, that makes you do this?"

I wasn't in a mood to talk. "Classified. Sorry."

"I'm not looking for the details," he said, his voice quiet but insistent. "I'm just curious why you feel compelled to do this."

I remembered the frantic call from Diane, and the shaking and teary face of Kara in the hospital examining room, and the flames that flickered up the Crescent House, and I said, "What makes you think I have a choice?"

Felix stayed quiet for a while, and I did, too, bringing up the scope every few minutes, looking to the access road in front of us, and the side road off to my right. The snowfields looked ghastly in the pale, fake light. By concentrating I could make out the sounds of traffic heading toward Plum Island. I put the glasses down and Felix's voice startled me, though it was quite low and even.

"Car coming down the access road."

I turned and saw the approaching headlights. Forgetting my old DoD training, I brought the scope up and was instantly blinded, the circuitry not being able to handle the sudden rush of light from the oncoming car. I brought the scope down and blinked hard a few times. There was a creaking noise as Felix shifted in his seat.

"Only one," he said, "That's good. And right on time."

He started to say something else, but I wasn't paying attention. I could now make out the sound of the approaching car, but there was something else. Metal creaking. Just the car settling in the cold, or Felix moving around? I picked up the night scope and looked out to the other access road. Empty. I scanned the fields. Nothing.

Metal. Creaking again.

I turned full in the seat and looked behind me, through the rear windshield. The quality was blurry, since my hands were shaking and I was looking through dirty glass, but it was clear enough to see, clear enough so I grabbed on to Felix's shoulder, hoping I could speak up soon enough, very soon, as the two men with shotguns worked their way through the abandoned airport hangar just a few score feet away, moving quick and sure, the shotguns now rising up to their shoulders.

"Felix!" I yelled. "Bad guys behind us! It looks like—"

I didn't have a chance to finish, as Felix shifted the Camry from park and slammed down on the accelerator, the tail end fishtailing as he spun around and headed out the other access road. I fell back against the seat and dropped the night scope, and I felt a hot flush of fear, wondering if I was overreacting.

I was still thinking that when there was an earsplitting *boom!* and the rear window was shot in.

24

Glass showered over me and Felix grunted, and I rolled back down, dropping my head behind the seat. The car fishtailed again, the rear end slamming into a frozen snowbank, and Felix cursed in Italian and yelled, "Are you hurt?"

"I don't think so," I yelled back. "How about you?"

"Just mightily pissed. Hold on."

The road was bumpy and Felix was speeding along, sliding and braking. I got up and spared a look to the rear. Most of the window was gone, broken glass littering the back seat. Headlights were back there in the darkness, following us, moving up and down as the other car speeded across the bumps. The interior of the car was colder and Felix drove like a whirling dervish, pumping the accelerator, braking and turning with a hard-edged fury, slamming the side of the steering wheel with his hands. We raced down the access road and I held on to my door handle and desperately tried to find my pistol with a free hand, moving across the fabric, finding nothing. My right foot nudged something and I reached down and came up with a night scope instead, and I got a cracked skull for my troubles as Felix whipped through a curve, another loud *bang!* echoing from inside the car as we broadsided a snowbank.

I looked up, head aching, tears in my eyes, as I made out a streetlight, and I yelled out, "Street's coming up!"

"I see it!" he shouted back. "How are we doing back there?"

I turned and said, "About sixty feet or so. They're moving pretty fast."

"Okay," he said, as we plowed through onto the main road, going about as fast as a landing space shuttle, "let's see if—damn it to hell!"

There was a screech of tires as Felix spun left and just as sharply spun right, sliding out into the street. There was a flash of headlights and the blare of horns and another fishtail, and then we were racing down the road, heading toward Plum Island. I finally sat up, heart pounding, my legs shaking. There was the roar of the engine and the rushing sound of the wind through the empty hole where the rear window had been, and I bent down and frantically rooted around, finally coming up with my Beretta.

"What the hell was that back there?" I demanded.

"Simple," he said, as we raced past the frozen fields and marshlands. "Just as we popped out on the street, I saw headlights from where we came in. Another car. If we had headed back to town, they could have boxed us in."

I looked back and saw one and then two sets of headlights charging behind us. "Shit," I said.

"Very perceptive," Felix said, glancing at the rearview mirror, "Mind reminding me what we got ahead of us? And make it quick."

Which was true. Ahead of us was the straight lane of the road, heading into the low lights of Plum Island. I stammered for a second and said, "Plum Island. Wildlife preserve to the south. The village is to the north. Probably just a few hundred people there in the winter. If we can get into the town, dump the car, we'll be all right. We'll dive into a cottage or something and call the cops."

"Are we still in Newburyport?" Felix said, voice grim. "That asshole police detective will give us a hard time."

I almost laughed. "Christ on a crutch, Tinios, we're being chased by two carloads of bad guys. I don't care if we're hassled by the ghost of J. Edgar Hoover. Look, after we cross over the bridge, either go straight or go left. That will bring us into town. Whatever you do, don't turn right."

There was a small drawbridge coming up and we were moving so fast that we were airborne just for a moment, long enough for me to hit my head again on the car roof as we rose up. We slammed down and there was a scraping sound, and I wondered what fool would ever rent a car to Felix ever again. I spared another glance back.

"Looks like they're gaining," I said.

Felix also glanced back. "Hate to say you're right. Okay, here we— "

Then he stopped, swearing again in Italian, as we flew by orange and black signs that said DETOUR and ROAD CLOSED and ONE LANE AHEAD and the intersection was blocked off, with only the road to the right and one lane straight ahead being open. Sets of headlights were screaming toward us and Felix jammed on the brakes and I slammed my hand forward on the dashboard as we skewed to the right.

"Felix!" I yelled, but there was nothing we could do.

We were now heading down a narrow road. Ahead were two signs: WELCOME TO THE PLUM ISLAND WILDLIFE REFUGE. And another: DEAD END.

For the first time I saw real fear on Felix's face. "Jesus, Lewis, I'm sorry."

I just stared ahead, not knowing what to say.

IN A MATTER of moments we were at a length of chain near a wooden guard shack, blocking the parking lot entrance. Another slam of the brakes, but we hit a patch of ice, and Felix turned and buried the front end into a snowbank. I bucked forward, injuring my head for the third time that night, and Felix got out, yelling, "Let's go, let's go!"

He had popped the trunk lid from inside and I was right with him, the soft interior light making everything look innocent. I had my Beretta in my coat pocket and a couple of spare magazines on the holster, and looking into the trunk, I made a quick choice. The zippered bag with the rifle went over my shoulder and the shotgun stayed behind. We would be running through snow and sand dunes, moving fast. A shotgun is good for close work and the rifle was good for long work, and I didn't want to be close to anyone. This took all of a second or two to decide, but I was still fairly slow, for by the time I stood up, with the heavy weight over my shoulder, Felix had already slammed the trunk lid and was running across the parking lot, spare ammo in his hands.

I joined him and saw the lights of our pursuers come roaring up the park road.

WE RAN past darkened park buildings, heading into the wildlife preserve, and with each step the pounding in my heart grew louder. Felix stopped as we reached a set of wooden boardwalks, and I said, "This isn't good, Felix, this isn't good at all."

"No shit."

"No, I mean this place. It's just sand dunes and beaches. No trees, no forests, nothing except sand, brush, and grass. Not a hell of a lot of hiding places."

From beyond the dark parking lot came the sounds of doors slamming and loud voices. I could just barely make out Felix's form in the dark. "Well, complaining's not going to do much tonight except waste air. You have any suggestions?"

"Yeah, let's get off the boardwalk, start going into the dunes."

"We just passed a sign that said stay on the boardwalks," he said, trying to make his voice sound light.

"We get any complaints, I'll take care of it."

"Deal."

We leaped from the boardwalk onto a nearby dune—no use painting a picture for our pursuers—and we scrambled up the sand and snow. The wind was starting to come up and I was breathing harshly as we climbed up the shifting sands. As we neared the crest I grabbed Felix's leg and said in a whisper, "Don't stand up as we get to the top. You'll be silhouetted from the moonlight. Hunch down and roll across."

He said nothing but did as I requested, and I joined him, rolling across the sands and snow. We went up two successive dunes like that, and then I grabbed his arm this time and said, "Quick rest break."

"You got it."

Felix lay next to me, his breathing slow and steady, while my own lungs were racing to keep up. The snow up here had been blown away by the constant winds, and the hardy dune grasses were still clinging to life. Felix shifted and then he had a night-vision scope in his hands, and I was flushed with embarrassment, knowing my own scope was left behind in the wrecked Camry.

"See anything?"

"Yeah, I do," he said, his voice slightly muffled. "At least eight or nine guys, and they're doing a pretty good job. They're moving in a skirmish line, beating their way here, taking their time. Damn it, this is one narrow island. They could practically hold hands and walk across."

He lowered the glasses. "You think we should split up?"

"No," I said instantly. "We'll be splitting up our firepower."

Felix paused. "Pretty bold words, Lewis. What have you got in mind?"

I tugged my bag free from my shoulder. "You're right, this is one damn narrow island. Eventually we're going to be at the south end, right on the beach with the ocean at our back, and this is no night for swimming."

The bag was free and I took the heavy FN 8mm rifle out, feeling the smoothness of the wooden stock. It's old, and when I had purchased it, I made the excuse that I was investing in an antique. But it's also Belgian-made (Fabrique Nationale) and quite accurate, and on this cold and lonely night with the sand against my belly and the sound of the winds and waves about my head, I was thankful for its ten-round magazine.

"Lewis—" Felix began.

"So they're chasing us south," I said, putting the rifle up to my shoulder. "So let's slow them down. Let's put the fear of God into them for a change. I'll rip off a few rounds and then we'll scurry back to the next dune. We'll make them hesitate before going up every dune. Damn it, I'm tired of being a target. You got a problem with that?"

"Hell, no," Felix said. "I was just going to offer to be a spotter, that's all. Let's get to it."

FELIX CRAWLED UP NEXT to me, night-vision scope to his eyes, and said, "Off to the left, boardwalk. Maybe a hundred yards. Two guys, talking and pointing. Got them?"

The FN had no scope, just open iron sights, which was fine. I clicked the sights to one hundred meters—being Belgian, it was metric—and breathed in. The wooden boardwalk was clear enough in the starlight and the light from the new moon, and I saw the dark shapes Felix had mentioned, just before a set of smaller dunes. I had no great expectations of marksmanship this winter night. I only wanted to keep their heads down, slow their advance until Felix and I could think of something else.

I breathed in and out, and said, "They still there?"

"Sure are."

"Okay, here goes," I said, and gently squeezed the trigger.

The first shot scared even me, the report quite loud and the muzzle flash looking like a tiny blowtorch in the night. I fired off three additional rounds, shifting my aim just a bit with each shot, the recoil no bother at all, and Felix slapped me on the back and said, "Let's go," and I moved down the slope of the dune with him, sand cascading around our feet, the smell of burnt gunpowder quite strong.

"Did you see anything?"

"They both dropped."

"But I probably missed."

"Probably," he said. "But they both dropped."

From the other side of the dunes came the sound of return gunfire, and a few yells, and the sounds made me smile. I felt good. We were fighting back.

ANOTHER TWO DUNES, and we were on our bellies again. Felix had the scope back up. "The little bastards are more cautious," he said. "They're moving real slow."

"Can you see what they've got for weapons?" I asked.

"Pistols and shotguns, best I can tell," he said.

"Good," I said. "No distance. All right, off to the left. Any target out there? I don't want them outflanking us."

He sighted in and scanned for a moment, and said, "Looks like a wooden trail sign. Kind of big. Can you make it out?"

I looked down over the rifle's sights. "No. Give me more."

"Straight ahead and straight down. Catch the boardwalk. Move to the left. Some scrub brush, some sand, another chunk of the boardwalk, and the sign."

Square, dark shape. "Got it."

I fired off three more rounds, then Felix and I scrambled off to the right. The FN doesn't have a muzzle flash guard, and with every shot, we were showing them our positions. When we stopped again, breathing hard, I said, "Anything?"

"You dropped him," Felix said, his voice a bit peculiar.

"You mean he fell?"

"No, I think you shot him. He fell back pretty hard."

"Oh."

I suppose I should have felt remorse, some regret at what I had just done. But blame it on the cold and the night's wild ride, and my own terrible walk the other night in North Tyler after being shot at, for what I truly felt: I was glad no one was coming up our left flank.

Felix kept moving the night scope back and forth, and said, "Damn it, they're too quick now. By the time I tell you where they are, they've moved somewhere else."

"Just give me a general direction, that's all I need."

"That's not going to work for long."

"I know. But it'll give us time."

"Time for what?"

"Time for someone to hear the gunshots and call the cops," I said.

Felix looked around at the scrub brush, the hills and ravines and dunes and sand piles, and said, "Well, they must be tripping over themselves to get there, 'cause I don't see a single damn person, except for the bastards trying to get us."

"Fishermen come out here at night, do some surf fishing."

"In January? With this wind?"

I raised up my rifle. "Damn it, Felix, if you can't agree with me, at least give me some targets. Where to?"

He muttered something and said, "A bit off to my right. Down where two dunes look like they intersect. I saw a couple of heads poke up."

"Got it."

Another shot, and then another, and then a *click*. Magazine was empty. Time to reload.

Return fire, a bit closer this time, and that awful bone-chilling *wheee!* that comes when a copper-jacketed slug of lead goes zipping over your head at several hundred feet per second. Felix joined in this time, the gunfire from his pistol very loud.

"Fools are getting better," Felix said, as we tumbled down the slope of the dune, heading to another rise of sand.

"I can handle them getting better," I said. "I can't handle them getting good. That would be terrible."

THREE MORE DUNES, and two more reloads on my part. The last time Felix had surprised me by pulling out his pistol and firing a half dozen shots off to the right.

"Jesus!" he had said when he was done and we had scampered off to another mass of sand. "That guy was good. He was coming right up the slope."

I didn't ask him the obvious question, if he had hit anything, I figured he'd tell me in his own good time. Right now I was on my stomach again, trying to keep my teeth from chattering. I would put one hand in my coat pocket to warm it up, and then repeat the process with the other. Hat and gloves were back in the Camry, along with the night scope. Sloppy. Felix had his pistol in one hand and the night scope up to his eyes.

"Anything?" I asked.

"Nothing. They're either hunkered down or they're making a wide sweep. That's what I would do. Get down to the beach on this side of the island, dog-trot down to the end, and then reverse and come back up on the dunes to the south of us."

"Nice thoughts."

"That's what they're probably doing."

"Well, they could be discussing how to surrender."

A short laugh. "Well, if that happens, you can be the gentlemen who handles the surrender terms. I'm getting too cold and cranky."

"It is getting cold."

"Too cold, and too tiring. How's your ammo?"

"One full magazine in the rifle, ten rounds," I said. "Haven't used anything from my Beretta. How about you?"

"One magazine in the pistol. That's it."

I reached under my jacket and tugged at my shoulder holster.

There were two full clips of 9mm ammunition hanging there, which I pulled free and passed over to Felix, along with my own pistol. "Here. Strip my ammo out and reload your clips."

"Lewis, you're going—"

"Felix, I'm going to need you armed more than anything else. Do it and shut up."

He said nothing in return, but his hands got busy as he ripped the 9mm rounds from my full magazines and loaded up his empty Smith & Wesson magazines for his own pistol. I burrowed both hands in my coat and rolled over and looked up at the stars, listening to the soft *click-click* sounds as Felix worked. The stars were nice and bright and maybe it was the lateness of the hour, or my exhaustion or fear, but everything seemed to be a mish-mash of lights in the sky, a random scattering that made no sense.

Sort of what we were in the middle of.

"Who are those guys?" I asked.

"Robert Redford and Paul Newman," Felix said.

"What?"

"Line from their movie, right? 'Butch Cassidy and the Sundance Kid.' Halfway through the movie they're outnumbered and they're being chased, and one line they say, over and over again. Who are those guys?"

"All right, so I stole the line. You tell me. Who are those guys?"

Felix grunted and handed me back my now-empty magazines and empty pistol. It was a scary feeling, right there, knowing that I was almost out of ammunition.

"No, you tell me. We start out looking for someone who raped your friend Kara, and a couple of weeks later we end up out here being shot at and being chased. So you answer the question. Who are those guys?"

"Friends of Doug Miles, it seems."

"A good guess, as good as any others."

"Time for another chat with the young Doug Miles, don't you think?"

Felix laughed. "If you and I are on speaking terms tomorrow, we'll chat about that. Right now, let's see if we can get out of here. Any more ideas? And don't tell me we're still relying on your phantom fishermen."

"Tell me what's going on down there."

He shifted and scanned the dunes below us. "Nothing."

"But they must be on the move."

"Sure. Circling around on the beaches. Half of them are also probably staying back, in case we double back."

"What's behind us? Any movements?"

Felix moved around on the dune, the sands shifting, making a comforting scraping sound. It reminded me of when I was impossibly young and innocent, and when a shovel and sand pail and being with my parents at old Tyler Beach could keep me happy for hours.

"Nothing. Just dunes and grass and scrub brush. And one utility pole."

"A utility pole?"

"Yep."

"Any streetlight on it?"

"Nope."

"You see any wires running to it?"

"Can't tell."

"Is there a junction box or something, about a third of the way up from the bottom?"

"Yeah, it looks like it."

Something stirred in me, something I seized and would not let go of. "Felix, let's get moving. And let's head to the utility pole."

"Why? You think there may be a phone booth there, something we can use?"

"Could be," I said, lying with ease, not wanting to tell him any more. "But let's get going."

He grumbled. "Hell, at least we'll be moving targets, and we'll be warmer."

ON OUR WAY south we were getting more tired from slogging through the snow and sand, and stopped more for quick rest stops, the Kevlar vests weighing us down. Felix moved nervously, constantly shifting the night vision scope up and down to his tired eyes. During our third or fourth rest stop he said, "You hear that?"

"No. All I hear is the ocean."

"That's what I meant. We're getting closer to the southern tip. We're running out of room."

"How far to the pole?"

"Oh, about a hundred yards or—"

The ridgeline on a dune to the east of us erupted with winking spurts of light that were followed by loud booming noises. Felix swore loudly and fired back, and I joined with a couple of shots myself, and the *whee! whee!* noises were louder and my face was pelted by sand tossed up by the bullets, and I fell back, tumbling down the side of the dune, and Felix joined me. We fell along the brush and snow and cold sand, and Felix yelped as he struggled at the bottom.

"You all right?"

"No, I'm not all right," he said through clenched teeth, "I got a piece of branch jammed into my thigh."

"Bleeding?"

"Like you wouldn't believe."

It was hard work in the dark, as I gave up a handkerchief and a shirt-sleeve to help bandage Felix's leg, stripping down and even removing the bulletproof vest, which steamed in the cold night air. I felt completely help-less. When I got my clothes back on we started moving south again, and Felix said, "What's up with that damn utility pole?"

"You tell me," I said. "Is there something large on top?" We were close. Felix leaned on me and raised up the night scope and said, "Yeah. Odd shape. Hey, isn't that one of—"

"Sure is."

"How in hell is that going to help us?"

I started moving, Felix's weight on my left shoulder. "It's going to give us a chance, that's all."

We hadn't moved far when gunfire erupted again, closer this time. We returned fire for just a moment and then Felix and I scampered up a smaller dune and collapsed in the snow and sand, I was soaking wet from perspiring and from melted snow, and Felix's breathing was getting labored. "How are you doing for ammo?" I asked.

"Down to the last magazine. And you?"

"Three or four in the rifle."

Felix coughed and said, "Listen, if they get close enough, I might be able to make a deal. Start them talking."

A gunshot boomed ahead of us, and the *whee!* sound of a slug whistled over our heads. "I don't think they're in the mood for talking."

"It was a thought."

I crept up to the crest of the dune, with Felix at my left side.

The utility pole was at my right, about fifty yards away. There was a boxy shape at the top of the pole, and a smaller, squarish shape about ten feet up from the base of the pole.

"Felix, look at that pole, will you?"

"Why, you see something moving there?"

"Just do it."

"All right," he said, leaning over my back. "It's one of those poles, and yes, it's got a siren on top and a metal control box about two-thirds down. Let's see—Oh, shit." He moved the scope around to our front. "I've got a couple of bad guys coming down the dunes, Lewis, can you see them?"

I could see movement out there and I moved the rifle over, but I could also make out the pole. Damn. Some choice. A gamble that could possibly save us, versus the certainty of fighting off a well-armed threat merely yards away.

"Lewis, what are you waiting for? Damn it, shoot!"

I said a quick prayer that probably made no sense, and I turned and aimed at the utility pole, firing off four rounds, all I had, aiming at the control box near the bottom of the pole, and then all that was in my arms was a harmless piece of wood and metal.

Felix was holding on to my shoulder, quietly screaming into my ear, "You idiot! What the hell were you shooting at it? There's nobody over there."

"You're absolutely right," I said. "But there's a siren pole from the Falconer nuclear power plant over there, and if we're lucky, I just shot out the control box. That means the plant's been alerted that they've lost one of their poles, and the guys at Falconer are starting to make calls. Especially to the police, to report another act of vandalism. If they're quick and if we're lucky, and if we can hold these guys off that long, there'll be a repair crew and a police cruiser here within ten to fifteen minutes."

Felix let go of my shoulder. "And if they're not quick and we're not lucky?"

"Then you'll get a chance to cut a deal," I said. "Right after you run out of ammo."

Felix breathed hard and lay down, night scope against his eyes. "You got a bayonet with that rifle?"

"Back home I do."

"Well, here's hoping we don't start regretting that it's at home and not here. Okay. Two bad guys, still coming our way. Guess you'll have to pretend your rifle's a club. Ready?"

God, no. "Yes, I am."

"Good."

And as the seconds dragged by and the shapes came closer, Felix turned to me and said, "For whatever it's worth, you did good tonight. Better than I thought."

"Shut up and keep watch," I said. "The night's not over yet."

I settled in, the useless rifle cold in my shaking hands, and listened to the waves, and the murmur of voices out there among the sands, of the men coming over to kill us.

Quick and lucky. Didn't seem much to ask for.

"They're right below us," Felix whispered.

25

Plum Island is within the jurisdiction of West Newbury, and the town's police station is a tiny white building, right next to the town hall. I was seated in an interrogation room at about two a.m., and with me was a West Newbury police sergeant who was not having a very good night. I sat on a wooden chair wearing my wet and soiled clothes, and feeling reasonably warm and happy, except for the fact that my hands were handcuffed behind me. Still, it was a small price to pay for the knowledge that at least for the next few hours I wouldn't be shot at, if I was lucky.

Luck. Lucky for us that a police cruiser was on Plum Island, checking out reports of shots being fired, when the call came in about the siren pole being disabled. It hadn't been ten or fifteen minutes, more like five or six, and that had been long enough.

The sergeant's nameplate said LES SEARLES. He was in uniform and his face was quite red with anger as he wrote out a report. He sat across from me, working on a table that was scarred with cigarette burns and old coffee stains. Behind him was a window that was mirrored with one-way glass.

"Name?" he demanded.

"Lewis Cole."

"Home address?"

"Atlantic Avenue, Tyler, New Hampshire."

He looked up from me. "I need a street number."

"Sorry, there isn't one. How about my mailing address? It's Post Office Box Nine-One-Nine in Tyler. Do you need the zip code?"

He was still staring at me. "Home phone number?"

I told him. When he asked for my work number, I shrugged and said, "Same as the home number."

"Occupation?"

"I write for a magazine called *Shoreline*."

"Hmph," he said. "Never heard of it. Date and place of birth?"

I told him that, too, and he smirked and said, "You sure look older, that's for sure."

Even though I knew he was baiting me, I still didn't appreciate the comment. He wrote some and said, "All right, what in hell were you and your friend doing out there?"

I looked straight back at him with a calm expression. "Star gazing."

Sergeant Searles tossed the pen down on the desk. "Stop the bullshit, will you? I'll tell you what we've got, and then I'll ask you one more time. All right?"

"If you insist."

A tough little grin. "Oh, I do insist. This is what we have. We have reports of shots being fired on Plum Island. Then we get a report that a siren pole for the nuke plant has been disabled. We get there and we find you and your buddy, one," he looked down at his pages, "Felix Tinios, who's got a very interesting record, by the way. The two of you are there, sitting nice and calm in the dunes. We find a rifle tossed behind some brush. We find both of you carrying nine-millimeter pistols. We also find a lot of empty shell casings and some blood trails. Get the picture?"

I tried moving my hands and found it tough going. Sergeant Searles had done a very good job with the handcuffs. "Sure. Picture is gotten."

"So I'll ask you again. What in hell was going on out there?"

My feet, though, at least I could move my feet. "We were star gazing."

His eyes were glaring right at me. "I don't believe you."

"Sorry about that."

"You're in some serious trouble, Mr. Cole."

Yes, but at least I wasn't being shot at. "You're probably right, which is why I want to call my lawyer."

His thick hands rested on the papers. "That's your right, but we could end this a lot easier if you cooperate. Come on, men were hurt out there. Maybe killed. That's assault, maybe attempted murder. Add on destruction of private property, trespassing on federal lands, and illegal discharge of firearms, and that's a lot of time. Talk to me, hell, talk to anybody you want, but let's work together. What do you say?"

"I want to call my lawyer."

He stood up, face still red, and he slammed the papers the desk. "You friggin' idiot, I'm trying to save your butt here, going out on a limb here, trying to work out a deal, and that's the thanks I get."

He was breathing hard. "Last chance."

"Thank you," I said. "I want to call my lawyer."

The sound of the door slamming hurt my ears, but I still felt warm and relaxed, though I was filthy and my clothes were probably destined for the dump when this was over. Some minutes dragged by and then the sergeant came back in, shaking his head.

"I tried to help you out, but your friend jumped the gun," he said, looking sorrowful. "I got a couple of EMTs in a holding cell, bandaging Felix up, and he's agreed to tell us what happened. This is your last chance to tell your side of the story."

I couldn't help it. I burst out laughing, which didn't improve the sergeant's mood. I didn't think it was possible, but he slammed the door harder the second time around.

A COUPLE OF HOURS LATER, after some more of the good cop/bad routine, I was finally given access to a telephone. I looked around for Felix and he wasn't there. I dialed a number he'd made me memorize out on the sands, and it was picked up on the first ring.

"Yes?" said a female voice.

"Is this...I'm looking for Raymond Drake."

"Who's calling?"

"Lewis Cole. I'm a friend of Felix Tinios."

"Hold, please."

There was dead air. No hold music, nothing to soothe you as you stood cold in the concrete-and-steel booking room of a police station.

She came back on the line. "What's the nature of your business?"

"I'm at the West Newbury police station. Felix and I need to be bailed out."

"Is that in Massachusetts?"

"Yes, it is."

"Attorney Drake will be there in one hour."

She hung up, and with handcuffs slapped back on, I was led back to the interrogation room for one more go-around with Sergeant Searles.

THE ATTORNEY WAS good to the word of his sleepless assistant. Within the hour he arrived, and after a lot of shouting and yelling that I could hear even through the walls of the interrogation room, Felix and I were taken out to a holding area. Handcuffs were removed and we were given back our shoelaces and belts. A lot of paperwork was signed and there were dark glares from the assembled cops, but Raymond Drake was the model of efficiency. He was dressed in an expensive-looking two-piece suit, Italian shoes, and a camel hair coat. He was about fifty or so, tanned, and with gold bracelets on both wrists.

When we were finally done the three of us went out into the parking lot. The sky was that dark gray that marks an approaching dawn, and Raymond Drake shook Felix's hand and then mine as we approached his dark blue BMW.

"I guess you fellows need a ride?" he said.

"We sure do," Felix said. "Where do we stand, Raymond?"

He flashed a smile as he held out his key chain and disabled his car alarm. *Blew-bleep.* "It took the usual talk of lawsuits and assorted other dire threats on my part, but I've got the two of you out on bail for gobs of money. They wanted to hold on to you until they've scoured Plum Island from one end to the next, looking for bodies. I convinced them that you'll be good boys in the future. Court date in two weeks. Don't miss it."

"We won't," I said, climbing into the back seat of the BMW, I eased against the plush seating, closing my eyes for just a moment. Felix got in front, and after the door slammed Raymond asked, "Where to?"

I spoke up. "North."

He turned on the engine. "North it is."

LATER THAT AFTERNOON I was in a bathrobe and sitting before a fireplace in a room at the Straggler Inn, one of the best bed and breakfast spots in Porter, a cup of coffee in my hands. Felix was with me, nibbling on a piece of toast. Going home for the both of us didn't seem to be too bright an option, and Felix's attorney was kind enough to stop at both of our residences so we could pick up some spare clothes and other supplies. One of the spare supplies I picked up was my .357 Ruger revolver. The West Newbury police were holding on to my 9mm Beretta, and I wasn't sure when I would ever get it back.

The room was a small suite, with a sitting room that had a great view of the harbor and the naval shipyard, and a few minutes earlier—after sleeping for most of the day—I had enjoyed a full and late breakfast, all the while watching seagulls and cormorant at play in the harbor. I was sore and tired and still shaky, but I was also warm and content at breathing and being alive. Felix was limping a bit—no stitches, but a few butterfly bandages from his run in with the tree branch—and he sat across from me, feet propped up on a coffee table. He had his own room down the hall.

"Some lawyer you've got there," I said. "We should be getting one hefty bill."

He finished the toast and reached down and grabbed a blueberry muffin from off the rapidly emptying breakfast tray. "Nope. Never got a bill, and never will. I gave Raymond a great gift one evening some years back."

"And what was that?"

"His life," Felix said, unwrapping the muffin. "When he was younger he was quite headstrong, poking his nose into things that weren't his business. He represented someone in a case against a relative of mine. Things deteriorated to the point that he was in the rear of a cabin cruiser one night, going out to Boston Harbor, one of those one-way trips. I thought that was a bit excessive, and I managed to convince my relative this wasn't going to take care of the problem. Rented a motorboat and got out there and set things straight, and ever since then, my legal help has been a phone call away."

I leaned back into the couch, feeling the muscles and tendons in my legs creak. "Too bad other problems can't be solved with just one phone call."

"Tell me about it," Felix said. "How are you feeling?"

"Sore. And you?"

"The same. So. What in hell's going on? Who were those guys?"

I looked over at him. "I was hoping you could tell me that."

His hands, which had been busy with the muffin, were now still. "What do you mean by that?"

"I mean this," I said. "Our young friend Doug Miles is involved in something illegal. I also think Doug has something to do with his sister's attack. Tonight we were chased around half an island by a gang of about nine or ten guys. That takes organization, discipline, and things very serious. Felix, when it comes to matters like those, you're the most serious guy I know. We were in your old home state. So who were those guys?"

He carefully broke off a piece of muffin and chewed on it. "Things can change pretty quickly, you know that, right?" he said, talking slowly. "One year some guy can be at the top of his game and have a good scam going with a few of his friends, and next year, they've been busted up. One's dead, one's moved out, and the others are doing time. A lot of stuff can happen."

"So I've been told."

Felix kept on eating, "I try not to get too involved in the day-to-day activities of what goes on around here and down south. I'm busy with the work commitments I already have. You get too friendly or too knowledge-able about what's going on, then you get on some radar screens. Your name gets recorded. Maybe your phone gets tapped. And maybe a subpoena or two arrives with your name on it. So it's in my own best interest—both personal and business—not to know everything that's going on."

"So you don't know who these guys might be."

He wiped his hands on a napkin. "No, I don't."

"I bet you could find out."

A smile. "You're right, I could. But it would take a few days and maybe a trip or two. But I can't do it right now. I'm leaving tomorrow. Remember?"

"Yeah, your business trip down south. It's still on, I imagine?"

"Quite on," he said, nodding. "A straight courier job, something that's going to start off the year right with a hefty payment. Some sensitive materials have to be brought down south, and then I have to make sure they get delivered. It might take three days, it might take three weeks. And when I get back, then I'll start trying to find out what Doug and his friends are up to. In the meantime, here's a suggestion."

"And what's that?"

"Stop."

I shook my head. "I don't think so."

He crumpled up the wrapper and tossed it. "I hope you don't think that the fact we both escaped last night with some scratches, bumps, and a possible criminal record has gone to your head. We—hell, you—might not be so lucky next time. You get involved in something over your head this next week or so, I'm not going to be around to provide backup. You could end up in some cold gravel pit with a couple of rounds in the back of your head, and that's all she wrote, Lewis. So stop."

I was getting tired. I raised up my coffee cup to him. "I'll think about it."

Felix shook his head, whether in disgust or despair I wasn't sure. "You better think pretty hard. I'd hate to miss your funeral service, among other things."

"Thanks for being so thoughtful," I said, and that was it.

LATER I STOOD by the window and looked out at the dim lights of Porter Harbor, still dressed in my bathrobe. Dinner had been a light snack and even though I had slept away most of the day, I was still tired. The bed was nice and wide and with thin, soft pillows, the kind that makes me fall right asleep. But I still had things to do, and I cranked open the window and let some of the cold air drift in, helping keep me awake.

There was a knock at the door. I looked at the clock. Eight p.m., right on the dot.

I walked over and opened the door and Diane Woods looked at me, her face cold and taut. She came in and I closed the door and I said, "Can I get you some coffee?"

She shook her head, staying a comfortable distance away from me. She tugged off a pair of gloves. Snow was melting around her leather boots, and she had on jeans and her thick parka. "I'm doing a surveillance tonight, down at the beach, so I can only stay for a minute. Some kids supposedly breaking into a house. What's going on?"

I looked over at her. "You hear about a fracas over at Plum Island last night?"

"Yeah, West Newbury cops arrested a couple of—Hold on. You?"

"And Felix."

She stared right at me. "You're getting close, right?"

I nodded. "Quite."

"What do you need?"

"Some support. Maybe to bail me out, maybe just a quick call for an extra set of hands. Felix is going out of town for a while."

"You've got it, any time of the day," and then she reached up with her fist and placed it against her mouth. "You sure you're getting close?"

"Yeah, I am. But no promises. It still might fall apart, just when I think I'm almost there."

She gave me a quick nod. "I understand."

"How's Kara?"

I think she pretended not to hear me. She looked down at her wrist and said, "Jesus, I'm running out of time. Lewis, thanks, thanks for everything."

Within a minute she was gone. The carpet was still wet where she had stood. I remained there for a while, and then walked back to the open window. The lights of the harbor were still there, but something new and heavy was in my chest, something that had just been left there when Diane departed. I took a deep breath, smelling a lot of things—the salt air, diesel fuel, old food, and things cooking—and I spoke out loud to Felix, who was hurrying his way south to Logan Airport. He wanted me to lay low, wanted me to do nothing, but I couldn't do that, not with Diane.

"Promises," I said quietly. "Promises."

26

Promises. Three days later I was back in Newburyport. I was now mobile, having rented a Ford Explorer from Felix's contact. I was also about twenty miles and several hundred dollars away from my lodgings at the Straggler Inn. I was staying at "The Lincoln House—Efficiency Rooms to Rent" and my room could have taken up half of the suite back in Porter.

There was a sagging bed against one wall, a counter with a hot plate and mini-fridge, and my own bathroom. The radiator clanked at night and the toilet often drained itself for no apparent reason, and my showers had to be quick, for the hot water lasted only a few minutes. I had to pay extra for the private bath and that was worth it, but the real value was the room's location: directly across the street from the Brick Yard Pub. I had pulled a chair up to the window and looked down at the building and the street. I had a good view and could see everyone moving in and out of the front door.

I had been here for two days and was content to stay just as long as I had to. So far Doug had not shown up, but I was sure he would. Everything had started from here. Everything. Felix and I had scoured Kara's neighborhood and had talked to friends, neighbors, family, and employers, and the only time anything got going was when I had followed Doug to this bar. Staying in the snow outside of his house on the other end of town hadn't done much. This was the center, the place that I was sure would hold, and I had books, magazines, radio, and enough food to last for quite a long while.

Felix might be gone, but I was certainly not going to wait.

With the help of a nap that afternoon and a shortwave radio that was bringing in an odd broadcast from Tennessee—some guy claiming thousands of Chinese troops were training in the high desert of Nevada, ready to help the government repeal the Second Amendment—I was awake when the pub began to get active. I sat in a tubular metal chair near the window, and there was a constant draft of cold air sliding past me. At my side was a tripod, and on it was a distant cousin of the night-vision scopes Felix and I had used a few nights ago. A quick drive to a sporting goods shop in Maine had provided the gear, which gave me the same ghostly green glow of the landscape below me.

I recognized Angela, the woman who had served me a couple of beers, and Harry, the muscular guy who had warned me away from the backroom. One or two of Doug's friends I also thought I recognized. But I was sure of one thing: no Doug.

I watched the people walk into the pub and, most often, stumble out. At about midnight a guy came out holding the hand of a younger woman. They embraced by the door and then slipped and walked to the parking lot, where they climbed into a van. The engine started up, but the van didn't move. After a few minutes it began gently swaying back and forth. "Such a cliché," I whispered, and my eyes went back to the pub's entrance.

About an hour later the door burst open and two guys flew out, and they tussled in the snow, moving almost in slow motion, fighting and cursing at each other. Lights from inside the pub made the snow brighter, and people gathered outside, cheering them on. Someone obviously made a call, for a Newburyport police cruiser came by, blue lights flashing, and the two guys got up from the snow, staggering a bit. The cop came over and talked to them, and there was a lot of head-shaking and finger-pointing. Then the cop went back into his cruiser, wrote up some paperwork, and then answered his radio and sped away, blue lights still flashing. A more important call, I'm sure.

The spectators either drifted back inside or went to their cars or trucks. The two guys that had been fighting were standing at the other end of the building by a snowbank, casually urinating into the snow. They talked to each other as they did their business, like two old New England farmers chatting over a stone wall. More people came out and then the lights were off and the parking lot was empty. I stood up and stretched, the muscles and ligaments in my back popping and creaking in protest.

After splashing some cold water on my face I stripped and crawled into the strange bed, and I slept fitfully, wondering how long it would be until I could get home.

Late in the afternoon on the next day, I came back from a walk along a plowed sidewalk near the Merrimack River and made a phone call from outside a convenience store. Two messages were on my answering machine, along with a bunch of hang-up clicks.

One message was from Diane and was to the point: "Call me if you have any news." The other was from Paula Quinn: "Give me a call, will you? It's been a while."

So I did, and I caught her at the paper. "How've you been?" she asked, and I had to pause for a moment, censoring through everything that had happened to me in the past few days. After this long pause, I said, "Okay, I guess. And you?"

"Bored out of my mind. Want to take me out to dinner tonight?"

I should have been dedicated and said no, but I was tired of eating out of cans and cooking on a hot plate, and dinner with Paula would mean real food from a restaurant, and even if I got back at seven, I would still be able to put in a few hours of surveillance.

"You've convinced me," I said.

"Great. Stop by the paper at around six. I'm trying to wrap up a feature story."

I said that was fine, and I hurried back to my rented room, hoping I would have enough hot water for a pre-dinner shower.

AT *THE TYLER CHRONICLE*, the back door was open, and I went past the circulation and distribution area, past bundled copies of the newspaper. Most of the lights were off and Paula was at her desk, tapping at her computer keyboard. She looked up and smiled and said, "Just a couple more minutes."

"Fine," I said, and I sat across from her and picked up an old *Union Leader* and started flipping through the pages.

It felt a bit odd, being in a newspaper office after hours. It was like you could sense the distant echo of phones ringing, the keyboards being tapped and stories being created, and the nervous energy of news being gathered and presented. There was a slight sense of power in this room, and I'm sure Paula thrived on it, as best she could on her paycheck. Except for a few places, newspaper work doesn't pay that much.

"I ran into Mike Ahern the other day at the town hall," she said, staring at her computer screen. "Didn't say much. Just sneered at me. Damn him."

I turned the page. "Can't hardly blame him, considering what we were thinking."

"Well, I'm still suspicious," she said, her fingers flying. "Ever since we started sniffing at him, nothing's burned down in Tyler. Maybe we spooked him."

I smiled. "Maybe so." I put the paper down and looked over at the desk in the center of the office, which was covered with papers and film rolls and scraps of paper towel. "Where's your photographer friend?"

She turned away from the screen for a moment. "Um, he's in Pennsylvania. Visiting his parents."

"Oh." Now the dinner invitation made more sense. I had done way too much sitting down these past few days, so I got up and went over to Jerry's desk. I looked over some of his stuff and saw a collection of contact sheets. I picked one up. It showed a series of photographs of the last arson fire, at the Crescent House. Little snapshots of the disaster that Paula and I had witnessed. Pictures of the fire trucks, of the firefighters dragging in hose along the snow, and the crowds of people out there watching.

So many faces. Watching the hotel burn. Faces. Watching.

"Paula?" I asked, trying to keep my voice level.

"Hmmm," she answered, still typing away.

"Almost done?"

"Yeah, why, are you hungry?"

I held on to the contact sheet. "No, curious. What do you know about arsonists?"

She stopped typing and looked up. "Besides the fact they usually do it for money or for thrills, and that this particular one is making my life miserable and is scaring the shit out of the residents, you tell me. What's there to know about arsonists?"

"Setting the fire is part of the adventure, but seeing the fire burn is where it's at. They enjoy seeing things burn, seeing the firefighters, seeing the lights and all the excitement. They get a kick out of knowing that they're responsible."

"Makes sense," she said. "You trying to make a point?"

"That I am," I said. "Once the fire is set, they usually stick around to see what's going on." I waved the contact sheet at her. "Your photographer friend, besides taking pictures of the fires, also takes pictures of the crowds. This is one of the contact sheets. You think you could get your hands on the others?"

She moved away from her desk, now nodding in excitement.

"I see what you mean. Sure, Jerry takes a lot of pictures, a lot. All we have to do is go through the contact sheets and see if there are any familiar faces, faces that show up more than once. Hell, Tyler's a small town, but not that small. All of these fires, late at night in winter...we see someone in every picture.."

"Still feel like going out of dinner?" I asked.

"The hell I do," she said, standing up. "Let's get to work."

A WHILE later we had moved into the newspaper's conference room and had spread the contact sheets out on the polished table. Paula had shuttled back and forth from the basement darkroom, bringing up black binders that contained the contact sheets.

"Jerry can be a bit of a slob, but he's a perfectionist when it comes to his photos," Paula explained, as she flipped through the stiff sheets of paper. "He keeps them all up to date and marks each sheet with the date and place that he shot."

Rocks Road Motel. The SeaView. The Tyler Tower Motel. The Snug

Harbor Inn. The Crescent House. It was like looking at old autopsy photos as we began scanning the contact sheets. We both used eye loupes to help magnify the images, and we both kept pads of paper, writing down faces we thought looked familiar from one fire to the next.

As we worked there was a creepy feeling along my back, seeing all those faces, all that emotion and anguish and curiosity, frozen forever on this nine-inch by twelve-inch piece of paper.

A COUPLE of hours later we were finished. The room smelled of old photo paper and pizza. We had gone into the work for an hour before we both realized dinnertime was slipping away, and Paula ordered us take-out pizza and drinks. The pizzas had arrived—and I had made sure that I paid for them and tipped the delivery boy well enough—and I had a plain cheese pizza while Paula had something called "the works."

I felt queasy as I saw her eat the mess of vegetables that was tossed across the cheese and tomato sauce. "How can you eat something like that?" I had asked.

"Easy," she had said. "I know pizza is fattening, so I convince myself that all of the vegetables I eat will cancel out the fattening stuff. Just like skipping breakfast means you can have a fudge sundae for dessert later on. Basic science of a woman's diet. Being a man, you wouldn't know."

Being a man, I had agreed, and we went back to work.

Now we were done, our eyes achy and watery, and my back was also groaning from the stress of bending over the table. The pads of paper were filled with scratched-out numbers and a collection of names, and the contact sheets had been placed into five piles, ready for their return to their binders.

"So," Paula said, stifling a yawn. "That's it."

"Certainly is."

"I gave up a good dinner and interesting conversation for messy pizza and three hours of overtime work that Rollie will never agree to pay for, and for what?"

I looked down at my pad. "For not much, it looks like."

"Yep. A face here and a face there, but there's no evil-eyed arsonist in the crowd, drooling with excitement."

"Your man Kyle shows up in two," I said.

She doodled on a pad. "Kyle Sinclair. Member of the zoning board, and someone who lived near the Rocks Road Motel and the SeaView. You'd expect him to show up. No mystery there, though I will check into it. It's the only thing we've got going."

"Sorry to kill a night."

She smiled that same damnable smile that could make something tingle inside of me. "Not to worry. It was a good idea. Here, let's clean up and get out of here, all right?"

"You've got it."

Paula got up and cleared away the remains of our dinner, and I started shuffling through the contact sheets. As I returned one set I looked again at the series of photos for the Rocks Road Motel. The first three frames were scenic shots of Tyler Beach—probably at the start of a new roll. Then a picture of the Rocks Road Motel, and then the subsequent photos of the fire engines, the spectators, the hoses, the burning building, and there, standing glum and alone, Mike Ahern.

Mike, on the job, just like in the other four sets of photographs.

I then snapped the binder shut, and as Paula walked out, I froze and looked again at the Rocks Road Motel pictures, and then at other four sets.

"Damn me," I whispered. There it was, in all five sets. Paula came back in, and I went back to work, my heart racing just a bit. A theory, that's all it was, but I wasn't going to say a word, I had struck out a couple of times before and had gotten Paula and me excited at the thought we were so close, and I didn't want to do that again.

But damn, there it was.

"All set?" she asked.

"Sure, let's get out of here."

Paula gathered up the binders and went out of the conference room and then downstairs, and I gathered up my coat and hers and walked with her to the back door. As we got dressed for the outdoors I asked, "Feel up to some coffee and dessert?"

Another quick smile. "How about a rain check?"

"A snow check?" I opened the door. "Being polite, or do you mean it?"

She closed the door behind us as we walked out into the parking lot and then she was in my arms, kissing me and holding me tight, and saying, "There. Believe me now?"

I was cold and felt like a bath and my back was still aching, but it was quite nice indeed to have her in my arms. "Gosh, I guess I do, Miss Quinn," and I kissed her again.

She giggled and said, "Lewis, really, good night."

"Fine. Your rain check's safe with me." We clasped hands briefly as we walked across the lot. "Your photographer friend? Are things all right?"

She squeezed my hand and sighed. "Oh, it's all right, but there are these odd stresses and strains. I mean, it's hard going out with someone that you work with day in and out. Sometimes you get at each other's throat."

"I imagine his beard must tickle."

"Stop imagining so much."

She got to her Ford Escort and looked around the lot.

"Where's the Rover?"

Oops. Time for another quick one. "Engine trouble. I'm renting for a few days."

"Oh, all right. Good night, then."

"Sure." I got into my own Ford product and followed her out of the lot, and then she turned north to her home, and I headed south to Newburyport.

Yes, all in all, a good night. If I could just prove it.

THE NEXT MORNING I woke up stiff and sore. I had gotten back to my rented room and had yawned through a couple of more hours of surveillance. Nothing much happened except for a fight between two women, and when the pub lights had sputtered out, I went to bed. But there was a loud television going from the room downstairs, and I suppose I should have complained, but that would have gotten me noticed. I didn't want any attention, not at all, so I tried to sleep with a pillow wrapped around my ears and I stared up at the ceiling, and little things kept racing through my head. The scent of Paula in my arms. The contact sheets with their black-

and-white secrets. Kara, shivering and alone in a hospital examining room. The damn snow and cold. Felix, winging his way south to the Cayman Islands. Me, alone in a smelly and dirty room in Newburyport.

I suppose I must have slept, though I would have been hard pressed to say when.

When I got up and did my morning bathroom routine, I sat on the edge of the bed, yawning and going through a duffel bag at my feet, trying to determine what to wear for the day. I was running out of clean clothes. I set a kettle of hot water on the hot plate for a cup of tea, and then I went to the window to check the weather outside, and when I looked down at the street, there was Doug Miles, standing all alone, outside of the Brick Yard Pub.

I went away from the window and burned my fingers, trying to get the kettle off the hot plate, and then I went back, sitting on a kitchen chair, looking at Doug through a pair of binoculars. He had on jeans, work boots, and a dull orange parka, and he stood alone, kicking his feet and breathing into his hands. He looked cold. He also looked up and down the street, and it was easy to see that he was waiting for someone.

Someone important, I hoped.

I quickly got dressed and I also tossed a few supplies in my duffel bag, and taking a gamble, I left the room and ran down the wooden stairs, making a hell of a racket, and then I walked across the rooming house's parking lot. I got into the Ford Explorer and switched on the engine and hunkered down, keeping an eye on Doug.

He was still there.

I left the radio off. No distractions.

Doug looked up and down the street, breathing again into his hands.

"Pretty impatient," I whispered. "Must be someone important enough to get you here alone by the pub. Someone who wants to see you, Dougie. Okay, then, who is it?"

The parking lot was empty, so he hadn't driven here. Dropped off? Or maybe he had spent the night in the Lincoln House. That would be funny in a perverse sense, if old Doug had cooped up last night and was the one with the loud television, someone with a sense of humor could have a lot of fun with that.

Doug stopped fidgeting. He put his hands in his pockets. A black Trans Am rolled by, and then glided to a stop. It looked like there was one guy in the car, the driver. Doug went around to the driver's side and started talking. Still hunched down, I lifted up my binoculars and tried to sneak a glance. Not much. Doug was shaking his head, talking a lot, moving his hands back and forth. I couldn't make out much of the guy in the car. Doug was blocking my view. Then Doug threw his hands up in the air and walked around to the other side of the car and got in.

I put the Ford into drive, and as I got out to the street, I was nearly rammed by the Trans Am as it went back into town. I held on to the steering wheel and took a deep breath, and then pulled out onto the road. Doug was still chatting, and he hadn't seen me.

Some luck.

I followed the Trans Am back into the center of town, and I was still lucky this morning, for traffic was light and I was able to keep one or two cars between me and the Trans Am. I was also high up enough to see what was going on, but the car had tinted windows, and all I could tell was that there were still two people inside.

After two turns, it quickly became obvious where they were going.

Back to Doug's home.

AFTER THE TRANS Am turned into the driveway to Doug's house, I drove up the adjacent road, back to my usual haunt. I raced through the knee-deep snow, carrying my duffel bag. No camp stool this time, so I hunkered down and watched as the two of them went in, Doug still arguing, it looked like.

I stayed out in the woods for long minutes, wishing I had the gumption and the available technology to have bugged Doug's home. Damn it, Paula and I had been bugged by Mike Ahern, and he was chasing after an arsonist. Didn't someone possibly connected to a rape merit the same attention?

Nothing much seemed to be going on at the house.

If not a bug, then maybe I should contact the UNH adult ed classes. Maybe it was time to take a course in lip reading.

Or something. Anything was better than living in a rooming house or shivering out in the snow.

I raised the binoculars again and the front door opened. A man strolled out, moving quite casually, going back to his Trans Am. He had a thick brown mustache and day-old stubble of beard, with thick, wide shoulders. His brown hair was done up in a tiny ponytail, and he had on pale blue jeans, white hooded sweatshirt, and a dungaree vest.

He got into the Trans Am and backed out, and in the quiet of the woods I made out the rumble of the heavy-duty engine.

Something started to tickle at me. Something about the car, something about the visitor, something...

I brought the binoculars back up. Funny how Doug hadn't seen the guy to his car, hadn't even come to the door. And then I remembered, all too well, the voice of a now-dead man. Muscle car, he had said. Muscle car.

I scanned the building. Nothing, nothing going on at all.

I looked to the garage door. Doug's car wasn't in the driveway. It must be inside.

I stood up, holding the binoculars fast in my hands, and I started running back to my rented Ford.

Smoke, gray smoke, was seeping out of the garage door.

27

Riding hard into the driveway of Doug's house, I bounced around as the Ford braked sloppily to a halt. I dove out and raced across the snow, slipping some, and I barreled through the front door. The odor was thick and it wasn't smoke, not quite right, but it was something bad. The living room was a mess as always and I spared the clutter a half-second glance as I moved to the right, to a door that led to the garage. It was locked and I had to heave against it twice before I broke through. The smell of exhaust was quite thick and it hurt my eyes. I coughed and went in, making sure I left the door open.

Doug's Colt was running and Doug was inside, slumped across the front seat. I tried the car door. It was locked. Damn. I didn't bother testing the other doors. This guy had been good.

I looked around and in a clutter of tools in the corner I found an ax handle, and in two quick smashes I had the driver's-side window broken. I reached in and unlocked the door and grabbed Doug around his shoulders.

"Doug!" I yelled. "Doug! Can you hear me?"

His head lolled around his shoulders, and there was a mat of blood and hair over his left ear. His lips were blue. I was probably way too late, but there were motions that had to be made.

After turning off the engine I grabbed him around his shoulders and pulled him out of the car. One of his feet caught on the brake pedal and I swore, sweating and with a headache coming on from the exhaust, and I yanked the foot free. I picked him up and dragged him out of the garage and through the living room and outside, then I dumped him in the snow. I suppose I should have taken the time to call for an ambulance, but I knew that seconds counted, seconds that were quickly melting away, and I got to work.

I tilted his head back and checked that his airway was clean, and I tried to find a pulse along the side of his neck.

No such luck.

I slapped his cheeks. "Doug!"

I stripped off his sweater and exposed his pale skin and bony chest. I felt up his ribs with shaking fingers, finding the breastbone, and the little place just below it. I tilted his head back again and was going to give him the first of two mouth-to-mouth blasts before starting CPR when he scared the shit out of me by coughing.

"Doug?" I asked, but there was still no answer, just a frenzy of coughing. I rolled him onto his side and his breathing got a bit easier, and then he gagged and threw up into the dirty snow. The sharp odor of bile made my own stomach do a few loop-de-loops and I wiped his face down with a handkerchief. He started shivering and whispered, "Christ, can I get inside? I'm freezing...."

"You need to see a doctor," I said.

"Later," he said, his voice slurred. "I gotta get inside 'fore I freeze."

"Doug—"

"Get me in, will ya!"

So I did.

A few minutes later he was on his couch and I was sitting across from him. He had a blanket wrapped around his thin shoulders and was holding a glass of water with one hand and a soiled handkerchief to the wound on his head with another. The door to the garage was shut and I insisted on keeping the front door open, to keep the air coming in. Even with the fresh air, though, the room reeked of exhaust and soiled clothing. He drank the water in a few shuddering gulps and I said, "What's his name, Doug?"

"Who?" he said, not looking at me. His hands were trembling.

"Who's the guy, Doug? The bad guy that just tried to kill you, and the very bad guy who raped your sister. Why are you protecting him?"

"You're crazy!" he said, weaving a bit on the couch. "It's not what you think...He's, he's—"

"He's the man that was with you that night, wasn't he?" I said, interrupting him. "Kara's landlord—now conveniently dead—said there were two men at her apartment that night, and that one of them was driving a muscle car. Kara also said the rapist was wearing a mustache. And you've got a piece of sculpture over there," I pointed to the crowded shelf, "that came from her apartment that night."

He refused to look at me, hands still trembling. I went over, moving the chair closer so I was in his space. "Come on, Doug," I said harshly. "Give it up! The guy just tried to kill you! What did he do, tap you on the side of the head and put you in there?"

Tears started streaming down his face and he just nodded. "I guess he decided you were an embarrassment, something that was getting in the way of business. Am I right?"

Another tearful nod.

"You're in a deep hole and I'm the only exit," I said. "You may have this bad guy after your behind, but if I make a phone call to Diane Woods, then there's no way out. You'll be hunted by people from both sides of the fence, and neither option looks good. Let me tell you one more thing—Diane is not in the mood for working within the criminal justice system. So you better start talking."

A mournful voice: "Jesus, I can't—"

"You better start, and start right now, Doug. Or I'm leaving and I'm making that phone call, and your friend will find out soon enough that you're not breathing carbon monoxide anymore. What's it going to be?"

Then Doug burst into tears.

I HAD BEEN PUTTING on a good act of the rough and tough guy who won't take no for an answer, and I had to force myself not to walk away or start making "there, there" noises when the crying eased down to sobbing. He let the empty water glass fall to the floor and started using the blood-stained handkerchief to wipe at the snot and saliva as he continued to weep.

"Oh, shit, I'm so screwed up it's not to be believed," he said. "Man, what I did to Kara...you shouldn't have gotten me out of that garage...I deserved to stay there..."

"Go on," I said. "Where did it start?"

Another round of sniffles. "A few months ago...I was working in Boston at one of the docks, real rough work, and I wasn't liking it, not at all. Some guy asked me if I'd come work for a friend of his. That's how I got in. Doing some light shit, nothing heavy."

"What's his name?"

"Seymour. Nick Seymour."

Nick.

A man bundled in clothes, with mustache and ponytail, walking out of a house in North Tyler a couple of weeks ago.

Nick.

Damn you, Felix.

"Go ahead," I said, trying to stay focused, not trying to let the sudden blossom of anger inside of me take hold. That could wait. Concentrate on what was going on here and now. Everything else could wait.

"It wasn't anything fancy," he said. "I was just a gofer, you know? Drive here and wait for Nick. Pick up so-and-so at the airport. Help break into a house out in Marblehead or Salem. Good work, too. I got paid all right and it beat working out on the docks all winter, that's for Christ sure. Then Nick began to trust me."

"So far, so good," I said, moving even closer. "Then what happened?"

He crossed his arms, soiled handkerchief clenched in one fist.

"Don't want to talk about it."

"I don't care what you want," I said. "I can still make that phone call, Doug. I'm your only way out."

He nodded, tears trembling down his cheeks, and he refused to look at me as he continued, "I still can't believe it happened. God, if I could take it all back. I should have never started."

"Started what?"

He coughed and wiped at his nose. "Along the way, doing shit for Nick and his guys, I started to get into the Andes magic a little, you know? Nice white stuff for topping out after a job...Sometimes Nick would pay me in cash and in blow...He had the best...I always looked forward to it."

Another hacking cough. "Then I really got to crave it. Man, you would not believe how much I wanted that white stuff...Then, back after Christmas, Nick gave me a package to hold on to. Said he had to make a delivery in a week and wanted it out of his house. He was getting nervous, you know? He didn't tell me much, but I knew from talking with the other guys that Nick's been working on a major score for this month. But he didn't want anything to screw it up, so he had me hold the package for him. So there it was, right in the kitchen, behind the cereal boxes, just sitting there..."

Doug brought up the handkerchief and wiped his cheeks and chin. "Christ, I was just doing nothing, sitting around. It had been snowing off and on and I couldn't go anywhere, and I was getting jumpy, and I said, shit, let's see what's in the package...Man, it was heaven...pure Andes flake. I just wanted a little taste, something to make the day go by, that's all...Then a couple of my friends stopped by and we started partying, and I didn't think a little bit more would be missed, I figured I could cut it a little with baby powder, who'd notice, and the partying really went on, some great-lookin' babes, and we tooted a bit more and a bit more..."

"All of it?" I asked.

A weak nod. "Nick came by the next day and I was passed out on the floor. The package was empty. Nick woke me up by throwing some water on me and then he was kneeling on my chest. I couldn't breathe. He had a knife to my throat and his eyes were kinda funny, and he said, 'Tell me why I shouldn't slit your worthless throat right now.'"

"What else?"

Doug closed his eyes for a minute. "I peed myself, that's what else. He was cursing me and swearing and spitting at me. Told me how I had fucked up. How the blow in that package was part of the negotiations he was dealing with...How I had pissed away six months of work in one night. He was getting ready to do it, ready to cut me...I was crying and beggin' him to stop...I said I would do anything, anything at all to get him off my chest and let me live. And that's when it happened..."

Though Doug was living and breathing in front of me, and a competent genetic scientist could search our cells and find similar DNA structures, I wasn't convinced he was human. Some psychiatrists and social workers would probably call me damn arrogant or something, and at that point, I didn't care.

"You gave him your sister," I said, trying to keep my voice steady.

A furtive nod.

"Why? Why would that make any difference?"

He folded his arms tight against his chest, rocked back and forth a bit. "I got to know Nick, got to know what he liked. He had a...a taste, something that involved hurting. That's all that mattered to him. Being in control and hurting. That's what he enjoyed. I saw a couple of hookers after he was done with them...He always had to pay extra, but that's what he liked. He knew my sister was a dyke, and that got him going, that he would be doing it with a broad that hated men...That got him going, and he got off my chest, and we went over there that night..."

Then he pulled the handkerchief to his mouth and bawled again. "God, I couldn't help it. He made me come with him and we went upstairs and I had the key to her place, one I copied from my parents last year. He went in and did it and I could hear her screaming and I stood there and I was in the living room, and I don't know, I had to have something in my hands. So I grabbed that damn dragon sculpture...I just held it and stared out the windows, and then Nick came back, grinning, zipping up his pants, and he said, 'Whaddya say, Dougie...you want a piece, too?'"

That was enough. I stood up and walked out of the house and stood in the snow, staring up at the cloudy sky. I was staring up, hoping that some flakes would begin falling, and quickly, for in looking up at the gray sky, I was working too hard at imagining what it must have been like that night in Kara's place, and to hear the voice after such an assault and know your brother was behind it.

"Snow," I murmured. "Damn it, start snowing..."

. . .

A WHILE later I was back inside. Doug had put on a gray sweatshirt, and I said, "I want Nick's home address, where he hangs out, and his business interests."

"Christ—"

"That wasn't a request, Doug. Start talking."

"You don't know—"

"But I do know this," I said. "He just tried to kill you an hour or so ago, so don't tell me you can't do it. You want to keep on breathing, start talking."

He sat on the couch, hands in his lap, then looked down at the floor and said, "When we was kids, Kara would always look out for me. Mom and Dad, they weren't much parents. Kara would put me to bed and make me lunch and make sure I did my homework. When the parents got to drinking and started fighting and yelling at each other, we'd hide upstairs and pretend not to hear them. We pretended we were far away and happy."

Doug looked up, face red and puffy, eyes still moist. "Will you for God's sake look what I've done?"

"No, I won't," I said. "I just want those addresses."

He sobbed and then started talking.

HOURS LATER, I was in my rented Ford in a parking lot near the Merrimack River, having a quick dinner in the front seat, half-listening to the radio. I had gone back to my rented room, had emptied everything out, and had also picked up some extra supplies. Now I was eating a chicken sandwich, not really tasting what was going into my mouth, just looking out at the lights of Salisbury, watching the cold waters of the river surge out into the Atlantic. At my side, among my possessions, was a handwritten list that I had made back at Doug's house, of various places that Nick Seymour might be. Most were bars or roadhouses, and it took some time for me to find them, for they were scattered along the narrow back roads of the Massachusetts North Shore. It had been a strange journey, of traveling into a world that I didn't belong to, of men and women working and living out there on the margins, drinking and partying and smoking after another mind-numbing day of work, and feeling that little gnawing fear in the pit of your stomach that the next day will bring nothing new, nothing wonderful, just the same dull stupor of being trapped and knowing of no way out.

I had searched the parking lots for Nick's Trans Am and had found nothing at all, but I had also entered each place to make sure. I pretended to use the pay phone as I scanned the bars and stools and pool tables, and I was tired and my head ached from the cigarette smoke, the loud music, and the same flat stares that came my way every time I opened a swinging door. A stranger among us, was the feeling I received, and now with everything still ahead of me, I was scared. No backup tonight, not at all. Felix was probably sunning himself and chasing airline attendants across warm sands, and I couldn't bring Diane into what I planned to do. Not yet, anyway, and I looked out at the lights and finished my sandwich and recalled the story Doug had told me, and I remembered seeing that jaunty confidence of Nick's a few weeks before, back at Felix's.

Nick and Felix. They knew each other, and as before, I was keeping my feelings toward Felix locked up and placed deep in a compartment inside me. I had to focus, and I couldn't waste time or energy wondering what Felix knew, and what he might be hiding.

On my own again, I started up the Ford and left the parking lot.

THE LAST ADDRESS on the list was Nick's home, out on the southern outskirts of Newburyport, and I drove there, trying to think of what I would do and how I would do it if I met him. And as I thought of those little strategies, I also knew if Nick wasn't home, I would start again at the list of pubs and roadhouses and resume my little journey along the back roads of Essex County.

Nick's neighborhood was Branson Drive, a quiet residential area with ranch-type houses and well-plowed driveways, and the snow-covered lawns were littered with sleds, plastic toys, and half-melted snowmen. An odd place for a bad man to live, and it made an eerie sense. The man was smart. Live in a rough neighborhood and you get plenty of attention and plenty of cruisers stopping by. Live in a place like Branson Street and the neighbors can all eventually repeat the same refrain: A quiet fella, no trouble at all, usually kept to himself.

Nick's house was a white ranch, set up a bit on a rise of land, and on a lot bigger than his neighbors. Unlit Christmas lights were still in the shrubbery, and the shutters of the house were painted a dull black.

A nice, quiet, and sober-looking house.

With a Trans Am in the driveway.

I DROVE SLOWLY BY, trying to see what I could through the well-lit windows, but I saw no movement. Not a thing. Doug had told me that Nick lived alone, and with no other vehicles in the driveway, well, it was possible that he was here tonight by himself.

What to do?

My hands slipped a bit on the steering wheel as I made a U-turn and came back up Branson Drive, and with a sudden impulse, I turned again and went up the driveway, my heart seeming to swell up right against my chest. Crazy, but it just might work. I checked on a few things before I got out of the Ford. My .357 Smith & Wesson went into a coat pocket, while a pair of police handcuffs went into another. A joke gift from Diane on my birthday last year, but they worked just fine, and I was sure they would work well tonight. Two more items—a clipboard with some blank sheets of paper and that day's *Boston Globe*—and I was out on the driveway of Nick's house. My heart seemed to want to burrow right out of my chest and through my heavy winter coat. I was in enemy territory, and for a quick moment, before I walked in, I looked up at the stars and they were so bright and beautiful I imagined they almost gave me solace.

Might work. Could work. I doubt he had noticed me much, sitting in the Range Rover back at Felix's house, and besides, tonight I was driving the rented Ford.

I walked up to the house, hand in the coat pocket and carrying the clipboard and newspaper, and up the steps I went, heart roaring along, my head almost shaking in the disbelief of what I was going to do, and I was seized with a brief triumph of joy, that in a very short few hours, I would be rid of this awful task.

I rang the doorbell and looked into a near window, and there was Nick Seymour, standing in front of a stove, stirring something in a saucepan. He had on jeans and black sweatshirt, sleeves rolled up to his muscled fore-arms. His ponytail looked freshly washed, and as I watched him, I reached over and rang the doorbell again.

Nick looked over in my direction and I gave him a half-wave, and he returned the favor with a friendly nod. He put down the wooden spoon, wiped his hands on a towel, and ambled over. Then the door opened up and he said, "Yes?" in a quiet voice.

I froze. His eyes. They reminded me of smiling concentration camp guards, of a merry Ted Bundy sitting in a courtroom, and the joy of a Ku Klux Klansman setting fire to a large wooden cross.

"Yes?" he repeated, still friendly, and I said, "Hello, sir, my name is Aaron Shaw and I'm from *The Boston Globe*." I passed over the newspaper and he took it and looked up and shrugged.

"Sorry, if you're here to sell me a subscription, I really don't have time to read."

Don't stare, I thought. "No, that's not it," I said. "I'm conducting a reader-ship survey, that's all, and I'd like to ask a few questions."

Nick shook his head. "I don't want to be rude, but I'm kinda busy with dinner."

Inside, I've got to get inside. Too many people could be watching from the other houses, and I don't want them to see me pulling out my .357 on their neighbor.

"I know you are, but for answering the survey, you'll get a free subscrip-tion for a month and a fifty-dollar gift certificate to the area restaurant of your choice."

He looked at the newspaper again. "Really? That's not a bad deal." Nick's smile got wider as he opened the door. "I sure as hell hate to cook. Tonight is spaghetti, and I had that twice last week, and I'm getting sick of that crap. C'mon in."

I walked into the warm and clean kitchen and self-consciously wiped my feet on a mat that said WELCOME FRIENDS, and Nick went over to the stove and turned off the burner and said, "If you'll excuse me for just a sec, Mr. Shaw. I've gotta make sure my VCR is set to record something tonight. I'll be right back."

"Sure."

I looked around for a second. The kitchen was small but well scrubbed, and before me was an entryway into the living room. Nick walked into the living room, heading over to the television, and I looked over at the stove and put my hand into my coat pocket, and when I looked up again, Nick wasn't smiling anymore.

He also had a shotgun in his hands.

"This is the way it's going to be, Lewis Cole," he said. "I'm going to start asking a few questions. You say something I don't like, you argue with me or you lie, and then I'm going to shoot you in the left knee. Then we'll keep going—right knee, right elbow, and left elbow—and we'll keep going until I'm done or you can't go on anymore. Do we have an understanding?"

Dear God. The kitchen was suddenly sweltering, and my heart seemed to deflate and start to settle toward my backbone.

"Yes," I finally said. "We have an understanding."

"Good." He stepped closer, shotgun at his shoulder, pointing down at my left leg. "Are you armed?"

"Yes."

"Where?"

"Revolver, in my right-hand pocket."

"Take your hand out of that pocket, real slow. I see anything else but fingers, you lose your left knee. Understand?"

"Yes," I said, hating what I was doing as I took out my hand. When my hand was out, Nick said, "Good. Now unbutton your coat and let it fall to the floor. That clipboard, too."

In another minute or two, my coat was around my ankles, Nick moved closer, shotgun unwavering. "Tell me, what kind of stupid fuck do you think I am?"

"You're a lot of things, but I've never thought you were stupid."

"Well, ain't you the bright one. Try this one on for size. Doug called me almost five hours ago, telling me that you were coming," I couldn't speak, couldn't move, could not believe what was happening. Nick was grinning. "You nitwit, you should know better than to trust a junkie, especially one who's so hard up. Hell, I tried to kill the little shit earlier today, and he dimed you right after you left, just for a few grams of magic powder. That make you feel good, author-man, knowing that little sniveling Doug thinks your life is only worth a few toots?"

Another step closer. "I asked you a question!" he said, voice rising. "And you know what I said I'd do if I didn't get an answer. So tell me, you fool. You feel pretty good?"

I was honest. "No, I don't."

A quick nod. "Well, I'm glad to hear that, and I'm glad you finally showed up."

He moved rattlesnake fast, slicing up the shotgun stock to my jaw. The sudden bone-shock of being hit made me snap my teeth up and I fell backward and to the floor, the hard tile no comfort at all, my eyes bugging out with the pain, my hands moving up to my face and feeling the slickness, and I was almost throwing up as I curled up on the floor, everything dim and rolling, and Nick came over and said, "And I had to wait, and I hate waiting!"

Then he stomped on my head.

28

Months of long and dark hours later, I was weaving on my feet in the kitchen, my clothes a mess, my eyes nearly swollen shut, my ribs on both sides throbbing with a burning pain. My hands were cuffed behind me and Nick had a hand on my elbow as he opened up a door.

"Time for a break, before I decide what to do with you next," he said.

He then shoved me down a flight of stairs into the cellar. I fell down, everything a rolling motion of pain and impact, tumbling, and sharp digs into my elbows and knees, and then I crumpled up on the concrete floor. Far off I heard the sound of Nick coming downstairs, and he grabbed my handcuffed arms and dragged me across the floor. I was breathing through my mouth, blood and saliva dribbling down my chin. My wrists ached where the handcuffs dug in and there didn't seem to be a joint or bone that didn't hurt.

Nick stopped and then kicked me again in the ribs. I groaned and tried to roll up in a ball, but it still didn't do anything for the pain. He said, "That was very thoughtful of you, bringing along the handcuffs. Saved me the trouble of tying you up."

I tried to open my eyes, and it hurt to do so. All I could make out was his booted feet and the dirty concrete. Nick said, "Sorry, but I don't buy the story you're just sniffing around 'cuz of that dyke I had a date with. Don't believe somebody would go to so much trouble for a piece of pussy, even though I put down that landlord later, figuring he might have heard something. Hell, you put up a hell of a fight back there on the island and hurt a couple of my boys, after I set that little fake meet-up with a friend of mine who called you. So I think you're up to something, Mr. Cole. I think you're working for someone, trying to screw up my deal, and I don't like that."

Another swift kick to the ribs, and I cried out, even though it didn't hurt as much as my jaw. Either I was on the verge of passing out, or Nick was getting tired of the fun. "So this is what we're going to do," he continued. "I'm going upstairs to take a shower and then have dinner, and then I'm coming back, and we're gonna talk some more. This time, I'm going to get the answers I want, and I'm not going to stop until I'm happy. Got it?"

I mumbled something and he said, "Fine. Just so there's no misunderstanding, I expect some good answers, or I'm not going to be so considerate. I mean, I haven't even touched your balls yet, and that's usually the best way to get what you want."

He laughed at his own superb sense of humor, and then I could hear him on the stairs again, and the cellar light went off and an upstairs door slammed shut and then was locked with a loud click.

Everything was now dark.

I CLOSED and opened my eyes a few times, trying to see something, anything, but there was just the black space about me. I slowed my breathing, tried to ease the terrible fears in the back of my brain that were threatening to break loose and paralyze me. Another breath, and another. Take stock, old boy, I thought. Just relax and start thinking, because when he's well-fed and well-washed, he's coming back. I closed my eyes, thankful I couldn't see his face anymore, those dull eyes that showed nothing, nothing at all, except a merry humor at being in control and being able to cause pain and terror. I moved my arms and groaned. It felt like my arms were slowly being pulled out of my shoulder blades. Relax, I thought, try to relax. My ribs ached and my jaw made clicking sounds as I moved around, and my tongue was sore where I had bit it. Both knees were throbbing from my tumble down the stairs, and beside it all, I was exhausted. If Nick had told me he would be back tomorrow, I'm sure I would have fallen asleep.

A thrumming sound overhead, and it was water moving through the pipes. Old Nick was in his shower. No doubt washing off blood, blood that didn't belong to him.

I opened my eyes. Shapes, this time. Shapes just outside my view. I blinked and thought they were people, waiting for me. The fabled dead friends in another dimension, waiting to bring you across? Had I suffered a brain injury falling down the stairs, and was that Cissy and Carl Socha and Trent Baker from my old job at the Pentagon, waiting for me on the Other Side?

I blinked again. No. Just a washing machine and dryer, and what looked like a workbench.

I rolled over and sat up, breathing hard from the exertion.

My head felt like it was loosely attached to my shoulders, by tendons and muscles that were fraying apart. I looked around again. The cellar wasn't completely dark. There was a sliver of light coming from the upstairs door, and another coming from a bulkhead door that led outside. I coughed up a wad of blood and spit. Water still moved through the pipes. Think, old boy, think hard and think fast, because no one knows you're here. Diane, Felix, Paula, the Newburyport cops, no one that matters, except for Nick and that pitiful creature that claimed to be Kara's brother. I took a couple of breaths and then stood up, grinding my teeth to prevent me from groaning again. I was getting sick of hearing myself. I shuffled painfully over to the stairs and walked up slowly, hearing each step creak as I went up, my knees complaining loudly about their treatment. I got to the last step and looked around, but I didn't see a light switch. Damn. Switch must be in the kitchen.

I moved down a couple steps and looked at the door. Well-built and solid. Not one of those particleboard jobs that could be punched through by a twelve-year-old. Still...I wondered how much energy I could put together, if I was down at the bottom of the stairs and raced up and hit the door with my shoulder. I winced at what might happen to my shoulder if I did that, but once in the kitchen, I could make a quick 911 call if I was dexterous enough or, with better luck, could get outside.

Then I noticed I didn't hear the water running anymore. Then Nick walked by on the other side of the door, whistling.

BACK STANDING ON THE FLOOR, I shivered from the cold and the exertion of trying to ease my way downstairs without Nick knowing I was there. Think, think, think, a voice inside of me screamed. Not much time left. I walked over to the bulkhead door. Locked, and not by one lock, either. Two. From upstairs the sounds of dishes rattling, as a table was being set. Over at the workbench, I looked for a length of rope or wire, something to string across the stairs. Maybe catch the son of a bitch as he came down.

Sure. Trip him up and then we'll beat him to death with our head. I flexed my fingers. Damn cuffs, and sure, even in this horrible place, I could almost admire the desperate amusement of being secured in a pair of my own handcuffs.

I coughed and leaned against the workbench. My head was woozy, and I fought against the urge to lie down, to give it all up, to look up in those dead eyes again and just surrender. A few moments of pain and terror, and, well, then it would be all over. Right?

I moved away from the bench. To hell with sitting down. As I shuffled across the concrete, I flexed my fingers. Cold and stiff. If we could get these damn shackles off, that would improve the situation.

Back on the floor. I remembered seeing a movie once in which the hero had been handcuffed. He had squatted down and had moved his legs through his arms, so that the cuffs were in front. Something like this...

"Jesus Christ," I whimpered, as I fell over on my side. My arms felt even worse, throbbing up and down with red-hot slivers of pain. No joy, none at all. No wonder they call movies make believe.

I sat up. No sound from upstairs. Probably eating. Or maybe he's piling the dishes in the sink. Either way, he's coming back down here soon enough. Damn it all to hell. Never again do something so stupid. Never again.

Another coughing fit, and I wiggled my fingers, and then I tugged.

Something moved.

I froze. Moved my right hand, and then the left. The left hand slipped through the cuff, just a bit.

Again, let's try it again.

A slight movement, and then my hand stopped. The left cuff wasn't closed quite as far as the right.

Don't try it again, I thought. Start tugging and moving and your hand will get swollen and you'll lose whatever advantage you've gained.

Okay. An advantage. Now what?

I looked across the cellar and saw the washer and dryer, and I knew.

THERE WAS a wooden shelf above the washer. Plastic bottles of some sort were up there. I boosted myself up and sat on the washer, and I grabbed the handle of one bottle with my teeth. I dragged it off the shelf and it fell in my lap, and I stopped, terrified I was making too much noise.

No sound.

I looked down. In the dim light I could make out the bright label of a liquid detergent.

"So glad you're not a powder man, Nick," I whispered. I kept the detergent bottle between my legs as I got off the washer and then knelt down, gently depositing the plastic container on the floor. I moved across the cellar, going to the far corner, moving the bottle with my feet. Using my teeth again and bracing the bottle against a cardboard box, I got the cap off. The smell of soap was strong and wonderful. I sat back and tipped the bottle back against my left wrist. It took some work because the bottle was half-empty, but in a few fumbled minutes, I had a stream of liquid soap running down my wrist.

Upstairs, the sound of water again, and the clinking noises of dishes being washed.

Stop listening! I shouted silently at myself, as the soap got down to my left wrist. I took a series of deep breaths and willed my left hand to relax, thought of each individual muscle and tendon, willed each cell to relax and let loose. I curled my thumb against my hand, and with my right hand I started pulling.

The same movement, just farther.

Then the searing pain of the metal cuff meeting a bone in my hand.

So close, so goddamn close.

Again. I tipped the bottle and gooped up my wrist again, and started over. A slow, steady tug with my right hand, pulling at the cuff. There was a scraping sensation, and I could feel something begin to give way, and feel the abrasiveness of the metal, and then I clenched my teeth and tears came to my eyes and I had to stop.

I was panting now, and my left hand felt like it was being gnawed on.

A flash of light, illuminating half the cellar, as the door opened up.

"Ready for some more fun, Cole?" came the taunting voice. "Just as soon as I take a crap, I'll be right down."

The door shut again. I clenched my teeth, breathed frantically through my nose, and I tugged and felt the skin give way and blood and the pain of the soap in the open wound, and then the cuff slipped off.

Mother of God, it hurt so much...

I looked up at the washer and dryer. The sound of flushing water, and I knew he would be here in a minute or two, and I got to work.

I WAS AGAINST THE WALL, slumped and with my legs splayed out, when the light came on. My hands were behind my back, and I kept my head down to my chest as he stomped down the stairs. I looked up, drool running down my chin, eyes half-open. He pranced over at me, a merry grin on his face, the shotgun carried casually in his right hand.

"Well, I see you moved all of five feet," he said. "Congratulations. You did better than I expected. Shall we begin?"

As he reached me, he bent over, and then I moved in a whiplash, shooting my right hand out from behind my back, the hand holding a large plastic cup, the cup containing a full load of chlorine bleach, which I tossed right into his smug, smiling face.

Nick shrieked and fell back, and I got up in a snap, forgetting all of the pain and soreness, and I tore away the shotgun from his hands—easy enough, since he was clawing at his face—and I took the shotgun and swung it up, connecting the stock solidly with his crotch. Another shriek and he was on the floor, and I was taking no chances, no chances at all, and I rose the stock up twice as I reconnected the shotgun with his groin.

With the lights on, I made out some jump rope over in another corner, hanging on a rack near an exercise machine, and panting loudly and moving fast, I went over and got it, and though he put up a bit of a struggle, within another few minutes his hands and legs were trussed.

I stood up, weaving and feeling faint, looking down at the moaning and tied-up figure, and I brought back my foot for a kick, and then thought better of it. I leaned onto the shotgun and tapped my foot against the side of his head.

"Yes, Nick," I said, my voice tired and raspy. "Let us begin."

I WENT UPSTAIRS and drank some water, then found the handcuff key on the kitchen counter and undid the sole remaining cuff on my wrist. I went out into the living room and found my .357, which I tucked in the rear of my waistband. Back in the kitchen, I tried not to look too much at the mess around my left hand, and I wrapped some paper towels around the bleeding and went back down to the cellar, dangling the cuffs in my right hand. Nick was curled up in a ball, moaning and crying, his face red and eyes swollen.

"Jesus," he moaned. "Please, please get me some water, man...Wash out my eyes, you've got to wash out my eyes..."

On some other day, hell, on some other planet, I would have done just that, but instead I got down on my knees and handcuffed his wrists, being extra sure to put the cuffs on tight. I then loosened the rope around his legs, and I said, "Here's the deal, Nick. We're going for a walk. You don't put up a struggle and then I'll wash out your eyes."

His eyes were screwed up in pain and his face was bright red. "Fuck you, asshole."

"Maybe so," I said, as I rolled him onto his side, "but this is one asshole who's going to keep his eyesight. If we don't wash your eyes pretty quick, you'll be blind. That's your choice. Help yourself and you keep your sight. Fight me and you go blind."

He cursed me again and said nasty things about my parentage and sexual habits, but I helped him up and he didn't put up a fight. We walked across the cement floor and going upstairs was a struggle, the two of us on the stairs, and as we went up, he tried to deal his way out.

"Come on, Cole, what's your number?" he muttered, as we reached the top of the stairs.

"Not for sale," I said, my joints and sides and tongue still aching with pain, one hand firm on a handcuffed wrist.

"There's always a price."

"No sale."

"Let me go," he said, his head moving, eyes screwed up tight. "Leave the key and make a call to a friend of mine and go into my bedroom. There's a wall safe, I'll give you the combination. There must be ten, twenty thousand in there. All yours."

In the kitchen I paused, thinking, and then I half-dragged him to the front door and then turned off all the lights. I didn't want his neighbors seeing anything. I picked up my coat and took out the car keys.

"'Fraid not," I said. "There's a price on your greasy head, and you can't match it."

"Of course I can!" he said. "Just tell me what it is."

I opened the kitchen door. My Ford was there, right where I had left it. "Nick, shut up, will you?"

"Cole, you bastard, you—"

"How's your eyes doing? Those corneas still burning? That bleach still eating its way through the pupils?"

My questions did the trick, and he didn't do a thing as I guided him outside to the driveway. I opened the rear door and tumbled him inside, forcing him to lie on his back. Using the seat belts and shoulder harnesses, I managed to fasten him. I didn't want him to sit up and start chewing on my ear or something as I drove away. I went around the front, the cold night air feeling fine on my skin, and I looked up at the beautiful and distant stars, and took a deep breath, and thanked all the gods—past, present, and future—for letting me breathe out in the night air again.

Inside, I cranked up the engine and drove out, and when we got on the road is when the shakes began. My legs were trembling and my hands were quaking on the steering wheel, and I had to empty my bladder so bad I thought it would burst. A damn close thing, a real damn close thing, and I was sure that the Greater Powers were probably wondering when in hell I would learn anything.

At a stop sign there was a plaintive voice from behind me, edged with pain: "You promised, Cole. You promised to wash out my eyes."

"So I did."

At my side were my overnight bags and bundles from my stay at the rooming house, and I unzipped a bag and pulled out a container of bottled water. After unscrewing the cap, I reached over the rear of the seat and poured the contents on his face. He blinked hard and moved his face back and forth, moaning some, and when the bottle was empty, I tossed it on the floor and kept on driving.

WHEN I GOT into Tyler I drove to the beach and headed up the nearly deserted Atlantic Avenue. By now the pains along my body were racing merrily along, and I wished I could just roll Nick out the rear door and head to a local emergency room for some serious painkillers. But there was a task to be done, and I was going to see it through. Even with the pain, there was a sense of contentment, of having finally done it. Nick now belonged to Diane, and the sooner I handed him over, the quicker I could get to something that would dull the red-hot sensations throbbing in my joints and side and wrist.

At Tyler Harbor Meadows I turned into the common parking area for Diane's condo unit, and I let the Ford Explorer slow to a halt.

No one was home.

Diane's Volkswagen was gone, and all of the lights were off in the unit, both upstairs and downstairs. I drove around the lot, past the mounds of snow, and backed into an empty spot, which allowed me a view of the condominium. I switched off the lights and let the engine rumble on. Damn.

A voice from the rear: "What the hell is going on?"

"Pipe down, will you?" I said. "Or I might have the urge to do some laundry again, real soon."

"You wouldn't dare."

"You're not in a position to dare anybody."

So he stayed quiet, and I turned on the radio, and I started thinking. Both of them were out, but where? Out for dinner or maybe a day trip to Boston or Northampton. I could call the Tyler dispatch, and they would politely tell me to mind my own business.

Cars started coming into the condo parking lot, and my heart raced a bit each time I saw a set of headlights. But no Volkswagen, no green car with Diane and Kara.

I chewed on a thumbnail for a bit. I didn't like this. People were getting out of their cars and were looking over at me, some with questioning faces. I'm sure I looked suspicious, and I didn't want some curious neighbor coming over to see what was up, and to also see Nick Seymour, trussed up in my back seat.

Hard to explain that one. But where to?

Not my house. No, sir. Nick Seymour wasn't going to soil my property, no matter what was going on.

I thought for a few moments more and then a man climbed out of a Lincoln, looked at me, looked again, and started walking in my direction.

Time to move.

And as I eased the Explorer out of the parking lot, I knew where I would go.

IT WAS QUITE dark when I reached Rosemount Lane in North Tyler, and I took one of the two spaces in front of Felix's house. The other space was empty, of course. Damn Felix. He was probably still whoring it up down there in the Cayman Islands. With this snow and cold and lousy job that we were involved with, who could blame him?

"Time for a rest stop," I announced, getting out of the front seat. I put the .357 into my coat pocket and went to the rear door of the Ford. Felix might not be home, but I knew where he kept a spare key, out back for the cellar door, and this was as good a place as any to drop Nick off, rest up, and decide what the hell to do next.

I unlocked the rear door on the driver's side and undid the seatbelt around his chest, and Nick moaned and said, "Damn it, my eyes are still burnin' awful."

"We'll get you washed up inside."

I moved to the other side of the Ford, unlocked that door, and repeated the seatbelt work. "Come along, Nick, it's time to—"

My jaw exploded, as his legs flew out and connected with my chin. I fell back against the snowbank and onto the snow-covered lawn as Nick squirmed his way out, getting his legs and then his torso out, trying to stand up, trying to make a run for it.

I rubbed my jaw, stood up, and kicked his legs out from underneath him. He fell with a *whoomph*! into the snow, and I rolled him over. He looked up at me, panting, and then spat in my direction.

I took in a deep breath. "Nick, old boy, you are beginning to piss me off."

With a free hand I picked up a handful of snow and rubbed it in his face, and I said, "Count that as the cleaning I promised you. Come along, or I swear I'll drag you through the snow, and you can be wet all night long."

He came along, cursing and muttering as we went along a shoveled side path to the rear of the house, and then he looked up at the building and said, "What the hell...you brought me to Tinios's place?"

"That I did."

"You know him?"

"Sure do," I said, turning to him and trying my best and fiercest smile, which was hard to do considering the recent assault to my chin. "You could say he's a real good friend of mine."

If I was trying to scare him, it failed. He just said, "Well, Christ, that's good. I know I can cut a deal with Felix."

"I don't think so."

We reached the back of the house, and there was the rear door, also shoveled free.

"You might be surprised," Nick said.

"So might you. Sit down and be quiet."

Another few curses, but I was hardly listening, and I pushed him down with a hand to the chest, and back he fell. The rear door was flanked on both sides by small windows, and I brushed the snow off the sill to the window on the left. I ran my fingers across the wood and pressed down, and a section slid free, leaving a gap of a few inches. I reached in and felt a long string and a key, and I was smiling quite broadly as I brought the key out.

My smile lasted all of a second. Something cold and metallic was being pressed against my right ear.

A voice: "Can I help you with something, pal?"

29

I froze right up, conscious of the power and death all wrapped up in that little piece of metal pressing into my skin. Besides my own breathing and the sound of the distant waves, there was also the low and steady laughter of Nick.

I cleared my throat. "Yeah, you can help me."

"I can?"

"Sure," I said, slowly turning. "Just tell me your hand isn't shaking, Felix."

And there he was, dressed in jeans and a black sweatshirt with a pistol in his hands. I felt a confusing rush of emotions: anger in wondering what was going on with him and Nick, and the anger tempered by the wonderful peace and joy of knowing Felix was here with his weapons and his ways, and I could relax, if only for a while.

Felix lowered his weapon. "No, my hand isn't shaking." He looked at me and at Nick, who had stopped laughing. "Looks like you've been busy."

"I have."

"Shall we get inside before we freeze, and try to figure out what in hell's going on?"

"No argument from me."

Eventually we all got into the cellar and Nick started blabbering on and Felix looked at him, and this time a look got Nick's attention.

"Nick, sit down and shut up," Felix said, going to a workbench and finding a length of chain and a combination lock. "You make any fuss, anything at all, then you're going to make me upset. Then I'll have to come back downstairs, and you won't like it."

"Felix, look, I can explain—"

Felix bent down and threaded the chain through the handcuffs and fastened the chain and lock around one of the steel pillars holding up the flooring, "Nick, you've just started down the path of making me upset. You still have time to walk back."

Nick shut up. Felix snapped the lock shut, looked at me, and said, "You look even worse than the time you ran back to the Lafayette House. Let's get you upstairs."

I followed Felix slowly upstairs, my ribs and legs complaining, and a lot of things were barreling through my mind as we got into the kitchen. Felix still had his 9mm in his hand, and he placed the weapon in an open drawer. The whole house was dark, the only light coming from the oven range. He sat on a high stool at the counter, and I sat across from him.

"I've been back about a day, just keeping low and quiet," Felix said. "I'm staying up in Dover and I was coming back here to get some clothes and stuff when I saw you drive in. I knew you had rented something, but I didn't know it was a Ford."

"The rental folks had run out of M-1 Abrams tanks."

Felix nodded with a slight smile. "Then I saw the two of you get up and there was a struggle or something, and then you went behind the house. I didn't know what the hell was going on. I just knew I had to get back there."

I looked up at him and slowly drew out my .357, and then I placed it on the counter. The kitchen drawer with Felix's own weapon was at my front. It was far out of reach. I looked again at Felix and his eyes narrowed, the dim light from the range making his eyes look heavy and hooded. There was a flicker of an expression on his face and a faint nod. He had gotten the point.

"Seems like you're upset," Felix said carefully.

"I am."

"What do you want?"

"For now, I want you to sit on your hands."

Felix looked at me and I looked right back at him, doing quite fine, thank you. As brooding a man as Felix is, I had gone stare-to-stare with the best of them.

He said, "I'm afraid I can't do that."

I slowly reached over and placed my hand on the revolver.

"I'm afraid you're going to have to."

He licked his lips and said, "What's the problem?"

"The problem is that creature locked up in your cellar. You know him, know him pretty well. Hell, he's even on a first-name basis with you. So. What's the story? You involved in his deal? You protecting Nick? You trying to tell me you didn't know anything about his little hobbies, didn't know he had raped Kara?"

My voice had been rising with every sentence, and I casually moved the .357 around so it was now pointing in Felix's general direction.

He kept on staring at me, and then there was a quiet movement, as he lifted one buttock and then another, sitting firmly on his hands. "I know Nick, but I'm not involved in his business."

"How do you know him?"

"Some guys I know, back in Boston," Felix said. "They recommended my services to Nick a couple of months ago. He's been by a couple of times, trying to get me signed up for a major smuggling action that's going to start in Newburyport. Fishing boats coming into the harbor at night. Relatively safe and with lots of profit. He wanted to hire me on, doing security work."

"But you said no."

"That's right, and you know it. I don't work with drugs, not at all. Too many crazy people out there."

"But you know Nick, and he seems to be right out there in craziness world. You mean to say you didn't know he liked to beat up women, liked a little rape action?"

He shook his head. "Didn't know and didn't care."

"Find that hard to believe, a man with your talents."

I think he was tempted to smile but didn't succumb to temptation. "Nick and I don't live in the same worlds. He's petty little crap jobs, like burglaries and smuggling, stuff I don't care about. He came to me with a straight job, and I turned him down. End of story. If I knew he had done that rape, I would have tracked him down myself and dropped him off at Diane's doorstep. Think of the mileage that would have gotten me."

I took some breaths and my ribs howled at me, and I was tired of it, tired of it all, and I looked at Felix and was surprised to find out my eyes were beginning to fill up.

"I guess I want to believe you, Felix."

His sharp look softened some and he gingerly freed his hands and placed them in his lap. "Look, I can take care of everything, right now, and prove I didn't know anything about what he did. You give me the word and I'll take him out back and he'll have a drowning accident, and it's taken care of. Do you want that?"

I was really hurting now, hurting something awful, and my ribs and jaw and wrist were all playing a concert of throbbing pain, of an agony I had never felt before, and with my hand on my revolver, I pushed it over the counter to him and sat back.

"No, he doesn't belong to us," I said. "He belongs to Diane."

A while later I was on his couch, sipping an Irish coffee, feeling the gentle numbness of painkillers work their magic across my bruised and battered body. Felix had cranked up the thermostat and the room was toasty warm, for I was only wearing a pair of loose shorts. Felix had taken a black jump bag out of his closet and had gone to work, wiping down my wounds, washing away the grime, and laying on a few butterfly bandages. He worked quickly and efficiently, and through all his gruff and bluster, his touch was gentle and sure.

The coffee was hot and stung a bit, but I did all right. "You'd make a great nurse, if only your bedside manner improved."

He finished taping a bit of gauze on my right side. "There's nothing wrong with my manners concerning the bedroom, and you should know that."

"Thankfully, I don't."

He laughed and gathered up his supplies and I said, "You do good work, Felix."

"Thanks," he said. "Nothing school-taught. Just fieldwork, all out of necessity. Sometimes...well, sometimes you get into a situation where either you or a buddy can't go to the local emergency room. So you do your own work, and you learn pretty quickly."

"You missed your calling."

"No, I didn't." He stood up and grabbed the bag, then looked down at me and said, "I think you're going to have a new scar or two by the time you heal."

"I think I'll get over it."

He rubbed at his chin. "You ever going to tell me where you got those old scars, back when you were at the Pentagon?"

The Irish coffee tasted wonderful, making everything warm "No, I won't."

"I figured." Then he bent over and put his hand to my cheek for a moment. "You just watch yourself. The ladies don't mind a scar or two, it gets them tingly, but anything more and they'll think you're a freak."

Then he moved his hand back and I said, "Thanks for the advice," but by then, a tad self-conscious, he had walked back to his bedroom.

ANOTHER TEN MINUTES later and I was feeling even better, a blanket across my lap, and Felix joined me in the living room with his own Irish coffee and said, "All right, what is to be done?"

"With our guest downstairs?"

"Among other things," Felix said. 'Why did you bring him here?"

"I went to Diane's place, but she wasn't home. I didn't feel like waiting in a parking lot with Nick trussed up in the back seat and I didn't want to take him to my place, so your place went right to the top of the list."

"Thanks, I think."

"Well, I figured you were still in the Caymans, and wouldn't mind me using the place for a while."

He leaned forward, coffee cup in his hands. "When we first started on this little adventure, you weren't too sure what we'd do if we found the bad guy. You wanted to protect Diane and her career, and you said when we got to this point, then you'd figure something out. I think you're figuring on giving him over to Diane, right?"

"Yeah."

"What changed your mind?"

The wind outside had risen some, and I was glad to be under the blanket and drinking the hot coffee and whiskey. I burrowed under the blanket a bit more.

"Not my decision," I said. "It's Diane's. She wanted this guy, and as her friend, I made a promise to her to do just that. I can't make her decisions about her career. That's her job. She wanted the rapist of her lover and best friend delivered to her for punishment, and that's what I'm giving her."

I glanced down at the empty coffee cup. "Kara will probably end up hating me, once Diane finds out what her brother did. That might break up the two of them, and then Diane will end up hating me, too." I looked up at Felix. "But I made a promise. That's what I'm going to do."

Felix nodded. "Promises can be pretty heavy."

"Yeah, well, this one is about ready to break my shoulders," and I started yawning, and my mouth was fuzzy with all the painkillers and coffee and whiskey I had imbibed.

Felix got up and took my cup from my not-so-strong fingers and said, "Why don't you stretch out there and go to sleep? It's late and you've had a hellish day."

"So I have," I said, moving around some. "And what about your cellar guest?"

"I'll bring down some blankets and make him comfortable, but he better hope he enjoys sleeping on concrete," Felix said from the kitchen.

I laid back and closed my eyes. "Make sure he doesn't go anywhere..."

"He won't," Felix said.

I closed my eyes and heard some footsteps downstairs, and the mutter of voices, and then felt a blanket being tossed about me.

I woke up, wincing from the pain and stiffness. Felix was in the kitchen cooking something up, and said, "You look like crap."

"And good morning to you."

"And you look like you need a shower and a meal, so why don't you get to it?"

So I did. I slowly made my way to the bathroom, grimacing from the little tugs and whispers in my body. I showered slowly and carefully, looking at the ugly black-and-blue marks along my ribs and legs, and at the bandages. Felix had left out a new toothbrush for me, but even brushing my teeth hurt. I looked at myself in the mirror, saw the haunted look in my eyes, and then I looked away.

When I got out of the bathroom some clothes were folded on the floor before me. I got dressed, went back down to the kitchen, and gingerly ate breakfast with Felix, letting the scrambled eggs and toast go down slowly. My jaw ached and my tongue was swollen.

We talked a bit about politics and when the weather would finally warm up, and when Felix had finished washing the dishes, he tossed a towel over his shoulder and said, "We need to talk about our downstairs guest."

"Not much to talk about," I said. "We make a call to Diane and set up a time and place, and his ass belongs to her."

He frowned and took the towel off his shoulder, then started rubbing his hands.

"You might want to talk to Nick," he said, looking a bit troubled.

The breakfast didn't seem to be settling so well. "Why's that?"

"He's got something to say, that's all. Something you might want to think through before you start calling Diane."

I didn't like what was going on. "Are we playing word and sentence games here, or can you tell me what's up?"

He wiped down the counter for the third time. "Let's go downstairs, and then we'll talk."

"Fine."

Felix led the way down to the cellar, and Nick looked up at us, his face sharp and tight and deeply stubbled. I could see where Felix had rearranged the chains and locks, so that his arms were in front, allowing him to sleep. A pillow and a couple of blankets were by his side. Felix grabbed two camp stools and we sat across from Nick. Felix looked over at me and said, "Are you ready?"

"Yeah."

Felix looked over to Nick. "Go ahead."

Nick licked his lips. "It's a good deal, Felix, and you know it."

He shook his head. "I'm not the man you have to convince. It's going to be Lewis, and I wish you luck, because he's definitely not putting you on his Christmas card list this year."

Nick looked up at me, and even with his chains and ropes about him, I had a twinge of fear and concern, that he could get loose, could hurt me again, and I clenched my fists and took a couple of deep breaths, and I said, "What do you want to say?"

"It's like this," he started. "This whole mess, this whole thing is over that dyke in Newburyport, right?"

I didn't feel like arguing with him or debating his choice of words, so I just nodded. "Go on."

He shook his head in disbelief. "Man, if I knew what trouble that would bring me, I would've stayed home and whacked off."

"Spare me," I said.

Nick went on. "It's like this, man. All my life, I've always scratched and worked for somebody else, no matter what jobs were being pulled. Last year, I started going independent, and then this past month I got something set up, something that would really set me for life. That's straight stuff, right, Felix?"

"Real straight," Felix said.

Nick nodded rapidly, as if pleased at Felix's agreement.

"Right, right. All set up, and I did it myself. Met up with a guy that needed a distribution center. There's too much heat up in Portland and down in Boston. So I worked the docks in Newburyport and got a couple of stand-up guys ready to do the work and some fishermen who need money to hold on to their boats, and everything is set, ready to begin next month."

I folded my arms. "Think there's going to be a conflict here, Nick, because I'm not sure where you're going to be next week."

"I know, I know," he said, looking at Felix and then looking at me. "Hey, I know about that broad in Newburyport, she's got a friend, and that friend's a cop in Tyler. I guess you're going to turn me over to her, right?"

"Not a bad guess," I said. "You've got a problem with that?"

An enthusiastic nod. "You're damn right! I've worked too hard to get sent up for rape and—"

"You've got a bigger problem than that," I interrupted with as cold a tone as I could. "That police detective is taking the whole matter personally. She's not inclined to use the criminal justice system this time. I think the justice system she's looking at is more frontier-like. Get the idea? I don't think you'll have to worry about jail time. I think you have to worry about something a bit more basic."

More looks toward me and Felix. "Listen, I've got a deal here, a deal you can work with. Man, I am so close to being set up for life, I can't let this screw me up."

I looked over at Felix and said, "I don't care what he has to offer. I'm going upstairs to call Diane."

I turned and started for the stairs when Nick yelled out, "The firebug!"

His words seemed to hit me at the shoulder blades and settle right into the base of my skull. I stopped and looked at the eagerness in his face. "What did you say?"

"The firebug, the arsonist, the guy that's been burning down Tyler Beach," Nick went on, his words tripping over each other. "I know who he is. You let me go, and I give up the guy. That's the deal."

I was now back in front of him, everything in the cellar seeming too sharp and too noisy. "Go on," I said. "Has he been burning down places for you, is that it? Is that how you know him?"

Nick moved away a bit. "No, no, not like that. Look, the guy's got a friend who works with me sometimes. Word gets spread around and the invitation ends up with me. The guy wants to know if I need some business-burning done, claims he's got the experience from everything he's been doing at Tyler Beach. I'm not really interested, not with what I got going on, but I got the name. You let me walk and you never tell that detective broad what I've done, and you get the name."

I looked over at Felix, my insides trembling. How in God's name had this happened?

"You and I need to talk," I said to Felix, and we went back upstairs. In the kitchen I got right to the point: "Can he be trusted?"

Felix shrugged, his tone somber. "On most things, no, I wouldn't trust him. But this isn't most things. Nick is ready to give you something you've been looking for a very long time. We could work something out, let him know that if he's dicking with us, we'll come back to his home and finish up our business. But I think the offer is for real. He's got a lot riding on his smuggling adventure opening up on time."

"So we cut him a deal?"

Another shrug. "Or we go along and still turn the little bastard in. Your choice."

Something tasted sour in my mouth. "That's not the way I do business. If we do get the name, we'll do it straight."

"Then you want to go ahead?"

My insides were still jumbling around, like they were busily rearranging themselves, the organs and tendons fastening and unfastening. "I don't know," I said, conscious my voice was sounding bleak. "I don't know what to say to Diane."

"Don't look to me," Felix said. "I'm afraid it's all yours."

"I know, I know," I said, and I remembered last week, and the photo contact sheets I saw, and something opened up to me. "Well, let's go back downstairs. I have an idea how to find out just how truthful Nick is."

Back in the cellar Nick looked up at us again, a questioning sense of hope about his face, and I said, "This arsonist. You know his name?"

"I do."

"And if we agree to go along, will you help set up a sting? Get him to agree to burn a property here in Tyler, so we can catch him in the act?"

He started smiling, the smile of a confident victory. "Yeah, I can do that. Real easy."

"Fine," I said. "One more thing. Is this gentleman the arsonist?"

I mentioned a name. Felix seemed to take a deep breath.

Nick's eyes widened for a moment. "You know," he said, his voice softer. "You know who he is."

"No," I said, feeling old and tired and hurtful. "I just suspected. You just confirmed it."

I turned to Felix, who looked like he was in shock himself. "We need to talk again," I said. "And longer, this time."

·   ·   ·

TWO DAYS LATER, after some rest, relaxation, and serious planning I gave Paula Quinn a call. After the usual polite chitchat, I said, "Your friend Jerry. Could you set up something with the two of us?"

Paula laughed. "What, a meeting? A lunch date?"

"A technical session," I said. "I need some photographic advice, and I was hoping you'd be able to smooth the way. What I know about cameras comes from those little sheets of paper they slip in each roll of film. I'm going to need some heavy-duty advice."

Paula laughed again. "This sounds quite spooky, Lewis. You plan to take some pictures in a high school cheerleader shower area?"

"Now, that's an idea."

She got another fit of the giggles, and after placing me on hold for a minute or so, she came back on the line. "Jerry can see you today at three, if it's convenient."

"Three's just fine," I said.

"So, tell me, what's up? You've got any more great ideas on where we go next on the arsons?"

Dear me. "Not now, but give me a couple of days, Paula. I just might at that."

"Fine. Jeez, got a deadline coming up. Let's do lunch next week."

"You've got it."

THAT AFTERNOON I was in the *Chronicle*'s office, sitting at the meeting room table and with Jerry Croteau across from me. He was wearing tan corduroys and a photographer's mesh vest, and his camera bag was on the far end of the table. Its shoulder strap was frayed and the pockets bulged with lenses and other mysteries of his profession.

"Paula tells me you're looking for some technical advice," he said, his hands clasped before him. They were thick and chapped—working with darkroom chemicals can do a number on your complexion.

"That I am," I said, holding a pen over a pad of paper. "Advice on both still and moving photography. I'll be using a thirty-five-millimeter and a standard camcorder."

He was still smiling widely. "Well, I can help you a lot with the first, and a little bit with the second. What do you need?"

"Nighttime photography," I said. "I want to take some night photos and be able to identify what's being photographed. But I don't want any flashes or anything to let anybody know that a picture's being taken."

"Hmmm," he said, rubbing at his beard. "What will you be taking photos of?"

I looked right at him. "Wildlife."

He nodded, as if understanding. "Um, okay. Wildlife. Fast moving, slow-moving?"

"Oh, relatively slow-moving."

"Um, can I guess here? Will this wildlife be, um, two legged?"

I nodded. "Very good. Two-legged it is."

"All right, then," Jerry said. "Start taking some notes. For your thirty-five-millimeter, I'd recommend the Kodak I-R Special. It's an infrared film but it's real fast, so you can pick up some good details. Especially if your subject's slow-moving. Will there be some ambient light?"

"A little, but not much," I said, scribbling away,

"Okay, that's good to know. For your camcorder, Sony puts out a special infrared film for scientists and nature specialists. It's called NightWorks. You should be able to do just fine."

"Glad to know that," I said, and after a few more minutes of technical talk, I capped my pen and shook his hand, thankful for what he had just done, and still a bit queasy with knowing he and Paula were sharing something special and intimate, something I was not a part of.

"Thanks for your help," I said, really meaning it. "I knew you'd be able to tell me what I need."

"Sure, no problem," Jerry said, getting up from behind the polished table. "I'm just curious what you're up to."

"Well, let's just say that next weekend I plan to do some documentary work."

"Sounds interesting. Um, can I ask you something?"

"Of course," I said, reaching for my coat.

"Paula tells me that sometimes you're involved in some...interesting things, things that can be newsworthy."

I put on the coat, wincing at the pain still in my arms and shoulder blades. "That's an interesting description, but yes, she's right."

He looked around the office for a moment. "Well, I guess what I'm asking is this. If whatever you're doing is something that's newsworthy, will you let me know?"

I thought for a moment and said, "No, you'll be the second to know."

He was grinning. "The second? Who'd be the first?"

"Paula," I said, heading out of the conference room. "She has first dibs, and always has."

He laughed and said, "Well, hell, that sounds just fine."

"Glad to hear it," and I went outside.

TWO NIGHTS LATER, after much more work and phone calls and a puzzled meeting with the president of the Tyler Beach Chamber of Commerce, I was in the office of the Black Cat Motel, on the beach and near the Falconer border. The room was cold, and even though I had a quartz heater humming along by my feet, every now and then I shivered.

At the desk near me I had some water and a package of cheese and crackers and nothing else, for I didn't expect a long night, not at all. Everything should be happening in the next fifteen minutes or so.

Before me was a window with venetian blinds, which were partially open, allowing the lens of my 35mm Nikon and the lens of a Sony camcorder to poke through. Both were on tripods and both were aiming across the tiny parking lot, at the Roscoe House Inn. The windows were dark and the night was cold, and the parking lot was unplowed. Both cameras were focused on the front door of the Roscoe House, which was conveniently unlocked.

I looked around for a minute at the empty office. I felt like I was in a haunted house, with the spirits and voices and scents of hundreds of guests still living in the walls around me. I rubbed my frigid hands and moved closer to the heater, still in awe of how everything was coming back together, was coming full circle. Almost there, almost there to finishing everything up.

Yeah, but what about Diane and Kara? came an insistent voice inside of me. What in hell are you doing with those two?

I tried to force those thoughts out of my mind as I bent over to look through the camera's viewfinder. I was doing the best I could. That's all I could do, and nothing else.

So shut up, I said to those insistent voices, and I kept watch out on the parking lot, and then I stopped breathing for a moment.

Motion, coming from the left. I kept my eye down, waiting, not moving.

A figure came out of the shadows, walking with some difficulty in the snow. In another five or six seconds, the shape would come out into the parking lot, where a streetlight was doing a fairly good job of lighting everything up.

Seconds, that's all.

The figure came closer. I dared not move.

Then it became clear. A man, dressed in a long coat, carrying something in his hands.

I focused the camera. There he was.

Mike Ahern, fire inspector for the town of Tyler, New Hampshire.

30

I backed up from the gear, my ears straining from listening and my leg muscles twitching from standing so long, and out by the entrance, a harsh whisper: "Cole?"

"Over here, and be careful, there's a lot of furniture along the way."

Mike Ahern glided into the room, unbuttoning his coat, and in one hand he held a police radio. He looked at my camera gear and said, "I still think this whole thing stinks. If it ever gets out that you set this up, if it goes down wrong, then—"

"Then you get my ass arrested and nothing else happens," I said, looking back out through the window. "But if it does work out, then you crack the case and you're a hero, with newspaper headlines across New England."

"Screw the headlines, I just want this asshole," he said, sitting down on the desk. "Are you sure he'll be here?"

"That's the arrangement I made," I said. "The burn is set for the next ten minutes. It was quite specific."

"And how about the man doing the hiring? How come I can't have him?"

"Because it was part of the deal. You get the guy who's been burning Tyler Beach, and that's a promise. The man with this deal has nothing to do with the earlier fires."

Mike grunted, looked at the camera gear, and said, "I take it the film belongs to me when the night is over?"

"You take it right," I said. "The film is all yours."

"And how did I get this wonderful gift of an arsonist in action?"

I turned back to the window. "You came here at the suggestion of an anonymous informant. This informant had specific information about the crime that no one else knew. With the cooperation of the hotel owners and the Chamber of Commerce, you've set up this sting. Now will you please shut up, or at least show some gratitude?"

Another noncommittal grunt and I returned to the camera gear, checking again for the fiftieth or hundredth time that everything was powered up, everything was in focus. I checked my pocket watch and when I looked up, there he was.

"Movement," I said. With no sound or apparent motion, Mike was at my side.

"Where?" he demanded, his voice firm but quiet.

"Over by the side of the hotel, left-hand side, by the door. He's going in."

I turned on the camcorder and bent down to the 35mm and started snapping off a series of pictures. The camera has a power winder, and the little whir-whir noises of the film advancing seemed very loud in the office. I could also hear Mike's breathing quicken, as he murmured, "That's right, darlin', you go right in here."

In looking through the viewfinder, I felt a brief moment of panic. The man was carrying a heavy duffel bag on his shoulder, and I couldn't make out his head, never mind his face. He moved quick and sure, and in seconds was through the front door.

"He's in," I said, and Mike murmured back, "I know."

"How long do you think for the setup?"

"Not long at all," he said, holding the police radio with both hands. "He's had quite the experience. I just hope he doesn't go out the rear door."

"No reason to," I said, looking again through the camera, "The front door is easy enough, and we're probably the only people around for a hundred yards."

From inside the Roscoe House Inn came the ghostly flickers of a flash-light being used, visible through the windows, and then the place got dark.

"Good boy," Mike said, keeping his voice low. "Don't want to make an impression, that's right. No need to shine a lot of lights and get people nervous. You do your business now, and then be on your way."

The place was now dark. My hands on the camera made the picture shake, and I tried to steel myself into not shaking, but I couldn't help it.

Mike suddenly said, "If this goes down tonight, Lewis, then I'm yours. You ever need anything from the town or the fire department, I'll take care of it. Personally."

I tried looking through the camera without using my hands.

"How about a reduction on my tax bill?"

"I'll take care of it."

"Mike, I was just joking."

His answer was plain and to the point: "I wasn't."

Then it just happened. Simple as that. No burst of fireworks, no flood-lights, no glare of publicity. Just the door opening up and a man stepping out, a man carrying a now-empty duffel bag in his hands.

Jerry Croteau, staff photographer for The Tyler *Chronicle*.

I kept on taking his picture, at least a half-dozen frames, before he moved out of view. Next to me Mike was slightly rocking back and forth on his heels.

"Got him?" he asked,

"Nailed him," I said, and Mike just nodded and started whistling to himself.

WE WAITED for another ten minutes and I kept the camcorder going, for Mike and the police would need solid evidence that could stand up in court. Since proving arson has always been so blessed difficult, a small sacrifice would have to occur tonight for the upcoming trial, one that happily the owner of the Roscoe House—set to be torn down next spring for a condominium project—was glad to provide.

I guess I should have felt happy or triumphant, but instead I felt tired and a little dirty. At this hour Paula Quinn was probably at home, reading a newspaper or working on the novel that all newspaper reporters claim they have within them, and within the next few hours, her life was going to be torn apart.

And there was nothing I could do.

"There," Mike said. "See that light over there?"

I did, an orange light that was flickering, and Mike brought up the radio to his mouth and said urgently, "Tyler Eye-One to Tyler fire."

The fire dispatcher came back instantly. "Go ahead, Tyler Eye-One."

"Reporting a structure fire at the Roscoe House Inn, eleven Monroe Place. Repeat, a structure fire, Roscoe House Inn, eleven Monroe Place."

The dispatcher acknowledged and from the radio came the chatter of fire crews responding, and Mike turned to me and surprised me by shaking my hand.

"You did just fine."

"Not bad for a civilian, right?"

"If it means anything to you, Lewis, I don't count you as a civilian. Now come on, let's see my boys take care of this one."

WITHIN A FEW MINUTES the parking lot was full of fire engines and hose lines stretched across the snow, but this evening was quite different. The first engine had been on the scene quickly and knocked down the fire before it had a good chance to start in a utility closet near the office. I went with Mike as we entered the dark and smoky hotel, his flashlight casting a bright beam that cut through the water mist and smoke. We went down a corridor, the carpeted floor squishy under our feet. "Here we go," Mike said, as he knelt down before an open closet. "No more secrets. Look here."

At his side was a charred piece of metal and wire with a power cord running out to an outlet. Nearby was a glob of melted plastic, and along the corridor, one-quart-size plastic milk jugs were lined up.

"I guess those plastic jugs held gasoline or something like that, but what's with the metal lump?" I asked. "Some kind of timer?"

"You should know," he said, poking at it with a clasp knife. "You were near something like this just a few minutes ago."

"I was? Oh. Quartz heater."

He looked up at me, eyes twinkling in triumph. "Yep. A quartz heater, but a small one, easy enough to carry in a duffel bag with a half dozen milk jugs filled with gasoline, the tops taped shut. You set the quartz heater and stuff it full of oily rags, and then you set the thermostat timer. Nearby you space out these milk jugs and you cut little holes near the bottom, so the gasoline starts dribbling out. You set everything up and leave, and then ten minutes or a half hour later, while you're enjoying a beer with some friends five miles away, the place you've set is beginning to burn."

He stood up. "Let's go outside. I think it's time for part two to start."

I followed him out of the dark and gloomy motel, knowing where we were heading and not looking forward to it one bit.

OUTSIDE THE WINTER night air was refreshing, but something began to squirm inside of me as I saw who was out among the cops and firefighters: Jerry Croteau and Paula Quinn. Paula was busy talking to a fire lieutenant and Jerry was taking photos of the firefighters rolling up the hose, and while they were both working, I could see they were keeping an eye on each other with little half-winks and smiles.

Paula.

Mike went over to one of the uniformed Tyler cops, who then went over to a Tyler police sergeant. I looked around. Diane Woods was not here. I was glad for that small gift. Paula noticed me and gave a little half-wave, and I tried to return the gesture though my hand felt like it was filled with molten lead.

Mike kept on talking to the police sergeant, moving his hands, until finally the sergeant nodded and went over to another officer, and then two of them went up behind Jerry Croteau. I held my breath. Jerry lowered his camera and talked to the cops, and he was smiling. I knew what he was thinking. He knew all of the cops and firefighters in Tyler, and this must be one major misunderstanding, that's all.

The sergeant shook his head, and the officer took away Jerry's camera and camera bag, and in a matter of seconds his hands were cuffed. He then seemed to sag, and his head fell forward as they led him to a police cruiser. This must have caught Paula's eye, for she turned and raised a hand to her mouth, and ran after the two Tyler cops and Jerry, but she didn't get there in time. Jerry was put in the rear of the cruiser and then driven off, and Paula stood there, arguing with the police sergeant, who pointed Paula over to Mike. She went over to Mike and he said something sharp in reply, for both hands were up to her face and then she ran over to me, trying to speak, tears running down her face.

"Lewis!" she cried. "You've got to help me! They've just arrested Jerry and charged him with setting the fire!"

"Paula..." I said, reaching out a hand to her, and she stepped back, almost yelling, "You don't understand. It's got to be a mistake! How could they do this to him?"

"Paula..."

"Look, you know Diane Woods, you know the chief, you can help me out, you can—"

"Paula, he's the one."

She stopped in mid-breath, her mouth open in shock, and then held herself tight with her arms. "No, you can't be right. There's got to be a mistake, he couldn't do anything like this—"

"Mike Ahern saw him do it, Paula. He's got film and pictures of Jerry going in and setting the fire. There's no doubt."

She nodded, gulped, and said, "So that's what it was all about, you bastard. All that happy talk about taking pictures at night. You set him up! You used me, you son of a bitch, to set him up!"

Paula kicked at me, still crying, and she turned and ran through the snow, slipping a bit in the wetness, heading for her car. I rubbed at my face, then felt a hand on my shoulder and turned and looked at Mike Ahern.

"Looked pretty rough," he said.

I nodded. "It was."

He looked around the lights and the noise and the firefighters at work. "Care to join me for a little ride?"

"What for?"

"We're going to interrogate the little weasel, before he starts remembering his rights and starts yapping about a lawyer. You being a writer, thought this might make a good article. I'll clear it so you can observe the interrogation."

About then all I wanted to do was go home and get drunk and crawl into bed, but for some reason I said, "Sure. Why not?"

So I walked through the snow myself, heading for one more sour little trip.

In the end it didn't take long at all, and I stood outside of the interrogation room with a cold coffee in my hand, watching Diane and Mike at work. It was right off the booking room, and the place was filling up with on- and off-duty cops who came in to see who had been arrested. There was the traditional one-way mirror looking into the room, and Mike and Diane were on one side of a table and Jerry was on the other.

Jerry had been all bluff and bluster for about ten minutes, until Mike had run the tape of him entering and leaving the Roscoe House Inn on a small TV in the interrogation room, and then he had put his head into his hands and had wept. And when he was finished crying, he started talking. Even though there was a tape recorder on the table, both Mike and Diane took notes as Jerry talked.

His story rambled on for a while, and in the end, it was a fairly pathetic one. I didn't think the owners of the burnt hotels would be feeling fine anytime soon.

"It's like this," Jerry said. "I'm stuck in a dead-end job, trying to get out, trying to get my stuff looked at by photo editors and up and down the East Coast. You think they care about seeing beach shots and pictures of people building snowmen? So I needed some action stuff, good pics that would sell. And after homicides, fire pictures do real well."

Once the decision had been made, everything else was easy.

He found small quartz heaters in hardware stores in small towns in Maine and New Hampshire. Gasoline was easy, empty milk jugs even easier. And targets, picked by sheer laziness from copies of the planning board minutes that had been lying around the office.

"Hell," he said, bravely smiling, "The whole beach is empty. I had my picks."

The first one did so fine, and the second one, too, and then, well, the firebug had seduced him. He couldn't explain it. He just enjoyed being alone in a building, feeling the empty rooms about him, and knowing he had the power to transform this enormous building into flames and smoke and a pile of rubble. Then, to make it even sweeter, to come back after the fire had been set and take pictures of what you've done, to record it for eternity, to print them up and to look at them, and then to have them forever.

But something came to disturb the feelings, the sense of power, and the wonderful trip that he had been taking.

"Money," he said sourly. "If you knew how much a photographer gets paid, you wouldn't believe me. My car is five years old, I live in a dump apartment, and even by padding my expense report, I had nothing. Hell, even if a New York paper wanted to interview me, I couldn't afford the airfare."

Jerry had a friend of a friend just over the border in Massachusetts who knew someone that lived in the shadows, and who could put Jerry in touch with someone else with connections. Jerry never knew who this shadow person was—he just made the offer. Jerry was the one who had been burning down Tyler Beach over the winter. Was there a business opportunity there? And then the word came back.

"One thousand dollars, in cash," Jerry said wistfully, and I kept my best poker face on, having set up this little deal just the other day with a manacled Nick Seymour. "I was to leave my car unlocked in the North Shore Mall parking lot and come back in two hours, and in a bag was the money and the motel's name. It was a test burn, just to prove my good faith and expertise. And that's where I was tonight..."

Then the emotions rose up and grabbed him again, and after he wept for a few more minutes, he sniffled and blew his nose and said, "Can I get a lawyer now?"

"Sure," Diane said, switching off the tape recorder and looking over at Mike. "I don't see why not."

THERE WAS STILL a press of people outside of the interrogation room and I was going to leave when there was a tug at my arm, and Diane was there, looking at me. "I was wondering if I could have a few minutes of your time."

"You look pretty busy," I said.

Her gaze was steady and direct. "I've got time enough to talk. Let's go."

She led me out of the crowded booking room and we went down a short corridor that led to her office. Just before closing the door she did something that made my heart ache: She put up a sign that said INTERVIEW IN PROCESS-DO NOT DISTURB. In lighter times Diane once told me this was her World War Three sign: Everybody in the department, from the police chief to the janitor, knew that when that sign was up, Diane was involved in something important and sensitive, and she was only to be interrupted when the sirens sounded and the Russian ICBMs were coming over the North Pole.

It was a sign for her work, and not once had she ever used it when talking to me.

She sat down at her desk, and I pulled over an empty chair.

Her office hadn't changed since the last time I had been there. Her desk and another one were covered with file folders, old newspapers, and notepads. Battered black filing cabinets and cardboard boxes held the case files, and a drug chart from the DEA covered up one cinder-block wall. There had once been a cheesecake poster of a bikinied blonde holding a revolver with the caption "Gun Control Means Being Able To Hit Your Target," but that had come down over the winter with no explanation. It had been put up as a joke by some uniforms, and Diane had gone them one better by keeping it up for a while, but maybe the joke had gotten old.

Right now, she was not laughing. The scar on her chin was blazing white. She folded her hands in her lap and said, "You pulled this off for Ahern, didn't you?"

"I did."

"Decided not to involve me at all?"

"I thought it was best to go with Mike on this one."

"Oh." She kept her hands still. "You and Mike now an item?"

"Hardly."

"Unh-hunh," she said, rocking her chair a bit. "This case sucked from beginning to end, you know that. I had to talk to families who saw their entire livelihoods go up in flames, and for what? Nothing, absolutely nothing. For some moron trying to make a name for himself. And I didn't like it turning out to be Jerry. The poor shit is good behind the camera, and he's treated the department well, and I don't feel good that this case is wrapped up. I feel sick and betrayed."

"So do a lot of his friends, I'm sure."

Diane glanced up at the ceiling for a moment. "This was my case, you know."

"I know."

"I worked it days, nights, and weekends," she said, her voice quiet but as sharp as broken glass. "I interviewed and re-interviewed witnesses, I put up with Mike Ahern's idiot moods, worked with the state, and went through hundreds of pages of documents. While I was going through that hellish time, I was also juggling another half-dozen felony cases. And, oh yeah, along the way, my lover was raped. So I had a full plate."

"I hear you, Diane."

"I'm sure you do. So you can probably appreciate the fact that you're not my favorite person right now. Mind telling me how Jerry Croteau got your attention, or do you need permission from Mike to tell me?"

My back was getting tingly, and I wished I could have found the right words to make it right. They weren't coming, so I tried to answer as best I could. "His photos."

"What about his photos?"

"I started going through his contact sheets, looking at the crowd shots he took of each fire. Knowing arsonists like to see their handiwork, I was trying to see if there were familiar faces in the crowd, trying to see if the same guy showed up in each shot."

"What did you find?"

"Nothing to do with people," I said. "Everything to do with buildings."

That same flat stare and tone of voice. "Go ahead."

"The Rocks Road Motel fire. I was there, and so was Jerry. We talked for a bit. He said he came on the scene after the fire trucks had gotten there, after the fire had broken out. I looked at the contact sheet for that motel fire. He had a lot of pictures of the place burning down. Also had a couple of beach scenic shots. But one picture really stood out, Diane. It was the Rocks Road Motel, standing all by itself."

She cocked her head. "So what?"

"The motel was all by itself. No fire trucks, no firefighters, no flames. It was a trophy shot, showing what it looked like before the fire started. I checked the other contact sheets. The same thing, for all fires."

"Who did you use to set up Jerry tonight?"

"I can't say."

Her fingers seemed to be turning pale from where she was squeezing them. "You knew about the photos, and you set him up tonight, but you didn't come to me."

"I wanted more proof."

"You wanted more proof? Where is it written that you have the right to make that kind of judgment?"

"That's how I work."

"Ah, how you work. You and your mysterious playing around, my ex-spook. Tell me about your other work. The rape matter."

Now it would begin. "I don't have him for you."

She slowly leaned forward, now resting her folded hands on the desk. "You don't."

"An arrangement," I said. "Look, it will all—"

She raised a hand. "I don't want to hear any more."

"Diane, please—"

"I'm serious," she said. "Shut your mouth. Now. Tell me this. Last time I saw you, at the bed and breakfast in Porter, you thought you were getting closer. Then you kept quiet. Now you've broken the arson case and you tell me you know the man's name, but you won't say anything else. Tell me one more thing. There's a link, right? Some sort of a deal, this whole case wrapped up and the rapist takes a walk. Right? But you know who he is. And he probably also did Kara's landlord, right?"

I swallowed. "Yes."

"His name?" she said, her voice a tad more sharp.

"I can't say, not right now."

"Why?"

"Because there's a..."

"A deal?"

Again I was frantic, trying to find the words, and I said, "Diane, it's—"

"You listen to me!" she shouted, slamming a hand onto the desktop for emphasis, the noise hurting my ears. "Just answer the question! Was there a deal? Yes or no!"

I felt like being sick. "Yes."

She slowly bent her head down to her hands and rubbed at her eyes, and I thought she was crying, but when she looked up a few moments later her eyes were clear and free of moisture. "Listen well, for I'm going to say this once."

I nodded, feeling miserable. No words would work tonight, not a single one.

"You and I have had some times together, and that's what I'm trying to remember right now. So listen right here. You get up from that chair and get out of my station and out of my way. You say one more word, you try to offer up one more excuse, and I'll arrest you here and now for obstruction of justice, and I will see your ass in jail. I don't want to talk to you, I don't want to listen to you, I don't want anything from you. Just get the fuck out or I'll have you in handcuffs and in a cell in thirty seconds."

And with that, she picked up a legal-size notepad and started scribbling furiously, and I got up from the chair, not looking back as I left the office and went out the rear door and to my car. I looked out across the parking lot and there was Paula Quinn out by the police station entrance, talking with some emotion to Ralph Porter, the local bail bondsman, and I left them all as I drove home by myself.

31

For the next several weeks, winter kept its icy stranglehold around Tyler and the surrounding towns. The news of Jerry's arrest made an initial splash in the media—especially since one of their own had been arrested—but in a few days, other stories had crowded it out. Arsonist arrested. Big deal. No one had been killed, and only a few motels had been burned down. The story went from page one to page three to news briefs and then to nothing.

I tried a few times to get in touch with Paula, but none of my calls were returned. I tried only once with Diane, and she hung up on me.

So there you go. I tried not to brood. I kept busy in my house, chipping away at the snow and ice, and fighting back the winter snow that seemed to arrive every few days. I skied into the Samson Point State Wildlife Preserve a few times and on still nights with no winds, I took out my telescope for late winter observations. But in all of my reading, writing, housework, exercise, and other interests, there was still a hollow and bitter taste in everything I did. When I had first come to Tyler Beach, after that disastrous training mission in Nevada, I had come to view this home and this beach as my lifeboat, a place where I would never be damaged, where I could always recuperate.

But on these long winter nights, with the stillness of the air about the telephone, I stared into the flames of the fireplace and thought about the past several weeks. I sat with an unread book in my hands and a comforter in my lap, and I wished for tiredness to descend upon me, so I could finally sleep.

FELIX KEPT IN TOUCH, taking me out for meals and trying to get me interested in ice hockey, and he came with me the day that I bought a Ford Explorer. I was tired of leasing and my poor old Range Rover was now junk for someone's scrap pile, and this time I decided the American autoworker needed help. One night in his house, sipping an after-dinner wine, he said, "It's tough, isn't it?"

"Sure is. Paula thinks I betrayed her by helping get Jerry arrested, and Diane thinks I betrayed her by not turning over Nick."

"You did the right thing."

"Did I?" I asked. "All I know is that two of my best friends won't return my calls, and I'm getting tired of winter."

"Take a trip south," he offered. "You can afford it. Find some new friends, especially those on the topless beaches."

"No," I said, turning my wineglass in my hands. "I want to stay home, and I want to get through this winter."

IN LATE MARCH I read in the *Tyler Chronicle* that Paula had won a first-place prize in news reporting from the New England Press Association, and in a fit of optimism, I sent a congratulatory bouquet to her at the Chronicle's offices.

I guess optimism has its place. The day after, Paula called me and invited me out to lunch. We had a leisurely meal at the Ashburn House and laughed and joked and talked about politics and current events, and through some unspoken agreement, we both stayed away from Topic A. When lunch was through, I suggested a walk and we went up the deserted and snow- and sand-covered sidewalk along Atlantic Avenue, past the Maid of the Seas statue, taking our time. It was a cold March day that gave no hint of spring, and as we walked, she looped her arm through mine and said, "I'm doing better."

"I'm glad."

"I haven't been angry with you in weeks," she said. "I've just been self-conscious about calling you up, after what happened. I'm glad you sent the flowers. You opened a door and I'm grateful."

I gave her arm a squeeze. "That's good to hear."

Eventually we ended up on a park bench, put our feet up on the metal railing, and looked out at the sands and the ever-attacking Atlantic Ocean. A few people were walking down there, and one determined kite flyer was losing his fight to the wind. Paula was hunched up in her coat with her hands in her pockets.

"I guess the worst thing that happened is that nothing makes sense," she said. "You see, I was beginning to fall seriously in love with Jerry. We would have some great times together, both on the job and off, and he would make these grand promises to me. He said he would become a famous photographer, go overseas and take pictures of hot spots, and be the very best. He said he would make tons of money, enough to support me so that I could take time off and write a book or something."

She looked up at me, the wind twisting her blond hair. "Some days, after I've been covering a four-hour zoning board meeting, those promises sounded pretty good."

"I can see why."

"Then you can see what happened next, after he was arrested," she said. "I was all in a fury, all properly shocked. I was going to do everything I could do to get my man out and prove his innocence. But then something made me take another look."

"Your reporter's instincts?"

"Exactly," she said, snuggling up against me a little. "I wanted to do some digging, try to find out what really happened, and in less than two days, I knew. Guilty, no doubt about it. I stayed home sick for three days. I couldn't stand it. It was like opening up your favorite candy bar, week after week, seeing everything the same then one day, you open up the candy bar wrapper and it's infested with worms. You wonder, how in hell did I screw this one up? How come I didn't see it coming?"

"What's going on now?"

"Hah," she said. "I cut off all contact with him, and you know what? Not a word. Not a peep. No jailhouse phone calls, begging for forgiveness. No desperate letters, promising true love forever. Nothing. So to hell with him."

So we sat for a few more minutes, the harsh wind playing across our faces, and Paula reached over and grabbed a hand tight. "It's been damn achy and lonely these past weeks. Promise me you won't do something stupid and go to jail."

"Promise," I said, and I bent over and kissed her, and she returned the favor with a touch of her hand against my cheek, and said, "I must be going. It's getting cold."

"Lunch tomorrow?"

"Why not dinner?" she asked.

I shrugged, smiling. "Why not?"

IN THE FIRST week of April I was with Felix in a parking lot south of us. We stood by the fender of his Mercedes-Benz and near us Route 2-A hummed with traffic. Before us was a squat and ugly brick structure, with lots of lights and barbed wire. The Massachusetts Correctional Institute in Concord, also known as M CI -Concord. Felix had an envelope in his hand and I kept my hands clasped together, for I was quite nervous.

"It's time, isn't it?" I asked.

"Sure is, but shut up, will you? The traffic's been thick the past hour or so. A few minutes late is no big deal."

After a while I was going to ask him the time again when the unmarked Ford LTD came in and parked in a visitors' spot. The driver's-side door opened up and Diane Woods stepped out. I gave her a half-wave and she looked a bit shocked, and then she looked into her car, as if debating whether to get back inside again. Instead, she strode across, wearing blue corduroy pants and a long leather jacket. Her face was damn near expressionless, but still I was happy to see her. It had been a long couple of months.

"Let me guess," she said. "There's no informant here to talk to me about a couple of bodies buried at Tyler Beach. You two have gotten me down here and made me waste near a half-day. Is that right?"

"Partially right," I said. "We did get you down here on pretense, and I'm sorry for that, but I think you'll really want to hear what we have to offer."

Her breath was coming out in little steam clouds. "And what are you boys offering me today?"

Felix said, "We're offering you Nick Seymour, the rapist of Kara Miles, and the murderer of her landlord."

She tucked her hands into the coat pocket. "Where? And how?"

"He's in there," I said, gesturing to the prison. "Beginning his second week of a ten-year prison term."

"What's he in for?"

Felix spoke up. "Major drug smuggling operation in Newburyport, the one that got busted a couple of months back? I'm sure you read about it. Nick was the captain behind the show. Word leaked out and the first major night he had, every cop from Customs to DEA was waiting for him."

She looked at me and then at Felix and said, "You croaked him, didn't you?"

Felix: "Yep."

"You're right, Diane, there was a deal," I said. "He would turn in the arsonist, in exchange for nothing happening to him regarding Kara. So we kept our word. But we never made any promises about his upcoming drug business."

For a brief moment she seemed amused, and then quickly recovered. "I see. So what's the point? There's no way I'm going to put Kara through the trauma of a trial, especially when it involves her brother."

"You know, then."

"Oh, I've known for weeks that she was protecting her brother. She was quite afraid of what I might do to Doug." She slowly nodded. "And with good reason. But Doug is now working on a salmon boat up near the Kodiak in Alaska, and he'll never be back. I've made that quite clear to him." She looked back at the prison walls. "In there, you say. Again, guys, what's the point?"

"Here," Felix said, handing over an envelope. She took it, puzzled, and held it in her hands and said, "What the hell is this?"

"Fake police documents," I said. "Felix had them made up. They say Nick was involved in child rapes, maybe even a kidnapping or killing of a child. You give the word, and Felix will get them into the prison and to the right people. By this weekend, Nick will be gone."

She turned the envelope over and looked at me. "Was this your idea, or Felix's?"

"It was a joint venture," I said.

"I guess the hell it was," she said. "You've kept this quiet all these months, just waiting for Nick to end up behind bars. Just waiting to hand this over to me."

Felix said, "Look at it as a weapon, Diane. All you have to do is tell us to pull the trigger, and we'll take care of it."

She looked again at the envelope, turning it over and over again in her hands, and then looked up at us, smiling, and said,

"Bang."

Then she tore the envelope in half and then in quarters, and after dropping the pieces of paper in the snow, she turned and walked back to her car. I sank back against the fender of Felix's car.

"Well, we tried," I said.

"We certainly did," Felix said. "There's not much more that we can do." He jingled his car keys in his hand. "I would really like to get going, if you don't mind. This place gives me the creeps."

I looked over at the concrete and bricks and the barbed wire, where Nick Seymour was warm and comfortable, and I said, "Then let's get the hell out."

About the middle of April the cold finally snapped, and the chilly winds retreated back up to Canada. The snow and ice around my house melted and for the first time in months I finally saw bare dirt on what was my front lawn. On one particularly warm Friday, I drove into town with the windows down, enjoying the smell and taste of the spring air. I stopped at the post office and, after a quick scan of the day's catch—a cable bill, an electric bill, and a supermarket flyer—I picked up an envelope. There was familiar handwriting on the outside, and inside was a handwritten card: "The

Honor Of Your Presence Is Requested At Dinner At 14 Tyler Harbor Meadows," and gave a time of seven p.m. for the next day, Saturday. And underneath, in smaller letters, was: "Regrets Only."

I had no regrets. I decided to go.

I GOT to Diane's condo promptly at seven, bearing a bottle of wine and a
bouquet of flowers. The parking lot was wet with melting snow and the
fresh ocean air tasted fine as I went up to the building. Most of the lights
were on, and I could see movement upstairs at Diane's window. I rang the
bell and waited, feeling like a kid asking out a young girl for a date for the
first time, and then the door opened up and there was Diane. She had on a
pale pink sweater and white slacks, and she was quite tanned.

She opened the door and stepped out onto the pavement.

"Hi," she said.

"Hi, yourself. You look great. Where did you go?"

A nice smile. "Kara and I went down to Key West for a week, and we got
drunk and made love and hung out on the sands, and had a wonderful
decadent time of it. Then we came back and spring is busting out all over. A
nice way to schedule the end of winter."

"I'll have to remember that," I said, still bearing the bottle of wine and
flowers. I looked at her and something inside of me just clicked away, and I
said, "Damn it, I've missed you."

Her expression changed, just as quick as the snow melting out there,
and she nodded and bit her lip and said, "I've missed you, too."

The flowers and the bottle of wine ended up in a half-melted snowbank
as we hugged, and I held her tight and a flood of memories just came
bursting over me, the times we had shared, the moments where she had
entered my life for the better, and the times I had helped her out, and I
think we were both a bit blubbery when we were done hugging with each
other. As we broke free, I kissed her on the cheek and she turned and said,
"Fool, kiss me right," and when our lips joined, I swore I felt as if my blood
had been switched with helium, I felt so fine.

I laughed and wiped at my eyes and she did the same, and said, "Let's go
for a quick walk. Kara's upstairs, finishing up dinner."

We held hands for a moment as we went across the parking lot and then onto the condo's dock that butted out into Tyler Harbor. The wood was warm and we sat on the dock's edge and dangled our feet. The sun had set some time ago, but there was a bright splash of pink out to the west, and we talked and watched the lights of Falconer and the cars going over the Felch Memorial Bridge, and I pointed out a bright dot of light that was a satellite of some sort, maybe the Hubble Space Telescope or the Russian space station.

Diane kept her hand in mine and said, "I've had a lot of time to think things through, and I want to chat with you for a bit, if you're up to it."

"Sure, so long as you don't intend to shove me into the harbor."

She nudged my ribs. "Hardly. It's just that I have a few things to say before dinner, to clear the air, and I want to do that before we go any further."

I squeezed her hand and she said, "I want to take you back for a second, back in January, when Kara was attacked. That was probably the worse month of my life."

"I know."

"No, you don't know. We all have our special pains and hells, and this one belonged to me. I don't mean that you haven't experienced similar things, Lewis, for I know you have, even when you don't talk about it. So that's my point. Kara was hurting and I was in such a rage, knowing I couldn't deal with this on my own. Which is where you enter the picture. But then there's pressures at work, there's the arsons, and then there's little doubts."

"What doubts?"

"Kara's story," she said, looking straight ahead, "I knew there were problems with the story after about a week, but I didn't want to hear that. And when you came to me with those doubts and others, I bit your head off. Like you said, you weren't dealing with Diane the detective. You were dealing with Diane the pissed-off woman, who wanted to know fast and to the point who had hurt her woman. I didn't want to hear doubts. I wanted names and addresses."

"Not a good time."

"Not by a long shot. So that's a pretty awful mix, and you take someone like me, who's both secretive and independent, and then, well, I got funny when I realized I was leaning on you and Felix to help me out. Two men. Now, you've known me for a while and you know I don't fit into any particular stereotype, no matter how many stereotypes are out there. Just because of who I love doesn't necessarily mean I pull a certain lever at the polling booth."

"But still it rankled, having Felix and me work the matter."

"Sure did," she said. "I was certain, if I didn't have the job or other pressures, that I could have done it all by myself, and not depend on, gasp, two men. So you can see where my head was at when the arson case broke and when you wouldn't say anything about the rapist. I swear to God, if you hadn't left the booking room right then and there, I would have arrested you. Hell, I might have even touched you up a bit with a nightstick, I was so angry."

I shuddered a bit, remembering the look on her face. "I'm sure you would have, Diane. I have no doubt."

She turned to me. "You should have told me what you were doing."

"I tried, but you weren't listening."

"You should have tried harder," she said.

I opened my mouth to argue and then I thought about her, being angry and frustrated and steaming, knowing the identity of Kara's rapist was known but was being hidden from her, and I gave up. "You're absolutely right. I should have tried harder."

A kiss to the cheek. "You're so right. Anyhow, I was wrong about something else."

"What's that?"

She sighed. "I should have put away the man-woman thing. I should have trusted you." Her voice broke a bit. "Damn it, you were doing your best, and you weren't doing it as a macho man thing. You were doing it as a friend, and I should have known that."

Well, that deserved a hug, and after a few more minutes of light watching, we went back inside, pausing for a moment for me to retrieve the wine and flowers. Inside, there was the smell of herbs and chicken and other wonderful things being cooked, and Kara greeted me at the head of the stairs. She was as deeply tanned as Diane and gave me a big hug, and Diane had to catch the flowers and wine before they fell to the ground.

Kara kissed my cheek and whispered, "I'm so glad to see you here," and I said, "Me, too," and it was a joy to see her smile and head back to the stove. I sat down at the round, glass-topped table, and we had a long and delightful meal of stir-fried chicken and rice, chased down by many glasses of wine. They hooted and laughed about their times in Key West, and about how one night at a dance club, a couple of male sailors had tried to pick them up, and Kara explained in graphic detail how they showed the two they weren't interested, and I laughed so hard that wine went up my nose.

Dessert was cheesecake and coffee, and Diane made a big show of presenting me with a T-shirt from Key West, one featuring Papa Heming-way, and I held it up and said, "Knowing the way he felt about women, I'm surprised you even let this get into your luggage."

"Don't worry," Diane said with a laugh. "He shared my luggage with a bunch of soiled panties and stockings."

I sniffed the shirt with apparent distaste, which was cause for another round of laughter, and Kara touched my hand and said, "There's one more gift."

"But only after the dishes are done," Diane ordered, and with that, we cleared the table and got to work.

Kara excused herself when we were nearly done and went upstairs. I was wiping down the last dinner plate when among the postcards and pictures that were stuck up on the refrigerator door I saw a newspaper clip-ping. I read the headline and the dish nearly slipped from my hands. Diane was looking at me, her face not betraying a thing as I reached over and picked up the clipping. It was from a *Boston Globe* of last week, and the item was quite short. The headline said, CONVICTED DRUG DEALER MURDERED AT MCI-CONCORD. The story said, "Prison officials are investigating the stabbing death of Nicholas Seymour, 29, of Newburyport, who was serving a 10- year sentence at MCI-Concord for drug smuggling. Officials said Seymour was found dead in his cell yesterday morning, having suffered from multiple stab wounds. There are no suspects in the case, and prison spokesman Mike O'Keefe said that while the case remains open, the prison is not hopeful that much progress will be made. 'Usually these type of killings occur to settle a grudge or a dispute: O'Keefe said.'"

I carefully put the clipping back on the refrigerator. Diane was wiping down the counter and still looking at me. I said, "Pretty convenient, this happening while you were out of the state."

"Yeah, funny how that happens," she said. "Prison's a violent place. There's no telling what might go on there at night. A word here, a word there."

"I get the feeling you might just know what happens there at night."

She folded up the towel neatly and placed it to the side of the sink. "Lewis, I'm a police officer, sworn to uphold the Constitution and the laws of the state of New Hampshire. What you're suggesting is that I was involved in a capital crime."

I looked at the clipping and then I looked at her. "No, what I'm saying is that I believe you settled this, just the way you wanted."

Diane walked over to me and then gently touched my cheek for a moment. "I have friends in other places, you know. Some women who share a common lifestyle, some who work in dangerous places, like the prison system. I wasn't going to allow Nick to leave prison. Not for a moment. And I wasn't going to let him go unpunished, and I wasn't going to have Kara hurt, ever again. And I was going to take care of it. By myself. So. What do you have to say about that?"

I stared at her calm expression, and I said, "Good for you." She grinned, and then Kara walked in, carrying a small brown box, and said, "Jesus, a couple more seconds, and I bet you I was going to find you on the table."

I turned and smiled and said, "You'll never know."

More laughter, and we went out to the dining room with more cups of coffee, and I sat on the couch and Diane sat near me, while Kara sat on the carpeted floor, looking up at the two of us. She gave me the box and said, "We wanted to give you something to remember, Lewis. Nothing fancy. Just a memento from our trip to remind you that you're our friend, and that we appreciate what you did, and that you can count on us for anything you need, tomorrow or next week or next year."

I began to undo the tape around the box. "Sounds special."

Diane rubbed the back of my neck. "It certainly is. I hope you like it."

And inside the gift box-past a collection of pink-and-white tissue papers-was an exotic-looking seashell, brown and pink and yellow, and wonderfully whole. I took the delicate structure out of the box and into my hand, and looked at the two smiling and happy faces, gazing with affection and love in my direction, knowing that at a point in my life just a few months ago, I had doubted that I would ever see them smile again. I was so glad to be wrong.

"It's perfect," I said.

KILLER WAVES
Book #4 of the Lewis Cole Series

With a lifeless body on his doorstep, ominous federal agents, and a deadly conspiracy looming, Lewis Cole finds himself in deep water that threatens to drown him...

When retired Department of Defense analyst Lewis Cole stumbles upon a murdered man in a quiet state park near his coastal home in Tyler Beach, New Hampshire, he's determined to stay out of the case. But his plans are derailed when a team of federal agents arrives, claiming the victim was a drug courier and demanding Cole's assistance.

With his life turned upside down, Cole reluctantly agrees to help, only to discover the agents have a hidden agenda. As he searches for answers, he's drawn into a web of intrigue involving a long-lost World War II secret, German U boats, and international conspiracies. But the deeper he digs, the closer he comes to his own secretive past—one that cost him friendships and now threatens his very life.

In *Killer Waves*, Brendan DuBois takes readers on a pulse-pounding journey filled with shocking twists, high-stakes danger, and unforgettable characters. Fans of James Patterson and Michael Connelly will be hooked on this heart-stopping crime thriller.

Get your copy today at
severnriverbooks.com/series/lewis-cole

AFTERWORD

Sharp-eyed readers of the Lewis Cole mystery series—yes, I'm talking to you!—should notice something missing from this third book in my private detective series. In DEAD SAND and BLACK TIDE, there were a number of flashback scenes, where Lewis recalled certain events that took place during his service in the Marginal Issues Section of the Department of Defense.

Such additional scenes were in the first draft of SHATTERED SHELL, when I sent the book out to my new editor, Ruth Cavin, at St. Martin's Press. Much to my great disappointment at the time, she advised (i.e., ordered) me to remove those scenes, saying they slowed down the action of the book and didn't add that much.

I thought she was wrong, and in one way, I was correct, because of the two of us, one of us had to be right...and after some time (and not much time at that) I agreed that she was right. Removing those flashbacks didn't detract at all from the overall book, and made it flow that much faster.

It was also a lesson learned. In each subsequent Lewis Cole novel, I made short and cryptic remarks about Lewis' Department of Defense background, but never again would I write lengthy flashback scenes about what he did.

Another thing I learned was how difficult it was to write this book. Lewis Cole's dearest friend, Diane Woods, suffers tremendously as does her lover, Kara Miles. There are sharp scenes among them and Lewis. Those were hard to write, but as William Faulkner once said, "In writing, you must kill all your darlings."

Meaning, of course, that you must kill your fancy writing, your flashbacks, and sometimes, you have to either challenge or kill off major characters.

Alas, Ruth left us way too soon in 2011, at the age of 92, leaving behind the legacy of helping scores and scores of mystery authors with her sharp eye and her love of the field.

Thanks so much again, Ruth.

ACKNOWLEDGMENTS

I would like to express my deep thanks and appreciation for my wife Mona, for her sharp eye and unflagging encouragement; to my agent, Jed Mattes, for keeping this book out there; to Ruth Cavin of St. Martin's Press for giving this book a home; to Don Murray, for showing me the way, years ago; to members of my family, for their continued support; and to Bill Blanning, for the extraordinary gift of STS-78.

ABOUT THE AUTHOR

Brendan DuBois is the award-winning New York Times bestselling author of twenty-six novels, including the Lewis Cole series. He has also written *The First Lady* and *The Cornwalls Are Gone* (March 2019), coauthored with James Patterson, *The Summer House* (June 2020), and *Blowback*, September 2022. His next coauthored novel with Patterson, *Countdown*, will be released in March 2023. He has also published nearly two hundred short stories.

His stories have won three Shamus Awards from the Private Eye Writers of America, two Barry Awards, two Derringer Awards, and the Ellery Queen Readers Award. He has also been nominated for three Edgar Allan Poe awards from the Mystery Writers of America.

In 2021 he received the Edward D. Hoch Memorial Golden Derringer for Lifetime Achievement from the Short Mystery Fiction Society.

He is also a "Jeopardy!" gameshow champion.

Printed in the United States
by Baker & Taylor Publisher Services